Under Ground

Under Ground

E. S. Thomson

CONSTABLE

CONSTABLE

First published in Great Britain in 2023 by Constable

A CIP catalogue record for this book
is available from the British Library.

ISBN: 978-1-47213-153-9

Typeset in ITC New Baskerville by SX Composing DTP, Rayleigh, Essex
Printed and bound in Great Britain by Clays Ltd, Elcograf S.p.A.

Papers used by Constable are from well-managed forests
and other responsible sources.

Constable
An imprint of
Little, Brown Book Group
Carmelite House
50 Victoria Embankment
London EC4Y 0DZ

An Hachette UK Company
www.hachette.co.uk

www.littlebrown.co.uk

For Guy and Carlo

The Times, 31st August 1854.

WE have today been informed that the cholera has, once again, reached our shores. How might we recognise him? From the ghastly blue of his hollow cheeks, the blue-black of his eyes and lips. How might we elude him? Might we shutter our doors and windows against the world? Avoid the touch and society of others? Even these count as nothing, for the very air we breathe carries with it his poisonous exhalations. He moves stealthily – a man may be fit and well at breakfast, and yet dead by noon, all life and dignity taken from him in an incessant purging of body and bowels. Twice before, the pestilence has stalked the streets of our towns and cities, indiscriminate in his plunder, without a care for the bonds of love and family, for the lives of young, old or infirm. May God deliver us from this dreaded plague.

Chapter One

I had known Mrs Roseplucker for years. The owner of a notorious brothel on Wicke Street, I had supplied her and her trollops with salves, balms and medicines since I had been apothecary at St Saviour's Infirmary. But St Saviour's had closed and moved to new buildings on the other side of the river. When I opened my own apothecary on Fishbait Lane, Mrs Roseplucker turned out to be my most loyal customer. Did I like her? I had a grudging respect for her ability to survive. Did I trust her? I had been forced to do so more than once, though everything has its price. Would I help her? How could I refuse?

And so, when she sent for us before it was even light on that cold October morning, when my question, 'What in God's name does she want at this hour?' was met with no answer, just a wide eyed, 'Come. You must come,' from the messenger, what choice did I have?

'Can't you tell us anything?' said Will, as he struggled into his boots and topcoat. The girl, Annie, was Mrs

Roseplucker's most loyal tart. Without her rouge and enamelling she looked to be no more than sixteen years old. She was in her nightgown, a shawl about her shoulders, her hair unbound like a madwoman. She shook her head, and shivered, even though Gabriel, my apprentice, kept the stove burning all night and the apothecary was as hot as a wash house. She drew her shawl tighter. Her pale face grew paler still and she shook her head again.

Wicke Street had once been a fine Georgian terrace. Now, it was a vile thoroughfare of scabrous town houses, their stucco streaked like the walls of a privy. Whatever louche charm the neighbourhood might possess had vanished with the night, the dawn's grey fingers pointing out the filth and decay that the darkness had mercifully concealed.

The door to Mrs Roseplucker's opened even before I had put my foot on the step, dragged open by a wan-faced maid I had never seen before. As it closed behind us Mrs Roseplucker herself emerged from the gloom. From the parlour I could hear crying and chattering, and behind this a muffled lowing sound, like the sound of an imprisoned bull.

'My God, Dr Flockhart, Mr Quartermain,' the woman said, though I could hardly hear her above the noise. 'What evil times have come to this house tonight!' She raised her candle in a theatrical gesture, peering at us through its dim glow. Her face was still daubed with the alum and arsenic mixture she favoured, though the vast horsehair wig she wore in the daytime had been replaced by a mobcap of stained linen. Its lace was torn in parts, the ties that hung down on either side of her face frayed and broken, dangling greasily like the tails of mice. Her nightdress was grey and billowing, her shawl ragged and mothed. A more hideous apparition I hoped never to see.

'What is it, madam?' I said. I looked past her. Through the open door of the parlour I could see Annie, her face streaked with tears, her arm around one of the other girls, who was wrapped in a blanket. 'What reason can you possibly have for summoning us at this hour?'

She put her finger to her lips. I could not think why, as the house was in uproar. But something was wrong. Will sensed it too, and I saw him looking about.

'Where's Mr Jobber?' he said. Mrs Roseplucker's doorman was usually crammed into a cubby hole beside the stairs. His role was to police the premises, ejecting those who stayed too long, or presumed too much. Now, his cubby hole was empty.

Mrs Roseplucker's chin quivered. She turned and vanished into the darkness. 'This way,' she said over her shoulder.

I could smell blood even before I opened the door. That unforgettable metallic tang, visceral and elemental – it is a smell that we know, in our hearts, to be wrong. No wonder the animals of Smithfield become so afraid as they near the slaughterhouse. As a medical man you'd think I'd be used to it. But I am not. And besides, even if I was, there was nothing that could have prepared me for what we saw next.

Beside me, Will fumbled in his pocket for his salts. I was tempted to ask him for a quick whiff of them myself, for the sight that met us as we pushed the door open would have made a butcher blanch. I strode to the window and pulled open the curtains – thick drapes of calico dyed a rich arsenic green but blotched and stained from years of being pulled open and closed by the greasy hands of maids and doxies. The room was warm, the coals in the grate still smouldering, so that the place was filled with a visceral fug. It was like standing inside a giant organism. And yet beneath the stink there was something else. Something fetid, and rotten. It was faint, almost imperceptible. But before I could place it Will clapped his handkerchief to his face. The silk, impregnated with his favourite scents from my apothecary – lavender, rose, lemon geranium – filled the room with the smell of a countryside summer, fleeting and delicious, and all too brief. I gave in, and pulled out my own handkerchief, holding it to my nose as if I were sniffing at a huge white rose.

On the bed, covered in a bloody sheet, was a body. I flung the sheet aside. A man, perhaps some thirty-five years old, lay on his back. His eyes were closed, his face was twisted into a terrible grin, and his throat had been torn out.

'Who is he?' I asked.

'Don't know,' Mrs Roseplucker replied. 'We don't ask. What use is a name in a house like this?' I nodded, staring down at the corpse. 'Well?' she said. 'Can you help or not?' She considered me a friend, though as I knew her to be a wily old slattern I was cautious about returning the compliment.

'My dear lady,' said Will before I could reply. 'The fellow is dead. There is little that will help him now.'

The woman glowered. 'I don't care two jots about *him*.'

I stepped close, leaning over that terrible grinning face, that ripped and bloody throat. The marks on the surrounding flesh looked like claw marks from a giant beast. And yet there were no signs of a struggle. I wondered why. 'What happened?' I said.

'Found 'im this way,' said Mrs Roseplucker. 'Annie saw to 'im last night. Came late. Last one in. He's been here before and he ain't no bother.'

'And he stayed?' I said. 'I thought Mr Jobber ejected the "gentlemen" promptly once their time was up.'

She pulled her ragged shawl closer about her shoulders. 'Sometimes I lets 'em stay. We're a hotel now, you know.' This last she delivered in as refined a voice as she could muster.

'This place? A *hotel*?' Will snorted.

'Yes, "a hotel"! Don't take that tone with me, Mr Quartermain!'

'And Annie left him here? Alone in this room?'

'Went up to her own room – he was alive then. Well, he was *sleeping*. Annie found him like this just now. Screamed fit to bring the house down. Woke *everyone* up, she did. And o' course Mr Jobber went in and tried to help. The poor lamb got himself all covered in blood.' Her chin trembled.

'Annie found him like this?' I said.

'Yes!' she cried. 'Found 'im dead. All that blood. No wonder Mr Jobber slipped. An' now Mary's run for the watch though I didn't tell her to go, and Mr Jobber's gone and locked himself in the parlour cupboard he's

5

that upset, so we ain't got long for you to look around, to work out what 'appened. I can't 'ave a dead man in my house, Dr Flockhart! It ain't good for business.'

'I'm sure,' I said. There was something she was not telling me. 'I assume you've been through the fellow's clothes. His pocketbook and so on?'

'Didn't have one,' said Mrs Roseplucker.

I sighed. 'Madam, if I am to help you, I expect you *not* to obstruct me.' I put out my hand. 'His pocketbook. And *all* its contents.'

'I'm tellin' you, he didn't 'ave one. See for yourself. His clothes are where 'e left 'em.'

I could see straight away that the coat and hat were of the finest quality, both well brushed and clean, the nap of the hat smooth and shining. The shirt was a thick luxurious cotton, the handkerchief silk, both soft as butter to the touch. I examined the cuffs of the coat and shirt – there was evidence of wear, and of careful maintenance, loose threads had been trimmed with sharp scissors. The shoes were polished, as far as I could tell beneath the dirt of the city, but the leather was well used, the soles worn to a point when most men would consider visiting a cobbler. I rooted through the pockets – nothing. Nothing at all. No pocketbook, no fob watch, no silver snuff box. Only his cufflinks remained – polished silver ovals that told me nothing other than that he had probably not been wearing his best ones.

'Come along, madam,' I said. 'Mrs Roseplucker, I can tell you are keeping something from me.'

'Not a thing, sir!' For once, the old slattern looked abashed. 'He's a gen'man, that's all I can say. Look at 'is 'at, look at 'is clothes. But I got no idea who 'e is, and not one of us has 'is pocketbook.'

'But you looked for it, didn't you?' I said.

'We did, sir. But it weren't there.'

'But I assume it was there last night,' said Will. 'It was there when the fellow paid.' Will was right. Mrs Roseplucker always took payment before the gentleman went in to her virgins and 'energetic girls'.

'O' course! No one gets to see my girls without I see their money. No exceptions.'

'So, whoever did this took the pocketbook – if you're quite sure it wasn't you or any of your girls. You know I can't help you if you keep things from me.'

Mrs Roseplucker drew herself up into a vision of righteous indignation. 'Would I tell a lie, Dr Flockhart? To you?'

'Definitely!' I said. 'Though on this occasion you are probably telling the truth.' I rooted in the dead man's trouser pockets. 'And you took nothing from him at all?'

'No, sir.'

I glanced at her. 'If you are lying it will go badly for Mr Jobber. You know he will be accused? I assume that noise I can hear is coming from him.'

Mrs Roseplucker's face sagged like a melted cheese. 'It weren't him, sir. Cross my heart, sir.'

'You don't have a heart,' muttered Will.

She wrung her hands. 'Mr Jobber won't come out. The watch is coming, sir. What'll they say? What'll they do to him if they sees him like that? All covered in blood and . . . and . . .' She sniffed, dabbing at dry eyes with the edge of her shawl. 'The poor lamb!'

'What's this?' From the watch pocket of the dead man's waistcoat I drew a fold of stiff yellow paper.

'Looks like a pawnbroker's ticket,' said Will.

'It is,' I said, opening it out. 'William Mowbray, St Saviour's Street.'

'Bill Mowbray is a wily old fox,' said Mrs Roseplucker. 'You don't want to trust him.'

'I'm not sure we have a great deal of choice,' I said. I turned to Will. 'Shall we pay him a visit?' The ticket bore a date from the previous week, and a number noting the item pawned. There was no indication or description of what it was, no mention of the ticket holder's name. That, we would have to find out for ourselves. But first, I had a corpse to examine.

The room was small and pokey, and I was relieved when Mrs Roseplucker bustled off to try to persuade Mr Jobber out of the cupboard.

'He might well be a poor lamb,' muttered Will, 'but he'll be off to the slaughter once the magistrate hears of this. Sounds to me as though Mr Jobber went a little too far.'

'It certainly looks that way, though let's not jump to conclusions just yet. Mr Jobber isn't usually violent.'

'He's assaulted many of the men who come here.'

'I know,' I said. 'We used to get them at the Infirmary. But I wouldn't say he was the murdering sort, would you? He always seems rather a gentle man, goaded to violence only when those he loves are hurt.'

'I agree,' said Will. 'And yet have you not just provided the perfect explanation? What if he was provoked? And you know how he adores Annie. If this fellow here had hurt her in some way—'

'Then he would have flung him out into the street, and his clothes after him, not clawed out his throat.' I stared down at the dead man. 'No, there is something else going on here, Will, but I don't yet know what it is. Unfortunately, the magistrate will likely take one look at Mr Jobber and send him to the scaffold. Unless we can provide him with a more convincing perpetrator.'

'In that case we have until Execution Day. Which gives us less than a week.' He had gone over to the window and was staring out balefully.

I bent over the body, my magnifying glass in my hand. The head was to one side, as if sleeping. There was blood everywhere – pooled beneath him on the bed, slathered about his neck and chest. I saw that the shoulders bore the marks of bloody handprints, as if someone had shaken the fellow. Bloody handprints were also on the door, and the doorknob – though whether these were from the assailant, or from Mr Jobber as he 'tried to help', we would never know. The bedding was neatly arranged, and there were no indications that the man had struggled. It was as if he had died in his sleep. Had he been dead before his throat was ripped out? The blood loss was copious, sprayed against the bedclothes as if it had pumped out of a living body rather than seeped out of a dead one. I moved his arms and legs, looking for the tell-tale discolouration of the skin that would show me whether he had lain in that position since death. His limbs were cold and stiff, *rigor mortis* well established.

'Four hours,' I said. 'Or thereabouts. He has lain here ever since.' I bent close to his hideously grinning mouth and sniffed at his lips. Beside his face, a length of sticky black cotton thread had adhered to the pillow.

9

I plucked it up between finger and thumb and sniffed at that too. I wrapped it in a fold of paper and put it into my pocketbook.

The dead man's face was handsome, despite that terrible frozen smile. He had thick dark hair, and there was a degree of hauteur to the arch of his nose, even in death. His nails were trimmed and polished, his hair neatly cut, his chin clean shaven.

'Anything?' said Will. He still had not looked at the corpse. I could hardly blame him, for it was a hideous vision, and Will was known to faint at the sight of blood. Since we had become friends – some four years ago now, when he had arrived at old St Saviour's Infirmary as a newly qualified architect tasked with the horrifying job of emptying the infirmary graveyard – he had become adept with the smelling salts. Now, we shared accommodation in my apothecary on Fishbait Lane and a better friend I knew I would never find. His company, and his opinion, were invaluable to me and I loved him more than I ever let on.

'What about a weapon?' he said now. He pulled his salts from his pocket once more, wafting them gently beneath his nostrils. 'A knife, or whatever?'

'It was no knife that did this,' I replied. I had looked everywhere and found nothing. 'These are claw marks. A frenzied attack too by the looks of it. Definitely claws. Possibly teeth. I will know more when I can see it in the light, when Dr Graves conducts the post-mortem. But there's no implement here that might account for this . . . this almost *animal* attack.'

'Perhaps there was no weapon,' said Will. 'Perhaps it *was* an animal.'

10

The sun sent a ray of pink light through the filthy windowpane. I looked up at an angry, blood-coloured sky, and then down at a yard full of black, oily-looking weeds and an overflowing midden. A pool of dark water glistened at its lip. Footsteps tip-toed across the dirt, from the kitchen door to the midden, from the yard gate to the kitchen door and back again. At the far end of the yard a small arch of crooked bricks framed a semi-circular hole in the wall. Beneath it ran the common sewer, a tributary to the River Fleet.

The Fleet bubbled up optimistically to the north of the city, far away on Hampstead Heath. Once, a long time ago, my father had taken me there. He said hemlock grew on the banks of the stream, and he wished to collect some. He used the stuff for lockjaw, for those with epilepsy, or mania. An inhalation of hemlock was, he said, good for bronchitis, toothache or whooping-cough. I was perhaps ten years old when my father made me walk all the way from St Saviour's Infirmary to Hampstead. At Ludgate he stopped and pointed out a vile stretch of trickling mud that ran beside the road. Blocked with offal and effluent, the waste from the tanneries, the dyers, the vinegar works and the emptyings of middens and drains, it was black and stinking.

'This is the Fleet ditch,' he said. 'And a nastier, filthier sewer cannot be found anywhere in the city.'

I followed him as he trudged onward, my handkerchief to my nose. Occasionally he would stop and point out a drain or a gully hole in the road or between the houses. 'It's down there. Beneath us. Trapped, poisoned, kept in the dark, but still going. Can you hear it?'

'Yes,' I said, listening to its solemn gurgle. I could smell it too, a putrid, eye-watering assault.

At last, we left the metropolis behind and walked up the grassy slope of Hampstead Heath. The light lost the sickly yellowish hue it always held in the city. I could hear birdsong, rather than the rattle of cabs, the rumble of drays and the shouts of street hawkers. And, at length, I could hear water too. Not the sluggish sickly gurgle of sewage and effluent but a bright, clear, joyful sound. He showed me the place where the hemlock grew, there on banks sprinkled with buttercups and marigolds and overhanging with redcurrant. Below, the Fleet ran in a silver stream. We sat on the grass, our linen bags filled with calendula and watercress, our feet lazily paddling the cool water. We ate some bread and cheese and an apple each. We dozed in the warm sun. Neither of us spoke. And then, as the day bled into a hazy twilight, we walked back to the apothecary. As we passed back over the Fleet ditch at Ludgate, I could not bring myself to look at it.

'It smells strange in here,' said Will. 'Not just blood and stink, but . . . . something else.'

'Rotten and fetid?' I said. 'Somewhat mousy? That'll be the hemlock. Water hemlock dropwort, to be precise.'

'He was poisoned?'

'Oh yes. Poisoned and then, as he died, his throat was set upon.' I could not tear my eyes from that dark arched hole in the wall at the end of the yard. As I looked, I saw shadows move within – rats perhaps? There was one mincing across the yard. All at once I saw a face – eyes blinking beneath a low oily hood that seemed a part of the dark, a part of the dank black shadows. And then just as it appeared it was gone. Had I imagined it? But I knew I had not. I felt a hand upon my arm.

'What is it, Jem?'

'Nothing,' I said. I looked again at that dark slippery hole. 'It's nothing.'

Suddenly there came a furious hammering on the door. The watch had arrived, a trio of burly constables shouldering their way into the house without waiting for anyone to let them in. They barged into the parlour. At the sight of them pandemonium erupted. Annie and Mrs Roseplucker started screeching and crying; three of the other girls launched themselves at the men, one of them clinging to the back of the smallest constable, beating him about the head and shoulders with her fists and knocking his tall hat to the ground. Will and I found ourselves pressed against the parlour wall while the girls, the policemen, and Old Mother Roseplucker screamed and fought. Inside the parlour cupboard, Mr Jobber began bellowing. The constables flung the women aside as if they were rag dolls. One of them produced a jemmy and levered the cupboard door open.

And there was Mr Jobber, backed away against the shelves inside the cupboard as far as he could go. His face was streaked with tears. He was dressed in a pair of long woollen combinations, and these, along with his hands, were covered in blood. He looked terrified. He tried to rush out into the room, to burst past the constables, but they were ready for him. They wrestled him into a large canvas sheet they had brought with them for that very purpose, and while he was discombobulated, they dragged his hands behind his back. In no time at all he was immobile upon the floor, wrapped in canvas like a huge pupa, his face pressed against the rug. Irons were clamped to his wrists, and he was hauled to his feet. And then he was gone, pitched into the Black Mariah, and driven away before anything could be said or done. One constable remained. He went through to the bedroom to view the body. I heard him vomiting into the chamber pot at the sight.

Next to arrive was Dr Graves. I heard the rumbling wheels of his corpse wagon even before it appeared outside the door, and then all at once he too was inside.

'Ah, Flockhart,' he said, conversationally. 'And you too, Quartermain. What on earth are you two doing here?' He leered at me and gave a theatrical wink. 'Need I ask?'

'Mrs Roseplucker asked us to help,' I said, my cheeks flushing at the suggestion that we had been there for our own purposes. 'The body—'

'Yes, yes,' he waved a hand, not really the slightest bit interested in why we were there. 'Where is it? Where's the corpse? Bloxham? Bloxham! Bring the winding sheet!' Dr Graves's assistant among the dead appeared carrying a shroud of grubby cream-coloured canvas. The reek of formaldehyde and decay seemed to follow Dr Graves and Bloxham wherever they went, and I saw Will clap his hand over his mouth and nose in revulsion as the two men pushed past him into Mrs Roseplucker's back room. The swathed corpse was carried out of the house feet first, like a rolled-up rug. And all the while Mrs Roseplucker and her girls were screaming and wailing, clawing at my arms, my hands, begging me to save Mr Jobber.

14

'I have some students this morning, but they'll be gone by midday,' Dr Graves bellowed over the noise. He sprang onto his corpse wagon and seized the reins. 'Come along to the mortuary when you're ready, Flockhart, and we can do this one together. Perhaps a spot of lunch while we work?'

Chapter Two

❦

I had an errand to run on the way to William Mowbray's
pawnshop and before I went to help Dr Graves. I had
work to do at my apothecary too, and I hoped Gabriel
and Jenny, my apprentices, were getting on with their
tasks and not lolling about reading penny dreadfuls in
front of the stove. All at once the day seemed to have
become very busy. Will too had work to do, though as the
mortuary was near Blackfriars he would surely be able to
check on his men while I attended to the post-mortem.
To add to all this, I had been meaning to drop in on my
solicitor, Mr Josiah Byrd of Water Lane, for some days
now. As we had to pass the place on the way to the pawnshop it made sense to call in. Mr Byrd had been a good
friend of my father's and I trusted him implicitly. I had
asked him to draw up a will for me. I was more concerned
by the reappearance of the cholera in the city than I let
on, and I wanted to make sure that Jenny and Gabriel, as
well as Will, were looked after should anything happen

to me. My affairs were simple to arrange – I would leave everything to the three of them.

I sank back into my corner of the hansom with my coat pulled up about my ears and considered my apprentices. They both concerned me, but in different ways. Jenny was almost as competent as I, and I was hoping she would be able to take the examinations at Apothecaries' Hall in a few years' time. In contrast to Jenny's extraordinary ability and curiosity, Gabriel was slow and clumsy, and gaining his licentiate seemed as far away as ever. I wondered whether his lack of progress had something to do with me. Should I work him harder? Should I beat him for his lack of diligence and progress, the way other masters did? But the lad was a dolt through and through. No amount of beating was ever going to sort that out.

Beside me, Will had pulled out a small vial of brown glass and uncorked the lid. He sprinkled some of the contents onto his hands and dabbed it onto his face and neck.

'You smell like a courtesan's boudoir,' I remarked, as the cab rattled over the uneven setts outside the bakery on Brass Street. 'I detect citrus, bergamot, jasmine and violet. Do you hope to impress Mr Byrd?'

'I hope to cover the stink of the city,' he replied. 'If I travel with my own fragrant nimbus I can deflect the worst of it and, I hope, offer some relief to those lucky enough to be in my immediate proximity.'

'Your nimbus is getting up my nose,' I said. 'The violet is far too pungent. I hope you don't plan to douse yourself from head to foot with the stuff?'

'More than that, Jem. And I carry fresh supplies, just in case.' He pulled out a handkerchief and buried his

17

face in it. 'It's an improvement, I think?' He breathed in deeply. 'And yet, I cannot deny that it's giving me a headache.'

I could not disagree. It *was* an improvement. But it was making *my* head pound too. The weather had been cold, and this usually dampened down the stench of the city. But not today, and the stink from the refuse in the streets and the sewers was inescapable. I took a small muslin pouch from my satchel and gave it a few squeezes before holding it to my nose.

'Lavender and attar of roses,' I said. 'Do you like it?'

'I can't say,' he replied. 'I am overwhelmed by my own mixture.'

'Do you take the stuff with you when you're with Mr Basilisk?' I asked. Will was a skilled architect, surveyor and draughtsman and had recently taken up a post with Mr Joseph Basilisk, the assistant engineer to the Metropolitan Sewer Commission. Will had a longstanding interest in drainage, though his attention to it so far had been theoretical rather than practical. Mr Basilisk, however, took a more applied approach.

'No,' Will said now. 'At least, not underground.' He shuddered. 'What's the point?' He turned to look out of the window. He had told me almost nothing about his work for the Commission, nothing about where he went and what he did. Clearly, he would not be drawn to speak about it now either.

It was hardly eight o'clock when we arrived at Mr Byrd's. Outside, against the kerb, a highly polished ebony brougham was parked. Its windows were curtained with black ruched silk, its door bearing a stylised animal of some sort along with a cluster of heraldic motifs, all in gold. The four horses – three more than necessary – were black and gleaming, with polished brass bells to their harnesses. I was just about to pay the cabby to wait when the door to Mr Byrd's chambers was flung open. I saw the office boy bow as a woman emerged to stand on the threshold. She looked up and down the lane to make sure she was being watched and admired, pulling on a pair of kidskin riding gloves as she did so. Her face was pale and proud, her red lips pressed together irritably. She swept down the steps, her blue-black silk skirt swirling about her ankles like the inky waves of a stormy sea. A coachman leaped down from the box to open the door to the carriage, but she brushed him away with a gesture of impatience.

'I'll drive, Philip,' she snapped. She readjusted her millinery – a riding hat of black velvet with a net to capture her dark hair – as the driver scuttled around to cling onto the back. A long slim leg clad in a white silk stocking flashed into view as she stepped onto the footplate and dragged herself into position. The junior clerk was peeping out of the window. The office boy was peeping out at the door. She knew we were all watching, I was sure of it, but she gave no indication that she had seen any of us. She seized the whip and cracked it in the air over the horses' heads, thundering off down the street as if the Devil himself were driving.

'A brougham with four-in-hand in the city?' said Will. 'She'd be better off in a hansom. Has she seen the traffic north of Fleet Street?'

I laughed. He was right, though I had the feeling the woman would drive on the pavement if she had to, if necessary over the legs of beggars and street urchins.

We went up the steps, and into Mr Byrd's chambers. Mr Byrd himself was in the antechamber warming his backside against the fire while his clerk scratched out a letter.

'Oh, Dr Flockhart, Mr Quartermain,' he said. He looked genuinely pleased to see us. 'Come in, come in. John, some coffee for the gentlemen, if you please.'

'Your office clerk seemed somewhat awestruck by the lady,' remarked Will.

'Ah, yes, yes, she is rather . . . rather . . . *modern*.' He cleared his throat noisily, as if the word 'modern' had become lodged in it. 'Now then, what can I help you with? It's certainly early in the day for business. I assume it's business? Oh!' He winced and put out a hand to steady himself on the polished mahogany mantelpiece. A frown creased his face.

'Are you well, sir?' I said.

'Oh yes!' He let his breath whistle out through his teeth. 'Yes, yes, quite well, thank you. Dr Liversidge has given me some powders. They are very good. Very good indeed.'

I did not comment on Dr Liversidge's powders, which were probably nothing more than sugared water and opium. Mr Byrd recovered himself and led us into his office. He sat down gingerly behind a large leather-topped desk scattered with papers, pen knife, paper weights. His inkstand bristled with quills. I had known Mr Byrd all my life. He was a burly man, with long arms compared to his height. He was always well dressed in crisply laundered and starched legal clothing – white stockings and black knee-britches and coat. He had dark curling whiskers and a kindly face. He was well read in all matters of philosophy, and marble busts of Plato and Socrates stood on either side of his fireplace. His library covered three of the four walls in his chamber, and he worked longer hours than anyone I had ever known. I had often passed his chambers and seen his light burning well beyond midnight.

Mr Byrd was one of the few people who knew who and what I was, but he kept my secret as closely as if it were his own. When my father had died – hanged, unjustly, outside Newgate – his will had come under some scrutiny. Not least because he had apparently left everything to his daughter, one Jemima Flockhart. Where was she? Dead, it was assumed, for no one had seen her since she was a baby, and her twin brother, Jeremiah, had been the sole survivor of that terrible birth. Only Mr Byrd was privy to the truth – that my father had swapped his living daughter for his dead son, and that I had been Jeremiah, 'Jem after my father', for my entire life. My father had wanted a fitting heir to his position as apothecary at St Saviour's Infirmary. But what did *I* want? No one had ever asked. Would I have preferred the life of a woman? I had asked myself this question many times, and the answer, always, was 'no'. It was not a difficult choice, though my life of deception had been a lonely one. Until I met Will.

But I had not come here to consider my past and present, I had come to safeguard the future of those I might leave behind should the worst happen. I asked Mr Byrd about the paperwork for my will. Everything was ready and completed in no time and all I had to do was to sign and witness the paper. Tea was brought in. Mr Byrd settled back in his chair and began to describe the way his sciatica was progressing. And yet the events at

Mrs Roseplucker's weighed heavily upon me. I could see from Will's face that he felt the same. Perhaps we should share our troubles?

'Mr Byrd,' I said. 'We have just come from a brothel.' His face turned pink, as if he feared I was about to share a manly anecdote. 'A man had been murdered there—'

'Good heavens!' Mr Byrd looked startled.

'Another fellow has been arrested, but it is our belief that he is not guilty. That the murderer remains at large.'

'Execution day is Monday,' said Will. 'So we don't have long to save him from the rope.'

'What manner of man is he?' said Mr Byrd.

'The dead man is wealthy,' I said. 'We know that much, though who he is, precisely, remains a mystery. The fellow who's been arrested lives in the brothel.'

'Are you looking for my advice, Flockhart?'

'It seems a sensible thing to do, now that we are here, sir.'

'Then my advice is this: you need to find the perpetrator,' said Mr Byrd. 'It will be no use attempting to proclaim this . . . this "brothel" fellow innocent, especially if the deceased is above him in rank and status. The courts will see him as a guilty man simply by dint of his character and history; that if he is not guilty of *this* crime then he is surely guilty of another, so may as well be sent to the gallows now, thereby forestalling further misdemeanours.' He shook his head. 'I'm afraid that a man who lives in a brothel is a man entirely without good character, and one less of them in the world will, in all likelihood, be seen by any magistrate as something to be applauded.'

I nodded. I had suspected as much. And yet we had so little time, so little evidence to draw upon. How were we even to find out the identity of the corpse? We could waste no more time with Mr Byrd. I stood up to leave, thanking him for his help and advice.

'Not at all,' he replied. 'I wish I could have been of more service to you.' He wrung my hand, seizing it from my side as if it were a bell-pull and pumping it up and down. 'I had no idea you involved yourself with murderers and prostitutes, Flockhart,' he added. 'And you, Quartermain.' He squeezed my hand, his face creased with worry. 'You are both trespassing in an illicit and dangerous twilight world. Are you sure it is a path you wish to take?'

How true his words were to prove. As for his question, what choice did we have?

***Excerpt from the Journal of William Quartermain, Esq., surveyor
and assistant architect, Metropolitan Sewer Commission.***

*Tonight, I dreamed of Puddle Dock again. Did I cry out in my
sleep, startling myself awake? I have no idea, but as my eyes
sprang open I had the impression that the night was ringing with
the last echo of a scream. I listened. Jem's room is next to mine.
He is a light sleeper and I have no desire to wake him, no wish
to explain myself or talk about my work. I know he has perceived
my anxiety. My fretfulness. And my sense of foreboding? Perhaps
that too – after all, he knows me better than anyone. Why else
might he ply me with camomile and valerian in the evenings
and sprinkle my pillow with lavender water if it were not to help
me find oblivion in sleep? He is a man haunted by insomnia
and knows that all seems hopeless in the small hours. I held my
breath, waiting for the creak of a bedframe, the sound of feet on
the floorboards, a door opening. But apart from the ticking of the
clock downstairs in the apothecary, there was nothing.*

24

I tried to return to sleep. Tried, in my mind, to draw a veil over my seething thoughts. But it was no use. And so here I am, once more at my desk in the darkest watches of the night, a candle to my left hand, an inkstand to my right, my pen scratching across the page in front of me.

It was my new master, Mr Basilisk, who suggested I keep a journal. Mr Basilisk selected me from scores of others; singling me out, he said, due to my combined proficiency as architect, draughtsman and engineer. It is true that I lay claim to those skills, though I have told him that my strength lies in drawing. I fear he does not listen and expects too much, for he waved my objections aside and said I just needed more confidence, more self-belief. He said that I should keep a journal as it is only by writing down one's ideas, one's thoughts and dreams, that one can capture the quicksilver of inspiration, pin it down, and give it life. 'Your typical engineer is often considered a dull fellow,' Mr Basilisk boomed on my first day. 'And, in many ways, he must be. But let me tell you, Quartermain, he has it in him to change the world if he will but look to his imagination.' And it is true, the mechanical action of moving the pen across the page, lifting one's hand to the inkstand and back, has a hypnotic effect, at once both magical and commonplace. The blank page becomes a friend to whom all thoughts can be confided without fear of judgement. Perhaps I will find imagination and inspiration here after all, and along with it the confidence to share ideas with my betters.

I started my work for Mr Basilisk and the fifth Metropolitan Sewer Commission some two weeks ago, the time before which I now regard as a time of innocence. It was a time when my vision for the city was all up . . . up . . . up! My ideas for transforming it into a place of light and air and beauty lay above ground – spires, boulevards, parks, tree-lined squares, spacious streets of

25

elegant buildings fringed with verdant gardens. How wrong I was. I see it clearly now. And so, in the manner of Mr Basilisk himself, I direct my gaze down . . . down . . . down . . . for it is there, underground, that our real salvation lies.

So far my work for Mr Basilisk has involved familiarising myself with the existing network of sewers, drains, underground rivers and passages that lie below the city streets. This I have done by examining any plans and drawings I can find that show these hidden structures. Unfortunately, they are of limited value, for the city has been built up, knocked down, re-arranged, modified and changed so often that what lies beneath is anyone's guess. Thus, I find myself required to create my own map, at least as far as I am able, of the city under ground. I have one of the most complicated sections of the city to navigate during these early weeks: from the Thames I am instructed to go as far north as Gray's Inn, as far east as St Paul's Churchyard, and as far west as Somerset House. At the malodorous heart of my enquiries is the River Fleet which starts pure and sweet up on Hampstead Heath and ends its journey as a sewer of the most vile and noxious kind, spewing out on the western side of the bridge at Blackfriars. I am required to make a detailed survey of the state of the sewers: what tunnels and passages exist, what rivers and watercourses flow beneath our feet, what is the size and condition of the tunnels, the brickwork and masonry, how is the whole system connected, the one to the other.

Yesterday, I jabbed at the mud for upwards of four hours. Most of the day – most of the week – has been about measurement. Measuring the speed of the water (slow), the height of the slime on the dock walls (high), the depth of the mud (deep). My companions in the waters are two hulking men, their names, unbelievably, are Fox and Badger. They have little to say for themselves. They are labourers for the Metropolitan Sewer

Commission, and there is no stink from which they recoil, no sight that makes them blanch, no hole or drain that they will not peer into or (as required) enter. I have taken to wearing the same clothes as my men, and I, like them, spend the day in oilskins and leather, caped, booted and gloved. My tall hat is safely stowed in the mortuary near Blackfriars Bridge, which has become our temporary storage area, and on my head I wear a sort of leather sou'wester. Fox and Badger wear the same, all distinctions of rank obliterated by our vile costumes.

Thus have the days passed. Me with my notebook and pencil in my hands, my tripod and level, they with their measuring sticks. Data is only the first step, but it is a necessary one. We must uncover all we can about the moods and vagaries of the city's watercourses. Not just the Thames, but the others – the Westbourne, the Tyburn, the Fleet, and so on. We measure and observe, count and quantify. And every few days I report my findings to Mr Basilisk, so that between us we might formulate a plan that will turn this town of foul and pestilential vapours into a vision of health and cleanliness. In the meantime, I must learn courage, stamina, hardiness – and how to beat a rat to death with a stick.

Chapter Three

I am fortunate enough never to have required the services of the pawnbroker. Given the great number of them that proliferate in the city, I am clearly in the minority. I knew of Mowbray's pawnshop as it was not far from my apothecary on Fishbait Lane. It had two doors – one opened onto St Saviour's Street, the other, around the corner, opened onto Pelican Street in Prior's Rents. The St Saviour's Street door was always slightly ajar, as if to welcome all comers. Its window was bow fronted, the small panes giving a view of the best wares available. The rings – garnet mostly – that studded a card glistened like insects skewered for display. Beside these, necklaces of coral and shell, and pewter fob watches. These gave way to stacks of crockery, bedpans, bales of sheets and bedding, clothes, footwear and cutlery, then a pair of children's shoes, a spinning top, a clockwork mouse. The other door, the one around the corner that opened out onto the slums of Prior's Rents, banged open and closed all day. Here, there was no window. The three golden balls that proclaimed the shop's purpose hung out at the corner – visible on both St Saviour's Street and Pelican Street. Inside, however, there was no distinction of rank. Desperation was the only currency.

'I've walked past this place many times,' said Will. 'There are always queues on a Monday.'

'Rent day,' I said.

'I've never stopped to look in the windows.'

'Why would you? You don't need to pawn anything.'

'How do you know? How do you know I'm not addicted to the horses? Or the dogs? Sorley's dog is a champion ratter. He says I should put a guinea on her next time she's in the ring.'

'*Are* you addicted to the horses and the dogs?' I stared at him in surprise.

'I'm just saying, Jem, that sometimes you make assumptions about me.'

'Then from now on I will do my best to expect the unexpected,' I replied. 'Especially when I'm in your company.'

Mr Mowbray's pawnshop was crowded with all manner of people, men and women, young and old. Many were what the philanthropists liked to call 'the respectable poor', shame-faced individuals carrying secret bundles, who strove to keep away from drink and crime, even though the odds were stacked against them. Others were evidently the worse for drink and had come to pawn their final possessions. I saw a man who looked like a school master carrying a box of wooden tools, and a woman clutching a basket with a child at her side, her face pink with shame that she had found herself in such a place.

Surrounding the customers were the items that they had brought in over many years. Boots and shoes of all shapes and sizes, clothes, furniture, musical instruments, stuffed birds, books, even chamber pots. High against the wall I saw a gentleman physician's travelling physic box, with labelled glass bottles and drawers of painted wood. Beside it, a double bassoon and a leather saddle. Greasy paper tickets hung like rats' tails from every item. Whatever tales might be told by this miscellanea, not one of them was happy. The place stank of unwashed bodies, of worry and despair.

Against the far wall was a long wooden counter divided into sections, each partitioned off with a wooden screen. Within these booths, customers were able to show their wares and discuss terms without the rest of the shop overhearing. All of them were currently occupied, the five assistants Mr Mowbray employed kept busy all day. The queue moved slowly. People shuffled forward to lay their wares on the counter, one after the other.

'No one seems to be redeeming their tickets,' said Will.

'Monday is a desperate day. I wonder how many of them come back on Friday to redeem their possessions for the weekend.'

'I find the whole undertaking rather dispiriting,' said Will. 'Imagine pawning your wife's shoes!'

'Or your child's only toy.'

At that moment one of the wooden booth doors opened and a woman crept out. She kept her head down, her bonnet drawn tightly about her face. She was fumbling a yellow ticket into a battered kid reticule. I noticed ink on her fingers, specks of it on the sleeve of her dress, and on the pale grey woollen shawl she wore over her shoulders. A governess, perhaps, or a lady's companion? Behind her, I saw the pawnbroker putting a silver patch box onto the shelf behind him. I just had time to catch her eye, note the anxiety on her face. Was it shame I saw? Shame that she had to supplement her meagre governess's pay by pawning her possessions? Or had she stolen the patch box from her employer? Did she hope to redeem it before its absence was noted?

'Yes please, sir?' It was Mr Mowbray himself. Will and I stepped into the booth and closed the wooden doors behind us.

William Mowbray was a tall thin man with an oval, completely symmetrical, bald head. His eyes, nose and mouth were clustered in the middle of his face, his ears flat against his head and hardly visible when he was facing forward, so that his face resembled something that might be etched onto a boiled egg by a child's inexpert hand.

'Hello, Dr Flockhart,' he said. 'I never thought to see you in here, sir.'

'I don't have stuff to pawn, Mowbray,' I said. 'But I do have a ticket. Not mine, you understand, but a fellow is dead and I need to know who he is. We found this in his pocket.' I produced the fold of yellow paper we had taken from the corpse's watch pocket.

Mr Mowbray looked at the ticket. 'You can't afford it, Dr Flockhart.'

'A gold fob watch and a signet ring. Both of great value, yes?'

Mr Mowbray nodded.

'How did you know?' said Will.

'From the skin on his little finger,' I said. 'And what gentleman does not have a gold watch?' I turned to the

31

pawnbroker. 'Don't suppose you remember the fellow, do you, Mowbray?'

'Yes, I remember him, Dr Flockhart. In a rather agitated state, he was. I remember him because he was a mite wealthier than we usually gets in here. Bit of a toff, like.'

'And what did you make of him?'

'Frightened, I'd say, sir. And furtive. Furtive more than they usually are.'

'Like the woman with the patch box? The woman in the dyed green dress who was in here before us. Governess, was she?'

'Yes, sir. At least, that's what she said, sir. Said she was pawning her mother's things now she was dead. I didn't believe her either, sir. No one looks that uneasy when they're pawning their dead mother's possessions. And no one usually offers up the information unless they're covering up for something else. What's it to me if their mother's just died?'

'Perhaps they hope for sympathy,' said Will. 'And more favourable rates.'

'You think it was stolen?' I said. 'The patch box?'

'Had to be,' said Mr Mowbray. 'Why else would she have accepted so little so quickly? Why else would she have acted so shifty? Not that it's any of my business.'

'Of course not,' I said. 'And the toff who owned this ticket?'

'I knew he'd take what I offered. If he had some other place where he could get more he'd have gone there. And I knew I'd not likely see him again neither.'

'Not see him again?' said Will. 'Why would you think that?'

'Seemed to me he was on a slippery slope. I can't say more than that, gentlemen, but you gets a nose for these things when you've been in the business as long as I have. Anyway, he had a month to pay back what I gave him, and after that, the stuff was mine. I must say, I'm sorry you've showed up.'

'I mean no offence when I ask this, Mr Mowbray,' said Will. 'But why would someone like that come to a shop at the edge of Prior's Rents to raise a loan?'

'I couldn't possibly say, sir. However, members o' the quality what come here usually have a secret. They don't want to take the family hair-looms to a jeweller – jewellers gossip, sir, gossip like you wouldn't believe. Why, it'd be all round London before you could say "lost my inheritance on the horses"!'

'I suppose there's not many who want that sort of wretched notoriety,' said Will.

'Indeed, sir. And he ain't the only one I've had here, sir. Not by a long chalk!'

'Don't suppose you can tell me his name, can you?' I asked.

'Gentlemen like that don't give their names, sir!'

'That's unfortunate,' said Will. 'We were hoping—'

'But his possessions may yet tell us something,' I said. I tapped my finger on the crumpled ticket I had handed to the pawnbroker. 'If you'd be so kind, Mr Mowbray.'

Mr Mowbray vanished into the back room of his shop.

'A gold watch and signet ring? That's several guineas' worth, I should imagine,' muttered Will.

'Let's see,' I said. 'Mowbray owes me a favour or two. I'm sure I can persuade him to part with the goods with a promise from an honest man to pay the bill.'

We were in the corner of the shop, at the very end of the long wooden counter. To our right was the wall of the adjacent booth. Above the constant shrill chatter of the shop, the bickering women and belligerent men, we could hear a muffled voice from behind the wooden partition. *Please, sir. Just a little more. My mother is dying.*

We turned away and stared blankly out of the window – a small aperture some eighteen inches square, barred like that of a prison cell. It looked out onto a court tucked away behind Pelican Street. On all sides the buildings loomed tall and misshapen. I glanced up to where the sky should be, but the window was too small, and I could see nothing but sooty walls and dirty windows, most of them broken or boarded up or stuffed with rags to keep out the wind and rain. The gutters sagged as if they were melting, the downpipes twisted and crooked. Doors opened onto the space, and here and there a pale unhappy face looked out. In the centre of the court a group of children were gathered about a pool of dirty water, three of them splashing in and out while a fourth attempted to float a stick on the murky surface. This was Well Court, and a more dilapidated, malodorous and wretched place could hardly be imagined. I had visited Well Court more than once. As apothecary to St Saviour's, I'd had patients who came from this place. I had visited them in their homes, bringing them physic from the hospital apothecary, or, more recently, from my premises on Fishbait Lane. Did I recognise any of the faces I saw now? It was hard to say as poverty and want rendered them all similarly gaunt and sunken.

'My God,' said Will. 'Look at this place. St Saviour's Street is a respected thoroughfare. How can such a foul den exist so close by?' He peered through the bars. 'I can see at least eight children,' he said. 'Three of them are no more than babies. The others look to be about six years old, though their faces are so wizened and sunken that they could well be younger. There are women standing in doorways over there, talking to one another while their children play in what looks like a midden.'

I peered over his shoulder. I saw a filthy child crawling towards a brown lumpen mass. One of the women called out, and a child that had been hitherto invisible to us, detached itself from the shadows on the far side of the court – a boy, perhaps ten years old. She picked her way through the refuse and plucked the child from the edge of the cesspit. She returned the child to its mother and, after a brief exchange, took up a pail of slops and emptied them into the overflowing midden. She rinsed the bucket at the pump – an antiquated thing with a greasy-looking handle that stood in the centre of the court not two yards from the cesspit – filled it up with water, and then staggered back across the mud and slime.

At length, Mr Mowbray returned, and I was relieved to turn away from the scenes of deprivation that were unfolding in Well Court. Will, I noticed, looked particularly anxious. His gaze was drawn again and again to the pump at the centre of the court. A heavy drop of water hung from its black greasy lip, plopping every now and again into the muddy puddle that had formed about its base.

'Here we are then, Dr Flockhart.' Mr Mowbray laid out a cloth of crimson velvet and, with gloved hands, carefully positioned two items upon it. A gold half hunter pocket watch, and a gold signet ring.

I picked up the pocket watch and pinged the case open. It was still ticking, a seven-day mechanism that had not yet wound down. I looked up at the pawnshop clock. The watch had kept perfect time. It was a beautiful thing, the gold back covered with curlicues and leaves, in the centre of which a single letter 'M' could be distinguished, the pattern sharp and clear from a life spent nestling in waistcoat pockets. Other than that, there was no clue as to who the owner might have been. The ring, however, had more to tell. It was small, designed for the little finger. It was made of gold, though it was clearly some years older than the watch. Its band was worn from being twisted around and around.

'I'm sure you'd like to see the stamp properly, Dr Flockhart, sir,' said Mr Mowbray. He produced a sheet of paper from beneath the counter and a stick of red sealing wax. He melted the end of the wax using a spill from the stove and dripped three splashes of the stuff into a blood-red blob on the paper. I pressed the face of the ring into the wax.

The impression it left was clear and sharp. I pulled my magnifying glass from my satchel and peered at the image, then handed the glass to Will.

'It's a rat,' he said, blinking. 'At least I think it's a rat. It's a rat in a shield.'

'I think they call it an escutcheon,' I said.

'Looks like a rat to me,' he muttered. 'And I should know.'

'I've seen it before,' I said. 'We both have. Recently too.'

Will frowned. Then, 'Byrd's!' he cried. 'That carriage!'

I thought of the woman who had burst out of Mr Byrd's office. The look in her eye, the way she had driven her coach and four through the city streets. The door to the carriage had had that same escutcheon, that same rat. She and I shared the same solicitor. And now we also had a dead man in common.

'I think we must visit this family,' I said. 'Whoever they might be.'

***Excerpt from the Journal of William Quartermain, Esq., surveyor
and assistant architect, Metropolitan Sewer Commission.***

*Yesterday, we spied a group of people out on the mud. The sun
was sinking, and their shadows were long. The foreshore had an
iridescence to it, at once black and blue and green, flecked here
and there with white and silver, but all the while shimmering
and changing as the fading light rippled across it. They walked
in a line, spread out each some two yards from the other. Four
of them were men, the fifth was a child. Each carried a stick – a
sort of hoe with which to sift and turn the mud. Four of them,
three adults and the boy, were in coats of dark moleskin. The
fifth was swathed in some sort of leathery cape. His hat sat close
on his head, with a long fan-tailed flap hanging down the back
not unlike the tail of a beaver. The crown he had encircled with
a wreath of ancient rope, speckled with barnacles that glittered
white as pearls. His face was black with dirt. His cape was hung
about with some of the spoils of his trade – bits of coloured rope,*

38

fragments of bones, several small bells – all affixed to his costume with twists of rag or twine. His hair was invisible beneath his hat, his beard long and matted. With his hoe held upwards like a halberd, and his proud demeanour, I felt as if I was in the presence of Old Father Thames himself. All but the boy wore heavy boots and improvised gaiters of canvas tied close to their knees and ankles with string, 'against the rats' I was informed by Fox afterwards. These fellows are known as Toshers, and they spend their lives poking about on the mud of the foreshore, or underground scouring the sewers for treasures.

Their names, when I asked, were given as One-Eyed Nathan (this is their leader), Jonny Smacked-Arse, Blind Billy (who is not actually blind), Tommy Two-Toes, and a boy called Thimble. Two of the men carried a round sieve each, and what looked like a large wooden spoon hanging from their belt. This, I have learned, is for mashing the filth in search of items of value – silver pins, gold teeth, small glass beads of the kind used by dressmakers.

Fox and Badger tell me that the Toshers know the sewers intimately. They are prohibited by law from going inside, but who would stop them? Despite their unsavoury work – sifting and scraping in the effluent – they appear remarkably healthy. Their work is fraught with danger. Although they did not regard Fox and Badger and me as an immediate threat to their livelihood, they recognised that we represent change and this they did not like.

'New sewers?' said Old Father Thames when I told him what we were about. 'What'll Toshers do wi' no tunnels? No Fleet? Take the bread out of our mouths, would you?' I thought for a moment he was about to seize the brass measuring instrument from my hands and dash it into the mud. But Fox cracked his knuckles with a sound like billiard balls rattling into a sack, and the fellow seemed to think better of it.

Night was drawing in, and with it a reeking dampness, as if the dark was rising, drawing its very essence from the black mud of the Thames. The man raised his head and sniffed at the air. With a swirl of his malodorous cape he turned from us without another word and led his followers towards the mouth of the Fleet.

'They go in at night?' I asked.

Badger nodded. 'Don't need light where they're goin'.'

I saw Master Thimble again this morning. He watched us from a distance while we floundered in the mud at the foot of the stairs between Water Street and Blackfriars. Later that day, as we approached the mouth of the Fleet, I saw him again. This time he crept closer. His appearance was more peculiar than ever. He had added to his outlandish attire a hat similar to those favoured by gamekeepers – not that any gamekeeper would wear such a hideous structure. It was round at the crown, but had a hole in the top, as if it had been chewed by a dog. It was green with mould and splattered with bird droppings. It was a good few sizes too big and came down over his ears. He put out a grubby hand to me as I adjusted the brass level atop its mahogany tripod. 'Show me, mister.' Fox rolled his eyes as I stepped back from the apparatus.

'Look through the eye piece,' I said. 'Can you see Mr Badger up ahead?'

The boy's face was a picture of delight. 'Hold still, Badger,' he cried. 'Stop waggling that stick. And get back a bit, can't you? Get back!' He stepped away from the level. 'She's a beauty,' he said, gazing at it appreciatively. Then, 'Want me to show you the Fleet? I knows all the best places.' I declined his invitation. He shrugged and retired to stand beside a rotten staithe that projected from the mud. 'You should arks me,' he said. 'If you really wants to see inside.'

He is persistent, I grant him that, for he appeared again in the afternoon as we were preparing to go into the sewer, and once more made his generous offer to guide us underground. This time, I agreed. Fox and Badger looked at me in disgust.

'Thing about Toshin',' said Thimble conversationally as we headed towards the mouth of the Fleet, 'you ain't ought to do it in less'n groups o' four. You're three. Now you got me it's four.' Fox and Badger regarded the lad warily.

'Steal your watch, he will,' said Fox.

'Push you under,' said Badger.

Mud

There are different types of mud, Thimble informed me today. These manifestations vary, depending on the weather, the tide and the seasons. Some of Thimble's Tosher typology is as follows:

'Glop' – dark mud with a sticky texture, like tar.

'Skin' – mud that has a dried surface, but that has yet to turn into 'pie' – mud that has developed a thick crust, but which still contains some soft and moist matter, or 'gravy', beneath.

'Swallower' – deep mud with an apparently firm surface that catches the unwary.

'Skid' – slippery mud with a loose, sliding consistency, and something he calls 'cobbler', the exact nature of which I have yet to fully understand.

'Lip' is mud at the water's edge that is moist and fresh.

Chapter Four

D r Graves was tall and thin, but stronger than he
looked. As a student he had been one of Edinburgh
University's most speedy and efficient resurrection-
ists. He kept his old grave-robbing paraphernalia in a
cupboard under the stairs in the police mortuary. A short
sharp spade for speedy digging, a crowbar for jemmying
open a coffin or – his preferred method – smashing a hole
in the lid and dragging the corpse out by the shoulders
using hooks and ropes.

A dead body is heavier than you might think, he'd said to
me once. I had not reminded him that, as the former
apothecary to one of the largest teaching hospitals in
the city, I had regularly dealt with the aftermath of his
colleagues' mistakes, and I was quite aware of how heavy
and unwieldy a corpse could be. The experience – digging,
dragging, carrying, running (on more than one occasion
he and his accomplices had fled from Greyfriars Kirkyard
with an angry mob at their heels) – had given him a

wiry strength. Coupled with years of anatomy, and an enthusiasm for his work that bordered on the obsessive, his approach to a post-mortem was both muscular and speedy.

Today, Dr Graves was working from the mortuary near Blackfriars Bridge. He was dining when I entered, perched on a high stool beside the sluice, gnawing on a ham bone. A rim of bloody water had gathered about the plughole, which, as we entered, gave a dark, gurgling belch as if it too has just digested a lunch of meat and claret. The place stank of effluent, drains, dead flesh and Dr Graves's lunch.

'Does that lead directly to the sewers?' said Will, peering into the sluice hole.

'No idea.' Dr Graves wiped his lips with the bloody rag that lay beside his knives on the tabletop. 'The Fleet passes underground nearby. Or is it the Tyburn?'

'It's the Fleet,' said Will. 'Do you put body parts down that drain?'

Dr Graves shrugged. 'Sometimes. Want some ham and cheese? And some relish too, perhaps? It's made from tomatoes. Very exotic!' Dr Graves was always generous with his victuals. He gestured with a mustard-smeared knife at the items set out before him. 'Radish, ham, cheese, onions, bread.'

Will shook his head. He was looking ill. 'What's this?' He picked up a bowl mounded with greyish matter that sat beside the ham.

'Brain tissue. Best not eat that.' Dr Graves grinned horribly and licked a smear of tomato relish from his knife. It was the knife he used for slitting the skin of a corpse's abdomen. Had he washed it in the minutes between finishing the post-mortem with the medical students and starting his luncheon? I didn't ask. He was looking pleased.

'The cholera is back,' he said. 'No surprise, given the state of the river. Should give us a few more bodies for the medical school. Mind you, stinks like the very Devil out there.' He turned to Will. 'I believe you're working on something that might be able to help with that, young man. Doing something useful at last, eh? Get that stench underground, not in the air, what?'

Will nodded. He hated talking about his new commission underground, though it exerted a strange fascination over everyone else. He shook Dr Graves's hand and excused himself. He had his own work to do, and he never enjoyed a post-mortem.

The corpse from Wicke Street was lying on the slab, untouched. I lifted the edge of the shroud and reached for the dead man's cold right hand. The signet ring we had found at Mowbray's pawnshop fitted his little finger perfectly. Taking a sheet of paper from Dr Graves's desk in the corner I scribbled a note, folded it up with the signet ring inside, and sealed the lot with wax and ribbon. I handed it to the mortuary boy and told him to take it up to Mr Byrd directly.

'You know who this fellow is then?' said Dr Graves, gesturing to the corpse with his knife. He had speared a square of cheese with its tip, which he then popped into his mouth.

'No,' I replied. 'But Mr Byrd of Water Lane does.' I shook my head at the proffered meats and relishes. 'No thank you, sir.' Like Will – indeed like most normal people – I had no idea how the man could bear to eat surrounded by death and decay. 'Shall we begin?'

I peeled back the canvas shroud and looked down at the corpse. The face was pale and waxy-looking, the cheek-bones sharp, the nostrils pinched as if in disapproval. The glimmer of teeth between his set, grinning leer was truly unsettling to behold, as if he found something horribly amusing about the situation in which he now found himself. His dead gaze was fixed upon the door, as if in expectation that someone more prepossessing than me might, at any moment, walk in. He was as white as alabaster, which was perhaps not surprising given that much of his blood had emptied out into Mrs Roseplucker's bedding, his hair as black and slick as wet onyx. He had taken pride in his appearance, his good looks, I thought. Had he lived a charmed life, the way so many did who were blessed with beauty? It was something I had never known, for I had been born with a port-wine birthmark that covered my eyes and the bridge of my nose in a rosy blindfold. It had served me well, disguising my identity, my sex, as effectively as my stovepipe hat, silk waistcoat and woollen britches. After six and twenty years I was well used to it, but it still made others stare. The claw marks about the site of the wound showed crimson against the pale skin of the dead man's throat.

'First impressions?' I said to Dr Graves.

'He's had his throat torn out by a dog of some kind,' said Dr Graves glancing over. 'Seems odd, given where the fellow was found. Do they have a dog at that place on Wicke Street? I've never seen one.'

'No,' I said. 'Besides, these don't look like teeth marks to me, they're more like the scrapes of long nails, or claws. This is a tear, not a bite. See the way the nails have dug into the skin then ripped right to left, right to left, right to left again? Three times. Five claw marks each time.'

Dr Graves nodded. 'Yes.' He bent closer. 'The trachea has been punctured and scratched. But what killed him was the tearing open of both carotid and jugular. Unless he was already dead, of course. You saw the scene, Flockhart. What're your thoughts?'

'Given the state of the bedclothes I'd say the poor fellow was alive when the assault on the throat occurred,' I said. 'Had he been dead already the blood would have seeped out. But the stuff was everywhere.'

'Must've been a deep sleeper,' said Dr Graves. 'One assumes the attack was swift and hard and the poor fellow simply didn't wake up in time to do anything about it.'

I shook my head. There was more to it than that. 'And yet he didn't cry out,' I said.

'Perhaps he did,' said Dr Graves. 'But no one heard him.'

'There were no signs of a struggle.'

'He may have been too drunk to fight back.'

It was a plausible suggestion. And yet neither Annie nor Mrs Roseplucker had said anything about the fellow being inebriated. But Dr Graves was growing impatient. 'Let's get on with it, shall we, Flockhart? I should really wait for the students, or give this one to the medical school, so if you want to be the first to get your hands on this fellow now's the time.' He removed the winding sheet as tenderly as if he were disrobing a sleeping lover. With a pale bony hand, he stroked the dead man's hair from his forehead. His face was so close to the corpse that for a moment I thought he was about to kiss it. Instead, 'Can you smell anything, Flockhart?' He frowned. 'I'm not certain but—'

Dr Graves had taught me anatomy, and he'd taught me well. *Use all the senses,* he'd always told us. *Not just what do you see, but what do you hear, taste, smell. That will lead you into the secrets of the body.*

'A mousy smell?' I said. 'Corrupt and stinking—'

'Yes.' Dr Graves looked up at me.

'Hemlock,' I said. 'That's my suspicion, sir. Perhaps the stomach will tell us more. Or the oesophagus. It would certainly explain the expression on the poor fellow's face, and the fact that he did not fight off his attacker.'

'I'm no expert on poisons, Flockhart,' said Dr Graves. 'That's your department.'

'If he was poisoned with water hemlock he will have been unable to fight off anyone. Water hemlock dropwort is the most poisonous plant in the kingdom. It paralyses the muscles causing death by asphyxiation and producing what's known as the "sardonic smile". The muscles contract and the face is pulled into this terrible leer. The dying victim has no choice but to grin at their own horrifying and imminent death, for they are alive as the poison takes effect. Perhaps he was sleeping when it was administered, but by the time he awoke it was already too late.' I pulled out my pocketbook and showed Dr Graves the length of sticky cotton I had found on the pillow beside the dead man. 'I think a hemlock mixture was dripped down this thread, against the fellow's lips, while he slept. It would not take much, if the concentration was right. The paralysis that hemlock induces means he would have been unable to move, unable to fight off his attacker, unable to cry out. He would have seen his murderer, and yet been utterly powerless to call out their name. As for the throat,' I shook my head. 'An unnecessary touch, I'd say.'

Dr Graves was both fast and efficient as an anatomist, but he had little curiosity beyond his immediate field of interest. 'Well, well,' he said now. 'Most unexpected. Shall we see what's inside?' He worked quickly, slitting the body from the sternum to the pubis and using his saw on the ribs. He lifted out the heart, the lungs, the liver and set them aside in earthenware bowls. 'Not much of a drinker,' he remarked poking his knife at the liver. 'And a user of opium, though not enough to render him costive.' The corpse's skin was cold and firm, like that of a pig's carcass. I never liked touching cadavers, despite the number of post-mortems I had attended with Dr Graves. To me, it felt like the very worst kind of failure. I had trained as a surgeon-apothecary so that I might save lives, not so that I might cut up the dead.

We had not been working on the corpse for more than twenty minutes before there came the scuffle of boots on the mortuary steps and a young man burst in. 'Where is he?' he cried. 'What have you done with him? Where is he? Edward! *Edward!*' At the sound of footsteps, Dr Graves had had the presence of mind to throw the shroud back over the corpse. Two men had entered the mortuary. One I recognised immediately.

His face was red and sweating with exhaustion, the effort of keeping up with his younger companion evidently causing him some distress. It was Mr Byrd the solicitor. He looked at me beseechingly. 'Unfortunately, your note arrived when Mr Henry Mortmain was with me,' he whispered. 'I'm afraid I . . . I mean I had to *tell* the fellow, Flockhart! It's his brother, after all. I hardly knew what else to do.'

'Sir,' I stepped forward and put my hand on the younger man's arm. 'Please,' I said. 'Allow us a moment.'

'For what?' he cried. 'You have my brother. It *is* my brother, isn't it? It *is* Edward?'

'We must make him decent before you can identify him,' I said. 'And there should be a constable present.'

'The constable is at the chop house, sir,' said Bloxham helpfully. 'He hadn't had any breakfast.' Bloxham had been skulking in the shadows, and I had quite forgotten he was even there. 'Shall I go and get 'im?'

Behind me, Dr Graves was busying himself about the corpse. Fortunately, we had not yet set about the head and face, and if we kept the corpse shrouded from the neck down it would not cause offence. Or so I hoped. 'Let him see it, Flockhart,' said Dr Graves. 'There's no dignity in death, no matter what.'

The young man barged past me and sprang towards the shrouded corpse, his arms outstretched as if he was about to seize it and drag it off the table altogether. Dr Graves evidently thought the same thing, for he cried out, 'Stand back, sir! Stand *back* this instant!' He held his bloody knife out, across the corpse, like a swordsman. 'This corpse is mine now, and you will approach it with care, sir. You will approach it with care or not at all.'

I had forgotten how authoritative Dr Graves could be. The young man, Henry Mortmain, flinched. 'Well, *is* it him?' His face was a picture of despair. 'You sent his ring, sir. It belonged to no one else. Unless it was stolen, of course.' For a moment, he looked relieved. 'That's it, isn't it? Someone stole the ring and he's the fellow under the sheet. It's the thief who's dead. Thank God!'

I shook my head. 'No, sir,' I said.

Mr Byrd seized my arm. 'I'm sorry, Flockhart,' he whispered. 'I *had* to tell him.'

I addressed the younger man. 'You think this man might be your brother, sir?'

'Half-brother,' whispered Mr Byrd.

'It *can't* be him,' said Henry Mortmain. 'I saw him not three days ago. There must be a mistake.' He stared at Dr Graves and me miserably. 'May I see him?'

Dr Graves pulled back the canvas sheeting to reveal the dead man's face – waxy skin, pale full lips, black hair. I could see a resemblance between the two. Mr Henry looked down at his half-brother. I saw him take a breath and let it out slowly. 'Does my father know?' he said at last.

'No one knows,' I replied.

'What happened?'

'Murdered, sir,' I said.

'Murdered? But how?'

'We're not sure. A violent death, I'm afraid. I can say no more at present.'

'Where was he found?'

'In . . . in a brothel, sir. On Wicke Street.'

'And the murderer?'

'The police have a man.' I did not tell him the man was innocent. I would take that matter up with his father.

Henry Mortmain looked down at the corpse again. He sighed and closed his eyes. Then he opened them again and drew himself up to his full height. 'Byrd,' he said. 'The ring if you please.' Mr Byrd came forward and handed over the signet ring. The young man held it between his fingers for a moment, turning it this way and that as if searching for its glint in the dim light of the mortuary. And then he slipped it onto the little finger of

50

his right hand. He clenched his fist, and let his arm fall back to his side. Without saying a word more to anyone, he vanished back up the mortuary steps.

'Well, well,' said Dr Graves, peering at me over the top of his glasses. 'Shall we continue, Flockhart?'

'Of course,' I said. 'If you'll excuse us, Mr Byrd?'

'Oh, indeed, indeed,' Mr Byrd pulled a handkerchief from his pocket and swabbed at his face. He was looking pale. 'So *this* is the fellow you were telling me about, Flockhart?' His eyes were round, his expression shocked. 'I can hardly believe it. If only I had known. Sir Thomas will be—' He pressed his handkerchief to his lips with a shaking hand and closed his eyes. 'I will have to tell him,' he whispered. He took a ragged breath. 'And may I ask . . . when did this . . . this attack occur?'

'In the small hours of the morning, sir,' I said. 'Perhaps three or four o'clock. The body was still warm when we came upon it—'

'Oh, dear me!' Mr Byrd blanched as Dr Graves drew out the pale pink bag of the stomach. He flopped it into a basin and put it to one side. The intestines followed, Dr Graves lifting pink and slippery handfuls of it clear of the body and slithering it into a large earthenware bowl.

'Oh, the poor fellow,' gasped Mr Byrd. 'Oh my word, gentlemen. Is this really necessary?'

'It is, sir,' I said. 'The magistrate has insisted. And Dr Graves does not waste any time when faced with such a horrific situation.' The truth was that Dr Graves did not waste any time because he preferred to have the job done before the family could object.

'And all that . . . that *stuff*. Is that the . . . the . . . '

'The bowels, sir?' boomed Dr Graves. 'It is indeed.'

'Perhaps you should leave, Mr Byrd,' I said. 'This is no place for you.'

'Yes.' Mr Byrd's face was sweating, even though the mortuary was mercifully cool. 'Yes, Flockhart, I think you are right. And I must find Mr Henry. The poor fellow—'

'And you can confirm that this is the body of Edward Mortmain?' I added.

'Oh yes,' he said. 'Quite definitely. This is Mr Edward Mortmain of Blackwater Hall, Hampstead, there is no doubt about it.'

Excerpt from the Journal of William Quartermain, Esq., surveyor and assistant architect, Metropolitan Sewer Commission.

Today, a gentleman was on the foreshore. I could tell by his clothing that he was ill-prepared for the horrors of low tide at Blackfriars. Thimble and I watched the fellow inch across the 'pie', sink into the 'gravy' and narrowly miss a 'swallower' before he made it to the 'lip' at the water's edge. Once there, he crouched down beside the water (if one might call such vile effluvium 'water'), appearing to examine it closely. The Portland stone of Blackfriars Bridge gleamed white against the murky water, which was the colour of stewed tea, and due to a recent outpouring from the Fleet had a rather glutinous texture.

I introduced myself and asked if I could be of any assistance. He said quite possibly I could. He said that, as far as he understood it, beneath the bridge, not two hundred yards from the mouth of the Fleet ditch, was the source of water for the Blackfriars Water

Company. When I agreed, he asked me whether I knew the route of the water pipes, what area of town it supplied specifically. I told him that the plans I had seen recently told me that the Blackfriars Water Company supplied Prior's Rents, and several houses on Wicke Street, St Saviour's Street, and some of the courts and lanes in the surrounding area.

He told me he had received a letter not three days earlier, delivered to him via his solicitor. 'It comes, I am ashamed to say it, from some tenants on my father's lands. It refers not only to their accommodation, but also to their water supply.' The sun was behind him, his face still smothered by his handkerchief, but I had the impression of a man some thirty or more years of age, dark haired, some five feet and eight inches in height. Jem has taught me that one may gain insights into an individual's profession and personality simply by observing their mannerisms, clothes and footwear. Unfortunately, I could make out very little with regards to the latter, for his boots were caked in mud. Yet his clothing, his voice and his bearing betrayed a man of some wealth, used to authority, used to being listened to. At the same time I thought I detected an anxiety to him. Perhaps due to the vile surroundings he found himself in, perhaps due to my bizarre appearance, there was something about his tone of voice, the way he looked out to the river and down at the mud, that gave me the impression that he harboured a deep-seated uneasiness.

I followed his gaze up to the stairs beside Blackfriars Bridge, and saw a carriage there, a long-faced woman in a vivid green bonnet staring down at him from the window. I had no idea whether he knew her or not for he made no move to acknowledge her presence. He handed me the letter he had taken from his pocket and said, 'Read it, sir, for I cannot bear to. And after you have done so I would like you to tell me what your views are concerning the River Thames as a source of drinking water.'

'I can tell you that already, sir,' I replied. 'Anyone who drinks from this pestilential Styx is drinking from an open sewer.' He nodded. For a moment he hesitated. I thought he was about to put his letter back into his pocket, but, like a man who hopes that by unburdening himself to a stranger his troubles will be lessened, he handed it over.

It was written on rough, thin paper with a jerky, uneven hand. The words were barely formed in places and scarcely legible. It was dated a week earlier and was addressed to 'Mr Sir Edward Mortmain', Blackfriars Waterworks. The gist of it is set out below as close to verbatim as I can remember it:

Sur,

We have ritten to your farther what owns the land and the waterworks but have got no reply. As our pitiable situashun has got wors sinse then, we is left wiv no chois but to come to you, who we hopes is less hard of hart and reddy to hear our plees.

Sur, this situashun is a terrible blighte on all of us, young and old. We are forced to liv in filth and sorrow. We ain't got no priviz, no drains, no water pipes. The water wot comes from the pump in Well Court is foul and stinkin, the stench of it as like to the open sewer what runs in the street, and the cess pool right beside it overflowin.

A horse-faced lady came yesterday. We have sin her many times. She tells us to cleer up the stink as that will be what proper Christian peeple do. But how can we do that? We ain't got no way to cleen nuffin.

The lady went in to Well Court and seed a celler room with a dead child in it and she seemed surprized. She said if we had cleened the celler the baby wuld still be alive. But how can we cleen anythin? The rent for that celler where that baby died is five shillins a week. Ten peeple are livin in it and it ain't big enough to swing a cat in.

Sur, we are left in stink like pigs, wiv ower water not fit for animals. Plees help us kind sur, may God preserv you.

from the sorrowful soles at Well Court. Pump Lane, Bell Court, Priors Rents.

He told me that he had visited Well Court and Pump Lane. He shuddered visibly at the very thought, and said, 'My God! what hell they endure, and so close to the gilded drawing rooms of my own kind too.' He stared out at the Thames. 'I would no more put a glass of that filth to my lips than I would sup from a privy.'

'It ain't so bad if you let it stand, sir,' offered Thimble. He went on to explain that the brown matter tended to sink, the liquid that remained being palatable enough.

The fellow Mortmain looked at him with horror and said to me, 'I have some pressing matters to attend to today, but I will see that my father answers this . . . this injustice.'

He made as if to return to the shore, but the mud had other ideas. His boots skittered on a patch of 'skid' and his tall hat slipped from head and plopped into a pool of black stinking liquid. Thimble scuttled forward across the mud the way a water boatman insect skims the meniscus. He seized the hat, rubbed at the filth with his coat sleeve, and reverently held it up to its owner. The fellow hesitated, then shook his head. I saw him squint at Thimble's own hat with what must surely have been disbelief and alarm. I saw his eyes twinkle, though his face was still buried in his handkerchief.

'Please take it, my friend,' he said. *'I think your need is greater than mine.'*

Chapter Five

Dr Graves and I worked on. All at once he stood up. 'Do you smell smoke, Flockhart?' he said. We looked to the corner, where a potbellied stove stood hard up against the wall. In front of it was Dr Graves's armchair, a pile of medical books and notes mounded on a table at its right hand. A blanket was rumpled on its seat. I had reason to suspect that Dr Graves often slept in his mortuary, though I had never asked him outright. The stove was stone cold; it was lit only in winter and then rarely, for a warm mortuary is a useless thing. But there was no mistaking it, there *was* a smell of smoke. To confirm the matter, all at once we heard the clattering of boots on the mortuary steps and Bloxham appeared.

'Fire!' he shouted. 'Dr Graves! Dr Flockhart! We are burning down!'

'What the devil?' Dr Graves threw down his knife in exasperation. 'There's no fire down here!'

But Bloxham's face was wild with fear. 'Come quickly,

sir. Come *now*!' Dr Graves and I followed Bloxham up
the mortuary steps and out into the street. A crowd had
gathered to watch the plumes of thick brown smoke that
were issuing from the mortuary building. Sparks and
whirling particles of ash filled the air.

I coughed and rubbed a smoke grit out of my eye. 'Smells
like straw,' I said. 'And paper.' I plucked a fragment of
ash from Dr Graves's post-mortem coat – a topcoat of
black worsted so old and greasy and stained with blood
and bodily fluid that it had the look and texture of damp
leather. 'This looks like newspaper.'

I went back down the area steps, my handkerchief
over my mouth, and groped my way round to the back
of the building. Smoke billowed thickly around me, the
fog that had drifted in adding to the choking grey pall
that filled the air. At the rear of the mortuary was a
yard that was used by the adjacent public house to store
crates and barrels. In the centre of the yard a brazier
stuffed with paper, wood shavings, straw and oily rags
was burning vigorously, releasing a heavy choking smoke
which drifted past the mortuary door. The impression
from the street was that the mortuary itself was burning
down. I seized a pail of dirty water from beneath a leaky
gutter and doused the fire. Dr Graves appeared beside
me. Usually he was in the mortuary, or it was night-time.
In the daylight his thin face was as white and luminous
as one of his beloved corpses.

'What in God's name is going on?' he said.

'Bloxham was useless,' I remarked. 'Why didn't he just
come round here and put it out?'

'Bloxham hates fire,' said Dr Graves. 'Haven't you seen
the skin on his face and hands? The fellow was burned

as a child. Badly burned. The fact that he ran down into the mortuary to alert us is exceptional. I'd have expected him to run away and leave us to our fate.'

Back on the street the crowd had thinned out, the onlookers evidently disappointed to be denied the spectacle of a conflagration.

'That's it cleared away now, Bloxham,' cried Dr Graves, spotting his assistant hanging about anxiously near the railings. 'Nothing to worry about. Why don't you go and get me a custard pie. You know the ones I like. And one for yourself too, my dear fellow. Whatever you desire.' He handed Bloxham a half crown. 'What about you, Flockhart? The apple tart from the bakery is quite excellent. Can't I tempt you?' I shook my head.

We went back down the mortuary stairs. It was below ground, lined with tiles and north facing, and the room was dark and chilly. I was looking forward to getting the job over with and going back up to my apothecary. The smell of the place was making me feel sick and I'd had more than enough of organs and innards for one day. Dr Graves threw back the sheet with which he had hastily covered over the body. 'Shall we continue? The brain, I think, is next.' He looked towards his workbench, where he had put the various earthenware receptacles into which he had placed Edward Mortmain's organs. He frowned. 'D'you have the colon, Flockhart?' He spoke in a matter-of-fact way, as if it might be quite usual to 'have' another man's colon.

'No, sir,' I said.

'You've taken it, haven't you?' He sounded cross, accusing. 'You only had to ask!'

'No, sir,' I said. Then added, 'Taken it from where?'

'From here, of course.' He gestured at a large empty bowl glistening with moisture. 'It's gone. Did you take it?'

I held out my hands. I could hardly believe what he was asking me. 'And put it *where*, sir? Around my neck? In my pocket?'

'Well, *someone* has taken it.' He clicked his tongue in annoyance. 'Bloxham,' he said as the man entered the mortuary. The smell of hot custard pie turned my stomach. 'Did *you* take the colon? And the bowels – rectum and so forth?'

'No, sir.' Bloxham looked unmoved.

Dr Graves scowled and threw down his knife. 'I don't know what's going on here,' he said, 'but when the constable returns I must speak with him directly. I want to report a theft!'

Chapter Six

After my time with Dr Graves in the mortuary I was mightily relieved to be going home. I was obliged to keep the apothecary stove on as we needed heat to use the condenser to boil and vaporise volatile oils. The place was delightfully fragrant and warm when I at last closed the door on the foggy day's damp chill. Jenny was preparing some liquorice pastilles, and an aniseed and clove tincture for those with toothache, and the whole apothecary was bursting with the fragrance. The smell of coffee was also powerful, for although my apprentice Gabriel was an indifferent apothecary, he was adept at roasting coffee beans. He had a supplier at the waterfront, and he roasted his beans himself on the stove top and ground them with his pestle and mortar. Occasionally he added cinnamon, or cardamom, or roasted cocoa beans. The coffee pot was on the stove as I entered. Will was already there. He was wiping mud off his favourite stovepipe hat with a damp chamois leather. There was a whiff of effluent about him, but I said nothing, and the smell was soon extinguished by the coffee and aniseed. I was impressed with his determination, especially as I knew his work for the Sewer Commission was giving him sleepless nights. I could hardly blame him – which of us would sleep easy in our bed after a day spent underground? When the next day promised more of the same? I clapped him on the shoulder and poured him a cup of Gabriel's coffee. Today it contained sugar, nutmeg and cinnamon and its aroma alone was delicious.

'Did your hours with Dr Graves bear fruit?' he said.

I told him about the water hemlock, about the claw marks at the dead man's throat. 'A rat, perhaps?' said Gabriel. 'There's a lot of 'em about these days.'

Will said nothing. By the look on his face, he evidently considered the idea that the dead man might have been mauled by a large rodent to be both horrifying, and not entirely impossible. 'The dead man's name is Edward Mortmain,' I went on. 'Son of Sir Thomas of Blackwater Hall.'

'Mortmain?' said Will. He looked up. 'Edward Mortmain?'

'Yes. D'you know him?'

'As a matter of fact I do. At least, I've met the fellow. He came to the foreshore a few days ago. He was concerned about the water supply to some of the properties in the town.'

'And you didn't think to mention this?'

'I had no idea it was the same person,' he said. 'And, if you recall, I didn't actually look at the corpse.'

'What do you know of him?'

'Very little, I'm afraid. The fellow appeared beside me at low tide, out on the mud. I exchanged a few words with him. He wanted to know about the quality of the water. Of course, I said it was of no quality whatsoever. His father owns the Blackfriars Waterworks.'

'How did he seem?' I asked.

'He *seemed* very well,' said Will. 'Very civil. Not at all what one might expect from a man of his apparent status – I mean, he was actually *standing* in the mud! His boots were ruined.' He shrugged. 'But he did not seem to care. It was my impression that he was disgusted with what he saw there – mind you, how could anyone feel anything but disgust? But he seemed genuinely shocked, appalled by what I told him. And then he went away.'

'I see,' I said. 'Well, that's something, I suppose. Anyway, we should go to Blackwater Hall and speak to the fellow's father. Perhaps we can tell him that you and his son were friends.'

'Friends?'

'Well, acquainted. It's sure to help.'

'It was my impression that Mr Edward Mortmain did not see eye to eye with his father,' said Will.

'That's perfectly usual,' I said. 'What son *does* see eye to eye with his father? But whatever their differences Sir Thomas Mortmain will surely want to find the truth.'

We took a cab up to Hampstead that afternoon. I had not been north of Camden Town for some time and how far the city had spread in that direction surprised me. Brick kilns smoked at the roadside as we left behind streets and villas, new built where I could remember not long ago there being market gardens, orchards and fruit trees.

A stream gurgled cheerily at the roadside, heading south from the Heath, bright and twinkling despite the fog that was drifting in from the east. As it reached the new houses it was forced into a conduit – a dark hole that sent it underground. I saw Will looking at it, his expression sorrowful.

'The next time that little brook sees the light of day it will be as black and pestilent as the Styx.' He sighed. 'What filth we humans create. What lazy disregard we have for Mother Nature. We throw our mess away and expect her to sort it out for us.' He closed his eyes. 'The River Thames is beyond all imagining. A poisoned pestilential sewer where once it was a river teeming with life. The only reason I can bring myself to go underground every day is the belief that I can do something to stop this . . . this *assault* on nature for we cannot carry on as we are.'

I nodded. How could I disagree? And yet I was born and bred here. I was used to the city and its dirty ways. But Will was from the West Country, from a village miles from anywhere. He had gone first to Bath, then to London. He had never got used to the metropolis. Perhaps he never would. I was glad we'd made the trip up to Hampstead for at least it took him far away from the river. It was just a pity that the fog seemed to have accompanied us.

We were approaching a screen of trees – rowan, ash, birch, oak – all of them gnarled and ancient, deeply rooted in the earth as if determined to cling on to the land they owned, even as the builders crept closer. Would they too be uprooted to make way for a sewer, a villa, a busy road down into the city? Probably. The sun came out, a low, autumn sun, golden and warm. But it did not last, for a moment later the fog thickened, and it was gone. Beside the trees a wall of red bricks, mottled with stains and patches, followed alongside the road. Once, long ago, when the air was not tainted with London smoke, these would have been lichens of green and grey. Now they were dead and had taken on a black scrofulous appearance, as if the wall itself was sick. We turned in at a pair of tall gateposts, about a half mile north of the village of Hampstead.

'What do you know of this place?' said Will.

'Nothing at all,' I replied. 'I had no idea it was even here.' We stared out at the grounds of Blackwater Hall. On either side of us were gardens – on the right, smooth lawns leading down towards ponds fringed with rushes. The stream accompanied us, flowing by the side of the path before it made off between banks of wildflowers – water hemlock, horsetail, fireweed. Its source was one of the large ponds I could see. On the left was an artificial wilderness with a stone grotto, a rockery, and a long herbaceous border, dying back now that the weather was growing colder. Beyond this a swathe of woodland made up of old, thick-set oaks followed the line of the red-brick wall. Directly ahead of us stood Blackwater Hall, an ancient manor house that looked as if it had been built during the reign of Elizabeth. It was a mass of small dark mullioned windows, crooked walls and dark beams of weathered oak set deep into patterned red-brick walls. The roof was smothered in lichen, the chimneys barley-sugar twists projecting like fingers. The trees around it – predominantly oak and yew – provided a dark background, the house seeming to be crouched among them, the glittering windows beneath their frowning wooden lintels giving it an angry, hostile air.

The door was opened by an aged butler. He was dressed in knee-britches, white stockings, shoes with brass buckles. His stockings were covered in smoke smuts, and there was a smear of what looked like dried egg on the lapel of his royal blue tailcoat. The man looked to be about eighty. 'We need to speak with Sir Thomas,' I said. 'It's a matter of some urgency.'

'Very good, sir,' said the fellow. I had the feeling he had been expecting us.

Inside, the air had a musty, acrid smell. Time, history, age – the place held them the way a goblet holds wine. We followed the old man into the gloom. His footsteps made hardly a sound, as if he'd walked that hallway so many times that he knew every creaking floorboard and loose panel. Will and I had no such knowledge, however, and our boots clattered upon the wooden floor, the ancient black floorboards creaking and groaning with every step so that it sounded as though a crowd was marching along rather than just the two of us. The walls were hung about with paintings depicting lumpen, brooding landscapes, or sallow faces with dead eyes and sunken cheeks and stiff ruffs about their necks. The gilding on the frames was dull and lustreless, as if the entire gallery was being gradually consumed by the dark Elizabethan panelling.

Our guide knocked on a low oak door and, in answer to a voice I did not hear, pushed it open. We found ourselves in a large muggy chamber. Heavy drapes covered the windows and a fire burned vigorously in a large iron basket in the grate. There was a wheeled chair standing to one side, a desk in front of the heavily curtained windows, and a general air of dust and neglect hanging about the place. On a sofa of worn brown brocade an old man in a grubby nightshirt was recumbent beneath a threadbare blanket. Beside him, on a stiff-backed office chair, sat another man.

'Mr Byrd!' I said, unable to keep the surprise out of my voice.

The man sprang to his feet. 'Flockhart! My dear fellow! We were just speaking of you. Sir Thomas, this is Dr Flockhart. A finer apothecary I have yet to meet. And this is his companion, Mr Quartermain.'

'You're the fellow who found my son.' The old man on the sofa did not move, but his eyes, pale as raw oysters, were fixed upon me. It was a statement, not a question. I had the feeling that Sir Thomas was not in the habit of asking anyone anything.

'Yes, sir—'

'Murdered, so Byrd tells me. His throat . . . his throat clawed out by a beast of some kind.' His face, I realised now, was white with fear.

'Most certainly he was murdered, sir,' I said. 'Obviously Mr Byrd has informed you of the manner of his passing.' I glared at Mr Byrd. Surely he had not told the old fellow his son's death was the result of 'a beast of some kind'.

'To some extent I have,' said Mr Byrd. 'Perhaps you might—'

'Your son was poisoned,' I said. 'He was poisoned and then he was assaulted. His throat was ripped out. Neither of these outrages was perpetrated by the man currently in Newgate accused of his murder. There's a far more intelligent hand behind this, sir.'

Sir Thomas stared at me. 'And you have proof of this?'

He sipped from a glass of water he had taken from an ebony table beside his sofa. A decanter of the stuff stood at the ready.

'He was poisoned by hemlock.' I could not bring myself to tell the old man about his dead son's grinning face. 'There is no doubt about it. I saw you have water hemlock in your grounds, sir. Beside the stream, and the ponds.'

'Do we?' He blinked. 'We have several special plants down by the ponds. They purify the water. They're one of the reasons our water here at Blackwater is so sweet and clear. My son Henry is the creator of the water garden. It is a triumph, and a great boon to all at Blackwater.' He frowned. 'Hemlock, you say?'

'Water hemlock dropwort, to be precise, sir. It is poison. One of the deadliest in England. Any member of your household might have got hold of the stuff from your garden. Might I suggest—'

'Poison?' Sir Thomas frowned. 'Are you sure? Are you *quite* sure?' He blinked suspiciously at the decanter of water at his side, and at the glass from which he had just been drinking. 'Ruskin!' he shouted. 'Ruskin!'

The door opened and the aged butler doddered in. 'Sir?'

'Do we have water hemlock in the ponds, Ruskin?'

'Quite possibly, sir,' came the reply.

'It will not taint the water itself,' I said.

But he was not listening. 'My God!' Sir Thomas's cadaverous face had assumed a haunted look. 'Edward was poisoned? With hemlock? You're quite certain?' His voice was a whisper.

'Quite certain, sir,' I said. 'The man who has been arrested does not have the knowledge to poison anyone.

He's a scapegoat, nothing more. If you let him swing then whoever did this to your son will still be at large.'

'The police—'

'Are fools. Jobber is an easy catch. I can assure you that this murder is more than the random handiwork of a man like him.'

He looked at us through narrowed eyes. 'Byrd says you're clever, Flockhart. Well, let's see if you are.' He waved a hand. 'Go on then. See what you can find out. Find out who did this. Ask what you like – of me, or anyone here. Anyone. You too, Byrd.'

'Sir Thomas, I can assure you that I had nothing whatever to do with this.'

'What are your assurances worth to me?' Sir Thomas gave a wheezing laugh, so that I was reminded of the sound of gently pumping bellows. 'Perhaps we'll leave it up to Dr Flockhart to decide, as he's so *clever.*'

'I'll have to ask you some questions too, sir.'

'You think I was stalking the brothels of St Saviour's with a bottle of hemlock in my pocket last night?'

'Not at all, sir,' I replied smoothly. 'But as a man of intelligence and experience there will be thoughts and observations you can share that will provide useful insights into the situation.'

He spread his pale hands wide on his emerald cushions, like a lizard. 'You'll not get the better of me with flattery,' he hissed. 'You must do better than that!'

'What sort of a man was your son, sir?' said Will.

'Edward? Soft-hearted. Foolish, some might say. Lacking in drive and ambition. A weak man. Venal. Dissipated.' Sir Thomas shrugged. 'No head for business, for what needs to be done if we are to continue to live

70

as we do. If our kind are to survive. Not unusual for an eldest son, I suppose. Mind you,' he muttered, half to himself, 'his brother Henry is even worse. Perhaps my dear wife, the Lady Mortmain, will help him to find the strength he needs to make the tough decisions.' He shook his head. 'She's a viper. And he a mouse caught in her teeth. By God, sir!' he started up from his pillows. 'I met my match with that one! Anyway, Flockhart, never mind them. What I was saying is that I am the second son, as was my father, and his father before him. The first-born of the Mortmains do not last long. Edward knew he was cursed. He knew his time was coming. I could see it in his face. There was little point in planning for the future.'

'What do you mean, sir?' said Will.

Sir Thomas smiled. 'You have a lot to learn about us,' he said. 'Ask my daughter Caroline about the rat. Yes, the rat. The Mortmain rat. *She'll* tell you. *Then* you'll understand.'

'May I ask, when did you last see your son?' I said.

'Two days ago.'

'Did he live here, at Blackwater?'

'He did, sir, when he was not at his club in town. But we had no wish to see one another. I kept to my chambers; he kept to his. As you can see, sir, *I* am always here. It's a pity I could not say the same about him.' He grinned at us then, his teeth long and yellow against his white wrinkled skin. 'I have not left this room since 1844. That's ten years, sir. Ten years!'

'And may we speak with the members of your family? They must be able to tell us something.'

'Oh yes. You must speak to *them*. Speak to them all! If it looked as though Edward died by the rat, then it *must* be one of them. I know which I'd put my money on!' He raised a finger, as if suddenly struck by an idea. 'I tell you what, I'll write you a note. A directive, if you will. Something that gives you leave to go about the place as you wish. Go anywhere and ask anything. If anyone objects, show them my note. I pay their allowances, damn them! If they object, then I shall tell Byrd to curtail all payments. I can, you know!'

'But, sir,' I said. 'To coerce people in this way, surely—'

'Have you met my family, sir? You, young man,' he waved a white bony hand towards Will, 'do you know any of them? No, I thought not. Well, sir, a nest of snakes is nothing compared to a nest of Mortmains.' He grinned again. 'I'd like to see you try to get the better of any of *them*.'

All at once he sat up and swung his legs to the floor. In one quick, sinuous movement he had slithered, unaided, from his sofa into his wheeled chair. He released the brake and propelled himself forward to the desk. The scratch of his pen was like the scrabble of rats' feet against the wainscoting. 'But Edward was my son, and I will not leave his death unanswered.' He seemed to be talking to himself as much as to Will and me as he blotted his page and reached for a stick of sealing wax. He melted an end in the flame of his candle and drew a large red welt with it beneath his signature. He pressed his signet ring hard against it. 'He deserved better. Better than "murdered in a brothel" on his gravestone, at any rate. Find out what you can, Flockhart. If you're as good as Byrd here says you are then I won't be disappointed. But I don't want you telling the police about it. Or the magistrate. Just you and me. And this fellow here. What's his name—'

'Quartermain, sir,' said Will.

'Quartermain, that's it. Just him. And Byrd, of course.'

'But, sir,' I began. 'I can't *not* tell the magistrate.'

'No! I must insist upon it.' He held the letter out. 'You may ask anyone in this house about my son, ask anyone in this house about anything at all – this letter gives you leave to ask, and obliges them to answer. But you will make no decisions concerning what to do with that information without first consulting me. Those are my terms. There can be no discussion and no argument. Will you take them?' The tongue that licked his lips was surprisingly red, as if he had just taken a sip of blood. I did not like the look in his eye as I shook his hand.

Excerpt from the Journal of William Quartermain, Esq., surveyor and assistant architect, Metropolitan Sewer Commission.

<u>*Thames water*</u>

What is the nature and appearance of Thames water? Not so many years ago it was lauded for its salubriousness. Fishermen made a living from its waters, and oysters grew. Now it is opaque. A sinister, dark brown fluid with a lumpen appearance and, at times, a gelatinous texture. The water itself is dead, its surface blighted by bobbing carcases of all kinds and scudded with drifting islands of jelly-like brown foam. If one stares into its murky depths, one can see the feculent matter churning up from below. The river is wide and slow, shallow at the edges, especially outwith the docks. There are mud flats at low tide, where the effluvium is deposited in layers, one on top of the other.

The problem

The population of our great metropolis is now some two million. Not since the glories of ancient Rome has any city been so populous. This teeming multitude is the creator of untold quantities of filth, from the tanneries, the butchers' stalls, the dye works, to the vinegar works, the match factories and the soap works, not to mention the contents of so many thousands of privies and cess pools. Where does this vile tide of filth go? Why, we fling it into the nearest watercourse and hope it will, eventually, find its way into the Thames. Once there, it is no longer the concern of the individual. Instead, it becomes of consequence to all, as it slops upriver, then down, carried on the ebb and flow, before finally being deposited on the banks not far from wherever it first emerged. The stink it creates is deemed responsible for the terrible scourge that is the cholera. I have my doubts about this idea, though I have, as yet, said nothing.

The solution

Mr Basilisk has the answer. He says we must drive the stink deep underground, direct it away from the streets and the river. Only then will the cholera become a stranger to us.

Chapter Seven

'Well,' I whispered. 'This is unexpected.'

'Unexpected?' Will hissed in my ear. 'It's bloody peculiar. What kind of a father asks a stranger to interrogate his family?'

'I'm hardly the Spanish Inquisition!'

'It might be better if you were. D'you think any of them'll speak to us?'

'I suppose we'll soon find out.'

We followed Ruskin back down the passageway. 'Ruskin,' I said, 'how old is this place?'

'Sixteen hundred and one, sir. But there was a house here before that date too. Indeed, I believe there's been a Mortmain living on this spot in one way or another since 1075. They came with the Norman invaders.'

By this time we had arrived at a door. Like the rest of the house interior, it was of a dark tarry-looking oak, black with age and smoke. Ruskin rapped upon it. 'Come!'

barked a voice. Whether it belonged to a man or a woman I could not tell.

The room we entered could not have presented a starker contrast to Sir Thomas's overheated sickroom, for the dark panelled walls had been replaced by wallpaper of vivid yolk-yellow silk. Hand painted with colourful birds and flowers – cranes, nightingales, lotus flowers, cherry blossoms and fruits – the effect was overwhelming. The bird motifs were repeated over and again, each rendition with its own unique qualities – here, a nightingale lifted a pair of dangling cherries from a bowl; there, the same bird pecked at a blossom. Cranes were depicted standing on lakesides, wings folded and necks drawn in, but also in flight, soaring over pagodas and weeping willows. Against the far wall a fire blazed and crackled merrily in the hearth, though the tall casement windows had been flung open to admit the autumn sun and the room had a fresh warmth to it. The fireplace, like the walls, had been modernised, and rather than the great basket of embers and rough stonework favoured by Sir Thomas in his grim, north facing chambers, this yellow room had a mantel of gleaming obsidian, a shining jet-black contrast to the teeming golden walls. A towering ormolu clock with a golden dial stood at its centre.

Before us, a woman reclined upon a chaise longue of bronze and gold brocade. She held a pen in her hand, a silver inkstand was balanced at her side on the sofa and a large heavy account book lay open on her lap. She was surrounded by piles of what looked like paper – letters and invoices – while an enamelled cash box and a stack of leather-bound ledgers stood before her on a low table carved with cherubs and vines and smothered with gold leaf.

'Miss Mortmain, these gentlemen come from your father,' said Ruskin blinking in the golden light. 'This is Dr Flockhart.' He gestured helplessly at Will, 'and Mr . . . erm . . .'

'Mr Quartermain,' said Will.

'Quartermain, I believe, ma'am. Yes, a Mr Quartermain and Dr Flockhart,' rambled Ruskin. 'They are just arrived, ma'am. I understand they wish to speak to you on the matter, most regrettable, of your brother's death, ma'am.'

Miss Mortmain's face clouded. 'I see.' She sighed and waved her pen towards another chaise of gold and bronze. Ink sprinkled the rug at her feet, though she appeared not to notice. 'Please, gentlemen, do sit down.' There were squares of black fabric of various textures and finishes scattered on the carpet at her feet.

'You must excuse me,' she said. 'My seamstress is due at any moment. She left me some swatches and I simply can't decide. The striped silk, black and a still darker black. The watered silk, the ruffled silk – black obviously. Black satin bows, I think. Black silk roses on a new bonnet of black. Ostrich feathers obviously – I love the height they give. And I think bombazines for all servants – or perhaps paramatta? I'm not sure. Father gave me the task. He knows I'm the only one capable. I have the energy for it, obviously, and the organisational ability. Henry is too vague, and my stepmother could hardly care less. She'll be in velvet, no doubt. And silk too. Tightly fitted, of course.' Her cheeks turned pink. She plucked a list from the golden tabletop. 'A carriage and six. Glass hearse. Twelve mutes, I think. The servants can follow on foot, obviously.'

'I'm sorry to interrupt your plans,' I said.

'Oh!' She put her list down. 'The undertaker will sort it all out, I'm just running through the necessary.'

She was a large, plain woman, some six-foot tall with a long equine face and close-set eyes a muddy hazel in colour. Her jaw was almost masculine, the brassy light of the late afternoon autumn sun illuminating a layer of down on her upper lip and the sides of her face. The colourful dress she was wearing – a vibrant red and white stripe in heavy silk whose many panels and flounces showed the art, if not the discernment, of her seamstress – made her appear huge against the golden chaise and yellow, bird-filled wallpaper. I was surprised she was not already in deepest mourning. Had not her brother just been murdered horribly, throwing the family into grief and turmoil?

'You are not yet in mourning, ma'am?' I said before I could stop myself.

'Me, wear black for a whole six months?' she said. 'I don't think I can. In church, yes, or in company, but here at home?' Will and I exchanged a glance. She frowned. 'I see your dark looks, Dr Flockhart, Mr Quartermain, but save your petty judgements. You're my father's visitors, not mine. I had no idea I was going to be obliged to receive you today. Had I *known* in advance I might have dressed in a way that satisfied your prejudices. Besides, the wearing of black is pure superstition. It is so that the living appear as shadows to death, and therefore won't attract his attention as he enters the home.' She flung the swatches aside. 'Such foolishness! Besides, death has not yet entered the home as Edward is still in the mortuary in London. And I do not suit black.' She looked down at her hands, her face momentarily shadowed in grief, and lowered her voice tremulously. 'Edward would not have wanted to see me in it.' Satisfied by this cursory display of sorrow, she threw her head back and waved an imperious hand. 'Pray, take a seat.'

The woman had mid-brown hair, thick, but wiry and lustreless, parted in the middle and looped about her ears in a dispiriting style that was considered fashionable, but which to me always looked both complicated and unflattering. She had added a trio of coloured bows to each side, which added a surprisingly juvenile element to her middle-aged appearance. Would I have worn my hair like that had I followed convention and dressed as befitted my sex? My father, whenever he had spoken of the choices he had imposed upon me – and that was rarely – said I would thank him for what he had done, once I realised the limitations from which he had saved me. So far, he had not been proved wrong, for I did not envy women their lot. How could I? What did any of them have that I might desire? Their poor education? Their cumbersome clothes? Their complicated, hideous hairstyles? Their lives spent bearing children over and again, their sons another generation of arrogant, brutish, entitled men – I felt my face glowing. Of course, there were many who were none of those things. My father for example. Or Will. Or myself, obviously.

'Yes, Dr Flockhart, as you see, I did not inherit my family's good looks,' Miss Mortmain smiled. Had I been staring? I should know better.

'Miss Mortmain,' I stammered. 'Madam, forgive me if I—'

'You were positively glowering at me, sir.' She tittered.

'Think nothing of it. Besides, you hardly have the look of someone who is wont to judge others by their appearance.' My red birthmark smarted under her curious gaze. And yet she was wrong, for I *had* judged her. I had looked for beauty, had expected beauty, and when I did not see it, I had somehow thought less of her. Perhaps I was not so different to most men after all.

'I am what is known as an old maid,' she said. 'At one and forty years of age it is impossible that anyone would take me for a wife. And as you can see, I did not inherit good looks from either of my parents.' She brushed invisible crumbs from her vivid striped skirts. '"Surplus", is how my stepmother describes me. Surplus to requirements. Too genteel for paid employment, too old and ugly to marry. But I have plenty of work to do, all the same.' She ran her hand lovingly over the cash box that sat before her on the golden table.

'Quartermain,' she said as we sat down. 'I know that name. Are you related to the Quartermains of Kensington?'

'No, ma'am,' said Will.

'Ah, well.' From her expression I was not sure whether she was relieved or disappointed. She sighed, spreading her skirts to their best advantage, that fearsome stripe billowing around her, so that I was reminded of a French hot air balloon that I had once seen drifting above the carnival crowds at Vauxhall's Cremorne Gardens. I could not get the idea out of my head.

'My poor brother,' she said.

'Your father said we should speak to you about him,' I said. I could not for the life of me think how to question her without seeming impolite and intrusive. At the same time, I could not bring myself to produce the letter her father had given me. And yet, she had made no effort to dress in mourning. Indeed, she seemed to have gone out of her way to clothe herself in the most garish costume she had. What was I – what was anyone – supposed to make of that? I glanced at Will. He was perched on the edge of the hard yellow sofa, his hands together on his lap like a naughty schoolboy expecting the strap.

But I needn't have worried, for it turned out that my problem lay not in getting Caroline Mortmain to speak, but in getting her to stop. 'My father sent you? Did he tell you to threaten me with a curtailment of my allowance if I did not co-operate?'

I blinked. How on earth could she know *that*? We had only just left her father's rooms. 'Ah . . . He said . . . that is, I have a letter explaining . . . ' I saw that the letter was now in my hand, though I had no recollection of taking it from my pocket. 'Yes,' I said at last. 'That is what he said.'

She smiled, a forced sweetness that sat awkwardly on her heavy features. 'Yes, well, he's getting very old and has developed some unexpected eccentricities. The letters are a particular oddity. He writes to me at least once a week to threaten me with financial ruin and reproach me for all manner of abominations. Last week he accused me of poisoning his favourite dog. I'm sure he told you. The dog died some five years ago of quite natural causes. At the time he hardly even noticed. He has so many dogs and pays them so little attention that he can hardly tell one from the other. He's not a well man, I'm sure you could see that much for yourselves. And, as he becomes more and more incapacitated, he becomes more and more . . . bizarre. The letters are the result of some fixation with contagion, he doesn't want to touch anyone, you see, or – far worse – doesn't want to *breathe them in*. His words, not mine. He usually sends Ruskin with the missives, and the poor fellow is always traipsing about the house with one of my father's notes in his pocket. And, as Papa so often forgets to write the recipient's name on the front, Ruskin, poor fellow, is obliged to remember, which of course he doesn't, and then the letters end up in the wrong hands. Last week he handed a note to my sister Charlotte telling her that her infidelities would ruin her and that she had better have a care. The tone was both menacing and lustful if you can imagine such a combination. It included a recipe for "a salve against the pox". One assumes *that* piece of advice was meant for one of my brothers rather than my young and innocent sister. You must excuse him – my father, obviously, not Ruskin. He rarely leaves his rooms now, which is a shame, as I'm sure he'd find it uplifting to spend some time in this one. I offered to wheel him here in his bath chair, but he won't even countenance the idea.' She gestured at the walls. 'It's lovely, isn't it? I saw your faces as you came in. It's hard not to be astonished by it, I know.'

'Lovely' was perhaps not quite the word I would have chosen. It was certainly striking, but the effect was garish, almost tawdry, and when the setting autumn sun shone directly in at the window, as it did now, the effect was stupefying. 'Are they nightingales?' I said.

'Yes, Dr Flockhart. And storks. Each one hand painted onto the silk. Chinese, obviously. Can you see the bamboo? I asked Old Fitz to grow some in the garden nearby, so that we might continue the motif in the grounds outside. He's been very successful. Perhaps a little too successful as the thicket has become rather extensive. You can see it from here.' She sat up straight and pointed into the garden through the open window. 'Down there, look. Towards the oaks. You can see Old Fitz too, he's taking a machete to it. Rather like an explorer, what?' She laughed, exposing large greyish teeth. Will and I exchanged a glance. His eyes were wide, his expression tense. The room would bring on one of his migraines, I was sure.

'Miss Mortmain,' I said, 'about your brother.'

'Ah, yes.' Her face became serious, as if she had suddenly remembered how she was supposed to be behaving. She frowned. Then, distracted once more, she turned again to Will. 'Are you *sure* we haven't met? Do I know you? I think I know you.'

'No, ma'am,' insisted Will. 'I don't believe so.'

'Madam,' I persisted, 'as you may know, a man has been arrested for your brother's murder.'

'So I believe,' she said. Her voice was now low, hushed and shocked. It was as if she were acting in a play. She put her hand to her breast. 'The brute!'

'We believe he's innocent,' I said. 'He is well known to us and although he is not what might be described as an honourable man, we cannot in all conscience see him hang for a crime he didn't commit. Not to mention that it would leave the real perpetrator at large and unpunished.'

'But how do you know this fellow is innocent? Just because he's an acquaintance? Dr Flockhart, Mr Quartermain, that's not an assumption you can make. How well do any of us know one another?'

'That's true enough, ma'am,' I said. 'But our conviction is based on evidence. I attended your brother's post-mortem, and there were facts presented by his . . . his remains that do not point in any way to the man accused of his murder.'

'What evidence?'

'I am not at liberty to discuss it, ma'am.' At that, her face coloured. At first I thought she was going to tell us to leave, or to insist that I described everything that I had learned from her brother's corpse.

'It is information of the most distressing kind, ma'am,' said Will smoothly. 'As a lady, with a lady's sensibilities, we must ask you to trust us. Trust us, as your father has done, and help us, if you can.'

She seemed mollified somewhat, and, as if to demonstrate that she did indeed have the sensibilities of a lady, she pulled out a handkerchief from her sleeve – which reminded me all at once of a barber's pole, the red and white stripes signalling the blood and bandages of surgery and tooth extraction, two activities in which they had once claimed expertise. She dabbed her nose with it. In her large meaty hand, it looked no more than a scrap of lace.

'Miss Mortmain,' I said. 'What can you tell us about your brother? What kind of a man was he?'

'Dear Edward.' Her eyes filled with tears. 'I am the eldest, by some seven years, and I was his earliest playmate, his nurse, his confidante – before he was sent to school of course. After that, because he so rarely came home, I became closer to the others. To Henry and Charlotte. The second Lady Mortmain, Lady Elizabeth, was their mother.' She dabbed at her eyes. 'But you want to know about Edward. What can I tell you? He was a difficult boy. Sensitive. Reserved – almost secretive, especially when he came home from Eton. When he was at school he wished he were home, but when he came home he longed for school – it was as if he were in conflict with himself. He found our father rather a brutish man, I'm afraid, which indeed he was. Papa was too hard on him. And then there's the legend, of course. The rat.' She shook her head again. 'He would take it to heart so.'

'Legend?' I said. 'Your father told us to speak to you about that. "Ask Caroline about the rat," he said.'

'It's just a foolish tale. So many families have them – families like ours that go back such a long way, obviously. I'm not sure about the others.'

'Can you tell us?'

'Stuff and nonsense as my governess used to say. But Edward developed something of a fascination with the tale. It's just a silly family story.'

'If you could, Miss Mortmain.' She saw I was determined, and, after all, it was she who had brought the subject up.

'It's the usual thing. A man behaves badly, and subsequent generations suffer the consequences.' She sighed and closed her eyes. 'Three hundred years ago, perhaps four, the head of the family at the time was ill. Dying, not unlike my own father is now, I suppose. His son, Hector Mortmain – no one in the family has had the name since – was a known villain.

'My family own land in town as well as up here, and Hector Mortmain terrorised the residents of both. He was a drinker, a gambler, a monstrous whoring fellow who put fear into everyone. One night he was with a group of his friends, minor aristocrats like himself, men with no principles, no morals, who cared about nothing but their own pleasures, whatever they might be. They were on a drunken spree down in the town, carousing through the streets along by the waterfront. Only the vilest dens would permit them entry and they visited them all. But gambling and drinking were not enough, they needs must attend to their beastly urges too.' She shuddered at the mention of the beastly urges, and her cheeks turned red.

'Of course, there are numerous women willing to sell themselves in the streets.' She raised her eyes heavenwards in the manner of a beatific Virgin Mary. 'In many ways it is my work among the fallen, the Magdalenes of Prior's Rents, that provides a salve. I sometimes think I was drawn to the work to atone for my forebears, to do something to expunge the stain on the family for Hector's behaviour. Do you think I'm right, Dr Flockhart?'

'I'm sure, ma'am,' I said.

She nodded. 'I said as much to Edward, but he only laughed. Anyway, it happened that on this night, wicked Hector Mortmain spied one such woman as he raged and bellowed his way through the neighbourhood. She was, so the legend has it, a rose set upon a dung heap. All around her was squalor, degradation and misery, and yet somehow she remained rosy cheeked and pure. Little more than a child, so it's said, though I find that *very* hard to believe as even the children don't remain innocent for long on that sort of street. And so, of course, he had to have her. His friends roared and cheered as he pursued this poor girl down the street. He caught at her skirt, and dragged her into his embrace, but she escaped, running from him down a narrow passageway. Inflamed by the feel of her in his arms and the sight of her at close quarters, the brute pursued her still. He bellowed at her to stop, by God, or he would stick her like a pig once he'd had his way, and he bounded after her between the tall, dark walls.

'Ahead, he could hear the pattering of the girl's frightened footsteps, behind him, the cries and roars of his comrades. He turned a corner. In the darkness ahead of him the girl was sobbing, for she had come to a dead end and there was no escape.

'Precisely what happened next is somewhat uncertain. Hector's villainous companions were still on the main thoroughfare. They seized a light from the lantern-bearer and, to view the spectacle and perhaps take their turn, they plunged after their master into the labyrinth of passages and courts into which he had vanished. All at once they heard a cry, a scream so fearful, so inhuman, that each one of them froze, their veins turned to ice. They crept forward in silence, their jeering boldness vanishing into the night, driven on by fear and curiosity.

'The shadows danced and leaped against the wet, black walls. Up ahead, they could see something moving upon the ground, something macabre, bestial and unholy. It seemed to heave and writhe before them, and they were seized by a crippling terror. There came another scream, gurgling and bloody, so terrible, so ghastly, that two of the party could stand it no more and fled into the night. The others, not wanting to go forward, but not willing to go back, held the lamp up high and peered into the reeking darkness.

'A pale smudge in the shadows, the light reflected off a soft white cheek, showed where the girl stood pressed against the wall, her face a picture of terror. Before her, on the ground, lay Hector Mortmain. The cries they had heard were his. The shadows seemed to have engulfed him for at first they could see nothing but a part of his face, and it seemed as though he was covered by something black and smothering. The leader of the group held his lantern closer. The sight which they beheld struck one of the party dumb with fear on the spot. Another ended his days raving in an asylum, for there, crouched upon the body of Hector Mortmain, was a huge rat. It was as black as the night, its tail a long silver whip of scaly flesh, its eyes black and glittering, its teeth worrying at the throat of their now lifeless comrade. And crawling over his body, ripping, tearing, scratching, were still more of the creatures. A teeming mass of them, smaller and greyer than their rat-king, but no less fierce. Hector's face was white and bloody in the lamplight, his dead gaze fixed upon his old drinking companions.'

'Well,' said Will. He licked his lips, his face pale and sweaty-looking. I knew he had seen what sort of creatures lived beneath the city. 'You certainly tell a good tale, Miss Mortmain.'

'Oh, we are all good at telling the story,' she said briskly. 'It's a pity Edward took it to heart so. But I'm not quite finished.'

'Do go on, ma'am,' said Will.

'Hector Mortmain's body was returned to Blackwater. It lay in the estate chapel for two days, as was the custom at the time, to allow the tenants to pay their respects. Not that any of them did, for Hector Mortmain was loathed and despised about the county. The two days passed, his sick and sorrowful father and his younger brother the only people to keep vigil over him. They saw and heard nothing, making sure to keep candles lit and fragrant herbs burning. But a fresh horror awaited them, a warning that the family had crossed beyond the pale and had no way of returning, for when the time came to fix the lid upon the casket, a huge black rat, with a long silvery tail, burst out from the winding sheet. It made off down the aisle and out into the courtyard and was last seen scuttling into the well at the far side of the park.' She stopped. 'We have a pump in the yard now and one in the kitchen and the scullery. No one's used the east well for years. I believe it's closed over and is hidden among the oaks which have encroached somewhat, as you'd expect. You can see them, and the remains of the well, in fact, from here—'

'And is *that* the end?' said Will. He sounded hopeful.

'Yes. Well, not quite. The legend goes on to say that since that time, no first son of the incumbent Mortmain has died peacefully in their bed.'

'And has this been the case?' I said. 'Have the firstborn Mortmains died in . . . less than peaceful circumstances?'

'There is some truth in it, yes. Hector's brother became Sir James Mortmain on the eventual death of his father. But then *his* first son died by falling from his horse when it reared up and threw him to the ground, startled by – so the story goes – a giant rat that ran across its path. The next died of the plague – apparently a rat was seen in his chambers not two nights before. After that, disease, accidents, battles finished them off one by one, and always a rat, large, black, with a long silver tail, was seen nearby. There have been a few exceptions, I believe. The sixth Sir Thomas's first son took his own life, for instance. I don't believe any rats were involved. But the legend seemed alive and well in my brother's mind. My father is the second son. His elder brother, my uncle, died when his carriage overturned on the London turnpike. It was most unfortunate as the fellow was practically a recluse and rarely went out. My father hates to speak of it.' She clapped her hands, like a schoolmistress dismissing a class. 'So that's the legend, gentlemen. It's macabre, certainly, but it's something my family takes seriously.'

'And you?' I said. 'Do you take it seriously?'

'No, Dr Flockhart. I blame bad luck, bad living and unhappy circumstances. But I don't blame rats and legends. After all, is not the rat a most ubiquitous animal? They live alongside humans wherever we might go. Besides, I am a daughter, despite being firstborn. I don't see that I have a great deal to worry about.' She gestured to the minute books and ledgers that surrounded her. 'And as you can see, it is the realities of life that concern me, not its fairy stories.'

'But your brother Edward did believe it?'

'It affected him deeply, though perhaps not in quite the way you might expect.'

'Can you explain?'

'To his mind, he had two options. He could live in fear, and become a recluse like my father's brother, or he could do the opposite. If the "curse of the Mortmains" was already a foregone conclusion my brother Edward decided he might as well abandon himself to . . . to *pleasure* while he had the chance. And so, as I understand it, that is precisely what he did.'

I had spent many evenings in the company of men, and I knew what they got up to when they were in search of pleasure. When I worked as an apothecary at St Saviour's Infirmary, Dr Bain, the hospital's most forward-thinking surgeon and my closest friend, had taken me out to all manner of degraded places – gambling dens, drinking clubs, cock fights, dog fights, brothels of all kinds. I was fully aware of what happened at Mrs Roseplucker's in those seedy rooms with her various 'virgins'. And yet, could I really discuss vice and debauchery with a woman like Caroline Mortmain? I had no choice. 'And what form did this . . . this *pleasure* take?' I said.

Caroline Mortmain shrugged. 'I am not at liberty to share that with you, Dr Flockhart; it might disturb your sensibilities.' Her face was impassive. For a moment there was silence between us. Then, quite unexpectedly, she grinned. 'Oh, goodness me, sir! Drinking, whoring, gambling. What did you think?'

She must have seen the surprise on our faces as she added, 'I'm sorry if that offends you, gentlemen. You asked me and I'm telling you. Are you not men of the world? Far more than I, to be sure. And those three words cover just about everything, do they not? I have spent a great deal of time in the darker parts of the city – not in search of entertainment, like my dear brother, but saving souls. I have seen and heard things in those streets, in my visits to Newgate, to the slums of Prior's Rents, that would make a sailor blanch.' She held her head up. 'I will not draw a veil over his behaviour. And certainly not if it helps you catch whoever it was who murdered him.' She dabbed at her eyes again. 'But he was a dear sweet boy once upon a time and he did not deserve to be murdered by a stranger in the back room of a brothel.'

I lowered my gaze to allow her to compose herself. For all her talk of rats and legends and dear sweet boys I had not finished with her yet. 'Miss Mortmain,' I said.

'Is there anything else you can tell us? Anything about your brother's friends and acquaintances, for example? Anything unusual that he said or did recently that you are aware of?'

'I didn't know his friends.'

'Was he in trouble of any kind?'

'Trouble?' she frowned.

'I don't know,' I said. 'Was he in debt, perhaps?'

'Of course,' she said. 'Aren't all young men in debt?'

'I'm not,' said Will.

'*You* are not heir to a fortune, Mr Quartermain,' she snapped. '*Especially* if you are not related to the Quartermains of Kensington.'

'Cards?' I said. 'Many a young blade has lost himself at the card table. I assume he relied on your father for his income?'

'Our mother had a little that was bequeathed to herself – though other than that all her money went to my father when they married. Edward and I inherited her moiety. I still have mine, plus some diamonds that my father keeps for me, but my brother's is all spent. After that he went to my father, but Papa became increasingly reluctant to pay his debts.'

I thought of the worn soles and heels of Edward Mortmain's boots, the artfully trimmed cuffs and collar, both of which spoke of a man who had reached the limit of his creditors' generosity. His features had been handsome, but his face had not exhibited the flabby bloated look and the thread veins of the drinker. His liver too had not betrayed a life of excess. I wondered now how much Caroline Mortmain really knew about her brother's habits? She struck me as a woman who

93

liked to know everything about those around her. And if she did *not* know? Why, perhaps she was not above filling in the gaps with her own suppositions and imaginings. Given the detail that had larded her account of the Mortmain rat, and the relish with which she had told the tale, she was clearly adept at embellishing what little she knew.

'Obviously he gambled, he drank, and given his final resting place, whored into the bargain,' she continued. 'In some ways it's a relief that it's over for him. One cannot live a life of such abandon, spend time in such low places and expect not to meet a violent end.'

'Do you have any idea whether someone might want him dead, Miss Mortmain?'

'*Want* him dead? I have no idea. I can't imagine that anyone *wanted* him dead. It must have been this fellow, what was his name? Jobber? Who else could it have been? Who else was there?' She frowned and fingered her looped ringlets. Her gaze strayed to the files that were piled on the golden table in front of her. She was clearly itching to get back to them. 'Oh!' she cried suddenly. '*There* it is!' She reached for a heavy leather-bound ledger with the date *1854* and the word *minutes* embossed in gold leaf on the spine. 'The minutes for the Committee for Lady Visitors. Newgate, obviously. I'm their most regular visitor. I like to keep busy, to be useful. I go on the days when I am not visiting the slum-dwellers. It's mostly Bible readings, advice about hygiene and godly behaviour, that sort of thing. We are always looking for donations and volunteers. Committee members.' She looked up at me, simperingly.

'Your brother, Miss Mortmain, if you please.'

Her hand fluttered to her breast once more. 'Dr Flockhart, my brother was a haunted man who let a fairy story get the better of his good sense and ended up owing money to many people.'

'He told you this? That he owed money to many people?'

'He did, sir. At least, not *as such*. But he certainly asked to borrow money from me. I helped him as best I could, but it was never enough.'

'When was the last time you saw him?'

'The day before he died, in fact. I was in Prior's Rents with some of my ladies. D'you know Prior's Rents?'

'I'm afraid so, ma'am,' I said.

'Of course, he'd been here at Blackwater the night before, but I'd not seen him then.'

'How do you know he'd been here?'

'I heard him arguing with my father. Besides, Blackwater holds no secrets from me.'

'I'm sure it does,' muttered Will.

'What do you mean by that, sir?' Her voice was sharp.

'Nothing, ma'am,' said Will. 'I just meant, there must surely be goings on in a large house like this that pass unnoticed.'

'*Goings on*?' She frowned. 'I can assure you, Mr Quartermain, that I am privy to *everything* that happens here.' Outside, a cloud slipped across the dying sun. The golden wallpaper took on a harsh, brassy appearance. I felt my head beginning to ache.

'If I may, ma'am,' I said. I jabbed Will in the ribs. What on earth was wrong with him? His dislike of the woman before us was almost palpable. Could he not keep his feelings hidden until we were out of her company? 'What Mr Quartermain means is that one cannot be privy to *all*

95

that happens within these walls, especially matters of a more mundane nature.' I hated toadying, but flattery and obsequiousness were sure to get us further than Will's veiled hostility, especially with a woman like Caroline Mortmain. 'But if we may, as it were, return to Prior's Rents. It is a place I have been to many times. My work as surgeon-apothecary takes me there and I make it one of my own philanthropic undertakings to provide physic, free of charge, to the suffering souls whose misfortune it is to dwell therein.' I grimaced inwardly at my own pompous phrasing. Beside me, Will snorted. I knew he would tease me about it later, especially the 'dwell therein' bit.

'The poor are everywhere.' She sighed. 'I applaud your kindness sir. The poor souls in Prior's Rents need my attention every week. My ladies and I are among them as often as possible. Last week I conducted a particularly robust rendition of the *Jubilate Deo* for the residents of Well Court. They were most appreciative.' She put her hand to her breast. 'Lord, but it is a repulsive place, sir. Up to six of them to a room. Sometimes more. One fellow lives with his family of seven in one room beside an open privy. The fellow makes pies – in that very room! Are you sure you would not like to become one of our regular subscribers, Dr Flockhart? Your name will appear in our annual report, next to the quantity of your subscription, of course, as it makes it worthwhile to contributors to see that their name and the bounty of their donation is visible to all.'

'I'm sure something might be arranged, Miss Mortmain.' I smiled unctuously. 'But to the purpose if I may. Your brother?'

'Oh, yes, him. Well, I had no idea what he was doing in a degraded slum like Prior's Rents, as I did not speak to him. And as far as I am aware he did not see me. But I saw *him*.'

'Doing what, ma'am?'

'Walking.'

'Which way was he walking?' said Will.

'Along Admiral Street. Southward.'

'Then he was heading in,' I said. 'Not out. Did you see where he went, Miss Mortmain?'

'No. At least, not specifically. As I said, I was with my ladies. But I was under the impression that . . . well I cannot be sure, but . . . there was another man. Not far behind. He was walking in the same direction at any rate, and he looked just as out of place as my brother.'

'Out of place?'

She shrugged. 'It was not a man from Prior's Rents, sir. That much was obvious. You say you have been in the Rents many times? Then you will know what I mean.'

'You mean he didn't look like a rat-catcher or a coster-monger?' supplied Will.

'Indeed, sir.'

'And what manner of fellow was he?' I said. 'Can you describe him?'

'He wore dark clothes. A dark topcoat, britches, boots, all black. One of those new hats, close fitting with a low rounded crown. I have no idea what they're called. He was tall, perhaps a little taller than is usual. His face was pale, with dark side whiskers.'

'Heavy-set or slender?'

'Neither. Perhaps heavier. Anyway, I had the distinct impression he was following Edward. Perhaps trying to catch up with him as his gaze seemed to be fixed upon my brother's back, though he remained some thirty or so paces behind, and did not call out. But it was only my impression. I was more perplexed by seeing my brother there. I've been to Prior's Rents on many occasions and not once have I seen Edward anywhere near the place.'

'And you would say that your brother seemed to know where he was going?'

'I would say he was walking purposefully, certainly.'

'Did you see where he went?'

'He disappeared – slipped between the houses, perhaps, down a passage or in at a door. But one moment he was there, the next moment he was not.'

'Whereabouts would you say the two of them disappeared?'

'It was just before the Dancing Cat public house. But I did not see exactly. I had my work to do, and my ladies look to me for leadership and guidance. And the poor are so delighted to receive us, I could not turn away from their happy faces to spy on my brother.'

'You work for the Humane Society also?' said Will gesturing to a stack of leather-bound ledgers beneath the golden table.

'I do, sir,' she replied. 'I am skilled in the art of resuscitation.' She took a deep breath. The seams of her already taut bodice groaned and creaked like the timbers of an ancient galleon. 'And I collect funds. It is a cause most dear to my heart,' she added. 'You know what our purpose is, I take it?'

'I do, ma'am,' I said, hoping to avert her exposition. All at once I was desperate to escape from that glaring golden chamber. But it was no use.

'The number of people wrongly taken for dead, Dr Flockhart. Drownings, sir. They are the curse of our waterways. The Serpentine alone claims many victims, especially unwary bathers. And the river – a place of sorrow and suicide. We do what we can to save souls and bring them to the Lord.'

'The mortuary at Blackfriars is a receiving house,' said Will. His remarks were directed to me. I had the feeling he was doing it deliberately, excluding Miss Mortmain while talking about a subject that concerned her. 'There are beds there for those pulled from the river alive or half-drowned, though given the state of the water at Blackfriars there is little hope for anyone who swallows even a mouthful. If they don't drown then they are poisoned beyond all saving.' He turned to the woman. 'Your father's water company draws from the Thames at that point, I believe, Miss Mortmain.' He spoke sharply. 'He supplies half of Prior's Rents.'

'My father's business concerns are his concerns alone,' she snapped.

'But I think your brother Edward did not share your indifference, did he?' Will went on. 'Or your father's.'

She clapped her hands and said briskly, 'Well then, gentlemen, I can see you are both men who care about fairness and justice for all. Especially *you*, Mr Quartermain. Would you care to donate to my most worthy philanthropic causes?'

'What, *all* of them?' said Will.

'Yes, sir, *all* of them!' From beside her sofa she produced a collection box, some six inches by eight, with a handle at one end that allowed her to shove the thing towards us, the slit in its wooden top ready to receive coins or folded notes.

'Would you like to know how your brother died, Miss Mortmain?' said Will suddenly. 'He was poisoned. And before he was dead he had his throat clawed out.'

She put her hand to her decolletage. 'Clawed out? Was it—'

'A rat?' he said. 'Do you think it might be?'

'I think—' Her face was white. 'I think—'

'He was a kind man, Miss Mortmain. I met him only once, but I could see he wanted to do good.'

She drew herself up. 'It is *I* who wish to do good,' she said. She gave her box a shake. I heard the rattle of shifting coins. It sounded full. 'The Humane Society suggests a guinea for saving a life.'

Will rooted in his pockets, his face sulky. 'I don't have a guinea. And there's the cab fare home to consider.'

'Here,' I said. 'Three shillings will have to do on this occasion, Miss Mortmain.' My coins rattled into her heavy wooden box.

'My brother Edward was an unhappy man, Dr Flockhart. Mr Quartermain,' she said, as if the coins I had donated had bought us additional information. 'And yes, he was also a good man. Whatever he was involved in, whatever he had done, I think there was no easy way out.'

Excerpt from the Journal of William Quartermain, Esq., surveyor and assistant architect, Metropolitan Sewer Commission.

The rats of the city are truly legion. I have, on occasion, seen one of their number skulking along the shelves in the apothecary. Jem has a mixture of arsenic and brimstone which he uses against them, however, so we are not sorely troubled here. But the rats of the waterfront are of infinite number and are not so easily eliminated. They are large, sleek, greasy-looking beasts; bold, agile and cunning. They can trot along the narrowest of ledges in the darkest of tunnels. They are fearless swimmers, and care nothing for the vileness of the waters they habitually navigate. Mostly they seek to avoid making our acquaintance, though they are, as a species, inescapable. They have a jaunty confidence, seeming to enjoy each other's company, and I have seen up to twenty of them together, sunning themselves beside an upturned skiff at low tide. I have watched them lightly dance, singly and in twos and threes, up a mooring rope to disappear into the belly of a merchant ship. Puddle Dock is home to a grain warehouse, and there they mill about behind sacks and under pallets quite out in the open. The rats of Puddle Dock are, due to their diet of spilled corn, the fattest of all, with well-oiled pelts, beady eyes and snaking, bony tails. Fox and Badger have a long acquaintance with these animals, for which they appear to have a grudging respect.

'I think some of 'em can read,' Fox said to me yesterday as we watched a sleek pair of the creatures peering up at an advertisement for Bile Beans that had been newly pasted to a wall beside the dock yard. I laughed, but Badger nodded.

'Yes'm,' he said. 'Some of 'em. Not all, but some.'

Chapter Eight

⸎

Caroline Mortmain reached out a hand and yanked on a tapestry bell-pull that dangled beside the fireplace. Ruskin, who had evidently been standing on the other side of the door the whole time, crept in. He grinned at us knowingly as he shepherded us from the room and back down the passage. I had learned not long ago that to underestimate the servants was a grave mistake. They were paid to work, to cook and clean, fetch and carry, but were they also paid to pretend all was well and turn a blind eye? Ruskin had been with the family for his entire life, but that did not necessarily mean that they had bought his silence, or his loyalty. I knew as well as he did that once he was too old or infirm to perform his duties there would be no place for him at Blackwater. The man had to be at least four score years, and yet he still traipsed the draughty, creaking corridors, up and down all day. No doubt one day they would find him dead, lying like a draught excluder at the foot of one of the doors. Perhaps Caroline Mortmain would attempt to resuscitate him so that the old fellow could keep walking, keep standing around awaiting instruction, keep bowing and nodding.

'What about you, Ruskin?' I said. 'What do you make of all this?'

'All this, sir?'

'The death of Sir Thomas's heir, what else?'

'I don't believe I have an opinion, sir.'

'Of course you do, Ruskin. You've been in service here since the first Lady Mortmain, perhaps longer, yes? There can't be a single thing you don't know about this family.'

'Oh yes, sir. I've been here since I was a boy, sir.'

'Well then. I'm sure you have a few tales to tell.'

'I don't tell tales, sir.' His voice had taken on a hard, brittle edge.

'That's understood,' said Will. 'But we would be so grateful if you could help us. We can't let an innocent man hang and leave a guilty one at large. And Sir Thomas deserves to have answers. His son is dead – it's your duty to talk to us, sir. Will you not give us the benefit of your knowledge and experience?'

'I don't know anything.' Ruskin looked from Will to me, and back again. His gaze slid over my shoulder, and for a moment I thought I saw something resembling fear chase across his features. I glanced back. In the gloom behind me I was sure – almost – that there was a movement in the shadows, a patch of darkness that seemed blacker than its surroundings. Man-shaped, perhaps, though I could not be certain. I blinked and tried to focus but whatever it was it had vanished. I could not even be certain that I had seen anything, so fleeting had my impression been.

'Did you see that?' I whispered. 'Will?'

Will shook his head. 'I didn't see anything.' He put his hand on the old man's arm and said, 'Come, sir, you must be tired. Is there somewhere we might go? Somewhere private where you might sit and talk with us a while?'

We followed Ruskin down a long dark passage, the worn stone floor striking chill through our boots. Up ahead I could hear voices and activity, the bustle of feet and the clatter of crockery and cutlery. Ruskin pushed open another door. The kitchen beyond was warm and noisy. At a long table of scrubbed deal, a fat woman was kneading a great lump of dough, while a maid stood at a stone sink scouring copper pans with sand and lemon juice. A boy sat beside the open door with a short-bladed knife in his hand, a basket of peelings on one side of him, a pan of white, naked potatoes on the other. Beyond the kitchen and down another corridor, I could see two women folding laundry. Hanging against the wall, being sponged by a girl in an apron that was far too big for her, was a gigantic dress of vivid green watered silk. One of Caroline Mortmain's, no doubt.

'Mr Ruskin,' said the woman kneading the dough. 'Have you had a bite to eat yet? We had to dine without you, sir, we couldn't wait. There are some cold meats in the larder if you've a mind, sir.'

'I don't have a need for cold meats, but I will take a pot of tea now, if I may, and these gentlemen too, no doubt.' Overhead a bell jangled.

'That's the yellow drawing room,' said the woman. 'Come along, Alice, get a move on, that's the second time, she won't stand for it! Mr Ruskin, that's one of the silvers gone. A fish server, would you believe it! Tom sleeps next to the silver cupboard for this very reason though he says no one was anywhere near it. I don't know what Mrs Grimshaw'll say.'

Ruskin held up a hand. 'Perhaps we can get to the bottom of it without worrying Mrs Grimshaw.'

At the table, a girl of about sixteen rattled some teacups into a tray. 'Break those saucers, Effie my girl, and I'll take it out of your wages,' thundered a tall thin woman, emerging from the shadows. She was dressed in black bombazine from head to toe. Her slick grey hair was severely parted above a pinched white face, a kerchief of black lace pinned to the back of her head and hanging down like a hank of winter weeds. She moved as silently as smoke, the chatelaine at her waist proclaiming her role as housekeeper.

'Yes, Mrs Grimshaw,' said the girl, Effie.

Another bell jangled. 'That'll be the master, can't you see the bell? Get along now. You don't want him complaining again, do you?' On and on it went, the voices and clatter, the sound of pans clanging as they were hung from hooks on the wall, the clump of boots, the jangle of cutlery, the rough hiss of knives being sharpened and the rhythmic grinding of the whetstone.

Ruskin's room looked out at the stable yard. In the corner, a small black arched fireplace cradled a mound of smouldering coals. A sagging armchair of damson-coloured brocade stood on one side of the fire, a hard chair on the other. A tarnished brass bedstead, slightly lopsided, its thin mattress covered with a threadbare counterpane of cotton patchwork, leaned against the wall. The place was heavy with the smell of smoke and damp, and the mustiness of old age.

'One of you'll have to stand,' said Ruskin. 'Though I suppose you could sit on the bed if you've a mind to.' He motioned to Will to close the door and he lowered himself gingerly into his armchair.

'I don't know either of you young gentlemen,' he said. 'But I knew your father, Dr Flockhart, and he was a good man. You'll be in the same mould, I should imagine.'

'In many ways, sir,' I said. 'I hope to measure up to him in time.'

'He made me a salve. Some years ago now.'

'For the joints? I think you have some of that very salve, don't you, Jem?' said Will.

'I do indeed!' I plunged a hand into my satchel. I was in the habit of carrying the stuff around with me, and so many suffered due to the damp that I was forever doling it out. No one was ever ungrateful. 'I have improved the mixture,' I said. 'Olive oil and beeswax with eucalyptus, frankincense, clove, willow bark extract, plus a few other special ingredients.' I winked. 'I can't give all my secrets away, can I?'

'It's your right ankle, I think, sir?' Will took the salve. He knelt before the old man. 'If I may?' He pulled off the man's shoe and stocking. 'Fetch some water, will you, Jem? And the tea?'

I went back into the kitchen. The girl Effie was lifting a copper pan onto a high shelf, the tea tray forgotten on the table.

'Let me help you, miss,' I said. 'It's no trouble.' Effie looked at me strangely as I turned back to face her, so that for a moment I thought she had seen through my disguise, had looked beyond the mask of red skin that covered my eyes and nose, and seen me for what I was, a woman in a man's clothing, pretending every day to be something they weren't.

I asked her for a basin of water and a towel. 'That for Mr Ruskin, sir?' she said. 'Poor old thing. He don't sit down nearly enough and the family sends him traipsing about the house at all hours.'

'Is this the first big house you worked in, Effie?' I said.

'Yes, sir.'

'What sort of a place is it?'

'It ain't so bad, sir. I'm just the parlour maid so it's mostly grate blackings and coal and such like.'

I slid a hand into my jacket pocket and drew out a small tin. 'This is my special salve,' I said. 'Beeswax, calendula, tallow and lavender. Put it on your hands at night just before bed. It'll soften the skin. Smells nice too and will help you to sleep.' I winked. 'Doctor's orders. Now pop it in your pocket, quick.'

She gasped, her cheeks turning red. 'For me? Thank you, sir!'

'What about upstairs? Have you ever noticed anything . . . strange or unexpected?'

'Ain't all rich folks strange, sir? They can't do a single thing for themselves. But it ain't for me to 'ave a thought about that.'

'Did you ever meet Mr Edward?'

'Oh yes, sir. I did his fire every morning when he stayed here. He never saw *me* though. He ain't *supposed* to see me, o'course. He's meant to just wake up and think, Lor! There's a fire! How did *that* magically kindle isself?'

'Which room belonged to Mr Edward?'

'Second floor, sir, east wing at the end opposite the man with the red face what's sitting on a horse.'

'Did you ever see or hear anything . . . anything about him that seemed unusual or out of character?'

'Like what, sir? Can't say I knowed anything about his character. And I never seed anything much but the grate.'

'Even the grate can tell a story, Effie.'

She smiled at that, a sly sideways smile, and said, 'You're right there, sir. You'd be surprised at the things I've seen in the fireplaces at this house.'

'Really?' I said. 'What things?'

'Nothing really.' She turned back to the tea tray. 'But he had a secret,' she whispered. 'I know that much.'

'He did?' I whispered back. 'What sort of secret?'

'He was in love.'

Caroline Mortmain had said nothing of this. So much for knowing everything that went on in the house. I knew I had been right to come to the servants if I wanted to learn what was really going on. 'Really?' I said. 'How do you know?'

'I saw a letter. In Mr Edward's grate.'

'A whole one?'

'Yes. He'd screwed it up and tossed it in, but it went behind the coal scuttle.'

'Can you remember what it said?'

'I can't read, sir,' she said. 'Well, not much. But I knowed it said "My darling Edward". I got a brother named Edward.'

'And you are sure it was "darling Edward", not "my dear Edward", like anyone might write?'

'No, it was D A R, those are easy, like at the end of Edward, and I knows an "el" when I sees one. The rest were obvious.'

'Can you tell me when this was?'

'Not two days ago, sir. Mr Edward was here for a couple of nights. Mr Ruskin'll tell you.'

'I don't suppose you . . . you took it, did you? The letter?'

'Why, no, sir!' She looked shocked. 'I used it for kindlin'.'

'Ah well.'

'Would it have been good if I had?'

'Yes, very good. It might have helped us discover who murdered the poor fellow.'

'Murdered?' Her eyes grew round.

'You didn't know?'

'I only knowed he were dead, sir.' Her face was pale now.

'I'm sorry,' I said. 'I didn't mean to frighten you.' I opened my pocketbook and took out a *carte de visite*. It had my name and address on it. This time my name was preceded by the title I had earned when I had become a Licentiate of the Society of Apothecaries and sat the examinations at the Royal College of Surgeons. I had not used it when my father was alive. To me, he had been the only Dr Flockhart. And the physicians and surgeons at St Saviour's had enjoyed calling me 'Mr', as if I was somehow diminished by the title. I had never felt the need to boast about my qualifications.

'It's not boasting, Jem,' Will had said to me. 'You earned those letters after your name. You might not have your MD, but you have as much right to the title "doctor" as any of them.' It was Will who had got the cards made. He had had the printer decorate the back with images of senna pods and willow leaves, 'to represent the two medicaments you are most regularly called upon to supply, Jem: laxatives and pain relief.' And on the front: *Dr Jeremiah Flockhart, LSA, MRCS, surgeon apothecary and purveyor of fine physic.*

'That's my name,' I said to Effie now, pointing as I read it out. 'And that's my address. 22 Fishbait Lane, St Saviour's. Oh, and you can have this too.' I handed her a small tube of card, the size and thickness of an index finger. It was plugged with a hard yellow substance. 'It's scented beeswax and almond oil,' I said. 'I mixed it with sandalwood and lavender. You can rub it on your wrists and give it a little sniff whenever you like. It's not physic,' I added. 'It just smells nice. Now put it in your pocket, quickly now, before old mother Grimshaw wants some.'

Ruskin plunged his foot into the bowl of warm water. He wriggled his toes. I knew Will for a kind and gentle man, and I'd seen him work his magic before. Old men brought out his tender side. He rubbed the man's ankles.

'My grandfather was just like you,' he said. 'I was brought up by him after my mother died. No doubt I'll be the same one day. It's the draughts, isn't it? My grandfather always said it was the draughts.'

'Yes, sir, and the pain is like gyves about my ankles.'

Will dried the old man's foot and reached for the pot of salve. 'I wonder how many miles you walk in a day, eh?'

'That's a good question, sir.' Ruskin closed his eyes as Will gently rubbed the salve into the man's swollen, thread-veined skin.

'What can you tell us, Mr Ruskin?' he murmured. 'You know all the secrets here. And Sir Thomas deserves to know what manner of a man his son was, and why he died.'

'Sir Thomas wasn't always the way he is now,' said Ruskin. 'The first Lady Mortmain, that's when things changed. She took her own life. Hanged herself. It was Miss Caroline who found her.' He shook his head. 'She didn't tell you *that*, did she? Some women go mad after the birth of a child, Dr Flockhart, you'll know that, and she was one such. Had to lock her in her room. And the baby, young master Edward, he was sent away soon after. Sir Thomas wouldn't have him in the house. Blamed the child for the death of his mother, though I could hardly see it was the child's fault any more than it was Sir Thomas's fault for fathering the lad, or the midwife's fault for birthing the baby.'

'And did Miss Caroline and Mr Edward meet very often as children?'

'Not often. Mr Edward was with his wet nurse, then at school, and then at Oxford. And of course, Sir Thomas married again and along came Mr Henry and Miss Charlotte. After Oxford Mr Edward came home but he never spent a great deal of time here.'

'When was he last here?'

'The day before he died.'

'Was there any reason to suspect that his relations with his family were anything less than cordial?'

'There was some . . . disagreement between Mr Edward and his father, sir. Over money, I believe, though perhaps I shouldn't say it.' He opened his eyes and lifted his foot from Will's hands. 'Feels so much better,' he said. 'Thank you. But I'd better get back—'

'But I haven't done the other one yet,' said Will. 'Sit

a while, Mr Ruskin. Whatever you say will be treated in the strictest confidence. And we need to know as much as we can – if we have some idea about Mr Edward's relationship with his family, some idea of how he lived, then this can only help us discover why he was murdered, and by whom.'

'He was always kind to me,' muttered Ruskin. 'Whatever he was.'

'What do you mean by that, sir?' I said.

'He was a dark horse, Dr Flockhart, sir. Spent money like you wouldn't believe. It was the cause of his arguments with his father. He wanted more, and then more still. One occasion, just before he was murdered it was, the strangest thing happened. It was about money, o'course. He came out from his father's rooms and found me in the corridor. "Listening at the door again, Ruskin?" he said. He sounded quite cross, which wasn't like him at all, and I said I was awaiting his father, as it was time for me to collect Sir Thomas's post bag.' He lowered his voice. 'I don't listen at doors, sirs. But I do hear things through them sometimes.'

'To be sure,' I said. 'It is your duty to be at the door. Anything overheard is purely coincidental.'

'Exactly, sir. Well, Mr Edward blushed at that, for he never had a cross word for me, not really, and he leaned towards me all conspiratorial-like and says, "Can't get the old miser to up the allowance, Ruskin. It's the blasted horses, don't ye know!"'

'The horses? So he was a gambling man?' It was no less than we had heard from Caroline Mortmain. After all, did not all landowners race and gamble? But there was more to come.

Ruskin lowered his voice, as if he was afraid his eavesdropping habits were also practised by his fellow servants. 'That's what he *said*, sir. He *said* he was a gambling man, but I don't think he was.'

'How so?' I said. 'It seems a curious thing to claim a vice one does not actually own.'

'Well, I'd never heard him mention the horses before, and Sir Thomas don't keep racers. He's just not interested, not even in the local steeplechase, though the current Lady Mortmain rides with the hunt and keeps a grand black stallion. Besides, I know a gambling man when I see one, sir. Why, young Mr Edward didn't even take *Bell's*!'

'Bell's?' said Will.

'*Bell's Sporting Life*,' I said. 'You know a dead cert when you see one, Mr Ruskin? I noticed the pink 'un in the grate as we came in.'

'I do, sir. And I've taken *Bell's* these last twenty years. Well, I thought I'd give Mr Edward the benefit of my expertise, what with him being the master's son and always nothing but kindness from him to me, and if he tells me he's a gambling man I take it that's what he is. And he was looking anxious and distracted and was biting his lip fit to bleed, and that's a look I've seen many-a-time, so just as he was about to walk away I ups and tells him to keep an eye on Virago, and he turns all pale and stops and says "What? Where?" and I said, "She's in the Oaks, sir," as that's exactly where she was to be and every sporting man in the country knew it.'

'The Oaks?' said Will.

'Yorkshire Oaks, sir,' supplied Ruskin. 'It's a flat race. One mile, three furlongs and one hundred and eighty-eight yards. Fillies only. Virago's set to win, sir, or my name's not John Ruskin.'

'And what did Mr Edward say?'

'Well, sir, he looked at me all strange and pale and he said, "My God, Ruskin, is she back already? Confound it! I came that way myself and didn't see her. Thank you, Ruskin," and then off he went.'

'And what did you make of that?' I said.

'What did I make of it? What I made of it is that it wasn't a word of sense! He didn't have no idea about Virago! How can he be a racing man if he's never heard of Virago?'

'That's true,' I said. 'Even I've heard of her.'

'Have you?' said Will. 'Why didn't you tell me?'

'When did the second Lady Mortmain die, Mr Ruskin?'

'Oh, some twenty years ago now. Sir Thomas was beside himself with grief – far worse than the first time. He's kept her room in town just as it was. Not that he goes there. He doesn't really go anywhere.'

'In town?' I said.

'Sir Thomas has a town house, sir. It's where she died. It's been boarded up these last twenty years. No one goes there. Not anymore.'

We made our way back along that dark passageway and up the flight of steep stairs into the main house.

'What was all that about?' said Will. 'Virago?'

'A horse,' I said. 'At least, for Ruskin "Virago" is a horse. But not to Edward Mortmain.' I stopped beside one of the small, mullioned windows. Across the lawn, in the gathering gloom, the ancient trees that bordered the park formed a dark fringe, wreathed in mist. 'I think Edward Mortmain was thinking of those oaks.'

'And the virago?'

'That remains to be seen. We've only met one possible candidate so far.'

'I'll be glad to get away from this gloomy old warren,' muttered Will. 'No wonder Miss Caroline stays in that abominable golden room. There's something oppressive about all this black wood, all these cold flagstones and uneven parquet floors. I need a warm snug, and a friendly publican to remind myself that the world is not such a bad place after all. Perhaps a plate of chops and a pint of ale at Sorley's. Or a beef and oyster pie. Mrs Sorley is back – thank the Lord. I'm not sure my digestion or my bowels could take another one of Sorley's pies.'

'Not just yet,' I murmured. 'We have a couple of places we need to go first.'

'Where?' said Will. 'Can't we go home now? I'm tired. All this traipsing about. I don't know how old Ruskin does it.'

'I'd like to take a look in Edward Mortmain's rooms.'

'Jem, we don't know where they are!'

'*You* don't, but *I* do. They're up the main staircase, second floor, east wing, opposite the man with the red face sitting on a horse.'

'They all have horses and red faces,' he muttered. 'And it's getting dark. We don't even have a candle.'

'I thought you always had a candle,' I said. 'Especially since you so often find yourself underground these days.'

He sighed. 'Do you have to remember everything I say, Jem?' He rummaged in his coat pocket and brought out a box of parlour matches and a candle end. 'Will these do?'

We crept up the stairs, every tread groaning beneath our feet. The evening was drawing in and the light of the setting sun bled through the stained-glass windows at the head of the stairs, the purples, reds and blues of the Mortmain coat of arms illuminating our faces like a bruise. I wondered who might hear us, who else might be at home? I remembered the dark shadow I had seen as we were speaking to Ruskin, and I could not help but look over my shoulder. Was someone watching us? I could not see them if they were. We had yet to meet the third Lady Mortmain, as well as the two other Mortmains, Henry and Charlotte. What would we say if one of them found us? Did the letter in my pocket cover our intrusion into private rooms?

We crept along the east passage on the second floor. At the end, as the girl Effie had said, was a full-length portrait of a red-faced man. He had the blobby nose and long face of the Mortmains. As in so many portraits from a hundred years earlier, he was wearing a huge white wig, curled and fluffed, which framed his face like the bouffant legs and buttocks of a well-brushed sheep. His eyes were small and beady and completely without lashes, which gave him a mean, pig-like appearance. He was sitting astride a cavorting horse, his right hand resting on the hilt of a sword. With his left he was pointing away, directing the viewer's gaze into the background, towards a dark thicket of trees in which a stone well was just about visible among the clustering trunks and branches. An ill-formed shadow, a creature of some kind, seemed to be emerging from it. The painting was six feet high in its curling golden frame, reaching up to a ceiling of yellowed plasterwork. Will struck a match and held it up to the image.

'What's that on the well?' I said.

'Can't really tell,' he murmured, peering so close that I feared the match might set the canvas alight. 'Just a formless shadow. But there are teeth. And tiny yellow eyes.'

'The family rat, no doubt.'

'Doesn't look like a rat. Looks like an angry otter.'

'Come along,' I hissed.

'I think it's coming out of the well, rather than going in.'

'For goodness' sake. One look at that fellow's wig and any creature would leap into a well.' I tugged his sleeve. 'Come *on*. Before someone sees!'

The brass handle to the room opposite was cool against my palm – was it locked? To my surprise, the door swung open without a sound. Inside, a still, dark silence.

Will lit another match as I groped my way towards the curtains. I pulled them aside, the scrape and jangle of their brass rings harsh in the crêpe-smothered silence. The twilight I let in made little difference, and Will's match flame flickered and wavered, reflected in the mullioned panes as a hundred dancing yellow lights.

We were in a large bedroom, some twenty feet square, with a heavy, four-poster bed against its north wall, and an ornate fireplace with a carved mantelpiece of polished slate. The mantel itself was artfully garnished in swathes of black paramatta, the grate cold and empty, with no trace of fire or cinder. The bed's damson drapery had been drawn closed and hung about with weeping lengths of mourning crêpe. The desk, a wide, leather-topped affair that stood before the window, was similarly dressed. The room was as cold and damp as the grave, with a dank, musty smell. I gestured Will towards the desk. He took one end of the crêpe, and I the other, and we lifted it clear.

I had no idea what I expected to find. And yet I could not leave that house without a look. Will had taken up a sheaf of letters from a mahogany letter rack. The wax had been hastily ripped apart on all of them, bits of the stuff carelessly scattering the desk's leather writing slope. Will opened one. Then another. 'Debt,' he said. 'All of them. He owes money to some angry people. This one sounds quite threatening.'

There were signs of industry about the desk. The ink in the inkstand had been pulled forward, the pen tossed aside as if a scribbled note had been dashed off. To one side lay a stick of sealing wax with its end melted and angrily squashed, a pen knife and the translucent shavings from a hastily whittled quill. I was not sure what to make of it.

'Whatever he did when he was here, evidently it involved opening his letters, and writing one, perhaps more, of his own. I assume he put them in his father's post bag, unless he took them with him to London. Either way they will be long gone by now, though we may yet learn something more.' I picked up a sheet of blotting paper that had fallen beneath the desk. It had been used many times and was dotted and marked with ghostly half-visible sentences, a palimpsest of lost notes and messages. *Sir, if you could . . . on the 1ˢᵗ inst. . . . road and weather permit . . .* It all seemed commonplace enough.

In addition, someone – I assumed Edward Mortmain himself – had doodled here and there upon it, wool-gathering, no doubt, as he considered his phrasing. On the other side of the paper, however, one line of words, half present half absent, appeared. Much of it was merely dots and dashes, splotches of darker ink showing where his pen had spluttered, the message the paper had blotted being written in haste perhaps, or anger. One thing I could make out, however, was a number – *18th*. The day before Edward was murdered.

'We need a mirror,' I said.

'The mirrors are all turned to the wall and covered in bombazine or crêpe,' whispered Will.

I went through a door to the right, which turned out to be a dressing room, complete with washstand and basin. Beside it, swathed in crêpe, was a mirror on a tall mahogany stand. Will lifted the candle as I held the blotting paper up to its reflection. The words were faint, and fragmented, but visible nonetheless.

18th October. My dear Byrd, I write to enquire about the properties in Well Court, Lade Passage and Back Glebe Passage . . . I will call on Wednesday inst. At 11am to discuss. Even though the words were blotted it was evident that they had been written in haste. The letters were large, ragged, dashed off, scattered with ink blots from where the pen had scratched and sprayed its contents. '*My dear Byrd,*' I said.

'He won't tell us anything.'

'Perhaps not, but he may well be able to tell us *something*, even if it is not what Edward Mortmain's business was.'

'Back Glebe Passage,' said Will. 'I know that name. That's—'

'Prior's Rents,' I said.

'Did you know the Mortmains owned property there?'

'Only since Miss Mortmain mentioned it. I assume the family have kept a hold of the streets wicked Hector Mortmain once roistered through,' I said. 'But who owns London is something of a mystery.'

'Would someone like Sir Thomas Mortmain bother with a place like the Rents?'

'Of course! It's seven shillings a week for a room in a house in Well Court. But there's a long line of people that lie between the poor wretches of Well Court and the golden rooms of the Mortmains. The tenant gives the rent to the rent collector, who gives the money to the leaseholder's agent. The agent answers to the leaseholder, the leaseholder is answerable to the solicitor. The solicitor knows the landowner's agent. The landowner's agent sees that the money goes to the landowner, perhaps via another solicitor.

'There are at least six people between the person who pays the rent and the person who owns the land. And it's a more profitable enterprise than you might think. Seven shillings for one room in a stinking slum like Well Court? How many rooms would there be in those subdivided buildings? There are four rooms in the basement alone! And then consider how many houses are crammed into those narrow streets and courts? You're looking at about a thousand souls in Well Court, each paying an average of two shillings. That's an income of £100 a week from one slum.'

'A better return than an address in Mayfair.'

'And you never have to fix the place either. Most of the leaseholders are on short term leases, so they don't have to make repairs – by the time the repairs are due, their lease has ended. Then someone else picks the lease up, and so the dance goes merrily on, the rent going up, the houses getting worse, no one responsible for anything. And if you do try to find the landowner, then there are so many solicitors and agents in the way it's practically impossible to call them to account. So, in answer to your question, Will, I am not at all surprised to learn that Sir Thomas owns at least part of Prior's Rents.'

I folded up the blotting paper and slipped it into my pocket. The bedroom had a feeling of abandonment. The air was stale, the bedsheets damp to the touch, the fireplace empty. Will was standing again beside the desk. There was a picture frame, face down, just visible beneath the fold of bombazine that we had pushed aside. Will picked it up. 'What a superstitious family,' he muttered.

'Death comes in so many guises. Perhaps it's not surprising to take every precaution – even if it means putting photographs of the living face down in case the spirit of the deceased takes revenge. This is a household that believes in a supernatural rat with a thirst for retribution. I think one cannot underestimate their superstition.'

Will was looking at the photograph. The frame was an ornate polished silver, the image crisp and focused. Will had tried his hand at photography not long ago. He had filled a few albums with his work – street scenes, the Thames at Blackfriars, images of the apothecary from different angles. Jenny and Gabriel had sat for him several times. I, however, had always refused. 'This is a daguerreotype,' he said now. 'Very well executed. A natural pose, and the clamp behind the head is invisible. I wonder who the sitter is?'

He turned the frame over. On the back was a label bearing the words *Thos. Golightly, 2 The Strand. Photography, taxidermy, scenery.* He removed the back, slipping the image from its casing. On the reverse of the photograph, handwritten in a flowing confident script were the words *For Edward. A secret kept. So shines a good deed in a naughty world. Affectionately, C.* I peered at the woman's face, the hooded eyes, the proud nose. A handsome woman in a modern dress peering over a boa of black feathers. I slipped the image into my satchel. Edward Mortmain had no further use for it.

Excerpt from the Journal of William Quartermain, Esq., surveyor and assistant architect, Metropolitan Sewer Commission.

The Fleet

The River Fleet springs far to the north. It has two tributaries, one rising in Hampstead, the other Highgate. There are tales of pigs inhabiting the sewers south of Hampstead, wild tribes of them spawned from a single lost pig who inadvertently wandered into the mouth of the sewer to farrow. Her offspring have been there ever since. Fox tells me that the pigs are wild and savage, that they wander around underground for miles. Thimble saw my expression, however, and was quick to reassure me. 'They don't never come this far. Pigs hate walkin' against the tide.'

I find the presence of my comrades reassuring. As doltish and teasing as Fox and Badger can be, they know intimately the moods of the tunnels and passages that lie beneath the city. Master Thimble, a lad no more than eight years old, is also entirely unconcerned by the darkness and the smell underground.

I cannot bear it, and I always have my neckerchief wound tightly about my lower face, the tall neck of my sewer-man costume drawn up as far as it will go. Fox, Badger and I have adapted some of the Toshers' own methods. Each of us carries a long sturdy hoe to stabilise ourselves in the flow of filth, and so that if we slip we might use the metal end to hook onto something – anything – and haul ourselves back upright. We each have a dark lantern affixed to the breast of our coats by means of leather laces and metal hooks. This allows our way forward to be illuminated. Equally, if we bend over to examine the flow, or the brickwork, the light will follow us. Thimble too has a lantern and hoe. He also wears his coat of many pockets in case he finds some useful items.

The Fleet, as it emerges into the Thames, is the vilest flood of filth and pestilence known to man. It has been consumed gradually by the city, first turned into a canal, then culverted, its lower reaches from Ludgate to the Thames finally entombed in 1769. The stink within is overpowering. I recognise it – sulphur, ammonia, decay, rotting vegetable matter, excrement – as being the same reek that drifts up into the city from the drains and gully holes that open onto it, especially those near Newgate, the Old Bailey and Temple Gardens. As we made our way inside today I looked over my shoulder. We had walked not fifty yards but already the entrance was no more than a glimmer of light, like a dirty full moon rising over a reeking Hades. The tide was on the ebb, and we had quite some time before it posed any threat to us. Nevertheless, the knowledge that the tunnel could, in a few hours, be flooded to the roof added to my rising sense of dread. What if I became lost? Separated from the others? I might wander for ever in those hideous tunnels until my light gave out. Until the waters flooded in. Until the rats come for me. When such are my daily thoughts, is it any wonder that I do not sleep at night? That my dreams are filled with darkness and fear?

125

I had a compass in my pocket and a map I had drawn of the known sewers: the substantial and well-built Georgian sewers, the modifications made in the Restoration era, the remains of the Tudor sewers, and the grim mediaeval traces of the sewers of King Edward. There are miles of them, old watercourses, drains, pipes, buried cisterns. Some are too narrow for us to walk or crawl down, but many are some four feet or more in height and easy to negotiate. The squelching of my boots makes me shudder, the squeaking of the rats appals me, and the shadows ahead and behind seem to seethe and jump with unseen horrors. Today, a rat dropped from the tunnel roof onto my neck, and I let out a scream so loud my own ears hurt. I dashed the animal to the water and it swam away into the darkness. Fox and Badger stared at me, their faces impassive. 'That's nothing,' said Badger. 'Nothing to what's up ahead.'

Thimble tugged at my sleeve. 'My old gaffer, One-Eyed Nathan, he lost an eye to a rat. Deaf Jack, he lost an ear. He weren't actually deaf, he were just pretendin', though the ear were quite gone. But you learn to fight 'em off. Or you gets fast with the stick.' He made a swift jab at the shadows with his hoe, and one of the creatures dropped into the effluent, stunned. 'Or you looks lively with your boots.'

Thimble does not have any boots. Tomorrow, I will buy him some from the chandler's on Bridge Street.

Chapter Nine

We crept back down the main staircase in silence, groping our way along the dark passage towards the door. Given that we had seen so many servants in the kitchen I was surprised that so few of them were visible above stairs. I was about to say as much when a door opened, and a young woman appeared. She was dressed in black silk from head to foot. Under her right arm she carried a book. In her left, she held a cage with a rat in it. The rat was not moving. She stopped dead when she saw us, her gaze darting from me to Will. She looked as if she would like to vanish back the way she had come. I sighed inwardly. Were we never to get out of this infernal place? She saw us looking at the cage.

'It's not dead,' she said, as if that was what we had been wondering. 'It's just sleeping. The gardener gave it to me. It's had some ether. I'm going to cut it open.' She flipped the book open with one hand. 'I've done a heart – a pig's heart. Cook gave me one. And I've done cows' eyes too. From the butcher. Now, it's his turn.' She held the rat up and shook the cage. 'Perhaps he is dead,' she muttered. 'It's easy to get it wrong.' The book, I noted, was a dog-eared copy of Bagshot's *Comparative Anatomy*.

'Where did you get that?' I said.

'Caroline gave it to me,' she replied. 'My sister.'

'Hunter's is better,' I said. 'Hunter's *Comparative Anatomy*, she should have got you that instead. The drawings are far clearer.'

'Are you a doctor?' said the girl. 'I hope you're more enlightened than father's physician. He thinks reading about anatomy will render me mad, or at least make me mentally exhausted. He thinks I'm not capable. I told him there's a woman doctor already. I thought I could become one too. What do you think?'

'I think it's a splendid idea,' I said.

'There is that Miss Nightingale too, these days,' said Will. 'I read about her in *The Times*.'

'That's no use,' said the woman. 'I don't want to be told what to do.'

'Nor should you,' said Will. 'And in the meantime, there's your rat to consider.'

She held up the cage. 'It's a big one. Old Fitz trapped it near the stables.'

'I'm Dr Flockhart,' I said. 'This is Mr Quartermain. You must be Miss Charlotte. Does your father know about your dissections?'

'Yes. No. Perhaps he does.' She shrugged. 'The point is he doesn't care. He said he's given up on his children. On all of us. My stepmother is a viper. Edward is – was – irresolute and immoral. Caroline is noisy and absurd.

Henry is weak and I, I am impossible.' She grinned. 'So he says. He's only partly wrong.'

'Which part?' said Will.

'Edward. Poor Edward. He wasn't either of those things. He was just unhappy.' She didn't look especially happy either. Her face was pale, her mouth a straight line. She had a similar look to Caroline, though she was slender, rather than a galleon like her sister. She had an earnestness about her too. I hoped she would not end up disappointed. 'Have you met Caroline yet?' she said.

'Yes,' I replied. 'She was wearing red and white striped clothes.'

'She reminds me of a circus tent when she wears that one.'

'Or a hot air balloon,' I said.

She gave a bark of laughter. 'What about the other two?' she said. 'My brother Henry and the third Lady Mortmain?' She grinned. 'Lady Veronica. "Lady Virago" is what my brother Edward called her. You probably don't want to meet her if you can help it.'

On the far side of the hall a door creaked open, and the tall black-clad figure of the housekeeper emerged. The chatelaine at her waist jangled like a gaoler's keys. I heard the faint 'click' of another door closing and when I glanced back Miss Charlotte had vanished. The housekeeper came towards us on silent feet.

'Sir Thomas has instructed me to inform you that the funeral of his late son Mr Edward Mortmain will take place in three days,' she said. 'His body is to be brought up to the house today. A vigil will take place for the deceased. Three days, sir. He hopes you will be done with your enquiries by then.' She gestured towards the door. 'Lipscombe has brought the carriage round for you.'

Sir Thomas's coach was a large mahogany box with the family arms emblazoned on the door. A pair of black horses gnashed and champed at their bits, as if they were furious to be sent back out into the night. I slid onto the sprung leather seat, as relieved as Will to be getting away from Blackwater.

Just as the coachman slammed the door and made to mount the box, I heard a knocking sound. A little white hand was tapping on the window. It was on the side that could not be seen from the house. I let down the window and peered out into the night.

'Effie,' I said. 'What are you doing here? Do you want to go to town?'

She shook her head, though the expression on her face suggested otherwise. She put her hand in her pocket and pulled out a fold of paper. It was grimy, crumpled, black with smuts and dirty fingerprints. 'It's Mr Edward's letter,' she said. 'I did take it, sir. I don't know why. I wish I hadn't. Mrs Grimshaw keeps watching me, I think she thinks I stole something. Perhaps the fish server, though I didn't touch it. I don't even know what a fish server looks like as they don't let the likes o' me touch the silver. And you was so kind to me, sir. Mrs Grimshaw, she's Miss Caroline's creature, sir. She didn't never like Mr Edward. Said he got what he deserved. But he were always nice to me, sir, so here's his letter. And there's something else there too. Something I found in the grate. Don't know what it is but it might help. Told you the grate has more secrets than anyone knows.' She fell back as the coachman cracked his whip, and vanished into the shadows.

The coach jerked forward. 'Thank God,' said Will. 'I don't think I could have stood another minute in that place.'

I could not disagree. The place had seemed ordinary enough on our arrival, but the more time we spent there, the more I had wanted to leave. And the feeling that someone unseen was watching us had grown until I felt as though my skin was itching. As the carriage rumbled off down the drive I looked back at the house. A final red beam of setting sun illuminated the Elizabethan bricks so that they glowed like the coals at the heart of a brazier. And then the clouds swept closed and the light was extinguished, the house nothing more than a grim, misshapen hulk. I stared up at its twisted chimney pots, the windows black bottomless pools – and then all at once a light appeared at one of them. It was a candle, dim and flickering. Behind it, reflected in its pale, yellow beam, was a face. I could not tell whether it was male or female, but it looked down at us with such loathing, such hatred, that I put my hand out and seized Will by the arm.

'Is that Edward Mortmain's room? The one on the second floor? D'you see, Will? D'you see the candle? And the face? Who—' I looked away for a split second, but when I looked back there was nothing, nothing at all, save for a single servant emerging from the oaken front door to light the lamps on either side. He watched us drive away, his lantern swinging in his hand, his face impassive.

Will was sprawled on the seat beside me. His eyes were closed and the roar of the wheels over the gravel surface of the drive had obliterated my words. 'What a family!' he said now. 'How does poor Ruskin stand it? That awful Mortmain woman!'

'Which one?'

'The striped one. All that rubbish about visiting rookeries and prisons and saving the near dead. As for her ladies, and her *jubilates*, and her advice. And imagine waking up after almost drowning and finding *her* leaning over you! I'd leap straight back into the water if it were me! I'd not let her resuscitate me if you paid me a hundred pounds. I'll tell you something else, too, Jem. I might not one of the Kensington Quartermains, but I've *definitely* seen her before.'

'Where?' I said. 'And when?'

'On the waterside,' he replied. 'When I met Edward Mortmain at low tide. She was waiting on Blackfriars Bridge in a carriage. I'm sure it was her. I'd recognise that face anywhere.'

Clouds had gathered darkly overhead. A squally wind had arisen, buffeting the coach so that it rocked and swayed as it hurtled into the night. The coachman lashed his whip above the horses' heads, the carriage bouncing as the wheels rattled angrily over the uneven surface.

'We can't talk here, Jem,' cried Will as we rocketed round a corner. I seized hold of the leather strap that hung down from the roof of the carriage to steady myself as the vehicle bounced and lurched. Will did the same. 'I think I prefer a hansom,' he shouted above the din. 'Remind me never to get a coach and four.'

I pulled down the window. Perhaps I could shout up to make the driver slow down. 'Mr Lipscombe?' I bellowed into the whirling twilight. 'Coachman? Mr Lipscombe?' But the fellow was hunched in a thick woollen travelling cloak, the collar pulled up around his ears and he seemed not to hear. I assumed he wanted to get to town and back before the storm broke, for he kept his eyes on the road, his hat pulled down, deaf to all but the sound of his horses and whip, and blind to all but the road ahead.

The road that led from Blackwater to the London turnpike was not like the straight, well-paved thorough-fares of town. It was hemmed in by high hedges of laurel and hawthorn, its surface a mixture of mud and cinder, heavily rutted from the passage of farm carts and wagons, with dips and bends that required skilful navigation if approached at speed. It was clear that Lipscombe and his horses had driven the route many times. I could hear nothing above the roar and clatter of the wheels, the creak of the carriage and the thunder of horses' hooves. The growing darkness whirled with leaves, birds exploding from the hedgerow as we rocketed by. And then, all at once, three things happened.

As the carriage swung around the corner, an animal sprang out from between two gate posts. I could not see what it was, but it was trampled by the first of our horses and flung, a blur of blood and fur, under the wheels of the carriage and into the hedge on the opposite side of the road. The horse stumbled, our coach rocked and lurched, careering to the right and tipping sideways as its wheels ran into the ditch. At that same moment a figure on horseback sprang out in front of us in furious pursuit of the animal that had leaped beneath our wheels. Unable to see us due to the high hedges and sunken road, the rider was forced to pull up with such sharpness that their horse pranced and whinnied, its teeth gnashing and foaming, its hooves flailing over our coachman's head. The horse's rider was flung back, somehow managing to remain seated even as their mount reared onto its hind legs. Lipscombe struggled to control his own horses, the animals bucking and screaming as the carriage slewed across the road. Will and I were flung from one side to the other, our heads knocking together like coconuts. Hardly had the coachman dragged his team to a standstill when another carriage careered around the corner. I saw lanterns glowing like the eyes of a beast as it rushed towards us, black horses racing as fast as their driver could manage. Behind them, a long box-like wagon of polished ebony. On its side, painted in glimmering gold, a skull, a pair of crossed bones, an hourglass. I heard the driver scream as he hauled on his reins. The horses reared and plunged, the air outside our carriage window now all kicking hooves and sable bellies and groaning leather, the air torn with shouts and whinnies, the sound of wood snapping, harnesses creaking and grinding.

Will was flung on top of me as our carriage jerked and bounced, the hooves striking home against roof and door like Thor's hammer. And then all at once a strange calm descended, horses huffing and snorting, bridles and reins jangling. I realised then that the whole time we had also been listening to another noise, a scream so agonised, so terrified, that it chilled my blood.

'What was it?' gasped Will. He seized me by the

sleeve. 'Did you see it? That creature that burst out of the hedgerow and under our wheels. It looked like a rat.'

'Rats aren't that big.'

'Oh yes they are, Jem.'

'Ho there!' cried a voice. The rider swung down from the black stallion. I could hardly believe that anyone could ride side-saddle and yet manage so large a horse with such skill. I had assumed that the rider must be a man. Instead, a tall, slim woman in a black riding habit stepped forward. 'Lipscombe, is that you? Where on earth were you going? Is anyone hurt?'

'Not I, your ladyship,' came the reply.

'Nor I,' said the driver of the hearse. The man at his side shook his head.

'Who in God's name is taking the carriage out so late?' she snapped. 'Henry, is that you? Damn it, Henry, you're supposed to be in mourning. You could at least *act* as though you're sorry he's dead – oh!'

My appearance at the carriage window stopped her short. 'Good evening, ma'am, my name is Flockhart. My companion here is Mr Quartermain. We have come from Sir Thomas. How are the horses, Lipscombe?'

'It's put the wind up them, sir, but nothing more,' the coachman replied.

The woman clicked her tongue. She gave Will and me the most cursory of nods in acknowledgement, and said, 'Well then, Lipscombe, best get the carriage out of the way. This hearse can't move backward, and we'll need your help to get it out of this ditch.'

The hearse was lopsided, both of its left wheels completely off the road. It was almost night, and the carriage lanterns gleamed darkly on the sweating backs of the horses, the gold skull and bones, the hourglass. Beneath, painted in gold, the words *de mortuis nil nisi bonum*. Do not speak ill of the dead.

Lady Mortmain frowned. 'And what the devil is making that infernal noise? Is that the fox I was after? The den is somewhere near Bateman's woods. We'll need to take the dogs out. My word, but he's a noisy one.' She jumped down into the ditch, reached forward and hauled a young fox into view. The animal screamed and thrashed, its eyes reflecting red in the light from the carriage lanterns. It tried to bite her, its teeth flashing, its eyes rolling. The woman held tight to the scruff of its neck, blood splattering her face from the creature's mangled legs as it wriggled in her grasp. Its cries grew louder, pitiful and wretched, but also filled with hatred and rage. Lady Mortmain seized it with both hands, and with a quick hard twist broke the creature's neck.

Chapter Ten

⁓

Will and I decided to walk back to the city. The night was clear, it was not far to the London turnpike and both of us were anxious to put our run-in with the speeding hearse behind us. And so, after Lady Mortmain had remounted her horse, our carriage turned around, the hearse continued its journey and Will and I set off for home.

By the time we reached the apothecary it was approaching ten o'clock. Mrs Speedicut was sprawled before the fire in my father's old armchair. She had been in the same position when we left that morning. I had a feeling that she had not moved at all, unless it had been to retrieve the gin bottle she kept hidden beneath the hops in the herb drying room. Did she really think I did not know about it? She reeked of the stuff as if it was oozing from her very pores.

'Come along, come along, you old slattern, make yourself useful,' cried Will. He kicked the side of her chair. 'Cut us a piece of that game pie I bought yesterday, can't you? It's in the larder. And some of that pickle you got from the market. And are there any apples? I've been thinking about a crisp red apple all the way home.'

I half expected Gabriel to have eaten the pie but there was plenty left, and Mrs Speedicut did as she was asked, heaving herself to her feet and setting about her duties with a sigh.

Will eased off his shoes and socks. 'Did you see the way she wrung the neck of that fox? She didn't even flinch.'

'Ruskin had intimated that there was a sporting quality to the woman.'

'Yes, well, I didn't expect a demonstration of that "sporting quality" so soon and at such close quarters,' said Will. 'What a singular family! And what did you make of the way Sir Thomas Mortmain spoke of them?'

'He obviously thinks, as we do, that Edward's death could only have been perpetrated by someone with an intimate knowledge of the rat legend. For that reason, he wants his family interrogated. What he intends to do with our discoveries is unclear, given that he insists that we don't inform the magistrate.'

'I think there is something he is not telling us. Something none of them is telling us.'

'I agree,' I said. 'And to make matters yet more perplexing, there's the matter of the stolen bowels. We never found them, you know. Dr Graves even went up to the lost property office at Bow Street!'

'Who would do such a thing?' said Will. 'A medical student, perhaps?'

'We have one such hopeful in Miss Charlotte Mortmain.'

'Yes, but she's just a girl.'

'Girls can do anything,' piped up Jenny. 'Leastways that's what you're always telling me, Mr Jem.'

'And so they can, Jenny. Certainly, I'm not ready to rule Miss Charlotte out yet. And she may look like a girl, but I can assure you she is no unwordly child and from what I can gather she is quite used to doing as she pleases.'

'But stealing her brother's bowels?'

'Her half-brother's bowels.'

'What difference does that make? I can hardly believe she would do such a thing to anyone, let alone to a blood relative.'

'She has dissected a heart and some eyeballs.'

'She's still a young woman. I just can't imagine it.'

'Then don't imagine it,' I said. 'Imagine her dissecting a rat that's still alive, for that was what she was planning. Or imagine her stepmother wringing the neck of a fox without even blinking.'

'Yes.' Will looked at me. 'That was quite surprising too.'

'And there is also the matter of Edward Mortmain's stomach contents. Edward Mortmain was poisoned, and the wound at his throat inflicted while the poison had taken effect but before he was dead. The blood spatter suggests that he was alive when his jugular was torn. I could smell the hemlock in his body – his mouth and oesophagus – not to mention the sight of his grinning rictus, which will haunt me for weeks. The lack of erythroderma suggests that he had not lain there for very long before he was discovered. The meal in his stomach suggested he dined not too long before death. The contents are of interest too. What would one expect such a man to dine upon? Claret, steak, oysters, the usual things? Well, our man does not eat any of that. Instead, what does he eat? Cherries and plums. A bit of meat certainly, a drop of brandy, but an unexpected quantity of cherries and plums. Now, what does that tell you?'

Will shook his head. 'I don't know.'

'Neither do I. Not yet. But it undoubtedly means *something.*'

I slid my hand into my jacket pocket and pulled out the grubby fold of paper that the parlour maid had thrust at me through the carriage window. 'This was found in Edward's fireplace just before he was murdered,' I said.

'I thought it had taken you rather a long time to fetch that basin of water for old Ruskin's feet,' said Will when I told him how I had come by it. 'We were right to speak to the servants.'

I handed it over. 'Read it out.'

He smoothed the paper as best he could, examined the nap, the thickness. He held it up to the candle and peered at the watermark. 'A high quality paper. A curious size though, not your typical notepaper.'

'English paper,' I said. 'Half a sheet of foolscap. Not the traditional choice for a love letter. Might you read it out?'

'*My darling Edward. I have said nothing. I will say nothing. I remain true to you and you alone. Come to me. Your own C.* It's dated 15th. Four days before Edward was murdered.'

'And the writer, the mysterious C, chose to send the letter to Blackwater, rather than to Edward's club. She clearly knew where he was likely to be, which suggests she saw him, or at least heard from him recently.'

The letter had been folded neatly and sealed before it had been crumpled up and tossed into the grate. I peered at the brittle blob of red wax. 'Sealed with a plain stamp, so nothing to help us there.' I folded the paper up. Edward Mortmain's name and 'Blackwater Hall, Hampstead' were written in the same bold hand as the letter itself. 'What do you make of it then?'

'Edward Mortmain had a lover, obviously.'

'A lover whose letter he throws away?'

Will shrugged. 'An argument? Perhaps one leading to murder?' He took the note from me once more and looked at it closely. 'I think it's the same handwriting as on the back of the daguerreotype. The long "s", the upright hand, the ornate tail to the "y". It's unmistakeable.'

'And there's also this.' I tossed him a small circular metal object. 'The parlour maid found it in the grate along with the ashes at the same time as she picked up this letter.'

Will examined the small silver disc I had taken from my pocket. A small hole had been punched in the top, so that it might be threaded onto something, a necklace or bracelet, perhaps, or the chain of a pocket watch. Once it had been a silver shilling. Now, both sides had been buffed smooth and shiny. On one side, engraved with delicacy and precision, the entwined initials 'E' and 'C'. On the other, some tiny forget-me-nots, distinctive for their small round petals, had been skilfully etched into the silver. In the centre were the words 'until death'.

From my satchel I pulled the photograph we had taken from Edward's desk. 'The mysterious C,' I said. 'Taken by Mr Thomas Golightly of number 2 The Strand. I think we must pay a visit to Mr Golightly, don't you?'

Chapter Eleven

⟨≋⟩

We spent the morning at work – we could not drop everything for Mr Jobber, even if he *was* about to hang – and Will spent an hour or two at his drawing board in the corner of the apothecary. He was drafting a plan of some sort, centred on the Fleet sewer – though he insisted on calling it the River Fleet.

'I must give it the dignity and respect it deserves, Jem,' he said. 'If it is a sewer, it is because we have made it so. We have taken a watercourse once filled with life and hope, a home to trout and sticklebacks, fringed by rushes and reeds, and we have polluted it and despoiled it and driven it underground. No wonder it poisons us with its stink and filth. It's no more than we deserve.'

I did not question his fanciful image of the unfortunate Fleet, which had not been the way he described it for perhaps a thousand years. Instead, I set a cup of Gabriel's finest coffee beside his drawing board and busied myself with my customers.

The next few hours passed quickly enough. I prescribed powders for worms, and for menstrual cramps. I doled out laxatives of varying strengths for constipation of varying degrees of stubbornness. I lanced two boils and applied poultices to two more. One patient with migraines came in asking if I might apply a leech to the back of his neck. I did as he asked. I had offered the same treatment to Will, though he had noticed little difference to his headaches as a result. I sold three jars of calendula and chickweed balm for eczema, six sachets of indigestion powders, four bottles of iron tonic for women with dysmenorrhoea, and two six-ounce bags of my pennyroyal, strawberry leaf and carrot seed herbal mixture for women who did not want any more children. I directed Mrs Speedicut in her cleaning of the apothecary and instructed Gabriel and Jenny in their work about the condenser. Gabriel sugared some pills, distilled lavender oil and roasted and ground some more coffee beans. Jenny had been reading about cholera and had suggestions of her own to make. She had devised a tisane of agrimony, raspberry and blackberry leaf, wild strawberry and rosehip and was selling it at a shilling a bag. Would it work? I hoped none of us would ever have to try it – especially as she had just run out of the mixture.

Jenny was awaiting the delivery of a parcel from Edinburgh, and it came that morning shortly after she had cleaned the leech tank and I had removed a cancerous mole from an old man's back. While Mrs Speedicut bound the fellow up, took his shillings, and told him to come back every two days so that she might change his dressings, Jenny and I sat together at the workbench with our newly arrived package. It was some eight inches by four in size, wrapped in brown paper and tied tightly with string. I let Jenny open it as she was now wriggling with excitement.

'Can I try one?' she said as she picked at the string. 'Will you let me? I think it'll be very hard to use.'

'Easy to get wrong,' I said. 'Easy to kill a man with one of these.'

'Best not let Gabriel anywhere near either of 'em, in that case,' she replied. 'D'you think they're the first ones in London? I bet they are. I bet no one else has one. Can I look after 'em? Go on, Mr Jem, let me look after 'em.'

Inside the package was a hinged box covered in brown kid leather. Two silver clasps kept the box tightly closed, the contents safe and snug inside on their bed of inky-blue velvet. Jenny opened the box the way a debutante might open a jewel case containing a prized heirloom, her eyes wide, her mouth open. 'Lor'!' she whispered. Lying side by side, glittering in the lamplight, were two of the glass syringes, direct from the finest surgical instrument maker in the country. 'The hollow needles!' she whispered. 'At last!' She put out a hand and took one up.

'I've been in correspondence with Dr Alexander Wood in Edinburgh for some months,' I said. 'There've been similar devices around for years, but this is an exceptional step forward. A hollow needle attached to a glass barrel and silver plunger. He used it for localised pain, injecting morphia into an area of neuralgia and the efficacy was most impressive – an almost instantaneous banishment of the pain. I believe he was inspired by the sting of a bee.' I took one of the syringes from the velvet cushion and held it up to the light. The needle was the finest I had ever seen, the end precisely bevelled, the tiny hole hardly visible against the sharp point. The glass barrel was marked with silver to indicate volume, the plunger a cork affixed to a silver rod with a tamped and flattened end. A wooden collar about the neck of the barrel allowed one to hold it steady between the fingers, guide the needle and press the plunger all in one easy movement. It was simple, ingenious and breathtakingly beautiful. It would change the nature of medicine for ever.

'Shall we practise?' I said.

Jenny looked surprised. 'You're not sticking that into me, Mr Jem, I don't care how clever and special it is.'

But I had been thinking about this for weeks, wondering what we might use to gain expertise. I reached into my satchel and produced an orange. I had picked it up from the fruit sellers at Covent Garden and had been saving it for this very occasion. Jenny blinked. 'An orange?'

'Yes,' I said. 'It has pores, like flesh. It is firm but softish, also like flesh. It has layers, like the epidermis, the dermis, the muscle beneath. Shall we try it?' And so we did, the two of us, sitting side by side jabbing the hollow needle into the orange, into its skin, down to the pith, through to the wet flesh beneath. I used ink, so that we might see what happened, and we each tried it several times.

Afterwards Jenny ate the inked orange. I washed out the hollow needle, and its glass barrel, dried them carefully on the stove top and put them back into their velvet-lined case. The whole undertaking was a delightful distraction and did something to take my mind off the horrors I had recently witnessed. I resolved to write to Dr Wood in Edinburgh that very evening and tell him how impressed I was with his new device. I wondered when we would get the chance to use it properly.

In the afternoon, we went out to visit the photographer, Mr Golightly. On the way, we stopped off at Mr Byrd's chambers in Water Street, not far from Temple Gardens beside the Thames. The gardens sloped down to the river, petering out at the foreshore. The tide was coming in, and the water was busy with barges and lighters and other small river craft. The water looked brown and sluggish. Will regarded it with disgust.

'You know,' he said, 'the problem – well, one of the problems – is that the river flows far too slowly. It means that the effluent – of which there is more than you could possibly imagine – drifts back and forth on the tide. It never goes away, not really. And every day more is added. No wonder it's such a foul mess. If the river channel were narrower, it would mean the water could flow faster. It would have a scouring effect and stop things silting up.' He pointed left and right, upriver and down. 'Huge embankments, obviously. Great walls that push the river into a channel at high tide – much better than letting it creep up over the foreshore like this. And we could fill in behind the walls, build it up, put buildings on top, with the sewers hidden inside. I've discussed it with Mr Basilisk. He thinks it's an excellent idea. He's going to incorporate it into his plan and show the sewer commissioners. It'll be expensive, a huge and complicated undertaking, but the results will be worth every penny.'

It was unusual for Will to mention his work and I was pleased to hear him sounding optimistic. The river stank abominably, and although we were far enough away on Fishbait Lane not to have to smell it, here it was not fifty yards from our noses. I could see pools of black iridescent water shimmering on the foreshore. Flies buzzed in great clouds while, despite its extreme repulsiveness, I saw people – three men and a boy – descending the steps that led down into the mud. The boy looked up and, seeing Will, ripped aside his hat – a ragged flap of canvas coiled around his head like a filthy bandage – and waved it in the air.

'Hi!' he cried. 'Hi! Mister! What you doin' up there? Ain't you comin' down today?'

'Not today, Thimble,' shouted Will. He raised his tall hat, as if saluting a lady. The lad waved cheerily and disappeared after his colleagues. His bare feet sank into the stinking mud up to his calves.

'Thimble?'

'Indeed,' said Will.

Mr Byrd's chambers looked out towards the river. The day was cold, the air bearing the tang of an incoming fog. Somehow, it made the smell worse than ever, as one could practically taste it, and feel it slick against one's cheek like a lick from a stale tongue. 'Makes me feel sick,' said Mr Byrd, who was indeed looking somewhat green.

'Never mind, sir,' I said. 'Will here will solve the city's effluent problem. He is working with Mr Basilisk of the Metropolitan Sewer Commission.'

Mr Byrd looked impressed. 'I know Basilisk. Full of ambitious ideas. Drive the stink underground, that's the ticket.' He frowned. 'The cholera's back, did you hear?'

'Yes, sir,' I said.

'Such a terrible smell. How can it be anything but pestilent?'

'I brought you some herbs to help,' I said. 'It is an oil I've prepared. A mixture of clove, eucalyptus and rosemary. Put a few drops onto a handkerchief—'

Mr Byrd seized the bottle before I had even finished my instructions. He slopped it all over his handkerchief, as if he were dousing a plate of fish and chips with vinegar. He buried his face in it and breathed deeply. 'Oh!' he said. 'Oh, thank God! That's better! Now then, Flockhart, Quartermain, what can I do for you?'

'Sir, as you know, Sir Thomas has asked me to find who is responsible for the murder of his son.' I pulled out the letter Sir Thomas had given me.

'Yes, Flockhart.' He sighed and waved a dismissive hand. 'I was witness to the proceedings, as you may recall.'

'Of course, sir.'

He shook his head. 'I cannot agree with his methods, though I understand his desire to uncover the truth.'

'Indeed,' I said. 'And whereas I am aware that this letter does not authorise you to tell us your client's business, I wondered whether we might ask you a few questions.'

'By all means, Flockhart. I don't know how you know this Jobber fellow to be innocent, but if the wrong man hangs and the right one walks free then it is a double misfortune.'

'Exactly so, sir. And so we wondered if you could help. Just a few questions. To begin with, may I ask, where you were the night Edward Mortmain was murdered?'

'You surely don't think that *I*—'

'Of course not, sir. But it can be useful to know everyone's whereabouts.'

'I was at Blackwater,' he said. He sighed, and shuffled papers about his desk, his expression petulant. 'When am I *not* at Blackwater, sir? I feel as though I am hardly away from the place. Sir Thomas is a most demanding client.'

'And you stayed?'

'Oh yes. Dinner was memorably excellent, for once, which did something to make up for it, I suppose. Salmon, fresh from Scotland.' He smacked his lips. 'You know the train can bring them down in less than a day? I could hardly believe it. The creatures might be taking an early morning swim down the Tay on Monday and be poached and dressed and on a Hampstead dinner table by Tuesday evening. Marvellous!'

'Yes, very good, sir,' I said. I had forgotten how much Mr Byrd liked the sound of his own voice. 'I wondered whether you could tell us about Sir Thomas's first wife. And his second. And his third, come to that. There are some uncertainties surrounding the death of both. And I did not like to ask Miss Mortmain herself—'

'Oh, indeed,' said Mr Byrd. 'Quite right not to ask Miss Caroline. Of course, the information is in the public domain, if you look in the right places.'

'I don't have time to look in the right places, sir.'

'Of course, of course, and it makes sense that you come to me, I suppose.' Mr Byrd sat back. 'I've been the Mortmain solicitor man and boy,' he said. 'I used to accompany my father on his visits to see Sir Thomas, and Sir Thomas's father, come to that. We have a long history with the family.'

'You must know all their secrets then?' I smiled.

Mr Byrd smiled back, his eyes twinkling. 'I suppose I do, Flockhart. Though I'm not sure there's anything to get excited about. It's mostly business – conveyancing, inheritance, property.' He shrugged. 'But to answer your question, yes, I can tell you about the death of the first Lady Mortmain. And the second. And about the third if you've a mind to hear it. If there is anything else I can tell you without compromising my clients, the family, then I will do so. But any questions pertaining precisely to the current fortunes, decisions and legal position of family members – those things I am not at liberty to discuss.'

'I quite understand, sir. If you could proceed?'

'Sir Thomas met his first wife, the mother of Caroline and Edward, in Antigua. He had some interests out there, though he has divested himself of them now. She was the daughter of a wealthy man, an aristocrat in her own right. Her father was Sir William Leatherall of the East India Company. She was always what you might call of a delicate disposition. The heat of the Indies did not suit her, and she was only too happy to return to England with her new husband. They lived at Blackwater, her portrait hangs on the stairs there. You've seen it, I imagine.'

'Yes, sir,' I said. I had tried to trace the shadow of her daughter's features in that beautiful face, but Miss Caroline Mortmain bore no resemblance at all to her mother. Her brother, Edward, on the other hand, was quite the opposite.

'Yes,' said Mr Byrd, as if reading my thoughts. 'Miss Caroline didn't fare well in that regard. Edward Mortmain, however, inherited all – his mother's tall slenderness, her large dark eyes, her pale clear skin. He had an almost feminine beauty, dark thick hair, sensual lips. I often wondered whether his father sent him away because he could not bear to look at the lad, so closely did he resemble his mother. But we can never know this for sure. Anyway, Miss Caroline came along some nine months after Sir Thomas and Lady Mortmain returned to Blackwater. She was the only child for quite some time – perhaps seven years or so. Lady Mortmain had several miscarriages. I suspect this did not help her health, and she had suffered a form of puerperal insanity after the birth of Miss Caroline. She recovered, of course. At least, that was how it seemed.'

'And the first Lady Mortmain, she was wealthy in her own right?'

'She was, sir. Sir Thomas's marriage to Miss Maria Leatherall considerably enriched the Mortmains' declining fortunes. Sir Thomas had made investments that had somewhat depleted his reserves. As you are aware, sir, a woman's fortune becomes the property of her husband on her marriage. There was a little bequeathed to the children, but no more than five hundred pounds each. And the jewels, of course.'

'The jewels?' said Will.

'They are known as the Chitra Golconda, Will,' I said. Even I had heard of them. A collection of India's finest gemstones, taken, as so many have been, by members of the Honourable East India Company.

'That's correct, Flockhart. The Golconda diamonds.

Twelve of them, to be exact, Mr Quartermain. A gift from Lady Maria Mortmain's father on her marriage to Sir Thomas. They were never set – her father thought to leave that up to her. But as far as I am aware they remain untouched. They are now the property of Miss Caroline, though her father has them locked in his strongbox for safekeeping.'

I thought of Caroline Mortmain and her garish appearance. 'I'm surprised she has not insisted on having them for herself,' I said.

'She would like them,' he replied. 'But Sir Thomas will not hand them over. The bequest stipulates that they are to be given to her on the event of her marriage.' He shrugged. 'And Sir Thomas is such a stickler for the law.'

'I'm sure he is,' murmured Will.

'But,' Mr Byrd clapped his hands, 'to continue! Had the first Lady Mortmain not taken her own life then the Chitra Golconda would have been mounted in gold and would have adorned the neck of Miss Caroline's mother to this day.' He took a fortifying sniff of his handkerchief. 'Sadly, that was not to be.'

'Can you tell us what happened, sir?' I said.

'Edward had just been born. Lady Mortmain became . . . insane. There is no other way to describe it. You're a doctor, Flockhart, you'll know what I mean, you'll know what effect childbirth can have on the mind of a woman. Unfortunately, Miss Caroline was witness to the whole sorry episode. She was only a child.' He shook his head. 'Anyway, young Edward was rarely in the house after that. Wet nurse. Eton. Oxford.'

'How long after the first Lady Mortmain died before Sir Thomas married again?' said Will.

Mr Byrd stroked his chin. 'Sir Thomas did not remarry for many years afterwards. *That* lady, unlike her predecessor, was a woman of more vulgar antecedents. Equally wealthy but the daughter of an industrialist – indeed, sir, I was somewhat surprised by the marriage, given Sir Thomas's views on the importance of heredity, but there it is. How can one account for love? One does not choose where one might bestow one's heart.' His face had assumed a sorrowful expression. 'Anyway, Lady Elizabeth Mortmain came to live at Blackwater Hall, dividing her time between there and the house in town. After a year or so Mr Henry was born. Two years after that it was Miss Charlotte. And then the cholera came – 1832, you will be old enough to remember it, Flockhart. The whole of London was in uproar. We'd watched it march across the globe, China, India, Russia, the Baltic, it was only a matter of time before it reached us, and reach us it did. It's not a death I would wish on anyone.' He sighed. 'Certainly, the family has had no shortage of tragedy.'

'And what of the third Lady Mortmain?' I said.

'A cousin of the second, I believe,' said Mr Byrd. 'She had come to act as a companion to Lady Elizabeth, to help with the children and so on. A few years after the death of her mistress she married Sir Thomas. She is, shall we say, very modern. Very beautiful. Very . . . ambitious.'

'Did she get along with Edward?'

'He tolerated her, I think,' he said.

'And the sisters?'

'Similar, Dr Flockhart. They are closer to one another than they are to their stepmother, with whom they have little in common. Miss Charlotte is a singular creature, often overlooked. An intelligent girl who, I think, wishes for a more fulfilling role than the one her sister has taken on. As for her sister, Caroline Mortmain – she was always an old maid. Sometimes it seems as if she was born to it.'

'She seems to keep herself well occupied,' said Will.

'Indeed she does, sir. I am treasurer for several of her philanthropic enterprises. She can be exceptionally persuasive.'

'And how does Mr Henry Mortmain get on with his stepmother?' I said.

Mr Byrd's cheeks coloured. All at once my questions seemed prurient and probing, as if I were hinting at something improper. I was asking him to gossip, and I could see that he was finding it uncomfortable. 'They are firm friends,' he said at last. 'She guides him, in so many ways. And he . . . he adores her.' He seemed relieved to have landed on a phrase that captured the ambiguity of the situation.

'The Mortmains still have a property in town, I take it?' I said.

'On Layton Square, off St Saviour's Street. At the western end. A town house, rather than a villa. It was closed up some time ago. You know Sir Thomas rarely leaves his rooms now? He's not been to town for many years. Not since the Lady Elizabeth died. I think he blames the place for her death. She was in town when she contracted the cholera. She died at the house, in fact. After that he never went back. The place is quite abandoned.'

'And the new Lady Mortmain? Did she never wish to open the place up?'

'She has not done so, sir. And believe me, as Sir Thomas's agent I would know about it if she had. I suspect its furnishings are too old-fashioned for milady. I believe Mr Henry is the only one of them who ever visits the place, and that's merely to preserve the memory of his mother. I understand she kept a rose garden there and he has endeavoured to maintain it as a memorial.' He sighed again, and ostentatiously pulled out his pocket watch. 'No one stays at the town house. As for Mr Henry Mortmain's visits, I've said nothing to his father, and I'd be grateful if you would honour that with your own discretion. Mr Henry asked for a key – a couple of years ago now – but he does not stay. I'm not sure what his purpose there is, he has never told me and I don't ask. But Rintoul assures me that he has seen him inside as well as out.'

'Rintoul?' I said.

'The caretaker, Dr Flockhart. In general, I would say that Mr Henry prefers the countryside. Especially the garden at Blackwater. The ponds and water garden are particularly fine, you'll have noticed them on your way in yesterday. He is its principal architect. Yes,' said Mr Byrd thoughtfully. 'He'd have been sorry to leave the place.'

Will frowned 'He was leaving?'

'Not any longer, sir. He was expecting to take up the living at St Bartolph's in Prior's Rents, in addition to the living at Blackwater. There are three livings held for Mr Henry, I believe, though now that he is the heir to Blackwater Hall, and not the second son, he will have to find someone else to take them on. He would have made an excellent clergyman, but,' he held up his hands, 'now he has other responsibilities to shoulder.'

Will shook his head. 'I have no family but Jem, sir. No work but what I gain for myself. There is something to be said for such simplicity.'

'Indeed, Mr Quartermain,' said Mr Byrd. 'My own life is similarly neat. Once I am gone the Mortmains will have to find themselves a new solicitor.'

'Mr Byrd, might it be possible for me to borrow the key to Sir Thomas's town house?' I said.

'Yes, yes, I daresay you're right to ask, Flockhart.' He rang the bell on his desk. 'No stone unturned, and so on. Mr Featherstone,' he addressed the clerk, who had appeared in the doorway, 'would you be so kind as to give Dr Flockhart the keys to Sir Thomas's town house? When do you plan to visit, sir?' He addressed this comment to me. 'I would prefer to let Rintoul know you are coming.'

'Perhaps before the funeral? Or perhaps after it?'

'If you might return the keys after you have seen what you wished to see.' The solicitor shook both of us by the hand. 'Do let me know if I can be of any more help,' he said.

Mr Featherstone ushered us to the door. As we left, I looked back. Mr Byrd was standing at the window. He was watching us, but his gaze was vacant, as if his mind was elsewhere, and when I raised my hand to him he gave no sign that he had seen. I felt suddenly uneasy. I could not say why, for he had been as helpful as I could have wished. And yet I had the feeling, despite all he had shared with us, that he had told us nothing, and we had told him everything.

Excerpt from the Journal of William Quartermain, Esq., surveyor and assistant architect, Metropolitan Sewer Commission.

The sewers have their own 'justice', so Badger tells me. They can bamboozle the unwary with their twists and turns, their slimed walls which, to the uninitiated, all look the same. The way one is cajoled into looking down at the rushing dark water as it flows past one's boots is like the call of a Siren. Once the gaze is drawn thither, one cannot look away so enthralling and beguiling is the poisonous flow. It makes the head spin, the waters illuminated only by the flickering light of the lantern so that all sense of direction is lost in a confusion of left and right, up and down. A sickening unquenchable dizziness sets in, until one longs to sink beneath. They are playful and cruel, the glimmering light thrown by the gully holes overhead affording glimpses of an unreachable world above ground that can turn a man mad with longing. The mind plays tricks, leading one deeper and deeper, away from hope and salvation, the chatter of the rats sounding almost human in those dark stinking places. Badger likes to bludgeon the creatures, and he collects them in a bag he has for this very purpose, hanging the corpses up by their tails from a beam on the dockside. He collects the larger specimens in another bag, stunning them with a single blow of his stick. These will enter the ring at the Dancing Cat public house in Prior's Rents, pitted against his prize bull mastiff.

I smile and laugh as Badger spins his tales of death and horror, of sewer men lost beneath the city, overwhelmed by rats, or caught by the opening of the sluice gates up near Kings Cross, or trapped before their own locked gratings at the mouth of a sewer as the tide rushes in. I clap him on the shoulder and say that I have been in worse places. But I have not. I have not and he knows it.

Chapter Twelve

Thomas Golightly's photography studio was on The Strand, not far from Simpson's dining room, in a tall brick-faced Georgian building up a long, narrow flight of stairs.

'Daguerreotypes are beautiful images,' said Will as we began to climb. 'You recall my dalliance with the camera? The whole process is extraordinary – delicate, time consuming, unique, intimate. No two daguerreotypes are ever the same. No reproductions can be made, the sitter must always be there, present and still. I have always felt that something of their soul enters the image itself. To capture exactly what lies before the camera's eye is a form of alchemy. Miraculous, in its way.'

'It's just chemicals,' I said.

'Don't spoil it! The process is a mystery of light and dark. It is as if nature herself had a paintbrush.'

'Nature needs no paintbrush,' I replied.

'You're so prosaic. How drab your life must be!

Everything atomised, reduced to this, or that. No mystery, no flights of fancy, no poetry.'

'Ah, but I have your musings to illuminate my mundane existence,' I said.

'I wish you'd have let me take your likeness,' he said after a moment. We were panting now. The stairs went on and on, we had passed doors to an accountant, a firm of shipping clerks, a bookkeeper, a dressmaker. No doubt our Thomas Golightly would be the last door at the very top of the stairs. I sighed. Will had indeed asked to photograph me numerous times. In the end, his work for Mr Basilisk had proved to be too time consuming for other interests. He had given all his plates and boxes, his chemicals and his camera to Gabriel, who had shown a passing interest. But Gabriel's interest in everything but penny dreadfuls was fleeting, and the photographic paraphernalia now lay unused in a corner of the apothecary.

'I'm too ugly,' I said now.

'That's true enough, Jem. But this fellow Golightly has a rare skill. I wish you would agree,' he went on. 'Why can't I have a memento of you?'

'Because you see me every day,' I said. 'You don't need a memento of someone you see every day. If you want to know what I look like you just need to tap me on the shoulder.' We kept on climbing. The stairs were steeper now, and narrower. The light was soft, the shadows pale and ghostly. 'Besides,' I added. 'It's maudlin.'

'How so?'

'A picture as a memento? I'm not dead and have no intention of being so any time soon!'

'I don't know why you are so obtuse.' He sounded cross. 'It's not as if it's going to take away your immortal soul.'

'And should I have a photograph of you?'

'If you'd like one, I'll sit for one.' He smiled. I knew I was prickly, brusque, arrogant. I tried not to be, but I could not help who I was. And yet, perhaps I could open myself up to him more than I did. Did he not deserve something other than just my friendship? Should I tell him the truth? That I loved him dearly, but that I could give him no more than those words?

'Perhaps we could get one taken together,' I said. 'After all, it is how we are. Together. We always will be, won't we?'

We had reached the top at last. Beside the door a brass plaque proclaimed it to be the premises of *Thos. Golightly. Daguerreotypes (licensed), et cetera. Aristocrats and professionals a speciality. Taxidermy. Appointments only.* 'We don't have an appointment,' I said.

'Then all is lost.' Will lifted his cane to rap on the door. Before he could do so it was flung open, and a man stood before us. At least . . . I blinked. Will and I exchanged a glance.

'Good day to you . . . sir,' I said. She was some twenty years of age, perhaps five feet two inches tall, her face heart-shaped, her eyes brown and laughing, her cheeks rosy and as untouched by the barber's razor as my own. She was wearing a stovepipe hat on a head of thick dark hair that had been cut into a ragged short-back-and-sides.

'Gentlemen,' she cried. 'How noisy you are! I could hear your conversation all the way up the stairs. Do come in.' She swept her hat off and bowed low as we entered.

'We're looking for Thomas Golightly,' I said.

'You want the photographer?'

'I believe that is his profession.'

161

'Then you are fortunate enough to have found him, sir,' she said.

'*You?*' I could not keep the incredulity out of my voice.

'I am Thomasina. My father is . . . away at the moment and I am filling in for him.'

'Does he know you are filling in?' said Will.

'I think he will not complain about it.' She shut the door behind us. She was wearing black woollen britches and a white collarless cotton shirt, a grey woollen waistcoat and a long brown canvas apron. Her feet were shod in a pair of old leather boots that looked as if they had been newly blacked.

'You are filling in his clothes too?' I said.

'What use might I have for a dress?' she replied. 'So cumbersome. I always wear these clothes nowadays. No one remarks on it hereabouts. They think I'm on the stage. The neighbourhood is full of music halls, so I just let them assume that's the case. Since I don't habitually find myself in drawing rooms I find I am able to avoid those people who might be the most judgemental.'

'What about the aristocrats?' said Will. 'And the professionals?'

'They don't mind. They don't look beyond my apron, and they don't tend to pay much attention to servants. Besides, I put a mirror up for them to look at when I'm focusing the camera and while they are sitting, and they spend most of their time gazing at that. People generally prefer to stare at themselves.' She shrugged. 'Probably why so many of them want a daguerreotype in the first place. They don't care what *I* look like. Got my hair cut up near Covent Garden a few months ago and that's helped somewhat. What about you?'

'Me?' I blinked. 'I . . . erm . . . '

'This is Dr Flockhart,' said Will. He was grinning widely at my discomfiture. '*He* gets his hair cut on St Saviour's Street.' He stuck out his hand. 'And I am William Quartermain, esquire. Surveyor for the Metropolitan Sewer Commission. Your servant, *sir.*'

'Thank the Lord someone is doing something about the sewers,' she said. 'I don't notice it as much up here, of course, but the city stinks.' Will and I were both gazing at Thomasina Golightly. From outside, across the city, I heard the bells of St Paul's chime the hour. She smiled, and her dark eyes twinkled. 'What can I do for you, gentlemen?'

'We're looking for some information,' said Will. 'Jem, do you have the image?'

I glanced about the place as I fumbled in my bag for the daguerreotype we had taken from Edward Mortmain's chamber. Thomasina Golightly's photographic studio was in an attic, high above the streets. Above us was only roof and rafters, which had been whitewashed to reflect the light. These were punctuated by large skylights, six of them in a row, each one gazing up at the dreary London sky. Blinds of fine white cotton were drawn over all but one of them, which gave the room a pearlescent brightness that was rare in the city. The floor was bare board, also painted white. A section beneath the skylights was carpeted and dressed to look like a library or drawing room, with a pair of armchairs, a mahogany table, a full bookcase, and an aspidistra on a tall slender stand. Behind, a swag of brocade was artfully draped across the wall. In a corner of the attic a cluster of head clamps and braces, designed to keep the sitter as stationary as possible, awaited use. Beside them, there was a variety of props – chairs, stools, children's toys, a stag's head mounted on a shield. In another corner, behind the door, a screen painted with birds and flowers concealed a brass bedstead, a ewer and pitcher, a wardrobe.

Against the far wall, a bench littered with feathers, coils of wire, boxes of straw and bottles of what looked to be glass eyes, showed where taxidermy was undertaken. On the beam overhead bags of leaves and dried lichen dangled. On the bench, a stuffed barn owl stood on a log beneath a glass dome, its beady gaze fixed on a fox's head mounted on a polished oak shield. The fox wore a disappointed expression. The owl looked intoxicated. Thomasina Golightly might be an excellent photographer, but she was an indifferent taxidermist.

Overhead, the skylight without the blind was open, and a breeze was blowing. Apart from a brisk tang from the vinegar works the air was fresh and clear. Bunches of lavender hung from the rafters here and there, and their fragrance caught the breeze. I knew photography to be an undertaking that involved several chemicals – bromide, iodine, mercury, among others – and there was an unmistakeable whiff of them about the place, despite the open window. A canvas tent stood to one side, its open flaps showing her workbench, bottles of fluids, buffing cloths, plates. The camera, a huge brown mahogany box with a great black cape at its back, stood at the ready, its lens pointing at the empty armchairs. I could see from the furnishings that this was the place where 'C' had had her likenesses taken.

I handed the daguerreotype to Thomasina Golightly. 'One of mine,' she said, glancing at it. 'There's no doubt on the matter.'

'Can you tell us who she is? The image was in the possession of Edward Mortmain.'

'The fellow who was found dead in the brothel?' she said. 'I read about it in the *Police Gazette* this morning.'

'Yes, that's him,' said Will. Then he added, 'You read the *Police Gazette*?'

'Of course!' she said. 'It's my firm belief that photography should be used to take the likeness of criminals of all kinds. Their faces, their hands, and so on. And perhaps places where crimes occur too. When there's a robbery, or a murder, for instance. Why should we not take an image of the scene? Would it not allow a greater degree of understanding? To be able to look again, in detail, at what was there at the time? An open window, perhaps? An upturned table? Perhaps a knife, or a blood stain? And what might be told by the position of the body? Images would aid reflection and stimulate interpretations and ideas. I have written to the magistrate about it, as well as the superintendent at Bow Street, and offered my services.'

'And they replied?'

'They did not, sir.'

'What fools!' I said.

'Quite so,' she replied. She sounded downhearted. 'But I will not give up. They will see that I am right, one day. And when that day comes, I will be there with my camera.'

'It's a heavy thing to carry about London,' said Will.

'It is, sir, though the art and craft of photography is improving all the time. One day, perhaps the apparatus required will be less incommodious. But enough about that, sirs. What is it you wish to know about this picture?'

'I suppose we were assuming that she paid for this and that you have a bill of some kind,' I said. 'We need to know who she is and where she lives.'

'Perhaps he paid,' she said. 'The dead man. He was heir to a vast estate, so I believe. And I'm very expensive, you know.'

'And your father?' I said.

'Thomas Golightly was my father. I used to help him, when he was alive, but now that he is dead I do everything. I pretend he's still alive because people seem to prefer to think that a man is in charge, even if they never see him. I don't know why. I suppose they aren't quite ready to imagine that a woman could execute photographs as well as a man.' She handed the image of 'C' back to me. 'You see each daguerreotype is unique. There is no copy. But the date is on the back, etched onto the plate, and that should help.'

She wiped her hands and went over to a desk that stood against the far wall beside an oak, roll-fronted filing cabinet. She rooted about for a moment, first in the drawers of the former, then the latter. 'Here we are!' she said. 'Your mysterious lady is . . . Mrs Christina Arnold of 12 Gilbert Place. Your Mr Edward Mortmain paid, but the photograph I took of him was sent to Mrs Arnold's address.'

'Thank you,' I said. 'I don't suppose you can remember anything about the commission? About Mrs Arnold, say?'

'It was three months ago now. Can't say I remember a great deal about it. But if I do remember anything, where can I find you?' She smiled, and the sun came out.

'You can find me at the Blackfriars' mortuary on most days of the week,' said Will quickly. 'Or on the foreshore beneath the bridge. Or—' He blushed, and sighed, as if he wished he had said something else, anything else, to tell her where he might be. But it was too late. 'Or underground.'

'An unsavoury location,' Thomasina Golightly replied solemnly. 'But necessary if you are to succeed in your mission.'

'Or you can find either of us here,' I said. I handed her one of my cards. Will looked downcast.

'Would you like me to take your likeness?' she said suddenly. 'Both of you together. You have an interesting physiognomy, Dr Flockhart.' I blushed. She was referring to my crimson birthmark. I had spent my life grateful for the disguise it gave me, and at the same time full of loathing for its ugliness. And yet, I had to admit that more recently I had made my peace with it. After all, it had made me who I was. Thomasina Golightly stared at me, and then at Will, with the practised eye of someone who is used to choosing the best way to present a subject.

'Jem refuses to be photographed,' said Will. 'I've given up asking.'

'You have a camera?' She turned her brown eyes to him. I saw him smile, his face lighting up with enchantment and admiration under the gaze of this confident, bizarrely dressed young woman. I felt a cold hollowness seep into my heart. And yet, as much as I might wish to keep him for myself for ever, I knew I had no right to expect such devotion. Was the time fast approaching when Will might find the love that I knew he craved? He might do worse than Thomasina Golightly, and was the cut of her jib not similar to my own?

She glanced from Will to me and back. 'I think the two of you,' she said. 'Together. What do you say?'

'Yes!' said Will. 'I say yes. Come along, Jem.'

Was it because Will was so insistent? We had been through much together and yet there was nothing but memories to mark our friendship, nothing to celebrate or immortalise it. The idea appealed, I had to admit. And if I were to share immortality with anyone then I would want it to be him.

'Don't you have other clients due, Mr Golightly?' I said. 'Aristocrats, and so forth?'

'Later,' said Thomasina. 'I have plenty of time.'

Chapter Thirteen

Mrs Christina Arnold lived not far from Russell Square. She was tall and stately. Around her the trappings of her life were worn and faded, so that I had a sense of past glory, a personal history laced with tragedy and disappointment. I watched her as she smoothed the silk of her dress, her hands anxiously plucking at the tight sleeves of her bodice, making sure the lace frills she wore at her wrists came low down over her hands. Her hair was invisible, her head wrapped in loose folds of a brocade turban. The curtains were drawn, and the lamps were lit and turned down low. The dim light softened her features and gave her skin a warm, youthful glow. She asked if we would like some tea, which we declined. I could not imagine sipping tea in silence with her after what I was about to ask. She was dressed in black. I assumed she knew that Edward Mortmain was dead, and she proved this by saying, as we sat down, 'I assume you are here to talk about poor Edward.'

'Indeed,' I said. 'Mrs Arnold, forgive the intrusion, but we're trying to understand why he was murdered and by whom. You were engaged to be married, I believe?'

'Yes, sir.' She did not offer anything more. Her gaze was wary, as if she wondered how much I knew about her relationship with the dead man.

'Did you see him before he died?' I said. 'Was there anything he said to you that led you to believe he was in trouble? That he had any concerns?'

'Edward was . . . troubled,' she said. 'Something was on his mind, though he did not say what. I think it was about money.'

'But he had plenty of money himself,' said Will.

'In a sense,' she replied. 'But his family's money would only be his when his father died. Sir Thomas kept a tight grip on the purse strings.'

'Did you love him, Mrs Arnold?'

'No,' she replied. 'And he did not love me. But we had an understanding. And we respected one another.' Her cheeks had flushed. She glanced towards the door as if she wished she could dart through it and leave us where we were, alone.

'Anything you tell us will be kept in the strictest confidence,' said Will. 'We know you're not a murderer.'

She smiled a little at that. 'Do you?'

I waited. The clocked ticked. But it seemed that reticence was something Mrs Arnold had mastered, and she made no attempt to say anything more. In the end, it was I who stepped into the silence.

'Mrs Arnold, as a widow you are, no doubt, a woman of the world. May I speak plainly?'

She sighed. 'I fear you will do so whether I like it or not.

And if it will help poor Edward, then—' She raised her hands in a gesture of resignation. 'And if . . . if I can rely on your discretion, then I will answer as best I can.' She sank back in her chair. 'What can I tell you, sir?'

'Perhaps you might tell me about your . . . arrangement with Edward Mortmain,' I said. 'I assume it was your first husband Mr Arnold who was responsible for your current unhappy situation.'

'Yes, sir,' she said. Her expression had turned cold and hard. Then after a moment she softened, and I had the feeling she was relieved to be able to speak. 'Yes, I believe I can trust you, Dr Flockhart.' A smile tweaked at the corners of her mouth. 'We all have secrets, do we not?'

'Yes, ma'am,' I said. I knew, as I spoke, that she understood my deception. What had alerted her? I had no idea. But perhaps a lifetime of holding a secret shame of her own had made her able to discern trickery in others.

'Mr Arnold was a dreadful man,' she said. 'I married him when I was eighteen years old. He was my father's friend. I had little choice in the matter, as you might imagine, and I did as I was told and married him. I had my objections, of course, but are we not expected to do what our fathers wish of us? And his money spoke louder than my objections ever could.' She did not wait for my reply. 'He was some seventeen years older than me. I did not know what he had been doing to slake his desires in the years before he decided he would make a wife of me, though I was to learn soon enough.' She held out her right arm and pulled up her lace cuff to reveal a whorl of scarred skin. 'The chancre appeared after two weeks of marriage, Dr Flockhart. Two weeks and I was a condemned woman. I had no idea what it was, not at first, but syphilis is well known to medical men and my diagnosis was swift.

'My health, my looks, my dignity.' She spoke slowly and clearly. 'My life, all gone because of that man. Fortunately, he died not long after. Died raving in Angel Meadow Asylum with the better part of his nose and forehead consumed by the disease he had gifted to me on our wedding night.'

'But you appear . . . you appear well,' said Will. It was true too. The turban gave her an exotic dignity, her loose dress lent her grace and elegance.

She inclined her head. 'The disease lies hidden inside me, sir. Despite the mercury, which has caused my hair to fall out and my teeth to loosen. But it will resurface in the end, I feel sure of it.'

I had not seen the chancre scar before she showed me, but I had noticed how dim the light was – no doubt it pained her eyes for it to be brighter. I had perceived too the gentle nod of her head from her damaged heart valves. She might never manifest the insanity that had characterised her husband's final years, but only if her heart gave out before then. Most asylum doctors did not connect the high incidence of insanity with syphilis contracted earlier in life, but to me the link had always seemed clear. And yet, Mrs Arnold might well live many years without losing her mind, without her face and nose being devoured by the disease. Perhaps the mercury was having its desired effect.

'How did you meet Edward?' I said.

'I met Edward Mortmain at the Royal Academy. I had some paintings exhibited.' She waved a hand. The artworks she gestured to were barely visible in the gloom, though I could make out a still life composition of pheasants and game birds, fruit and polished tankards. Another showed a vase of flowers, opulent and jewel-like against a black background. 'Suffice to say that our engagement was not what anyone might expect.' She closed her eyes. 'He said he had no wish ever to consummate our marriage, but that he would keep me in a manner that was appropriate to a woman who was to be Lady Mortmain one day. Obviously, there would be no children. We were to be married in name only. I did not object. He wanted nothing from marriage but that it would stop his family from expecting it of him. And, in turn, my financial worries – and let me assure you, sir, the widow of a wastrel who sustains herself by painting is in a very precarious financial position indeed – would be removed.' She shrugged. 'The arrangement struck me as both desirable and pleasing. Edward and I enjoyed each other's company very much. And so I did not hesitate to agree. He insisted I had my photograph taken.' She pointed to the mantelpiece. 'You see, I have his too.'

I picked up the framed daguerreotype of Edward Mortmain. He appeared happy, though there was a wariness in his eyes as he looked out at me from among the trappings of Thomasina Golightly's photographic studio. 'And did you understand why he . . . did not choose a more appropriate woman to be his wife?'

I saw her recoil slightly, as if I had slapped her face. 'Appropriate, Dr Flockhart? We were friends. Good friends. There are far worse marriages.'

I took from my pocket the letter the parlour maid at Blackwater had given me, the words written hastily, truthfully. *My darling Edward. I have said nothing. I will say nothing. I remain true to you and you alone. Come to me. Your own C.* 'Did you write this, ma'am?' I said.

'Yes,' she said. She blushed. 'Yes, I did. Miss Caroline Mortmain came here. Three days before Edward died. She was . . . insistent that I cut off all relations with her brother. She was most forceful.'

'How so?' said Will.

'She had written me a letter. I burned it of course. I did not respond to it, and I did not show it to Edward.'

'What did it say?'

'One phrase was particularly memorable, especially under the current circumstances.' She smoothed her dress. '"My dear Mrs Arnold, you will marry him over my dead body. Or over his."'

The clock ticked disapprovingly in the silence that followed. Caroline Mortmain had said nothing of this. I was not surprised. No doubt she hoped we would not find our way to Mrs Arnold. 'It seems an extreme response,' I said.

'She is an extreme woman. Have you met her?'

'Yes—'

'Well then, you have seen what she is like. Edward called her "the termagant". One can see why.'

'*I have said nothing. I will say nothing,*' I said. 'You wrote this in your note to him. What did you mean by it?'

She hesitated for a moment and then said, 'Edward Mortmain was not the man people thought he was.'

'How so, madam?'

'He had secrets, Dr Flockhart, as do so many of us. I believe he understood mine, though he never asked about them directly. And he never divulged his own.'

'But you knew what it was?'

174

'No.'

I did not believe her. 'But you suspected.' I saw from her face that I was correct. 'You suspected, but you will not tell us?'

'I respected his privacy then, and I respect it now.' She stood up, our interview clearly over. 'He did not tell me, so anything else is pure conjecture. *De mortuis nil nisi bonum*,' she said.

It was a common enough aphorism. Did she realise it was also emblazoned on the Mortmain hearse? 'I'm not asking you to speak ill of the dead,' I said. 'I'm asking you to help us find his murderer.'

She was ringing the bell now, glancing anxiously at the door for the maid. She seemed almost afraid. But I had not finished with her just yet. I put my hand into my pocket, my fingers finding the cold circle of smoothed and engraved silver that the maid had given me as we left Blackwater. I held it out in the palm of my hand, the metal glinting darkly in the drawing room's dim light. 'Is this yours, madam?'

Her pale cheeks coloured as she stared at the entwined initials: E and C. 'No, sir,' she said.

'It is not from you?'

'No, sir.'

'Might Edward Mortmain have had it engraved for you?'

'This is a love token, Dr Flockhart, something that might be worn close to the heart. Edward and I had no reason to exchange such intimate trifles. I can assure you, I am not the "C" referred to here.'

'Did he ever speak to you about the Mortmain rat?' asked Will suddenly.

She nodded. 'From time to time. In fact, the last time I saw him . . . he was rather agitated about it. He said he was sure he was being followed. He seemed to believe it was the Mortmain rat, though I have no idea why. The city is full of rats, I told him. One should not be surprised if one looked round and such a creature was in sight. But he would not be persuaded. He said he was a guilty man who deserved his fate, and he was sure his time had come.'

'Guilty of what?'

'I don't know.' She frowned. 'But he said that he would rather die by the rat than by the rope.'

Outside, the fog had rolled in once more, the afternoon growing dark and choking. Mrs Arnold's street was not a well traversed thoroughfare, and we were obliged to walk to the end of it to pick up a cab. Will shivered, and he pulled his collar up against his ears, his hands thrust deep into his pockets. I took his arm, and we sauntered off into the gloom. But there was something not quite right. At first I was not entirely sure what it was. I felt the hair prickle on the back of my neck, and that same feeling I'd had when we'd left Blackwater Hall the previous day stole over me: the sensation – both disquieting and intrusive – that we were being watched. Behind us, as we walked, I could hear the soft *clop* . . . *clop* . . . *clop* . . . of a creeping vehicle, the faint creak of carriage leather. I stopped to look back, but the sound stopped too, and I could see nothing. Whoever or whatever it was it had no lamps, no shape, no obvious presence. Had I imagined it? I stared into the fog. For a moment I thought that

I could make out a dark hulking shape. But then the choking atmosphere thickened once more, and I could not be certain that I had seen anything. We walked on. Once again, the invisible carriage crept after us, hidden, but present. *Clop . . . clop . . . clop . . .*

'What is it?' said Will, who seemed not to have noticed anything.

Perhaps I *was* imagining it. 'I'm not sure,' I said. 'There's something there. Something or some*one*, hiding out of sight. Behind us in the fog. Creeping.'

Will sighed. 'I can't see anything. I can't *hear* anything. Come along Jem. There's a cab stand at the end of the street.'

He was right, of course, and we did not have far to go until we reached it. But there were many dangers when the fog crept in, when it lay like this as thick as broth upon the city. Thieves and footpads relished the concealment it gave them; pickpockets plied their trade without fear of apprehension. There were accidents too. People fell into the river, or off the dockside. They mistakenly wandered down streets that are best avoided or got caught far from home without a scarf to cover their face and were smothered by the fog. Or they were run down by vehicles, vehicles moving swiftly without lights in dark and silent streets.

I stopped again and stared back the way we had come. We had walked only about ten yards since leaving Mrs Arnold's house but already the light from her windows was invisible. The sounds from behind us had also stopped. Someone, something, was waiting for us. Waiting out of sight, hidden in the gloom . . . And then all at once it came at us. Suddenly and without warning. I heard the crack of the whip, the rumble of the wheels and the sound of hooves pounding onto the road. A great dark shape, two black horses in shining harnesses, burst out of the fog. Behind them a coach, the driver on his box, black-clad and muffled against the cold, appeared faceless beneath his tall hat. The horses champed and whinnied as they rushed towards us. I raised my stick and cried out, the driver hauled on the reins as I sprang forward and seized the horses' bridles, my arm almost torn from its socket as I dragged them to a standstill. Will bounded forward, his stick held above his head like a club. I saw the dark glitter of the rat and the escutcheon, and a pale face appeared from between the dark silk curtains.

'Dr Flockhart? Good heavens, sir! What manner of greeting is this?'

'What in God's name were you doing, madam?' cried Will. 'You drove straight at us. You almost ran us down!'

'Don't blaspheme at me, young man!' she said, her expression scandalised. She held her hand to her breast as if to still her beating heart. 'I was merely taking precautions in the fog. Our lamps are out. Something must have startled the horses – perhaps the sight of *you* coming towards them brandishing a stick like a cutthroat, Mr Quartermain! Get in, sirs.' She pushed the carriage door open. 'It's a nasty night to be out.'

We trundled along in silence for a moment, Miss Mortmain bundled up in furs in a corner of the carriage, her hands thrust deep into an ermine muff. 'What were you doing in town, ma'am?' I said at last.

'I was here to see my milliner,' she replied.

'Does your milliner live in this street, madam? Near to Mrs Arnold?'

Caroline Mortmain's cheeks burned. 'You judge me, Dr Flockhart. And you, Mr Quarterman. And yet you should not.'

'Were you going to call in on Mrs Arnold?'

'I was,' she said. 'I was going to try to make amends for my . . . behaviour. Before my brother was murdered, I mean. I was wrong to . . . menace her as I did. I just wanted to . . . to tell her I was sorry. But I didn't in the end. I just left her a note about the funeral.'

She sighed. All at once, it was as if the mask she wore every day had suddenly become too tiring to keep in place. She sagged visibly, as far as she was able to when so tightly laced, and her long plain face beneath her outlandish fur-trimmed bonnet became longer and more unhappy than ever. A petulant frown creased her brow, and I thought for a moment that she was about to stamp her foot and say something churlish. She pulled out a handkerchief and dabbed her eyes. When she looked at us again, the mask was back in place.

'My relationship with my brother was fraught with sorrow,' she said. 'Much of it due to our mother's death – something he knew nothing of, but which I witnessed, and which has tainted my entire life.' She stared out of the window at the grey curtain of fog that blocked out the city and sealed us in with her, as if we were lost at sea.

'I was seven years old when Edward was born,' she said. 'Old enough to feel excited at the prospect of a baby, a sibling that I could look after with my mother. My beloved mother. She was the light of my life, a constant loving presence. We were the best of friends, the two of us. My father was rarely home in those days. My mother seemed happier when he was not home. At the time I did not know why, though I shared her feelings and preferred Blackwater Hall when he was absent from it. When my father came home, I was sent up to the nursery. He wanted my mother for himself. I was a precocious presence he had no need of and saw no value in. I understood that she had been ill after my birth. I learned later, much later, that she had been cared for by a mad-doctor after I was born and had spent some months in Angel Meadow Asylum down in the town. She never spoke of that time, only ever referring to her illness in the vaguest of terms. Somehow, I knew it was linked to my birth, and to my father, and she both dreaded and feared his return. And then one day my father came.

'Soon afterwards, my mother said I was to have a baby brother or sister. She hoped it might be a brother, she said, as every man wanted an heir and that it must be a boy, and in her case, she must get him two as the rat was sure to get one of them. I knew the legend, of course I did, but I did not think of it as something I should be frightened of. I was a girl after all, and the monstrous rat was no concern of mine.

'And so my brother Edward was born. My impression of him was of a pink, screaming, wrinkled little face. My mother seemed obsessed with him – always holding him and crooning over him. He hardly seemed worth it. So noisy and smelly and selfish, always mewling and squealing. And then my poor mother became ill. I knew he had caused it. He and my father, the pair of them. She was perfect before he came along, the two of us happy without *them*. But he ruined everything.'

Will and I sat before her in silence, neither of us daring to interrupt. I sensed that she had half forgotten we were even there, for her gaze was still fixed on the window, and the dark fog that rubbed against the glass.

'I was not allowed to see her,' she continued. 'Not even for a minute. A woman came to look after Edward. My father had gone back to London and left the doctor in charge. My poor mother was locked in her room. I heard her sobbing and screaming, and her cries tore at my heart.' She put her hands to her head. 'I have never forgotten it. I *will* never forget it. I could not bear to hear her so sad and wretched, and so I stole the key from the housekeeper and went into her room.

'The woman in that bed was hardly recognisable to me, her face red and puffy, her eyes glittering, her hair in tangles about her head. Some of it had fallen out and was on the pillow like clumps of water weed and I could see the white patches of her scalp. She did not know who I was, but screamed at me to bring her baby, her precious baby Edward. I ran from the room, and down the stairs. Behind me, I heard the housekeeper's footsteps, the jangle of her chatelaine, her angry voice as she scolded me, told me I shouldn't have gone in, that the sight of me would only make my mother worse. I heard my mother shouting and screaming, the door slamming and the key rattling in the lock. The noise of it all dinned in my ears as if I were in a mad-house, and I ran away, out into the garden.

'Once there, I looked back, up at the window to my mother's room. I saw her standing there at the open window, in her nightdress with her arms outstretched. At first, I thought she was going to call to me. And then I saw that she had something about her neck, something white and tight against her skin, like a necklace of silk. Before

I could say or do anything she had climbed out of the window onto the windowsill and slipped over the edge.

'It was not a long drop. In fact, it was hardly a drop at all for the noose she had prepared was insufficient for that. Instead, she just hung there, the back of her head against the stone sill, the white rope about her neck getting tighter and tighter, her face turning purple, her body jerking in her white chemise.'

Caroline screwed her eyes shut. 'I can see her even now. Her thin legs, her white nightdress, her hand clutching at her neck as her feet smacked against the stonework.' Her face was wet with tears. 'What child should witness such a sight, watching every second of . . . of . . . '

She could not finish. Her hands clenched into fists, and she took a breath. 'I ran into the woods,' she said. 'I crawled into the base of the hollow oak that grows beside the old well. I curled up there, in the dark and damp, and waited for the weight of the tree to crush me down, down into the grave where I wanted to be. I believed it was my fault, you see. It is hard for a child *not* to perceive that one action does not necessarily lead to the one that follows directly after. I had entered my mother's room, even though I had been expressly told *not* to do so. Her next act was to take her own life. You can see how a child might connect the two events.'

'Yes, ma'am,' I said gently.

She seemed not to hear. 'And so I curled up, as small as I could make myself, inside the oak. I heard them calling for me – Ruskin, the gardener and his boys. But I stayed where I was, my eyes fixed upon the tumbledown wall of the old well, staring at the toadstools that sprouted from the moss and roots that smothered its stones. I told myself that these queer little creatures were my friends, my companions in the earth. Some were small and thin, faded purple and crooked as little old men, others were pale and fat with big brown hats, like tiny washer women. Another seemed as a white angel, slender and alone, watching over me from beneath the branches of an ancient yew. Those in a cluster beside my head were round and red as strawberries. And when night fell there were others, out in the woods, that glowed in the darkness.'

She dashed a hand across her eyes and sat up straight, as if determined to throw off the dark clutches of the reverie she had found herself in. 'They call them the Jack O'Lantern, I believe. Quite ordinary, Dr Flockhart, and to be found everywhere in the autumn. Their gills contain a primitive phosphorescence. But as I lay there that night, a child alone in the cold and the dark, I told myself that the gentle luminescence I could see was the ghost of my beloved mother come to take me with her.'

I stole a glance at Will. His face was almost invisible so dark had the carriage become, and I could see only the white of his eyes, staring at Caroline Mortmain as she told her tale of sorrow and despair.

'It was all Edward's fault, of course. *He* took her from me. From that moment I hated him with every shred of my being.' She looked from me to Will, her gaze steady, her eyes still glittering with tears. 'But I am not a monster, Dr Flockhart, Mr Quartermain, and I kept my feelings well hidden. Perhaps my father suspected my animus for he had his precious firstborn son sent out to a wet nurse in London. After that my brother was kept in my father's house in town, and I did not see him for some years. Later, he was sent out to school, away in the country,

183

and it was only when he was older, perhaps some seven years of age, that he began coming home to us for the holidays. I told him the story of the Mortmain rat. How I used to enjoy watching the fear on his face! I could see that it troubled him. And why would it not? He was only a child, far too young for such horror stories. And yet he was drawn to it as much as he was repelled, for he asked me to tell the story over and over again.

'And so we grew up, he and I. I was no longer a child, and I knew that my mother had suffered from puerperal insanity. I tried to be a good person, to do good deeds, to prove to myself that I *was* good, that the dark thoughts that I sometimes had, about my father, my brother, about myself, could be overcome. And then my father married again. Lady Elizabeth was young and beautiful, and before long there were two more children. Henry, a gentle boy nothing like his father. And Charlotte. A runt, my father said. He did not like his female children.'

Caroline shrugged. 'The second Lady Mortmain died when Charlotte was two years old. She was not a kind woman and was no mother to me. Not that I needed one. I was some twenty years old by then. She might have been like a sister to me – but she chose not to be. I was not sorry when she died.'

'Cholera?' I said.

She nodded. 'She was in London with the children. The sickness burst into the city with a violence no one had predicted – 1832 was a year like no other. You're younger than me, Dr Flockhart, but you must surely remember it all the same. My father's wife shut herself up in the house in the hope that she could leave the pestilence outside but—' She held up her hands. 'Alas.'

'I made a special effort to love Edward, to be his friend,' she went on. 'But every time I saw him I was reminded of our mother, how she had looked. I saw her in him, you see, though not everyone agrees. And then I saw her again in my mind's eye – leaning over me smiling with the sun in her hair, reading to me before the fire, her cheeks pink, her eyes sparkling. And then I saw her face livid and swollen, her face screaming at me to go away, that she wanted Edward, Edward, *Edward*! I saw her body sliding out over the windowsill, hanging there white as a lily against the dark stone. It was that last sight of her that I could never erase. And the others, those happier memories, became harder and harder to retain.'

She turned to me. Even in the gloom of the carriage I could see that her expression had grown harder, angrier. 'He did so many things that were unacceptable,' she cried. 'That "Mrs Arnold" woman! She is far from appropriate. His visits to low places, no wonder he was found dead in one such! His *interference* with business matters he did not understand.'

We stayed silent, neither of us willing to interrupt her flow of bile. 'D'you know, one day last week Edward came to me and said that he had been making enquiries about Prior's Rents. Did I know that it was land owned by our family? That it was *our* waterworks at Blackfriars that pumped Thames water into their homes? I said that of *course* I knew! But they could live elsewhere if they did not like it, they could use *other* water companies if they wished, *other* pumps supplied by *other* companies if they chose to. I told him that the houses were nothing to do with us, that building was not what we did, not what Mortmains had *ever* done. He said the poor were people like any other, that they deserved better. What on earth he meant by *that* I have no idea. The *deserving* poor do not have homes in Prior's Rents. The poor who live in Prior's Rents are poor because they are lazy, profligate, sinful. I do my best to help them, but they simply do not *listen*. I have spent my life among them – far more than *him*. I *know* what they are like. I *know* what they need. I *know* what will save them.' She shook her head. 'My father would agree. He always said Edward was weak. Always said he was naive, a fool. He was right about *that* much at least.'

'Did you murder him, Miss Caroline?' said Will. 'Did you murder your brother Edward?'

'What?' It was as if he had slapped her face. '*Murder* him? Me? Of course not! What do you take me for? I try to explain my innermost thoughts and feelings to you, to give you some insight into my relationship with Edward, what kind of man he was, and you jump to the worst of all possible conclusions?' She reached up a muscular arm and pounded on the roof of the carriage. It jerked to a halt. 'We have arrived, I believe,' she said. Her voice was hard, and brittle. Cold. Furious. The atmosphere in that enclosed space felt charged with static, as if we were sitting at the heart of a thunder cloud. I had no idea where we were, the fog outside so thick I could see no houses, no landmarks. I have never been so relieved to get out of a carriage as I was then. My feet had hardly touched the ground before the door slammed, the coachman cracked his whip and the horses plunged forward, vanishing into the fog.

***Excerpt from the Journal of William Quartermain, Esq., surveyor
and assistant architect, Metropolitan Sewer Commission.***

*In the afternoon today I received an unexpected visitor. The tide
was incoming, and I was sitting with Thimble looking out at
the brown effluvia, watching the flow, waiting to measure the
height of the spring tide. When I told Thimble that was what we
were doing, he laughed and said it was October, and therefore
autumn, not spring. 'Ah, yes,' said a voice behind us, 'but the
phrase "spring tide" refers to the leap that the tide makes due to
the alignment of the earth, the moon and the sun, rather than
the time of year, does it not, Mr Quartermain?' Thimble stared
at her, open mouthed. I must admit, I suspect my own expression
was not dissimilar. I felt myself blush with pleasure to see her.*

   *'Quite so, Miss Golightly,' I said. I scrambled to my feet, tore
off my dreadful sewer-hat and made her a clumsy sort of bow.*

   *What a bizarre figure I must have looked, in my brown sewer
costume, my huge muddy boots with the string tied about my*

knees 'against the rats'. And yet she seemed entirely unperturbed by it. Perhaps because her own costume was far from orthodox: although she was, on this occasion, dressed in women's clothing – a grey dress somewhat hitched up at the hem for walking purposes so that it did not trail in the mud. Her cropped hair peeped out from beneath a baker boy's cap in a delightful fringe, and her sturdy black lace-up boots gave her a military look. Added to this impression was the fact that she was wearing what looked like an old military coat, scarlet with gold buttons, over her dress. I asked how she fared and where she was going, and she replied that she had closed her studio for the day and had come out to stretch her legs and take the air. Thimble and I looked at one another and laughed. She grinned too and said that it was indeed more pungent at the waterside than she had expected.

The day was bright and clear, but I knew the fog was coming. I could taste it on the air, in addition to the usual stink from the river. I burrowed a hand into my pocket and produced a spare pocket handkerchief. Jem always makes sure I have a supply. He douses them with fragrance for me, and this one released a refreshing cloud of citrus, thyme and sandalwood. Of course, it was jealously swallowed up almost immediately by the stench of the river, but if held to the nose it would do its work. I hoped she would take it, that she would find it useful and remember me because of it. What else might I do to endear myself to her? I had no idea. And yet I so badly wanted her good opinion.

I felt myself sinking into a doltish silence. I am never like this with Jem, nor with the likes of Thimble, or even Mrs Roseplucker. But the sight of Miss Thomasina Golightly filled my thoughts, my mind, my heart, so much that it seemed to smother me, and I fell completely silent.

'Cat got yer tongue?' said Thimble, staring at me critically. I shook my head and commenced to say that, of course, the phrase

'cat got your tongue' referred not to a real cat, but to Khat, a cancerous leaf beloved by fakirs and their countrymen, which might cause cancers of the tongue if chewed regularly and often. 'Jem told me,' I muttered at the conclusion of this unnecessary information, as if it somehow excused me from any responsibility for the ridiculous words I had just uttered.

Miss Golightly sniffed at my handkerchief, her eyes twinkling at me over its white folds. She asked whether the mortuary had taken anyone in recently, whether she might attend with her camera. I said it had not. She asked whether, if any came in, she might be informed.

'Could a boy be sent for me?' She looked at Thimble and winked. His mouth fell open (as, I think, did mine). I told her I would see what might be possible, though the mortuary keeper – an indolent man rarely seen sober – was paid by Dr Graves from the new St Saviour's Infirmary, and that between him and the anatomy students there was fierce competition over any corpses. We discussed once more the value of photographing the murdered dead. I could not disagree with her arguments. I suggested she speak to Dr Graves, who I knew shared her enthusiasm, even though he might not be so keen to share the bodies.

The fog was drawing in and the streets were growing dark, and I offered to escort her back to her lodgings. I left Thimble in charge of the measuring stick, the level and the notebook (perhaps a rather reckless decision as I have seen neither him nor my apparatus since), hastily changed my bizarre costume for something more appropriate to the task, and walked with Miss Golightly back west to her lodgings and studio.

Chapter Fourteen

Wicke Street in the daytime was a sorry sight. The road was thick with filth of all kinds, horse dung being an especial feature of the neighbourhood, and the stuff was churned into runnels by the passing of carts and hansoms. Household refuse, potato peelings and straw added texture. As we walked past the flat-fronted Georgian terrace houses, the stink of nightsoil intensified. I pulled out my handkerchief and buried my face in it. Usually, Will was the first to complain, the first to pull out a bag of lavender, a clove-studded orange or a square of silk doused in sandalwood. Now, he seemed hardly to notice. He glanced balefully at a drain – a gully hole sunken in the gutter beside an overgrown gap-site that lay between the houses like a neglected farmyard.

'It's the Fleet,' he muttered. He pointed to the hole. 'It's down there. Or at least, one of the old sewers that leads to the Fleet is down there. The stink is coming from below ground, as much as above. D'you know, there's every chance the stuff will explode one day? It's happened before. In '46. So much filth and effluent squeezed into the Fleet that gas built up inside it like a powder keg. Then the tide came in, the river backed up and all at once it just burst out. *BOOM!* Like a giant carbuncle of ordure. Kings Cross was sprayed with the stuff. So Badger says anyway.' His voice was matter of fact, as if he were describing something perfectly ordinary. 'Can you imagine it?'

'I don't wish to imagine it.'

He pointed to the patch of nettles, weeds and dried mud that lay between the two rows of terrace houses. I assumed it had once been a public green of some sort, though time and decay had rendered it nothing but a wilderness, scratched at by skinny chickens and rummaged by pigs.

'You see, the sewer runs below this ground here, probably not more than six feet under. That's why they haven't built houses here, as they'd subside. If you look,' he pointed left, and then right, 'you can see the buildings on either side leaning inwards.' It was true too, for the houses to the east and west of the gap site sagged drunkenly, their roofs missing slates, clumps of plaster crumbling as the brickwork cracked and strained. The house on the right had its outer wall supported by giant beams of wood, thrust at an angle into the earth. Curtains still fluttered in the crooked windows. It would take more than the prospect of imminent collapse into a sewer to render a house on Wicke Street uninhabitable.

In recent months Mrs Roseplucker had made some changes to her property, though rather than improving matters, she had merely accentuated its woebegone façade. The outside of the house was an ancient stucco.

191

Once white, it had turned yellow, and then brown, mottled and steaked by the sulphurous London rain so that Mrs Roseplucker's terrace now looked like a row of neglected teeth, crooked and discoloured.

The maid opened the door. She looked angry and harassed. 'Mistress ain't seein' no one,' she snapped. 'She's a-sleepin' at this hour, and says I ain't to let no gen'men in, neither.'

'And Annie?'

'Sleepin'.'

There were other girls I could have asked for, but I did not know them for they came and went from one week to the next. None were as ever-present as Annie, who had been Mrs Roseplucker's most loyal virgin for years. 'Is the other maid here?' I said. 'Mary, the parlour maid.'

'We ain't got *parlour* maids,' replied the girl. 'We ain't got *chamber* maids neither. We only got *a* maid, and that's me. There *was* two of us, but now there ain't, and so I gets to do everything – includin' cleanin' up all that *blood*.' She scowled. I could hardly blame her for there had indeed been a great deal of the stuff and the bed would have been ruined.

'So where's Mary?' said Will.

'Mary don't work here no more. Mistress kicked her out. She said she'd as good as killed Mr Jobber by goin' for the watch like that. Reckon she's right too as he'll hang for what he did, there ain't two ways about it.'

'Can we come in?'

'No.'

'Can you get Mrs Roseplucker for us?'

'Dint you hear? No gen'men. I don't want a black eye for doin' what she says *not* to.'

'Do you know where Mary went?'

'Number six.' She jerked her head up the street, back the way we had come.

'Very well,' I said. 'But tell Mrs Roseplucker we called, will you? Dr Flockhart and Mr Quartermain.'

'I don't remember no names.'

'Well, describe us then!' I was tempted to give the girl a black eye myself. She watched us through a crack in the door as we walked back down the street. To be honest I was somewhat relieved to find that Mrs Roseplucker was in bed. I disliked the inside of her home – the hideous décor, the tangy, salty stink of the place. I always felt as though I were submerged in a warm fishy broth. Somehow I doubted number six would be any better.

The house where Mary had gone was halfway down the terrace, some five doors away from Mrs Roseplucker's. There was a notice in one of the windows, a dirty rectangle of stained and warped card that had the word 'RoomS' scrawled upon it. A lodging house, evidently. The door was standing ajar. The smell of onions, old meat and over-cooked cabbage drifted out to meet us. From within came the sound of children crying, a baby screaming and a woman shouting. A dog barked. I rapped on the door with the head of my stick. 'Mary!' screamed a woman's voice from inside. 'Mary, get that, can't you!'

'I'm upstairs,' came the bellowed reply. 'Ask Roger.'

'Roger!' The voice shrilled in the air. 'Roger!'

All at once the door was flung open and a boy in ragged cap and trousers burst out. He had a hoop in one hand and a stick in the other.

'I'm outside, Mam,' he shouted. 'Ask Mary!' He grinned as he bounded past us into the street. 'Mam,

it's some men!' he shouted over his shoulder. And then
he was off, joining a throng of other ragged children
and vanishing into a gap between the houses opposite.
I pushed the door wide. The smell grew stronger, now
also heavy with the reek of a soiled child. The walls were
a grim distemper, the waist-high panelling stained and
blotched with blooms of mould and damp.

'Good day to you, madam,' I shouted into the passage.
'May I speak with you a moment?'

A woman appeared, thin and anxious-faced with a baby
on her hip. The baby was silent, its face pale and drawn,
its eyes sunken. 'What do you want?' she said. 'Do you
want a room? It's ten shillin's a week for the basement,
but you'll have to share a privy with Mr Blumenthal. He's
in cutlery. Want me to show you? Or there's one on the
top but it'll cost you, plus Mary's extra and you'll need
her for water and the chamber pot.' She adjusted the
baby. Its lips were blue. I could smell its napkin and see
the stains upon it from the door.

'I need to speak to Mary, madam,' I said. 'It shouldn't
take long.'

'Oh, we *all* need to speak to Mary, sir. And you're
welcome to do so if you can get her to come downstairs.
Mary!' she shrieked over her shoulder. '*Mary!*' My head
began to ache.

The girl Mary appeared in the cabbagy darkness at
the top of the stairs. Her expression was sulky. Her hair
was tied up with string and she was sporting a bruise
under her right eye. I wondered whether she would be
better off at Mrs Roseplucker's, though only she could
answer that. Annie had once been the maid of all work
but had been promoted to the role of 'energetic virgin'

on her fifteenth birthday. 'Much easier than kindling fires and emptying chamber pots,' she'd once told me. Given the expression of mutinous fury on Mary's face she might well be of the same opinion. I saw that she recognised who we were straight away. Her expression became cunning.

'Mary,' I said, 'you need to tell us what happened at Mrs Roseplucker's. I know she's been keeping something from us.'

'That Mrs Roseplucker!' muttered the woman. The baby's bowels gurgled ominously. 'Ain't it enough that the constables took that big spoony Mr Jobber away in the Mariah? Stabbed one o' them tarts' fancy men, that's what I heard. Jealous rage. He seemed the quiet sort, to be fair, but ain't it always the quiet ones what's the problem?'

'Still waters, madam,' said Will.

'Eh?' The woman frowned. The baby whimpered. Will looked at it and backed away.

'Mary,' I said, 'if you could step outside with us for a moment.'

'I ain't got nothing to say,' she said. 'I told the constable what I seed.'

'There's a shilling in it,' I said. 'Perhaps more.'

'P'raps I can help,' said the woman with the baby.

'It's *me* they're wantin',' said Mary. 'Not *you*.' The girl threw the woman a withering look as I ushered her into the street. Will had already fled, and was smoking his pipe outside, leaning against the railings. The smoke was a relief after the cabbage and baby.

'I want you to tell me exactly what you did that morning,' I said, ' and what you *saw* in the order in which you saw it. Was it usual for a gentleman to stay the night?'

'Not really, sir, though some of 'em pays extra to stay longer. Some of 'em likes to pretend the girls is a wife to them, sir. Mrs R charges those gen'men for the whole night. But most of 'em can't wait to leave once they done their business.'

'What's your job, in the mornings, Mary?' I said.

'I go in quiet as the girls is sleepin'. I lay the fire and do the chamber pots, and sometimes I has to make chops and eggs for breakfast and take it up. Mrs Roseplucker telled the neighbours she's runnin' a hotel, but she ain't.'

'I imagine the neighbours have enough worries of their own,' said Will.

'Mrs R likes a clean and orderly house, sir. Mr Jobber made sure there weren't no trouble. Fights and such. Drunkenness. Hitting the girls.' She put her hand to her face. 'Hittin' the girls was for Mrs Roseplucker to do.'

'I'm sure she's sorry about that,' I said. 'You know how she dotes on Mr Jobber.'

'There were a dead man stabbed in the back room, sir. Someone 'ad to call the watch.' She scowled. 'I dint see *nuthin.*'

But she must have seen something, and we needed to know what it was. The explanation as to what had happened there had been relayed to us by Mrs Roseplucker and Annie – both the most unreliable witnesses one might come across. Was Mary any better?

Will jangled the coins in his pockets. 'I'll pay you a week's wages if you tell us everything you did that morning and everything you saw.'

Her eyes gleamed. 'Four shillings!'

He pulled a pair of half crowns from his pocket. 'Five!'

'And I'll get your old job back for you if you want it,'

I said. I rummaged in my satchel and extracted a small tin of arnica salve. 'Here, let me see to those bruises.' Mary held her face up to me as I dabbed the stuff on her cheek and beneath her eye. The girl sighed with pleasure to receive a gentle touch, even for a moment.

'I were maid o' all work at Mrs Roseplucker's,' she said. 'I gets up when the clock in the kitchen strikes six. I washes my face and hands and put the pinny on. I chases the mice out and sees what state the bread's in and if the chops is gone off. Then I goes about the house. I'm to empty the chamber pots as Mrs R's girls uses them a lot, what with the washing out o' the gen'men and such like. I got a pail and I traipse up and down the stairs. I goes into the rooms and tips the pot into the pail.'

'None of the rooms are locked?'

'No. Mr Jobber might need to go in and see to a gen'man if he ain't behavin'.'

'And the last room was the back bedroom on the ground floor? The room where the man was found?'

'Yes. I took the chamber pot from under the bed.'

'How could you see it if it was dark?'

'There were some light coming through the curtain from the dawn breakin'. And my eyes were that used to the dark. I can always see it under the bed.'

'Did you see anyone in the bed with the man?'

'Annie.'

'I thought it was too dark to see.'

Mary frowned. She said nothing.

'Did you hear anything?'

'Like what?'

'Like anything. Snoring. Or breathing.'

She blinked. 'O'course there were *breathing*,' she said.

197

'From whom?' I said. 'If the man was dead, who was breathing?'

'Annie,' said the girl again. She looked doubtful. 'I think. I didn't *see*. But it *must* o' been her!'

'What happened next?' said Will. 'After you emptied the chamber pot?'

'Then I took the pail, and I went out into the yard and tipped it into the sewer at the end. After that I went into the court round the back of Wicke Street and washed the pail out at the pump. I likes to take my time at that as it were always nice not to be inside when it ain't raining. That's when I heard screaming.'

'And then?'

'I dropped the pail, dint I? Dropped it and ran back. By the time I got inside the others were all there. Mrs R and Annie out o' the bed and Mr Jobber. The door to the back room were open and the curtain were pulled aside and there he was, a dead man just a-lyin' there. Everyone knowed Annie were Mr Jobber's favourite, but he ain't never seemed the jealous type before. Well, I took one look at Mr Jobber an' I ran, sir. I'm sorry I did it now. I wish I'd asked Mrs R what to do, but . . . but . . .' Her eyes were round with horror. 'All that blood! And Mr Jobber were making that terrible sound, like a bull lowing. I thought he were going to come at me too!'

'I don't blame you,' I said. 'I think most people would have done the same. How long had you been working at Mrs Roseplucker's?'

'Not two weeks, sir. I came from Mrs Lovibond. Mrs Lovibond didn't want me, she said I were too cross-eyed, so she sent me up to Wicke Street.'

Will handed her the five shillings. She fingered the

coins in disbelief, before stuffing them into her pocket. I saw the woman with the baby watching from the window, and I wondered how long Mary would get to keep her treasure. I rooted in my satchel and pulled out a length of green silk ribbon. I'd had it for months, tucked into one of the pockets. I'd found it outside the haberdasher's on Fishbait Lane, no doubt dropped by one of the lady customers.

'Here,' I said. 'Let's get rid of that string, shall we?' Her eyes lit up as she saw what I was about, and she smiled bashfully, her bruised and sullen features transformed. She put the string into her pocket for future use.

Ahead of us, down the street, I saw Mrs Roseplucker and Annie emerge from the Home for Girls of an Energetic Disposition. Will and I bounded after them.

'Mrs Roseplucker, I need to speak with you,' I gasped as we caught them up.

'Well, you can speak all you want,' she replied. 'But speak while we're on the way.'

'To where?' said Will.

'Newgate, o' course! Mr Jobber's up in front of the magistrate in two days, and as far as I can see you two ain't done nothing to help him.'

'We're *trying* to help him, madam,' I said. 'How can I get to the truth if you're not honest with me?'

'About what?'

'About Mr Jobber, madam.'

'What about him?'

'That he is a Sodomite.'

Mrs Roseplucker shot us a look, her face a mask of cold fury. Annie looked alarmed. She glanced at Mrs Roseplucker and bit her lip.

'Well?' I hissed. 'It's true, isn't it? Tell the truth, or I *will* let him hang.'

'And if anyone finds out, then he'll hang for it anyway,' Mrs Roseplucker hissed back at me. 'You know *that* sort o' thing's a capital offence.' She looked at me, her eyes yellow and crafty. 'We all have secrets, don't we, *sir*? So I should think you'd be very happy to say *nothing* about Mr Jobber's tastes to *anyone*.' She leaned forward. 'And should you want your own secret to remain known to only a select few, present company included, I suggest that you do your best to get Mr Jobber out of Newgate and back here to Wicke Street where he belongs!' I felt my skin grow cold and my scalp prickle. I had known Mrs Roseplucker all my life. We had, over that time, developed a mutual respect and understanding. I knew her for a wily old bag, though I admired her survival instinct. She had helped me more than once and had even saved Will's life, something for which I would be forever grateful. Now, I realised that she would do whatever she had to do to ensure the survival of herself and those she loved. She would thank me if I saved Mr Jobber, but she would bring me down if I did not.

'Look,' Annie stepped up and put her hand on my arm. 'Dr Flockhart – you're right. Mr Jobber, he ain't like most men. It's one of the reasons we all love 'im. He ain't mean or cruel. He don't want to hurt us, or fuck us, or sell us, or do anything but keep us company and make sure no one hurts us. I know he's a big lump. I know he don't say much. But you must look beyond how he *seems* at first.'

'He ain't got a bad bone in his body,' piped up Mrs Roseplucker. 'Not unless someone lifts a hand to me and my girls. But he's got sap in 'im, like any man. He just has different . . . needs than such as the like o' you an' me.'

I shuddered to think what Mrs Roseplucker's 'needs' might be, and I could see by Will's expression that he was thinking the same. But Mrs Roseplucker was still talking. 'He goes with men, Dr Flockhart. Not *any* men, but them what likes him back. Seems like he can spot them – least ways, they can spot each other. And so they goes in the back room with him. They knows to come late – when all the others is gone. Usually, I don't see them. I told Mr Jobber he might do what he pleases, as long as he's happy and as long as they pays.' She pressed her lips together. 'Everyone pays at Mrs Roseplucker's.'

'And so Mr Jobber was in bed with Edward Mortmain that night?' said Will.

'He was.'

'So the fellow was not alone, and he was not with you, Annie?'

She shook her head.

I sighed. 'I see. Why did no one tell me this earlier?'

'Mr Jobber didn't kill no one,' said Mrs Roseplucker. 'You'd find *that* out easy enough, a sharp one like you, Mr Jem. And I weren't going to let no jury hang him for being a Sodomite once they seed he weren't a murderer. Magistrates like a hangin'. They likes to show justice is bein' done. And they likes to make an example of folks from time to time. They'd not need much of an excuse to send Mr Jobber to the gallows. Why, he's seen the naked arse o' more than one o' them, and that's more than enough to put him straight on the rope.' She scowled.

'Besides, there weren't no time to think o' a better plan, as that minx Mary'd gone for the constable.'

With hangings on the Monday, time was running out.

'Have you seen this before?' I held out my palm. In the middle of it was Edward Mortmain's love token. Mrs Roseplucker's hand shot out. As she held it to her eye I could see she was disappointed it wasn't gold. She bit down on it with what remained of her teeth. I clicked my tongue. 'It's a shilling,' I said, 'not a sovereign.'

'I can see *that*!' she snapped. 'I 'ad one once that *were* a gold sovereign! The Duke o' Wellington gave it me. He often asked for me. Used to like me to dance in front of 'im wearing nothing but a pair of cavalry man's boots.'

'What a picture!' said Will.

Mrs Roseplucker threw him a bitter look. Her bonnet – a grey mass of ragged grey ribbons than hung down in festoons on either side of her face – had slipped forward over her forehead, so that she looked like an angry tortoise emerging from a sack of laundry. 'I've seen lots o' these sorts o' things,' she said. 'I've 'ad lots of them. Love tokens. I bet *you* ain't.'

'No, madam, I have not,' I said.

'Would you like one, Jem?' said Will. 'An entwined "J" and "W" on one side and a poem on the other? *My love for you is deeper than a well, more lasting that the pox when I forget the calomel.*' We looked at one another and burst out laughing.

'Or how about, *My darling, you are all the world to me, although you roam the sewers, no one smells as sweet as thee.*' We shouted with laughter. I wiped my eye.

Mrs Roseplucker regarded us in silence. 'Perhaps you should,' she said after a moment. 'Love's not something to be laughed at. Both of *you* should know *that*. Even Mr Jobber knew it.' She turned the token in her grubby fingers. 'Can't say much about it,' she said. 'There ain't much love to be had in my business, you all knows that much.'

'Edward Mortmain told his family that he was engaged to be married to a woman. But it was a sham marriage, an arrangement to stop them from asking questions. He had another love. I think we can assume it was a man. Perhaps the "C" on this token? The woman he was to marry swears this was not meant for her. But he had tossed this into the fire, so we must also assume something had gone wrong between them. Betrayal? A change of heart? Perhaps Edward sought solace – relief, comfort, whatever it was – with Mr Jobber.'

'We must speak to Mr Jobber,' said Will.

I considered what Caroline Mortmain had said, how she had seen her brother on Admiral Street, disappearing into a passage beside the Dancing Cat public house. 'Is there a molly house in Prior's Rents?' I said.

'Couple,' said Mrs Roseplucker.

'One down Admiral Street, past the Dancing Cat?'

'That'll take you to it.'

'How would we know it?'

'It's a house,' she said. 'A red door. Ask for Mother Allcock.'

***Excerpt from the Journal of William Quartermain, Esq., surveyor
and assistant architect, Metropolitan Sewer Commission.***

*This morning I told Thimble that the man we had met on
the riverbank not two days earlier, the fellow whose hat he
was wearing, had been found murdered. When I said that he
appeared to have been murdered by a giant rat, the lad nodded
sagely, as if such an end were entirely normal. He asked me
whereabouts 'the Lord' had been found. When I told him it was
in Wicke Street, adjacent to the very sewer we had traversed the
previous week, his eyes grew round with alarm. 'Lor!' he said.
'Perhaps the giant rat came out o' that very sewer pipe!'*

*'Perhaps it went into it,' I replied. He told me then that the
cholera was on Wicke Street too, as if this eventuality was
somehow connected to the presence of the 'giant rat'. He thought
for a while, and then added that the sickness on Wicke Street was
nowhere near as bad as it was in Bermondsey. He told me that
in Bermondsey they 'drinks from the river', whereas those living*

204

*north of the Thames, himself included, only drink pump water.
I am not sure that there is much difference between the two.*

Chapter Fifteen

Newgate. The word itself is enough to fill the heart with fear. I had been there twice, once as a prisoner, and once to visit my father, condemned for a crime he did not commit. I put these thoughts from my mind. If I were to help anyone, I would be no use if I could hardly bring myself to walk up the prison steps. Will reached for my hand and gave it a squeeze as we turned into Fleet Lane.

Up ahead, the prison was hidden partly by the edifice of the Old Bailey, and partly by a thick pall of smoke. Someone had been burning refuse in St Paul's Churchyard and it hung in the air in an acrid cloud. Beneath this, the stench of the prison – ammonia, decay, excrement, fear – laced the air like poison. It was said that the smell of Newgate was enough to kill a man, that a labourer who had helped to install the ventilation system had died when he was overcome by its fumes. The building was one of the most feared and forbidding in the entire kingdom. It had been burned down many times, but each time it had grown back bigger and blacker than ever, like a poisonous fungus, its roots entwined around the bones of the dead. Its blood-stained history stretched back over a thousand years and was sure to last for a thousand more. Above us, its looming walls were smothered in soot and weeping with moisture, as if the captured sighs of those imprisoned within had leached through its stones. It seemed impossible to me that anyone could look upon it and not feel their heart jump into their throat. Even Mrs Roseplucker had fallen silent, Annie too, though all the way from Wicke Street they had been squabbling about the ownership of a hideous orange shawl as if their very lives depended on it. And yet as we drew close, still we could hear laughter and singing. A gaggle of roistering cab men stood drinking half-and-half outside a public house opposite the site of the scaffold. The chatter of drovers' voices, and the bellow of animals echoed down from Smithfield. A group of cheering urchins, bootless and hatless, burst out of an entry between two crooked houses in pursuit of a pig. Street hawkers cried their wares, drays rattled past, children, washer women, messenger boys shouted and whistled and sang, all the noise and bustle of an indifferent city.

Tiny windows peered down blindly on either side of the small, thick-set central doorway. Above it, a carved frieze depicted a giant pair of leg irons, which appeared to dangle there as if abandoned by some monstrous stone goaler. It was visiting day, and a steady stream of people were shuffling in and out. We joined their ranks and passed into the reeking darkness.

It took a moment or two to get used to the dim light, the press of bodies, the stink and the noise. Groans, screams, the sound of weeping reverberated off the walls up ahead as if we were inching towards the seventh circlet of Dante's Inferno. My mouth turned dry. But Mrs Roseplucker was no stranger to Newgate, and she stalked forward now with her head held high, Annie on her arm.

'Well, well, if it ain't young George Dyer!' she crooned. Her face split into a grin like a rotten apple. The subject of her attentions was, in fact, anything but young. He was some five and a half feet tall with bandy legs, a large round belly, a thick neck and small head. One of his eyes was missing, along with the greater number of his teeth. He wore a leather apron, which was bound to his body by a wide, heavy-buckled belt. A bunch of black keys dangled from it on an iron chain.

'Mrs Roseplucker.' He nodded a greeting, and stared at Annie, appraising her with his bloodshot eye.

'Now then, George, you keep making things nice for Mr Jobber and p'raps my Annie'll make things nice for you.'

'He ain't got no cause to complain about his situation,' replied the turnkey. He had not taken his eye off Annie. For her part it seemed that Annie had not been warned that she was there as part of a transaction to ensure Mr Jobber's comfort.

'Oh, not '*im*, Mrs R!' she said, rolling her eyes. 'I got my best hat on!'

'Well you don't need to take it off,' she replied. 'I'm sure Mr Dyer don't mind.'

George Dyer licked his lips. 'You know your way by now, Mrs R,' he said. He fumbled a key into his great meaty fingers. As he moved I could smell the rich fishy stink of his leather apron. Annie glanced at Will and me around the side of her bonnet, her cheeks pink with shame. We knew what she did for a living, but to have her mistress offer her so openly was something even Annie felt the indignity of. Will and I kept our faces impassive, looking the other way as Mrs Roseplucker cried, 'Get along, Annie! Mr Dyer won't wait all day.'

The turnkey unlocked the gate – a small door of riveted iron lattice as black and thick as liquorice. 'You know the way,' he said. He drew back the heavy bolts. 'It's busy today, so keep your wits about you.' He ushered us through, keeping a proprietorial hand on Annie's arm, and slammed the gate closed.

On the other side was another turnkey, this one bigger than George Dyer by about eighteen inches. His arms swung at his sides; his small blunt head seemed to rest on his shoulders without the aid of a neck. I hoped for Annie's sake that she was not expected to service all of them.

And so we proceeded, each gate taking us deeper into the black heart of Newgate. Others walked ahead of us, shuffling along in the gloom, following the turnkeys, waiting at the gates, moving onwards again. The noise grew in volume and intensity. Up ahead someone was screaming in pain and fear. To my right, unseen in the shadows of a barred cell, I heard a rhythmic grunting, like the sound of a rutting beast. On all sides children wailed, men swore and spat, women bickered and moaned. And then all at once we were out in the open – at least, it was as open as anywhere could be in Newgate, as it was no more than a walled roofless yard. Stretched across it was a twenty-foot-high iron gate. On one side the visitors were clustered, on the other side the prisoners.

The visitors were a mixed bunch, here a respectable-looking woman dressed from head to foot in black clung to the bars, weeping and babbling to a man in curate's clothes; there a woman held up a screaming baby and shouted imprecations at a small wiry man with a scarred face and greasy hair. The curate's spectacles were broken, his necktie filthy, his coat torn and stained. He and his wife looked terrified, as well they might for on either side of them huge men loomed, shouting and swearing to their drunken womenfolk.

And where was Mr Jobber in all this? At first we could not see him. And then one of the turnkeys appeared, shoving the prisoners aside as he strode his way forward. A huge man, some six and a half feet tall, trailed in his wake. It was Mr Jobber, his pale face impassive, his huge arms straining at the seams of his coat.

Mrs Roseplucker let out a cry – a sound not unlike that made by rooks as they circled their nests in the evening – and shouted, 'There he is!' She made to shove her way forward. Will and I tried to follow, Will making his apologies: 'Excuse me, madam. Do excuse me, sir. If I might just step through?'

'Get back, you bastard!' Mrs Roseplucker shrieked into a man's startled face. 'Let a poor old lady through!' She produced a short leather truncheon from one of the hidden pockets in her skirt and thwacked him on the side of the head with it. '*Stand aside!*' She jabbed another in the guts and kicked a third on the shins. 'Let me *through*!' The crowd seemed to swell and heave about her. For a moment I thought she was about to be punched on the nose for her pains – but one look at her battered syphilitic face creased up in fury, and people did just as she asked and stepped aside. I pulled Will close, and we shuffled in behind until we were standing on either side of her, hard up against the metal grille that separated us from the prisoners. The tang of fresh ammonia seared my nostrils, and I felt a warmth against my boot. I did not look round. Hopefully our conversation with Mr Jobber would be a short one.

When Mr Jobber saw Mrs Roseplucker his face burst into a smile. He surged forward, rudely shoving his turnkey handler into the dust. No doubt he would pay for it later, but for now, it was clear that his heart was filled with joy. He seized the bars in his huge fists. 'Mrs R!' he cried. Tears sprang from his eyes. 'Mrs R!'

Mrs Roseplucker put her dirty claw-like fingers over his meaty paws. 'Dear Mr Jobber,' she crooned. 'Don't you worry. Dr Flockhart here'll get you out. He 'as a few questions he'd like to ask you, but first,' she peered up into his large moon face. 'Are you eatin' proper?'

Mr Jobber nodded. 'Yes, ma'am.'

'Well, I've brought you some things.'

'Where's Annie?' Mr Jobber peered over Mrs Rose-plucker's shoulder, his anxious eyes searching the crowd.

'She's . . . she's coming in a moment, ducky. Now, take this.' She put a hand into her pocket and brought out a long, cured sausage, reddish-brown in colour and studded with lumps of fat. She forced it through the bars into Mr Jobber's hands. Mr Jobber sniffed it appreciatively. Next she produced a pair of small brown apples, a bag of sugared almonds, a lump of cold ham, and a kipper wrapped in newspaper. Mr Jobber secreted the various items of contraband about his person.

'There now,' said Mrs Roseplucker, stepping back. 'Mr Jobber's ready for you now, Dr Flockhart.'

'Mr Jobber,' my face was inches from the bars. I looked up at him. 'I need to speak to you about Edward Mortmain.'

'Who?' came the reply.

I gritted my teeth. 'The dead man, Mr Jobber. Remember? The man they think you murdered?'

His face became fearful. 'Didn't murder him, sir.'

'I see,' I said. 'But you will hang as surely as if you *did* murder him if you do not tell me *exactly* what happened that night.'

'Ask Mrs R,' he whispered. '*She* knows.'

Mrs Roseplucker jabbed a finger in my face. 'Tell *him*,' she shouted. 'Tell *Dr Flockhart*. He *knows* what you are. He don't *care*. He ain't no better than you! Just *tell* him.'

'Well, sir?' I said. 'Let us start with the fellow's name, at least.'

Mr Jobber blinked. 'I didn't know his name,' he said. He looked so downcast that I felt quite sorry for him. 'I seed him a few times before. I met 'im when he came to see Betty – she ain't at Wicke Street no more. Betty said he didn't do nothing but smoke his pipe while his friends was in with Annie and Ruby. But then the next night he came back. He came back for me. I only seed him on bath night,' he said. 'Only when I'm all clean and soft.' He smiled and ran a hand across his broad chest at the memory. 'I get a proper bath once a month in the kitchen, Mrs R soaps me all over—'

'Good,' I said, anxious to forestall any description of Mrs Roseplucker's soapings. 'It's a most hygienic approach. And then?'

'And when I'm all clean and dry, sometimes I get some o' that rose water you give to Annie, Dr Flockhart, and

I splashes it on my chest. Then I'd put on my special clothes. I gets a clean shirt every first Saturday, and there's a green velvet waistcoat with golden buttons and a green velvet jacket. Mrs R had them made for me special. *Very* special.' He smiled. I could not help but smile back. All around us there was vice and debauchery, misery and sorrow, and yet somehow Mr Jobber stood alone in a bubble of innocence, reflecting on the pleasure of his monthly bath and his suit of clean clothes. I knew him for a silent, doltish man. I had never heard him utter more than a few sentences at a time. Had I been wrong to assume that he had no emotional depth, no delight in anything, no inner life other than that afforded him by his role as Mrs Roseplucker's doorman?

'The rose water is a delightful fragrance, Mr Jobber,' I said. 'You are not alone in your love of it. Mr Quartermain uses it by the bucketful. That and sandalwood. And lemon verbena. And geranium.'

'Steady on, Jem,' said Will.

Mr Jobber looked at Will appraisingly. It was the first time I had seen any kind of intelligence in his eyes. 'I like the sound o' *that*!'

'I will be sure to bring you some,' I said. 'But to the night in question, sir. You are cleansed, Mr Jobber. You smell of roses and you are wearing green velvet. What next?'

'Then I wait.'

'How often had you done this for this particular gentleman?'

'About six times, sir.'

'And he never gave a name?'

'No, sir. He never said very much.'

'I doubt he came for the conversation, Jem,' muttered Will. He was getting anxious. I was keen to get away from the place myself, but I was nowhere near done with Mr Jobber.

'And on the night the man came to you that last time,' I said. 'What happened then? Can you tell me, step by step?'

'I were ready. I lit my candle. All the gen'men were gone, and the girls was in bed. Mrs R went to bed and left me alone. Then *my* special gen'man came.'

'Do you know what time?'

'It were after three,' said Mr Jobber. 'I heard the St Saviour's clock chime the hour. I thought he weren't coming but then 'e did.'

'Did you lock the door after him?'

'Yes, sir. I always locks the door. That's my job.'

'And did you see anyone else outside? In the street, or nearby?'

'No, sir. But I weren't lookin' for anyone else. He knew to come and I were expectin' 'im, more or less.'

'What did he say?'

'Not much. Just, "Well, David", 'e always called me David.'

'That ain't his real name,' chimed in Mrs Roseplucker.

'But my gen'man liked to call me that.'

'Yes, yes,' I said. 'For the purposes of this meeting you were David. Do continue. He said – what?'

'He said, "Well, David, here we are again. At least I can rely on you." He looked sad. And I said "Yes, sir, that you can." And then he followed me to the back room. The sheets was all clean too. I does that for my gen'man.'

'And does he pay you?' I said.

'Course 'e pays,' spat Mrs Roseplucker. 'Ain't nothing for nothin' at Mrs Roseplucker's. An' it's four times as much for Mr Jobber.'

'He took a ten shillin' note from 'is pocketbook and put it on the washstand, like always,' said Mr Jobber.

'So he definitely had his pocketbook at that time,' said Will.

'All gen'men has pocketbooks, sir,' said Mr Jobber, looking puzzled.

'And then you went to bed with him,' I said.

'Yes, sir. 'E likes to—'

I held up a hand. 'Let me stop you there, Mr Jobber. The precise details are unnecessary. Does he usually stay the night?'

'No, sir. Usually afterwards we go to sleep for a bit and then when I wake up 'e's gone.'

'And that's it?'

'That's all he wants, sir.'

'That's it?' I said. 'Nothing more complicated?'

'Mr Jobber scrubs up nice,' said Mrs Roseplucker, proudly.

'I suit green velvet,' said Mr Jobber.

'And I brush his hair and puts some pomade in it. He's a big handsome man, ain't you, sweetie?' She leered up at him. 'Makes more in one night with your dead Sir What's-Is-Name than our Annie does with all of them ordinary gen'men.' She stroked his pale smooth cheek through the bars with a long, withered finger. 'You just ain't never seen 'im that way, Dr Flockhart. You think you're so observant, but you don't see half of what's goin' on around you. There's gen'men all over town who'd want Mr Jobber. He don't say much, so he ain't goin' to

215

blab, ain't goin' to get expectations, ain't goin' to give no one the pox.'

'But you have other . . . other gentlemen, Mr Jobber?' I said.

'This one wanted to be exclusive,' said Mrs Roseplucker. 'Paid for it.'

'Exclusive,' whispered Mr Jobber.

'What happened next?' said Will.

'Next?' Mr Jobber's face turned paler still. Its expression of fondness and pride at the recollection of his velvet waistcoat and evening of pleasure evaporated. 'Nuffin!' he said. 'Next was Mary comin' in for the chamber pot and I woke up cos she always slams the door and rattles the curtain rings, and there was all this blood!' His chin trembled. 'And I don't know *how*, sir. All I knowed is that my gentleman was dead and there was blood everywhere. And then I was screamin' and screamin', and Mrs R and Annie came, and there were noise and voices, and the girls were all on the stairs.' He clutched at the prison bars, his face a picture of horror. 'I dint do nothing! I did what he wanted. What he always wanted. I'd not do murder to any man! Oh God, Dr Flockhart, it's terrible in here.' His voice was a whisper. 'I ain't a murderer, but there's plenty in here who is. They ask me to do things, sir. Things I would never do to anyone, but if I says "no", what then? Why, knives, sir. Knives and buckles and belts, *that's* what. They calls me a Molly-Mae. They *knows*, sir, and I ain't said a word about it.'

'Keep silent, Mr Jobber,' I hissed. 'Say nothing to any of them and I'll help you all I can. And if they come for you, then you must fight them.' I pointed a finger through the bars and stared up at him, my red mask hideous in the gloom. I had been in Newgate and my name was known there. 'Tell them you are the friend of Flockhart the surgeon-apothecary, and if they so much as touch you then I will poison them so cruelly that they will beg for the gallows.'

Excerpt from the Journal of William Quartermain, Esq., surveyor and assistant architect, Metropolitan Sewer Commission.

I have visited the sewers several times now. On each occasion I am accompanied by Fox, Badger and Thimble. Thimble tells me that he can make five shillings a day as a Tosher. I have offered to give him three every time he helps us navigate the Fleet and its adjoining passages. I have said he can carry my brass level. He agreed to my proposal with alacrity. He now wears with pride the boots I have given him and carries the level in its box whenever he can. Fox and Badger do not understand my affection for the lad. Badger calls the boy a 'dirty sewer rat'. Thimble calls me 'Mr Cat'main'. This is his corruption of 'Quartermain', frequently abbreviated yet further to 'Mr Cat'. He considers us to be 'Cat and Thimble', as if we are united in some unspoken rivalry with Fox and Badger. Perhaps we are.

Today we followed a tributary sewer to the Fleet as far up as the junction between Wicke Street and St Saviour's. The tunnel narrows at this point, and it is difficult to make progress. The Georgian brickwork is sometimes in good condition, but often it is not. Here and there are pipes of great antiquity that vomit their effluvia in a continual stream over a lip of decaying clay. Side tunnels are low and broad, their floors are flat, and their roofs are narrower, as if whoever laid them had no idea what he was about for they have been put in upside down. The result is that the matter then pools and solidifies, preventing the stuff from moving fast enough, reducing scouring and leading to stagnation and blockages. A terrible depth of slime accumulates, breathing its foul stink up through the gully holes in the street. The sewers here are close to the surface, and we could stand on a ledge of brick and peer up into the daylight. I recognised my location too – how curious it was to peer out from beneath the earth and see the backs of houses! The brickwork here is soft and friable. At best it is like cheese, hard, but with a softish, yielding texture. At worse it crumbles like damp gingerbread. The mortar disintegrates beneath our fingers.

The mud contains numerous treasures. Today, as I was preparing to leave, Thimble presented me with his best find of the day: a large bronze crotal bell. It is an inch in diameter and must have fallen from the harness of a horse, perhaps centuries ago as it has a smooth, worn appearance. I tried to refuse, but he insisted that I keep it. 'Put it on a ribbon,' he said. 'Wear it around your neck, so's I can hear where you are in the dark.' He grinned fiendishly. 'Ain't you Mr Cat? Well then, you needs must 'ave a bell!' I replied that I hoped never to need such a thing. Nonetheless, the bell sits beside me as I write. I have washed it free of dirt and it has a tinkle as lively as when it was affixed, with others, to a bridle. I have threaded it through with a length of ribbon and will wear it beneath my sewer costume tomorrow.

219

His other finds included a silver buckle, six vertebrae, a roman coin, three shards of blue and red mosaic, a pewter whistle, a length of rope, the skull of a dog, a musket ball and the leather sole of a child's shoe.

Chapter Sixteen

I had never been so glad to be out of a place as when we emerged, at last, from Newgate. There was a cab stand directly opposite, and we jumped into the first hansom in the line. We sat in silence as the wheels rattled over the road, the stink of offal and blood from Smithfield a relief after the intolerable fetor of the prison. It was only when the physic garden gate had slammed shut behind us, when we had skirted the lavender bushes, retrieved two bottles of ale and a bag of new apples from the shed and were sprawled on the camomile lawn in a rare patch of autumn sunshine, that either of us spoke.

'I had no idea Mr Jobber was one of Mrs Roseplucker's "virgins",' said Will. 'Did you?'

'It is somewhat unexpected, certainly,' I said. 'I suppose I have never seen him when he's washed and scrubbed.'

'I can't really see his appeal.'

'Physical attraction is something of a mystery,' I said. 'And I doubt he was required for his scintillating conversation. If a man moves in exalted circles, judged on his wealth, his financial acumen, his sociability, perhaps there is comfort to be found in someone who expects none of these things. Mr Jobber is immune to wit, and drollery. He has no idea about politics, trade or the economy. He isn't a rascal, or a rogue or a schemer. What he does offer is discretion. Complete privacy. He's a big, gentle, silent man. He only throws men out into the street when Mrs R and the girls tell him to. He'd defend any of them with his life, Will, you know that. People fear him because of his size, and because, when he is required to, he can cause pain. But I think the latter does not come easily to him. Perhaps he is a kind and gentle lover too, despite how his appearance and demeanour might be judged by others. Whatever Mr Jobber had to offer, Edward Mortmain desired it. I'm sure there are many men – aristocrats or not – who would be happy to spend the night in the unquestioning embrace of a big warm giant of a man.'

'I suppose Mr Jobber has as much right to pleasure as anyone else,' said Will. He was lying on his side, propped up on his elbow. He took a gulp from his ale. 'Still, it's a surprise. How did you know?'

'It was evident after we'd seen Mrs Arnold that Edward Mortmain's secret – one of them at least – was whom he preferred to take to bed. If he married a woman who had no intention of ever consummating her relationship with a man again, it would at least give him protection, of sorts, from gossip, and from his father's matchmaking. He didn't tell Mrs Arnold about his love for his fellow men and, being a woman who respects the privacy of others, she had not asked. The fewer people who know that your sexual proclivities might lead you to the gallows, or hard labour, the better. And Edward Mortmain is a well-known figure in his way. The scandal was something I imagine his father would not have countenanced, even if he'd been able to avoid the hangman.

'I believe Edward Mortmain was being blackmailed,' I went on. 'I'm not sure by whom. Not by Mrs Arnold; she strikes me as a sympathetic woman who has her own tribulations. The relationship with Edward was platonic – they were two people who helped and respected one another. Mrs Roseplucker? She is always on the lookout for ways of earning more money, but would she try her hand at blackmail?'

'I don't think so,' said Will. 'Nothing about the way she behaved towards Mr Jobber, or the finding of Edward Mortmain in her back room, suggest that she was trying to extort money from him.'

'Exactly. She loves Mr Jobber. She accepts all manner of sexual peccadilloes – in her game, one has no choice. You saw her face when she talked of it, she was proud to think that her beloved Mr Jobber had a lover from among "the quality".'

'But since when does a man of that class go to a place like Mrs Roseplucker's?' said Will.

'The Mortmains are an old family, they worry that they are losing land and status due to the rise in prominence of grubby bankers, traders and industrialists. Their values are wrapped up with their obsession with heirs and inheritance. Look at Sir Thomas and his three wives! Even the rat legend is based on a roistering rapist, and they celebrated him in their coat of arms! But Edward Mortmain was not like that. What might he do, where might he go to fulfil his desires without his tastes being known and judged? And so he went to Wicke Street. And other places.'

'The more plebeian a place might be, the less judgemental?'

'I suspect so. Though as an intensely private man these other places did not suit him so well, I think. Especially since one of them provided him with a blackmailer.'

'And you think this blackmailer murdered him?'

'No blackmailer would want to kill the goose that lays the golden egg, Will.'

'Then we have two separate crimes: the blackmailer and the murderer.'

'Quite so. But whether, and how, they are connected is unclear. It's my belief that Edward had been blackmailed for quite some weeks now. Ruskin said as much when he told us that Edward was always short of money, always worried about it but was pretending that it was for gaming debts.'

'And you think this love token will help us?'

'I hope so, as we are running out of time and options.'

'Who does it belong to?' Will held the love token up between his finger and thumb. 'It is evidently not Mr Jobber, nor is "C" Mrs Christina Arnold. So who might it be?'

'To answer that question, and some others we have yet to even ask, we must follow Edward Mortmain to Prior's Rents.'

'Prior's Rents?' said a voice. 'What reason might my stepson have had to be going anywhere near such a place?'

Both of us leaped to our feet like scalded cats. 'What the devil—'

Standing behind the lavender bushes looking down her nose at us was Lady Veronica Mortmain. She was dressed in a black silk dress and long silk cloak that gleamed as if she were clothed from head to foot in polished jet. Henry Mortmain stood tall and slender beside her, a glum expression on his handsome face.

'Well?' she said.

I knew that we had been followed since we left the apothecary that morning. I'd seen two men hanging about outside the haberdasher's opposite when we left, one a watcher and one a runner. The larger of the pair had been a man of average height in bowler hat and nondescript clothes, perhaps a groom from Blackwater, or a footman dressed for the city. The other had been smaller, weasel-faced, skittish and wiry. The former had been pretending to read *The Times*, as if standing outside a women's fabric shop with a newspaper held to one's face were a completely normal undertaking for a man who looked like a gamekeeper on his day off. The latter had been standing with his back to me, smoking a short pipe, watching my apothecary via the reflection in the haberdasher's window. Had he run to tell Lady Mortmain and her stepson Henry where we were? Where we had been? I remembered how the two of them had been described to us: Lady Mortmain was a viper; Mr Henry was weak. But they would not get the better of us. The only thing that puzzled me was how they had got into the garden. I had closed the gate behind us – I'd heard it clang shut myself. In addition there was only one key, and it belonged to me.

Then I saw that Lady Mortmain was jiggling something in her left hand. 'No doubt you are wondering how we got in, sir? Of course, we have every right to be here, every right to come and go as we please. The Mortmains were among the founders of St Saviour's Infirmary.' She held up a key identical to the one in my pocket. 'We have a long connection with the old hospital. I'm surprised you didn't know.'

'I was the apothecary there, madam. I was more concerned with the patients than the accounts.' In truth, I had always been aware who the Infirmary's principal benefactors were, and although the name 'Mortmain' had been on the garden's deeds no member of that family had contributed to it, or to St Saviour's Infirmary, in cash or kind during my entire tenure as apothecary.

'As I'm sure you know,' she went on now, 'Old St Saviour's was built entirely on land endowed by my husband's estate. This physic garden included. It is ours, sir.'

'My family have worked this garden for five generations,' I said. 'It was gifted to me when the old infirmary was demolished. I have the deeds to prove it and you are trespassing.'

She waved the key, choosing to ignore what I had just said as if my remarks were of no value or concern to her at all. 'And so my stepson and I thought we'd just come by to make sure all was well. And here you both are, talking about our poor Edward. His death, his *murder*, I should say, has nothing to do with you. The police have arrested a man and that is an end to it. We do not need the scandal, the disgrace, the *pain*, of further enquiry.'

I said nothing. I knew she would not have listened to me if I had. 'I know my husband tasked you with finding out what happened to poor dear Edward,' she went on.

'I am informed that, *somehow*, you have persuaded him that the man arrested for the crime is innocent.'

'And so he is,' said Will.

'And who do you propose *is* the murderer?'

'Why do you wish to know?'

'How dare you answer my question with a question of your own! Impudent fellow. I have a *right* to know!'

I was pleased to find that she could be so easily riled. I thought for a moment that she was about to stamp her foot, but she mastered her pique and looked down instead at the soil in front of her. The fog crocus, *Colchicum autumnale*, was in bloom, a welcome splash of colour in an otherwise drab autumn garden. It had appeared a few days earlier, and clumps of the slender, leafless flowers were facing the direction of the watery October sun. They were curious blooms, distinctly crocus-like, but with a pale and etiolated appearance, and without foliage of any kind which gave them an unsettling, incomplete look – no wonder they were also known as 'naked boys'. They were a washed-out mauve in colour, but despite their aesthetic limitations they were a cheery sight at the fringe of the camomile lawn. I grew them for their corms, which, once carefully prepared and the dose measured minutely, were an ancient but effective treatment for the gout. I had several patients who suffered from the condition, and my recipe for gout pills was reliable – if the patient did not take too many. Death via multiple organ failure was almost inevitable if my prescription was not followed to the letter. But Lady Mortmain was interested in neither gout nor physic. I watched as she put out a small, patent-leather shod foot, and pressed it firmly into the centre of one of the nodding clumps of purple flowers. She pressed her weight upon it, and screwed her toe this way and that, mashing the delicate heads and their pale slender stems into the dark earth. She lifted her foot, stepped sideways, and screwed her toe into the second clump.

'Oh, come, my dear,' said Henry Mortmain. 'What use is that? You have muddied your boot too!' He whipped out a handkerchief and made to bend down and wipe the offending matter off her foot, but she shook her head sharply. Will and I watched this exchange with interest.

'I see, Dr Flockhart, that you are upset at the fragility of your flowers, and the ease with which they can be destroyed,' she said, although I had betrayed no such emotion. The fog crocus is a robust little thing, despite its insubstantial appearance, and it would take more than Lady Mortmain's boot to finish it off. 'What a shame it would be if something far worse happened to your beloved garden.'

'You have some rare plants, it's true, Flockhart,' said Henry. He looked about admiringly. 'Why didn't anyone tell me we owned this garden?'

'But you do not own it,' I said.

He stepped over the ruined crocuses. 'Is that a red gardenia?' He strode across the camomile lawn and put out a hand to the evergreen shrub I had cultivated against a south facing wall. 'What a marvellous specimen.' He plucked one of its blooms and held it to his nose. 'Delightful,' he said. He had taken the only flower that was not turning brown, for although I managed to keep the red gardenia flowering into the autumn, the weather had turned too cold and damp for it now. 'I can't get mine to grow,' he said. He sniffed at it again, a whorl of thick crimson petals second only to the rose in loveliness. He smiled and held it out to his stepmother, who had still not moved her foot off the crocuses. 'For you, my dear?' he said. 'It represents respect and admiration. A secret love. Will you not accept it?' She shook her head and frowned. Henry shrugged and slipped it into his buttonhole. 'I've tried everything to make mine thrive,' he went on. 'But it seems a most contrary evergreen. Hates too much sun, or too little. Too much water, or too little. One asks oneself whether it is worth the effort it takes to keep it happy.' He caressed the red flower, then turned to absently finger one of the shrub's dark leaves. 'Beautiful, but temperamental. Capricious, even. Not unlike my dear stepmother, perhaps?' He spoke under his breath, as if he had forgotten I was standing beside him, and the smile he had attempted fell away from his face almost immediately. Then he cleared his throat and said briskly, 'I believe it prefers an acidic soil. Is yours acidic, Flockhart?'

'It is for that particular plant, sir,' I said. 'It's what the gardenia favours and I've done my best to accommodate it. The gardenia is excellent for liver disorders, swelling, inflammation in general. Or applied to the skin as a salve for burns. It's hard to grow outside but it is worth the effort as it's a useful addition to the apothecary's pharmacopoeia.'

'London earth is predominantly clay, is it not? How do you manage?' The fellow seemed genuinely interested, and I had the impression that he was relieved to be immersed, however briefly, in a subject that was both close to his heart and took him far away from his current situation as heir to a cruelly murdered brother.

'Years of cultivation, sir,' I said. 'And I have the best compost in the city. This was formerly the physic garden to a monastery. Its soil is the finest in London and its walls keep out the worst of the weather. Only the fog hinders us, though I suspect its sulphurous content is enjoyed by this particular gardenia, for it thrives well despite everything.'

'Yes, we have less fog up at Blackwater,' he said. 'Nevertheless, my gardenias are a failure and I have tried everything. I wonder if the soil is too wet—'

'Oh for goodness' *sake*, Henry!' snapped his stepmother. 'Never mind the gardenias! Look, Flockhart, my husband is old. He hardly knows what he is saying these days. If you have any information about this family, about Edward, about who murdered him, then you must bring it to me. To us. And you will *not* take it to the magistrate, or the police. Is that understood?'

'Perfectly well, madam,' I said.

'You did my brother's post-mortem,' said Henry, looking up at me suddenly. 'I remember you.'

'I did, sir,' I said.

'Hm.' I thought he was about to ask me something, or tell me something, but he changed his mind. His face was glum. 'Lovely garden,' he said.

'Your garden at Blackwater is very impressive. The ponds and water garden especially.'

'My own innovation.' He smiled. 'The water lilies in the summer would lift even a heart of stone—'

'Oh, come *along*, Henry.' Lady Mortmain sounded exasperated. She turned on her heel and stalked towards the gate, slicing off the dead heads of foxgloves with an angry twitch of her riding crop as she went.

Henry sighed. 'She's just upset,' he muttered.

'They needed to be cut back anyway.' I watched as he fiddled fretfully with the Mortmain signet ring that his brother had once worn, twisting it around and around his little finger, his eyes mesmerised by the action of his own hands. 'Your brother used to do that,' I said. 'Twist his ring about his finger. I could tell from the skin beneath; the way the metal was dull on the outside but brilliant elsewhere.'

'Yes,' he said without looking up. 'He did not enjoy the role he played.'

'You think he was acting a part?' I said. 'A part he was supposed to play, but which he did not relish?'

'Doesn't everyone? Everyone who inherits wealth, responsibility. Everyone who inherits wickedness.'

'And you?' I said. 'Does it sit easier on your shoulders?'

'I'll get used to it, I suppose,' he said glumly. 'She insists upon it, so I suppose I'll have to. She's right, of course—' He looked up, seeming suddenly to realise where he was, and who he was talking to. He saw that Lady Mortmain had disappeared and a look of alarm flitted across his features. 'Stepmother?' His anxious gaze darted towards the open gate. 'Veronica? Veronica!' And then he was gone too. Striding after her, almost running to catch up.

'I wonder if she will put him over her knee for being a naughty boy,' said Will as the gate slammed shut behind him.

'I think she was hoping he would project a more strong-armed version of himself to us,' I said. 'Not that she needed an enforcer. She is perfectly capable of being menacing all on her own.'

231

'The only thing Mr Henry Mortmain could strong-arm would be a barrow of compost,' said Will. 'But she exerts a Siren's lure over him, that much is evident.'

'Is she the mother he never had, or the mistress he cannot bring himself to leave?' I said.

'Perhaps she is both.'

I nodded. The last red gardenia of the year that Henry Mortmain had plucked and put into his buttonhole had come apart as he fled, its petals scattered across the camomile lawn like clots of blood. 'It's a powerful combination, Will. What deeds might a weak man under-take to earn the approval of such a woman?'

**Excerpt from the Journal of William Quartermain, Esq., surveyor
and assistant architect, Metropolitan Sewer Commission.**

*I must take a moment to record my thoughts, my feelings, as they
arise at the memory of a second afternoon I have spent in the
company of Miss Thomasina Golightly. At the conclusion of our
last meeting, I had asked whether she would care to meet me at
Lincoln's Inn Fields the following day, and she had agreed with
what I interpreted as an encouraging degree of enthusiasm. Today
I left Fox and Badger at Blackfriars and went up into the town.
Miss Golightly and I walked about the gardens a while, talking
the whole time about this and that. About her father, and her late
brother, whose clothes she now wears (indeed, she was wearing them
when we met, though I betrayed no concern whatsoever about it).
She asked about my work for the Commission, about my friendship
with Jem, our investigations into the death of Edward Mortmain
and the wrongful arrest of Mr Jobber. She is a lively interlocutor,
and the hour spent in her company slipped past like gossamer.*

Today's saunter was only the third time I have met her, but already she steals into my thoughts more than I care to admit anywhere but in these pages. She is not like any woman I have ever come across. She is outspoken and knowledgeable; she is curious and independent. She does not conform to expectations, but picks and chooses from convention those elements which may suit her, and rejects those that do not, depending on circumstance and occasion. She dresses in whatever way she pleases. She has the face of a pixie and the hair of a street urchin. I must see more of her, for I am quite enraptured! I wonder what she makes of me. Good things, I hope, and I draw optimism from the fact that she came to find me at the riverside, even if it was to ask me about photographing corpses. I suspect that Jem is similarly enthralled. I saw the way he stared at her when we met her in her studio. I have seen that expression on his face before – a furtive admiration and longing – though never, unfortunately, when he is looking at me.

Ah, Jem, my dearest and most beloved friend. What would I say to you if you were here before me now? If you were able to read the pages of this journal? I would tell you that you are not the easiest person to love, and yet love you I do. I would say that without knowing you and sharing your life I would be but half the man I am. That you are the cleverest and wisest man I know, and the bravest too, for I know the lie that you live. Your prickliness and arrogance frustrate and infuriate me in equal measure, but I would not change a single item about you. I was so alone when I met you, alone and, I will admit it, heart-sick; my soul, and my purpose here lost and crushed by this unforgiving city. But you saw in me what others did not. You became my lodestar, so that now I cannot be without you, no matter what. And yet, my love for you is no longer the wild flame it was when we first met. For your part, I know that you could never love me like man and wife, but I know that you do love me. No one will ever be dearer to my heart and soul than you, but today I found myself asking whether you could agree to share that position. Could you share it with Thomasina Golightly? I wonder what answer you would give.

Chapter Seventeen

Prior's Rents is the most vile and neglected rookery in the whole of St Saviour's ward. Like so many places in the city, however, it is not far from more elevated addresses. One may walk down Admiral Street, for instance, and after passing through houses of the most filthy and degraded appearance down beside the Dancing Cat public house, one might cross the open sewer at Blake's Passage, traverse a terrace of mews cottages at Wrights Lane, pass through a stable yard, and all at once one is staring into the backyards of the grand houses on Eagle Square. Despite this proximity, few of the better off make any effort to improve the lot of those who spend their lives crammed into the rookeries of Prior's Rents, and as long as the ditch, the stable yard and the mews cottages act as a buffer between rich and poor there is little anyone will do to alter that.

The molly house we were heading towards could have been approached easily via the houses on Eagle

Square. It struck me as we walked towards it that Edward
Mortmain would have been able to slip through the
stable yard and past the mews cottages without anyone
thinking very much of it. The route that Will and I took,
however, was more direct, leading as it did through the
heart of Prior's Rents. We walked quickly, following the
directions Caroline Mortmain had given us, heading
down Admiral Street then looking for an opening beside
the Dancing Cat public house.

The passage we found there was dark. The daylight
should have been visible high overhead in a narrow
ribbon between the tops of the tenement buildings,
but the fog had crept in, and instead there was nothing
but grey above, grey fore and aft. The passage was
punctuated with doorways but most of them appeared
to be boarded up, for which I was very grateful, the fewer
apertures in which villains and footpads might hide,
the better. I gripped my stick in my right hand, quite
prepared to use it to ward off an attacker if I had to. I saw
that Will had done the same. The passage was some five
feet wide. Here and there men stood in small groups,
their shapes lumpen in the fog, their faces pale blurs
beneath their ragged caps. They stood motionless, as if
with no purpose other than to lurk there in the gloom.
We strode forward.

'I'm beginning to wonder at the wisdom of this, Jem,'
muttered Will. 'And . . . I think we're being followed.
Can you hear those footsteps?'

'Assuredly we are,' I replied. 'He's been following us
since we left the apothecary. Medium height, stocky
build, wearing one of those bowler hats beloved by
gamekeepers. And yet I believe this is a different fellow

to the two men who pursued us this morning. Those were in the pay of Lady Mortmain. *This* fellow – it remains to be seen whose bidding *he* is doing.'

'Shall we find out?'

We turned a corner, and Will pulled me into a recess, hard up against a boarded-up door deep in the dark greasy wall. He held his stick up, his face a mask of concentration. His knuckles were white. And then all at once our pursuer rounded the corner. Will leaped out and shoved the fellow against the wall. He knocked his hat to the ground and shouldered him hard against the wet sooty bricks. He pressed his stick to the man's throat. I noticed that he had kicked the fellow's feet apart so that he stood with his legs wide, unable to move for fear of falling over. I wondered where he had learned such slick violence. Will was usually averse to attack, leaving such decisiveness to me. But he was a changed man, in many ways, since he had taken up his work in the sewers. Perhaps he had been obliged to learn a few tricks to defend himself.

'What do you want with us?' he hissed into the man's ear. The bowler hat rolled in the dirt at our feet.

'Nothing, sir,' stammered the man. 'I wasn't—'

'Yes you were,' I said. 'And you followed Edward Mortmain down here, didn't you? Two days before he was murdered?'

'No . . . I—'

Will pressed his stick against the man's throat. 'Do we look like we want to hear lies?' I could hear the fear in his voice. Violence did not come naturally to him, and I knew that he was afraid of Prior's Rents. 'Cough it out, man! Or shall we trample this lovely new hat of yours into the mud?'

'Please, no!' The man tried to look for his hat. I was standing with my stick over my shoulder, my right foot poised upon the crown of his new bowler. '*Don't!*' he screamed.

'Well?' said Will.

'Sir Thomas sent me,' he said.

'Sir Thomas has better things to do,' I replied.

'Well . . . Not him *exactly*, sir. More like his agent. A member o' the aristocracy don't want to dirty his hands with speaking to the likes o' me.'

'And you were tasked with doing what, exactly?'

'With finding out what his son was doing. What sort of life he was living. Where he went, what he did and with whom. That sort o' thing. Pretty low stuff if I'm honest, sir, but times is hard, and I do what I'm told.'

'That's all?' said Will.

'That's all, sir.'

'And so now you are following us too? Did Sir Thomas authorise that too?'

'He did, sir. That is, his *agent*—'

'Why?'

'How should I know? I don't get told why. I just get told to do it.'

'And what have you told him so far?'

'Nothing much,' he said. 'Visits to brothels, to Newgate, to that garden.' He shrugged. 'I tell him where you've been, that's all.'

'Let him down, Will,' I said. 'You followed Edward Mortmain down here, didn't you?'

'I did, sir. He went in the red door at the end.'

'And do you know what happened behind that door?'

'No, sir. I ain't told to go inside, just to report on his whereabouts. On your whereabouts. Just like I don't go into his club with him, or into the tobacconist's, or any other place. I just see where he goes and wait for him to come out again.'

'And was he in there for long?'

'Not ten minutes,' he replied.

'And on previous occasions?'

'Longer. Over an hour usually.'

'And did you follow him to Wicke Street? On the night he died?'

'I did, sir. But he never came out again. I waited till about four o'clock in the morning, then I went home. Can't stay up all night, they don't pay me enough.'

'And did you see anyone else go in after him?'

'It's a brothel, sir. There was plenty of people sneaking in and out.'

'Sneaking?'

'Don't everyone look furtive when calling on such places?'

I shrugged. 'I don't think we need to detain you any longer Mr—?'

'Sackville, sir.'

'Of course.' The man's name was no more Sackville than mine was. 'Well . . . Sackville . . . You can be sure to let your master know that we are making progress, and we will apprise him of our discoveries in due course.'

'We better hurry up and make some discoveries, Jem,' said Will as the man scampered back the way he had come. 'Jobber hangs on Monday.'

I had the impression the fellow was relieved to be done with us. But we had at least learned something useful from him. 'So, Sir Thomas Mortmain knew about Edward's fondness for men all along,' said Will.

'Perhaps,' I said. 'Assuming the information was passed along. As for what is going on behind this door – a molly house is a molly house. They've not changed in fifty years despite what anyone might think. Are you ready for what we may find?'

Will tipped his hat. 'Lead on!'

I rapped on the door with the head of my stick. A shutter opened in the middle of it and a pair of eyes peered out.

'We're looking for Mrs Allcock,' I said. 'Mrs Roseplucker of Wicke Street sent us.'

The shutter slammed closed, and we heard keys turning, and bolts being drawn back. The front door opened directly onto a large low-ceilinged parlour. Its windows had been boarded over and the apertures hung about with velvet swags and drapes. The dark cave that had resulted from these modifications was illuminated only by candles. The place was hot, with a cloying dampness to the air. Sagging armchairs and chaise longues squatted here and there in the broiling gloom, like huge overgrown toadstools. As it was only one o'clock in the afternoon the place was quiet. Aside from the thin young man who opened the door, a woman sitting on a huge green divan-like sofa with an account book open on the cushion beside her, and a maid who was loading cheap brown coal into the fireplace, there was no one.

'I'm Mrs Allcock,' said the woman, surveying us critically from her nest among the cushions. 'This is Francis,' she jerked her head towards the man who had let us in. He was dressed in a loose silk dressing gown.

His eyes were dark and languorous and ringed with kohl.
His lips bore traces of paint, as did his cheeks. His hair
was slicked back, and I had the impression that not so
long ago it had been hidden beneath a wig of some kind.
There was one such made of glossy jet-black horsehair
ringlets sitting on a stool beside Mrs Allcock's divan like
a sleeping spaniel.

'Put some clothes on, Francis,' she said. 'Now then, my
ducks, what can Mrs Allcock do for you that Mrs Roseplucker couldn't?' Francis pulled his silk closer around
himself, but otherwise ignored her. He folded himself
onto a large velvet armchair and pulled out a pipe.

'We are here on behalf of Mrs Roseplucker,' I said.
'You heard that a man was found dead in her house?'

'I did, sir.' The woman's face was blank. 'That has
nothing to do with me, nor with anyone here.'

'Indeed, madam. And you heard who he was? Edward
Mortmain. Mr Jobber has been arrested. He will hang on
Monday unless we can help him. He is innocent of course.'

'I've known Mrs Roseplucker a long time,' said Mrs
Allcock. 'I was one of her girls once. I got no complaints
about her on that score.'

'We understand that Edward Mortmain was, at times,
one of your gentlemen visitors,' I said. 'We have reason
to believe that he had a lover, someone he was especially
fond of, in this establishment.'

'They don't use their names here,' she said. 'You can
imagine why.'

I had the silver and velvet frame containing the
daguerreotype that Mrs Arnold had given us, and I produced it now, wiping the glass free of dust as I handed it
over. 'This gentleman,' I said. 'Do you know him?'

She located the pair of pince-nez that were hanging from a chain around her neck and peered down at Edward Mortmain's silvery likeness. 'I seen him,' she said. 'Came here quite a few times. Called himself Elijah Mathers. Ellie Mathers. You remember him, Francis?'

'Course I do, Mother,' drawled the supine Francis.

Mother Allcock narrowed her eyes. 'I heard they put Mr Jobber in the clink. Now you tellin' me it ain't him what done it? Don't see how I can help you. I ain't sayin' nothin' that's goin' to bring the Peelers down here. So if you don't mind, I believe I ain't got nothin' else to say to you two young gents.' She nodded to the door. 'You can find your own way out.'

'I have no intention of bringing the Peelers down here, ma'am,' I said. 'I just wanted to know what you could tell us about the man you know as Ellie Mathers. If you *don't* tell me, then the Peelers is what you will most certainly get.'

For a moment, she hesitated, her reptilian gaze focused on our faces. Then, 'Ellie Mathers weren't the only toff we get here.' She sat forward. 'In case you were in any doubt on the matter, we're what's called a molly house. I cater for gen'men that likes other gen'men. Some of 'em likes to dress up as ladies, some of 'em don't. Some likes to have their boys dress as ladies, some don't. Like Francis here.'

'Fanny Cumming at your service, gentlemen,' said Francis, flourishing a hand as he took a mock bow from his chair.

'Either way they can do what they like with each other as far as I'm concerned, as long as no one gets hurt, and as long as I get paid. We don't ask for their names, we just take their money – there ain't nothing in this house that's free. Your Mrs Roseplucker knows *that* as well as anyone does. As for your dead man, I don't remember much about him. He ain't been here for a while.'

'Came last week, Mother,' said Francis. 'I saw him. Came lookin' for Charlie.' Francis uncurled himself and blew a long plume of smoke across the room. He gazed at Will with appraising eyes. 'Ain't I seen you before?' he said suddenly.

'No,' said Will. 'At least, I don't think so. I've not been here before.'

'Perhaps you should come,' Francis smiled and licked his lips.

I produced the shilling love token from my pocket. 'E and C,' I said.

'Ellie Mathers and Charlie Abbot,' Francis shrugged. 'Charlie did them for all his regulars. Made them think they was special.'

'What was going on between them?'

He rolled his eyes. 'Oh, they're *all* in love with Charlie. Your man, Edward what's-his-name weren't no different. He wanted Charlie all to himself. They fell out over it.' He turned the token between his fingers. 'Lots o' boys do these for their husbands, though Charlie's are always the best.'

'Was Charlie blackmailing Edward Mortmain?' I said.

'There ain't none of that here,' said Mother Allcock sharply. 'Can't have my reputation ruined. No one'd come if they thought that'd happen. If there's any blackmail going on, and I ain't sayin' it don't happen, then it ain't from this house.'

'It weren't Charlie,' said Francis.

'Is Charlie here?' said Will. 'Can we speak with him?'

Mother Allcock and Francis exchanged a glance. She gave the faintest of nods. Francis sighed. He stood up and went to the foot of the stairs. 'Charlie!' he screamed up into the gloom. 'Charlie!'

We waited in silence. At length we heard feet on the boards overhead. There came the sound of urine thundering into an evidently already full chamber pot, then a door opened. There were more footsteps, this time on the stairs, and a young man with a mass of blond curls appeared. He was well built, tall and broad, with a smooth pale face, rosebud lips and an angry expression. He was wrapped in a crimson robe tied at his waist. 'What's so important you wake me up before it's even six o'clock?' he said. He was better spoken than his fellow residents at Mother Allcock's, his teeth white and even, his posture confident and proud. It was clear to me that he was not from these streets, even if he had ended up on them.

'Ellie Mathers is dead, Charlie,' said Francis.

The lad Charlie blinked. 'Well it wasn't *me*!' he said. 'I've got nothing to do with anything like that!'

'These gen'men want to know about him,' said Francis.

'When was the last time you saw him?' I said.

Charlie shrugged. 'I don't pay much attention to the passing of the days and nights. It's impossible to say where one ends and the other begins in this place. Though he *was* here a few days ago too. Didn't stay long.'

'He was worried about something,' said Will. 'Do you know what it was?'

'Said he was being followed,' said Charlie. 'I knew that much.'

'And you made him this token?' I held it out.

'Ellie said he was in love with me. Perhaps he was, perhaps he wasn't. I made him a token with our initials on it.' The lad shrugged again. 'It was just part of the game.'

'Did he think it was a game?'

'Don't know,' said Charlie sulkily. 'Yes, he knew but . . . but he didn't want it to be a game.' He sighed. 'Look, I knew this place worried him. It was too noisy for him. Too boisterous. We know how to have fun here, don't we, Fan? Right on this here carpet on our hands and knees if that's how the fancy takes us. But Ellie didn't like that. Wanted to be more . . . *quiet*. Invisible, is what he said. Well, I'm not invisible, not at Mother Allcock's at any rate! And I don't want to *belong* to anyone. And so we fell out. He knew I went with other mollys, and he didn't like it. And then two weeks ago he accused me of blackmailing him. Said it could only be me as he was always so careful. But it *wasn't* me.'

'Can you prove it?'

'Can I prove I wasn't blackmailing Ellie Mathers? I don't see how I can, sir. You either believe me, or you don't.'

'Did he say what these blackmailers wanted?'

'Money,' he said. 'Everything. "They want the stars, Charlie", that's what he said. He was always a bit poetic in the way he talked.' He smiled faintly. 'I liked it.'

'What about a name?' said Will.

'Do blackmailers give their names?' said Francis. He smirked.

Charlie ignored him. 'Cock Robin,' he said. 'That was the name on the letters.' He shrugged. 'I never saw him again after that.'

Excerpt from the Journal of William Quartermain, Esq., surveyor and assistant architect, Metropolitan Sewer Commission.

Yesterday the sun came out. Underground, in the wider tunnels such as those that lead south from the old Fleet Bridge, a greyish veil hangs on the air, like a wraith above the putrid flow. Even here the fog creeps in. Today, however, this visible miasma had all but vanished. Instead, as we passed a gully hole the sun shone in. The effect was surprising to me. Perhaps I have spent too many hours beneath the city for I must confess that it lifted my spirits. The filth took on a myriad dark and shimmering hues, a burnished bronze upon the walls; a deep black-green the colour of a mallard's neck around my boots; and streaked through the waters like a vein and artery side by side, a dark throbbing red mingled with lustrous peacock blue from the dyeworks near Prior's Rents. A fringe of fungus grew against the lip of the gully hole, vivid orange caps that glowed luminous in the sunlight like tiny lanterns. Thimble,

*who monitors my face for signs of distress or pleasure, grinned
at me.*

*'Ain't it pretty, sir?' he said. 'Like the windows what's inside
a church. 'Specially with the bricks all arched overhead like.'*

*My eyes smarted in the ammonia, and the breeze that blew in
through the aperture seemed like nectar.*

Chapter Eighteen

꧁

We left Mother Allcock's after that. There was nothing more to be gained there. Two of the men we had seen idling in the passage outside the place had disappeared. A third was now lying insensible upon the ground, another was engaged in sexual congress with a filthy-looking woman who appeared to be dressed in a bundle of coloured rags. Her grubby knees and stick-legs flailed about on either side of his jerking buttocks as he did his business. The air was heavy with the smell of offal and pig shit as there was an abattoir not far away and the wind was blowing straight across it. The stink seemed to coat my tongue like butter.

'I need a drink,' I said.

'There's a pump on Mort Street,' said Will.

'Is there?' I said. 'I don't think I want a drink that badly.' I could not imagine a worse place than the pump on Mort Street and I said as much to him now.

'There's one in Bishop's Court if you prefer,' he replied.

'I'd no idea you were so well informed.'

'I know where all the pumps and wells are,' he said. 'All the pumps and wells from here to Wicke Street. Prior's Rents is my area of expertise. I've marked them on a map for Mr Basilisk.'

'Then perhaps we might—'

'I'd not drink water from a single one of them.'

'I was going to recommend a pot of ale,' I said. I pointed with my stick to a dingy doorway above which was a painted board bearing the image of an orange tom cat. 'What'd you say to the Dancing Cat?'

'I was about to suggest that very establishment.'

The Dancing Cat was not as attractive as its name suggested. It was illuminated by a couple of small, dirty windows. What little daylight they let in was supplemented by the dim yellow glow afforded by a few tallow candles that had been stuck onto saucers and were positioned here and there about the room. Men sat hunched and silent over their pots of ale. The tables were low and greasy, the floor matted with dirty grey sawdust. The fireplace was a dark hole with a mound of smoking brown coals clumped in its tumbledown grate, above which, pinned to the chimney breast, dangled a stuffed cat, a hangman's noose tight about its mangy neck. A more grotesque piece of taxidermy I had never seen. The air was thick with the smell of fried fish, sweat, smoke and stale beer.

'Two half pots,' I said to the publican – a slatternly woman with an aggressive air. She slammed the pots down and snatched my pennies from the counter. We took a seat in the corner with a commanding view of the fire and the dead cat.

'An excellent choice, Jem.' Will sipped at his ale.

'A picture is forming in my mind,' I said. 'A picture of what happened to Edward Mortmain.'

'Are you ready to share your thoughts?'

'Perhaps you can share yours,' I said. 'Your observations are invaluable.'

'Mine?' He sat back. 'Very well. Edward Mortmain was a good man. He had questions about his family's business, about their ownership of Prior's Rents and their connections to its slums and water supply. But he had vices of his own, private vices, for which he was being blackmailed. He obviously needed money to pay his blackmailer and he pawned his ring and watch to do so. Unhappy in love, he sought solace with Mr Jobber, a trusted bedfellow. While he was there, someone stole in and murdered him, using poison and a weapon we have yet to find.' He frowned. 'Poison is perceived as a common choice for women. If you remember your Euripides, Jem, and I know you do: "I prefer the old way best, the way of poison, where we are as strong as men."'

'Well said,' I replied. 'Do go on.'

'But to rip out a man's throat, that is a brutal act. So my question is this: are we looking for two attackers, or one? One male and one female? Are they working together? One might assume so, though if we are to avoid assumptions then it is also possible that the first person poisoned him, then left the scene assuming the deed to have been done. Then the second person arrived later, but before the poison had finished its work, and committed the assault on his throat – the act which finally killed him. In this version of events the two actions are not undertaken by the same person, or persons.'

251

'An interesting theory,' I said. 'There is also the matter of who stands to gain from the death of Edward Mortmain.'

'At the moment I can think of only one individual.'

'Brother Henry?'

'Precisely. Brother Henry stands to inherit everything. And is he not allied with his stepmother?'

'That was my impression,' I said.

'And yet, Edward's death also means that the Mortmain family no longer teeters on the brink of scandal. And it halts any steps he might have wanted to take to expose Sir Thomas, his father, as a man who supplies foul water and squalid tenements to those who cannot afford to live elsewhere, a wicked parasite who lives royally on the misery and desperation of others less fortunate. It's my firm belief that the cholera comes from the water the poor are forced to drink, and not from the air they breathe, though God knows the stink is enough to make anyone sick. I told Edward Mortmain as much when I met him beside the Thames, though what he intended to do with the information we will never know. So perhaps we should consider the unexpected proposition that Sir Thomas himself had much to gain from the death of his son. A son whom, it seems to me, he had already consigned to the grave. You remember his comments? "The first-born of the Mortmains do not last long." And "there was little point in Edward planning for the future". What father says such things about his son?'

'Your arguments are all entirely logical,' I replied. 'But do we have evidence for any of them?'

'Not as such.' He looked downhearted. He drained his pot and slammed it down on the tabletop. 'We must *find* the evidence!'

'We will do our best, should any of your theories prove to be correct. But first . . . might I ask whether you know the gentleman at the tap? The fellow with the sack?'

Will glanced over. A man was looking over at us from beneath the brim of a filthy cap. He was short and stocky, dressed in a dirty coat of boiled wool and a pair of canvas trousers tied with string beneath the knees. At his feet was a sack bound at the neck with a coil of greasy rope. The sack heaved and squeaked as if it were alive.

'Badger!' Will exclaimed. He raised a hand. 'What brings you here, sir?'

The fellow picked up his sack and shuffled over to us. 'Arfternoon, Mr Quartermain, sir.' His gaze was shifty, darting to the door and back, as if he was expecting someone.

'Got some rats?' said Will, pointing to the sack. He had adopted a cheery, enquiring tone, though I knew him well enough to tell that the very sight of the man made him uneasy.

'Yes, sir,' the fellow replied. 'Big 'uns.'

Will swallowed, though the smile stayed on his face. 'Plenty to choose from, down at Blackfriars, ha ha!'

'Zatcly, sir! Want to see?' The man Badger made as if to untie the sack's fastenings.

Will held out his hands. 'Oh no, no, Badger, that won't be necessary. But look, I'm glad we bumped into you,' he went on. 'I won't be down tomorrow afternoon. Can you manage without me? We have a funeral to attend.'

Edward Mortmain's funeral. I was hoping I would be able to draw some meaningful conclusions after that event. Will began talking earnestly to the fellow Badger about mud and flow and water depth. It did not interest me, and I sat back for a moment to consider how best to proceed. I fell to musing about pumps and poison, about the dead man's corpse, about cherries and blackmail and signet rings, and about the legend of the Mortmain rat, which somehow stretched its long black shadow over the whole murderous business. But there was worse to come before we saw an end to it. Far, far worse.

Chapter Nineteen

Our route back to the apothecary led through the direst streets that Prior's Rents had to offer. The mud, offal and straw that habitually filled the streets in a rotten slurry had dried into a hard crust. Flies buzzed about our ears, the piles of refuse seething with maggots promising a never-ending supply of the infernal creatures. At the corner, where Mort Street met Admiral Street, someone had gathered a mound of street sweepings in a barrow, as if with a view to carting it away to the fields – which was where the stuff used to go before London's growing sprawl pushed the fields too far away to be worth any carter's while to go there. Now, instead, the refuse was simply flung into the river – the Thames or the Fleet ditch – if it did not remain where it was. As we skirted this fly-blown nuisance, all at once I heard a voice cry out. 'Oh, Dr Flockhart, Dr Flockhart!' Will and I exchanged a glance.

'It's you she wants,' said Will. He grinned. 'Go to her. I have work to do at the waterside.'

I seized his arm. 'You don't escape that easily!'

'Oh yes I do!'

'You too Mr Quartermain!' shrilled the voice. 'The more the merrier.'

'Remember to smile,' I said. I turned around, dragging Will with me. 'Miss Mortmain!' I cried. 'What a pleasure to see you. And yet how unexpected!'

Caroline Mortmain was surging towards us. Behind her, she had left a gaggle of ladies standing on the corner, outside the Pelican Street entrance to William Mowbray's pawnbroker's.

'We were just beginning today's mission,' she said. 'We are going to Well Court. Do you know it?' She did not wait for a reply. 'We thought perhaps some hymns. And then Mrs Bleasdale is going to give a talk about Christian values. After that I am to speak on the evils of drink and the importance of cleanliness.'

'That's all very well, Miss Mortmain,' said Will, his smooth tone belying his criticism. 'But what use is all this to the residents of Well Court?'

She blinked at him in disbelief. 'It is soothing to the spirit, Mr Quartermain and, *obviously*, shows them the pathway out of poverty and degradation. The poor are the victims of their own indolence and moral weakness, sir. If they but stopped their abuse of hard liquor, swept their houses, engaged in hard work and catechised their children, they would all lead happier and more healthful lives. The workhouse would have far fewer inhabitants. Apathy, sir, is what corrodes self-belief and ingenuity, and thence comes moral laxity – sin and so forth, obviously.'

All at once a smaller, slighter, figure appeared. 'Come

along, sister,' she said. 'You made me traipse all the way into town, so let us do what we came to do, and return home.'

'I believe you have already met my sister Charlotte,' said Caroline.

Will and I tipped our hats. 'Miss Charlotte,' I said. 'How are you enjoying your mission in the Rents?'

'It stinks,' she said. 'I wanted to go to see Hunter's Anatomy Museum, but Caroline says it's not appropriate.'

'If you want to be a doctor then you could do worse than examine those places that are the source of disease,' I said. 'Well Court is an excellent example of pestilence.'

'Will you join us, gentlemen?' Caroline went on. She was dressed in black, perhaps as a gesture to acknowledge her brother's passing, perhaps because the grime of Prior's Rents was likely to stain her more colourful dresses. She seized my arm, and Will's, and before we could object she was marching us down the road.

Caroline Mortmain's troop of Bible women were each clutching a leather-bound hymnbook in readiness for the work ahead. Most of them were also pressing handkerchiefs to their noses, and the smell of rose water was thick in the air as we approached.

'Ladies, ladies, ladies, our work is upon us!' cried Caroline. She began ushering the women down the passage behind the pawnbroker's.

'I believe your family has a long connection with Prior's Rents,' said Will.

'Indeed,' she replied. 'This is land owned by my family. It has been so for years.'

'And your family have never thought it appropriate to provide better housing for the people who live here?'

'It is partly for that reason that I come here with my missionary work. Bible readings and so forth bring light into the darkness.'

'And yet perhaps the light might penetrate more effectively if their homes were of better quality?'

'I see you are quite the improver, Mr Quartermain. Quite the revolutionary. But you do not understand, sir. These people *choose* squalor and degradation. Look, you see the rotten vegetable matter and filth in this courtyard? They could take it away, but they do not. They might burn it, but they do not. If they had even an ounce of desire to improve their environment and perhaps make a little money into the bargain, they might sell it to a market garden. But they do not. Instead, they leave it there, an offence to all. Equally, the cesspool over yonder.' She gestured towards a brimming pool of shimmering black liquid. 'They could get it emptied, or empty it themselves, or shovel it into a cart and sell it to a farmer, but they do not. Indolence, sir. It is the curse of the age. It leads to squalor, and thence to vice and disease.'

We watched as a child picked its way through the mud. A scrawny chicken and a pig pecked and rooted among a pile of decaying matter, though what nutrition might be gleaned therein it was impossible to say. The child – a boy – was dressed in a woollen jacket, its fabric so stained and greasy that it had the appearance of wet canvas. Beneath this he wore a ragged grey shirt and a pair of britches that came to his knees and ended in tatters. His stick legs were bare, streaked with filth and studded with scabs and sores. In his right hand he was dragging an empty bucket – wooden, bound with hoops of iron, its handle a twist of oily-looking rags. He was heading towards the pump. Across the court, the fluid from the midden and cesspool had oozed a slick channel through the refuse – snaking past mounds of rubble to coalesce in a shining black pool at the base of the pump. The boy shoved his bucket beneath the spout and began to crank the handle.

Will shook his head. He stalked across the yard. 'Let me help you,' he said. The boy stared at him in disbelief.

'Mr Quartermain?' cried Caroline. 'Mr Quartermain, you prevent them from developing initiative, self-reliance and fortitude, if you help them like this. *Advise* them, certainly, but material assistance is to deny them the chance to find determination within *themselves*.'

Will ignored her. 'Where are you heading?' he asked the boy. I saw him look down at the bucket with disgust and wrinkle his nose. The boy pointed to a doorway flanked by two boarded-up windows.

'Your family could do much to help,' I said.

'Oh, I don't think so, sir,' she said briskly. 'At least, not in the sense that you imply. These streets are owned by the poor. They are made by the poor and the poor keep them thus. Still, I do what I can. Ladies!' she trilled. 'Your hymn books, if you please. Will you join us, Dr Flockhart? We would benefit from the gravitas of a gentleman's voice. You are a tenor, I presume? And Mr Quartermain a baritone?' She began to shepherd her friends into position on the only patch of ground that was not sodden with ooze, gesturing to a servant she had brought with her to lay down sacks so that the ladies might stand on something other than mud and effluent. Flies buzzed about our ears.

'I have chosen a children's favourite. "All Things Bright and Beautiful". A new hymn but a cheery one. The third verse your friend Mr Quartermain would do well to heed. Do you know it? Allow me.' She began to sing, her voice high pitched and grating. '*The rich man in his castle, the poor man at his gate, God made them high or lowly, and ordered their estate.*' She simpered up at me. 'I think that's true, don't you? Now then, ladies, Dr Flockhart, are we ready?'

'Jem,' Will's voice came from the door to the hovel he had just entered. He was standing with a handkerchief over his mouth. I could see that something was wrong. I made my excuses, Caroline Mortmain watching me as I stumbled away across the courtyard.

Behind me, the women started up their caterwauling. About the court, on all sides faces began appearing in windows, men and women emerging to stand in doorways, frowning and muttering darkly to one another. How could human beings live in such places and retain any degree of health, I thought, as I skittered my way towards Will. What use was singing? Or readings from the Bible? All the physic in the world would not save them if they did not have basic comforts – clean water, sanitation, dry housing, unadulterated food. I did what I could, as an apothecary, as a doctor, but the problem was so great, so monumental, that my individual ministrations were all but useless. Where might hope lie for places like Well Court? I looked at Will. Dwarfed by the great black tenement behind him, his face pale in the gloom, he did not look like a man who could save anyone. And yet surely his work for the Sewer Commission would enable him to achieve things that were impossible for the rest of us?

Will ducked back inside, pulling me after him. Within, it was as dark as the grave. The windows, without a single pane of glass that remained unbroken, were boarded over. The only light came in through the open door or seeped in at the cracks where the boards met. It took a moment for my eyes to get used to it. Outside, the voices of Caroline Mortmain and her troop of Bible women rose and fell. I saw her looming over the others. She had found a box and was standing upon it, swinging her arms as she conducted her choir. In her huge black dress and large cup-shaped bonnet, she reminded me of a monstrous stag beetle, up on its hind legs.

Inside the room I could make out dim shapes. The boy we had seen was sitting on the floor upon a nest of rags. In the corner, on another mass of filthy bedding, lay a woman. Beside her, on the damp earth floor, was a tin cup half full of water. It was my impression that the boy had filled this cup from the bucket Will had brought in and left it at his mother's bedside. The smell in the room was indescribable.

'Look at her,' whispered Will. 'Her face.'

In the darkness, in the grey light of the open door, the woman's face glimmered like polished bone, white, but with a bluish tinge. Her lips were dry and cracked. I saw them move, saw a white tongue pass over them as if she was trying to speak, but she made no sound. I thought I recognised her. Had I not seen her from the window of the pawnbroker's not two days earlier? The boy too was the same boy I had seen from the window of William Mowbray's pawnshop, lifting another child out of the midden.

There was no doubt in my mind about what I was looking at. Of all the diseases in the city, in the kingdom, this was the most feared. It was the fastest to act, the most violent, the least dignified. Consumption killed many more, but cholera, cholera was dreaded more than the Devil himself.

The skin of her face – the only part of her flesh that I could see – had a parchment-like appearance, as if every ounce of moisture had been sucked from her body. It clung to her skull so that her teeth protruded, her cheekbones rendered sharp as blades seemed about to burst from the skin. Her eyes had sunk into dark hollows, glittering between lids as pale and membranous as moth wings. Her dress was soaked with the watery stool that had spilled from her, unchecked. The boy crawled over to his mother and applied the rim of the tin cup to her lips. The stuff trickled down her cheek and onto the rags beneath her head. She did not move.

From outside, the voices of the Bible women rose and fell in unison. But now their song had been joined by another sound, by discordant yowlings and raucous bellows. The residents of Well Court were adding their own voices to the cacophony.

'I think we should leave,' I muttered to Will. 'There's nothing we can do for her.'

'We can't abandon him here.' He knelt before the boy. 'What's your name, soldier?' The boy made no reply. His eyes darted to the bed, and then to the door. Will held out a hand. 'Will you come with us?'

'Will, you can't save them all,' I murmured.

Outside, the singing had grown in volume. A noisy drunken roar, no hymn, but a bawdy popular song. *'Nancy Dawson, she's a whore, son. Keep yer pecker in yer hand. Wipe her fanny with yer hankie if yer cock won't make a*

262

stand.' Louder and louder, on and on, each line lewder than the last. The Bible women's voices faltered. I saw a piece of rotten fruit, hurled from an upstairs window, smash into the ground in front of Caroline Mortmain. She waved her arms to keep her ladies in time and raised her voice.

Before us, the boy scrambled to his feet. For a moment I thought he was going to take Will's hand, but instead he shouted, 'Fuck off, mister!' and plunged past us out into the courtyard.

Will turned back to the woman on the bed. 'Should we help—'

'No,' I said. 'There is nothing we can do.' In the dark, the woman's eyes glittered between her half-closed eyelids. 'Besides, she's dead.'

'And we just leave her here?'

'We can hardly take her with us.' I handed him a handkerchief. 'Here,' I said. 'I have more than one. It's impregnated with lemon verbena, cedar and rosemary.'

'You don't still subscribe to the idea that this is spread by miasma, do you, Jem?'

'I don't know what spreads it,' I said. 'But let us take every precaution.' I flapped the silk square in his face.

'I have my own—'

'No, you don't. I'm afraid our water carrier snatched it from your pocket as he ran past.'

'I didn't even notice!'

'That's the idea,' I said. 'They train them young.'

Outside, Caroline Mortmain's Bible women were beginning to fragment. Caroline was doing her best to stay in control and had dismounted from her box onto a piece of sacking. She held her skirts up, out of the mire.

'Let us consider our work done for today,' she cried. 'We shall pray for a more receptive audience on our next visit. Perhaps, ladies, we might bring some gifts with us to sweeten the message. I have a spare Bible, and a copy of Blake's "Catechisms for the Young" that I might bequeath. And some plums and cherries from the garden, perhaps?'

The ladies were chattering among themselves, their faces white with fear. 'Such ingratitude,' I heard one of them mutter as another rotten apple smacked into the mire. 'Miss Mortmain, my dear, I fear the residents of this particular place are beyond redemption.'

They began to make their way towards the court entrance, their faces set, their lips thin with disapproval. 'Such is the fight, ladies,' boomed Miss Mortmain. She seized my arm, her face radiant. 'Can you not feel it, Dr Flockhart? The thrill of it, sir? The surge of blood in the veins, just the way my forebears felt at Waterloo. At Naseby. At Agincourt!' She turned back to her friends, arms spread wide. 'The fight against squalor and degradation continues, ladies. *"For there will never cease to be poor in the land; that is why I am commanding you to open wide your hand,"* Deuteronomy, chapter fifteen, verse eleven. We know we have an uphill battle. These people do not know temperance, industry, continence. It is up to us to teach them. And so we shall, my sisters. So we *shall*!'

When we got back to the apothecary there was a note awaiting me. It was from Dr Graves, and it contained only three words. 'Missing bowels returned.'

*Excerpt from the Journal of William Quartermain, Esq., surveyor
and assistant architect, Metropolitan Sewer Commission.*

<u>Problems</u>

1.) Cess pools are now dug so deep that they reach the
sand below the clay, and thus the liquid matter
seeps through to the water courses and thence to
wells and pumps.

2.) Excessive use of water closets in the wealthier areas
floods cess pits and causes offensive matter to
make its way into sewers intended only for surface
water.

3.) The tidal nature of the river (often misunderstood
by members of the Sewer Commission, and
Parliament) prevents removal of nuisances that
are dumped into it.

4.) Several water companies supply water that is
taken directly from the Thames.

Chapter Twenty

The following morning we went back to see Mr Byrd. 'I don't know why we have to go to see him again,' said Will. 'Besides, won't he be at the funeral? Whatever you need to speak to him about surely it can wait.'

'I think there's something he'd like to tell us.'

'Such as?'

'Wait and see,' I said. 'But it might solve at least one part of the puzzle.'

Mr Byrd looked less than pleased to see us, though his innate politeness made him greet us with his usual good humour. 'Good day, Flockhart, Quartermain,' he said, shaking our hands vigorously. He'd had a mirror brought into his chambers and he was examining himself in it, critically casting an eye over his middle-aged physique and the clothes he had dressed it in. 'You see me preparing to leave for Blackwater, sirs. Is my mourning appropriate, d'you think? Would you say it is sufficiently deep? As deep as the occasion requires? I wanted silk, but without the slightest bit of sheen. Sheen would be disrespectful. I was most particular about it and the tailor was reassuring on the matter, but now I have it on I wonder whether it is altogether as sombre as it should be. Would you say I am sufficiently *ad dolorem*?'

He was dressed from head to toe in black, including his stockings and shirt, a black wool cut-away coat, black silk neckerchief, shoes, handkerchief. He wrung his hands.

'So much could go wrong today that I am all knotted up inside. I have not had a wink of sleep and my digestion is quite vile, sir! I fear Lady Mortmain will insist on attending, and that will enflame Miss Caroline to do the same. Sir Thomas is sure to be displeased. A funeral is no place for a lady, as well you know, gentlemen, but the ladies in question are distinctly hard to control.' He smiled nervously. His face was pale, and he had purplish circles beneath his eyes, as if he had not slept for days. He retreated to the safety of his desk and sank into his chair, his hands resting on the leather desktop. 'Well, well, let us put those thoughts aside for a moment. What is it that I can help you with, gentlemen?'

It was not an audience I had been looking forward to. In fact, I had been awake most of the night worrying about it. I'd heard Will moving about in his room in the dead of night, and more than once I'd been tempted to go in and speak to him, to share my thoughts and deductions, to ask his opinion on the dreadful logic of what I was about to say. But in the end, I had left him in peace. Will had enough on his mind, I did not want to add to his worries. And so, what I was about to say would no doubt come as a surprise to him too. I took a breath.

'Mr Byrd, how long were you blackmailing Edward Mortmain?'

'I beg your pardon?' Mr Byrd stared at me in disbelief.

'You are "Cock Robin" are you not, sir?'

'How did you know—' began Will.

'A little byrd told me,' I said. 'You're vain enough to enjoy teasing your victim with an oblique reference to your own name, are you not, sir? And yet he never guessed it, did he? Never once suspected.'

'This is absurd!' cried Mr Byrd. 'I have no idea what you're talking about, Flockhart. Blackmail? How dare you, sir! Why, I could have you thrown out of this office, out of this town, for such a vile insinuation!'

'I can assure you, sir, it is not an insinuation. It is a question based on a fact and I will and *must* repeat it. How long were you blackmailing Edward Mortmain?'

Mr Byrd closed his mouth. For a moment he continued to stare at us. I saw his Adam's apple bob in his neck as he swallowed. And then all at once he let out a curious wheezing moaning sound, like a sigh escaping from the depths of his soul. He seemed to deflate before us, his head slowly sinking into his hands. 'It's not what you think,' he muttered. 'Oh, Flockhart, it's not at all how it seems.'

'Is it not?' I said. 'And yet you *are* Cock Robin?'

'I am, sir.'

'Then pray explain.' I knew I sounded angry, but I could not help it. I had known Mr Byrd all my life. How dare he deceive me, pretend he was my friend, furnish me with information about a murdered man, and yet all along be misleading me. I tried to keep the rage out of my voice when I said, 'An innocent man will die, Mr Byrd, and every moment that you lie and bluster is a moment that brings that closer.'

'Sir Thomas told me to do it,' blurted Mr Byrd. 'He said I must. He wanted it *done*. How could I refuse? I am his agent, his solicitor, I *must* do as he asks.'

'Even when it is breaking the law, even when it might have such consequences? A man's life?'

'*I* didn't kill Edward Mortmain!'

'I didn't say you did,' I replied.

Mr Byrd's face was ashen. 'You do not know Sir Thomas as I do. As Edward did. If you refuse him, he *will* find a way to punish you. He . . . he *enjoys* punishing people. And you will not even know it is him!'

'That's because he gets people like you to do it!' said Will.

'Your explanation, sir, if you please,' I snapped. 'Or would you prefer me to speak to the magistrate? His view of your actions will be far less sanguine than Sir Thomas's, I can assure you.'

Mr Byrd threw himself back in his chair. 'Sir Thomas told me that he had some concerns, misgivings even, about his son Edward's behaviour. Sir Thomas likes to be informed of his family's interests, their activities. The name of Mortmain is a watchword for probity and privacy, and he is determined to keep it that way.'

'Sounds as though it's a watchword for tyranny and unkindness,' I said.

'You may think what you like, Dr Flockhart,' he replied, 'but my family have served the Mortmains for one hundred years and I was not about to break that bond of trust. Sir Thomas is a highly respected man. Although, you are right, he can be somewhat censorious. Cruel almost. And he is feared as a result.'

'Even though he is a recluse who can't move without being pushed about in a bath chair?' said Will.

'Yes, sir, even despite his infirmity. And he is less bound to that chair than you, or anyone, might suppose,' he added bitterly. 'Anyway, when he told me that he had concerns surrounding Edward's undertakings in the city – "creeping about behind my back" was the phrase he used – he wanted not only to know what his son was doing and why he was doing it, but also to . . . to *correct* that behaviour once he had learned of it. His first request was that I have Edward followed. And once I had reported back my findings—'

'Which were what, exactly?' I said.

'Edward's questions about Prior's Rents, his interest in the work undertaken by the Metropolitan Sewer Commission, his visits to Mrs Arnold and to Mrs Allcock's.'

'To Mrs Roseplucker's?'

'Precisely.'

'Why would Sir Thomas not just have a conversation with Edward, like any normal father?' said Will.

Mr Byrd gave a hollow laugh. 'Can you not see, Mr Quartermain? He is not "any normal father". A mere "conversation" would never do. No, no, no. Sir Thomas wanted to pursue Edward, to punish him and frighten him and bring him to heel all at once – and derive some pleasure from it into the bargain. "Watch him wriggle, like a worm on a fish-hook" were his exact words. "A little bit of blackmail will do nicely. Make him dance to our tune, eh?" He even laughed as he said it. "See to it, Byrd!"' Mr Byrd closed his eyes. 'And so I did.'

'So, *you're* the agent who paid that fellow to follow

Edward, and then to follow us, on behalf of Sir Thomas?'
said Will.

'I am, sir.'

'Did Sir Thomas believe in the rat?' I asked.

'What?'

'You must know of it, sir. The family legend? The
Mortmain Rat.'

'Oh, that stuff. Yes, yes, they all pay it lip service,
I suppose.' Mr Byrd chewed his lip. 'I did not kill Edward
Mortmain,' he said again.

'But your blackmailing did get out of hand?'

He nodded. 'Sir Thomas's idea was to get him to see
how dangerous his . . . his proclivities were. That his
attendance at molly houses would bring his family into
disrepute and open him up to *real* blackmail, to ruin and
disgrace. We hoped to make him stop of his own accord
by teaching him by his own experience how dangerous
such activities are. I take it you do *know* it's a felony, sir,
what Edward Mortmain did with other men? One can be
hanged for . . . for *that*.'

'Yes, Mr Byrd, I was aware of the possible consequences,'
I said. 'Pray continue.'

'Well, Edward paid my demands without demur and
yet continued with his . . . affairs. I gave the money to
his father and made sure to keep him fully cognisant of
the situation. And then, as if to deflect attention away
from his true nature, all at once Edward brought Mrs
Arnold into the equation. And yet *still* he pursued that
young fellow at Mrs Allcock's. He could not see where
it all might lead.' He dabbed at his lips with a folded
handkerchief. It was doused in lavender and rose water,
and he sniffed at it and closed his eyes. 'At his father's

271

request I pushed him for more,' he said. 'He *had* to stop, had to give up *men*. Sir Thomas was adamant.'

'And so you asked him for the Chitra Golconda,' I said.

'Sir Thomas's idea.' Mr Byrd dabbed his eye.

'How did you know?' said Will to me.

'Charlie told us,' I replied. '"They want the stars, Charlie." D'you remember? It wasn't poetic at all, it was entirely prosaic. The Chitra Golconda is their name in Hindi. They are known in English as the bright Golconda or the Golconda stars.'

'We thought to tempt him with just a couple of them,' said Mr Byrd. 'The Golconda stars are in Sir Thomas's possession – in the strongbox he keeps in his room. They belonged to the first Lady Mortmain. Each the size of a plum stone, they were cut but never set. Caroline should possess them, but her father said he would keep them for her until she married. Sir Thomas made no secret of the fact that he thought her too ugly to marry, or to wear anything so beautiful. "Like putting a tiara on an ox", he used to say.' Mr Byrd took a deep breath. 'Anyway, last week Edward came to me, and told me he was being blackmailed.'

'And you confessed?' said Will.

'Of course I didn't!' snapped Mr Byrd. 'I couldn't tell him, not without his father's permission.'

'Sir,' said Will gently, 'I think you could have.'

'Well, I didn't.' Mr Byrd wrung his hands together. 'It was the first time he had come to me. The first time it seemed as though he might be about to tell us that he would stop. That he knew he *had* to stop. Edward said he had taken two of the diamonds – he had been visiting his father, the strongbox was open, they had quarrelled, his father had turned away—'

'Was it usual to have the strongbox open?' I said.

'Does not a miser like to look at his riches?' he replied. 'And besides, it was Sir Thomas's intention to test his son, to see if he had the courage, or the desperation, to attempt this most heinous of family betrayals. And try he did. Through some sleight of hand when his father glanced away, I believe. I hardly know how as the poor fellow was talking so quickly and was so agitated that his explanation was unclear to say the least. Suffice to say, he was able to palm the jewels. There are twelve altogether and he hoped his father wouldn't notice the loss of a couple. He popped them in his mouth and swallowed.'

'Good grief!' said Will. 'What size are these things? A plum stone, you say? Would a pocket not have been a more convenient place to stash them?'

'No, sir. Sir Thomas is a suspicious man. One never knows whether he will ask one to turn out one's pockets, or demand to see what is in one's hands. Especially if one has been anywhere near his strongbox. Or his desk. Or indeed, near his bed or the door to his dressing room. It is an invasion of privacy and trust, I agree, but if one is an employee, or a family member, one does his bidding no matter how outrageous the request might be. And so Edward took what he considered to be the ultimate precaution. As it happens his father *did* ask to search his pockets.'

'And what was your advice to him,' said Will. 'When he came to you that day with five thousand guineas-worth of diamonds in his belly?'

'I told him to eat some fruit,' said Mr Byrd. 'Are you not always telling me to do so, Flockhart? Is not constipation the scourge of the age?'

'Among other things,' I replied.

'And I take it that he was killed – murdered – before he got the chance to . . . become reacquainted with these diamonds?' said Will.

'Yes,' said Mr Byrd.

'And so you set a fire to drive us from the mortuary, and then stole the bowels in which you hoped to find them,' I said.

'I did indeed, sir,' he whispered. His face had turned pale. 'But they were not there.' Mr Byrd put his head in his hands once more. 'They are lost for ever.'

Chapter Twenty-One

We left Mr Byrd after that. I asked Will whether he
thought we should tell Sir Thomas what we knew.
That we were aware of the part he had played in
terrorising his own son.

'It seems like the correct thing to do,' he replied. 'And
yet, although blackmail is a crime, Edward stole from his
father – in some ways it's a perfect circle. And to call him
to account at his son's funeral seems a harsh judgement.
Besides, no doubt Byrd will tell him anyway, and the real
question of who killed Edward remains as unanswered
as ever.'

'I think the murderer is close,' I said. 'Why else use
the motif of the rat? It seems unquestionably to point to
the family.'

'True enough,' said Will. 'And if we return to first principles and ask ourselves who stands to gain from Edward's
death the answer is still Henry. And yet he seems the
most affable of fellows, the least likely to turn to murder.'

'But did we not think Mr Byrd was the most affable of fellows? Look what sort of a man he turned out to be.' I pulled my scarf tighter about my neck and huddled into my coat. 'Perhaps Henry is a little *too* obvious,' I muttered.

'There are reasons why any of the other members of this family might wish to murder Edward,' I went on. 'For a start, no matter what they say, and regardless of blood, they are a self-serving lot. The waterworks could not be moved upriver, they *must* not be moved down, their current location means they draw from the most polluted stretch of the river. The fact that Edward wished to close his family's waterworks threatened to cut off one stream of easy income for them. Which of them would have supported him? Consider Caroline, for instance. She is, I believe, capable of anything. Her philanthropy is her lifeblood. What if Edward had had his way? What if the waterworks were closed and the rookeries of Prior's Rents cleared? What role would she see for herself then? I am concerned that there is nothing she would not do to preserve the status quo. Does she not see her ultimate purpose as a beacon of moral superiority? Without her charitable causes, her philanthropy, what is she? Just another old maid lolling on a golden sofa twiddling her thumbs. She sees her mission as helping the poor – but in her own particular way. A way that ensures she is *always* indispensable. She likes to judge the recipients of her munificence, to judge them and yet always find them wanting. She is not in the least bit concerned with improving their lives materially. That, she believes, is up to them. As bizarre as it might seem, I believe she would regard any move towards improving the lot of those unfortunate enough to live in Prior's Rents to be a personal attack on her own *raison d'être*. Without the poor, without dirt and squalor, disease and poverty, she has nothing.'

'And she would kill her brother over that?' said Will. 'Over his desire for slum clearance and sanitary reform? You paint a picture of an unhinged mind if that is her motive for murder.'

'Who can say what rage – rational or otherwise – burns inside her? Does she seem sensible to you? And we cannot forget that her mother went mad. It would be remiss to overlook that fact.'

'You think madness is hereditary? Even when childbirth is its cause?'

It had been a long time since I had considered the hereditary nature of madness. Insanity was something that ran in my own veins, perhaps, for my father had run mad, driven out of his mind by a sickness that caused sleep to become impossible. I had yet to manifest any such tendency, and it was my most earnest hope I would not share my father's fate. But I had given the causes of insanity a great deal of thought, and my current ideas about what types of madness might pass from parent to child were based on observation, and on the conversations I'd had with the doctors at Angel Meadow Asylum.

'I believe madness *can* be hereditary,' I said. 'Depending on what form it takes. From what Mr Byrd told us, and Caroline herself, the first Lady Mortmain took her own life due to puerperal insanity, a common affliction for many women after childbirth. It is caused by circumstance, so I don't assume that Caroline Mortmain is mad just because her mother suffered from a temporary mental derangement. But it *is* a possibility. And her behaviour, what we have seen of it, is unusual. Her colourful clothing when the rest of the house is in mourning, for example. Her behaviour in Well Court. Such zealousness in the face of hostility – how did she describe her feelings? *"The surge of blood in the veins, just the way my forebears felt it at Waterloo. At Naseby. At Agincourt!"* It is preposterous. *She* is preposterous. But that doesn't mean she is not dangerous. Clearly, her passions – whatever they might be, however misguided they might be – run deep.'

'Even so, Jem—'

'You see that it *is* possible? And whatever she might say, the Mortmain rat has shaped her thinking as much as anyone else's in this callous family. What better way to shock them all than with a brutal reminder of their own wickedness, their own mortality. And I believe she is perfectly capable of ripping someone's throat out.'

'But how might she have got into Wicke Street? How did she know where Edward was?'

'The kitchen door at Wicke Street was not locked. Anyone might have found their way in. And why might she not know where he was? Mr Byrd told her father. Could she not have listened in? She says she knows everything that goes on at Blackwater and I am sure that, by and large, she does. She could have had her own man follow him. She could have followed him herself. She knows Prior's Rents better than anyone. She does not fear those streets. They are in her blood – she said as much. And did you not see her on the bridge at Blackfriars that time when you met her brother?'

'I did.' Will sighed. 'I suppose so. And yet—'

'And yet, I do not find myself convinced by any of it,' I said. 'Any more than you do.'

'Indeed,' he said. 'And yet it *is* entirely plausible.'

'Perhaps our ideas will be clarified when we see the whole family together,' I said.

Will shivered. Once more I could taste the Thames on the gritty air; it was the taste of mud and low tide, effluent, coal smoke, decay. Looking to the east, the air over the city had taken on a yellowish hue. The breeze was slight, but had a coldness to it, like a draught from an open sepulchre, and it would bring the weather with it. In an hour's time, two if we were lucky, the city would scarcely be visible. I wondered whether the fog would reach Hampstead. Perhaps they were too far north, the ground of the heath high enough to preserve them from the worst of it. Mr Byrd had informed us of the time and location of Edward Mortmain's funeral. Family members and trusted servants had been keeping watch over the coffin as it lay at rest in the family chapel at Blackwater. The coffin was to be loaded into a hearse and marched through the lanes of the village before returning to Blackwater for the service, and the interment of the casket in the chapel vault. Sir Thomas had made it clear to us that he wanted an answer by the time his son was buried. Our time had all but run out. Will and I sat side-by-side in silence as our hansom rattled north.

The mourners were awaiting the sad event in the library – a large chamber, with two slender casement windows looking out across the lawn to the side of the house. I had the impression that no one had used the place for some time. It had a musty scent, as if of dust that had

recently been disturbed. I looked along the shelves –
copies of *Hansard, Blackwood's Magazine,* and *Chambers's
Journal* sat alongside mysterious volumes in Greek and
Latin, the poetry of Keats and Byron and gardening
manuals, none of them looking as if they had been
touched for generations. The leather of their spines
was cracked and dull with neglect, the tops of the pages
dusty, and when I pulled one off the shelf to examine
it – a copy of McGregor's *Manual of Horticulture* – the
pages were spotted and foxed. Beside this, a shelf of
books on physic looked somewhat less dusty than the
others. I saw Christison *On Poisons,* Anstruther's *Elements
of Materia Medica,* and Munro's *Anatomy.* All somewhat
elderly editions, and well used. Charlotte Mortmain's
collection, no doubt. I plucked one from the shelf, a well-
thumbed copy of Jaffne's *Flora and Fauna of the British
Isles,* and flipped it open. *C. Mortmain* had been written
in a childish hand on the frontispiece. From across the
room the girl Charlotte glared at me, and for a moment
I thought she was going to plunge through the crowd of
silent mourners to snatch it from my hand. I slipped it
back into place and turned my attention to the rest of
the room.

The room was quiet, as if none of the mourners had
anything to say to one another. A couple of maids were
in attendance. One of them I recognised as Effie, the
parlour maid. They passed among us with glasses of
warm brandy, and negus. I was partial to a glass or two
of negus. I prefer it made with port rather than wine,
lemon rather than orange, and a good dash of sugar and
cinnamon. What I sipped now was delicious – strongly
flavoured, the lemon and cinnamon cleansing and

powerful on the palate, but nonetheless a delicious and warming beverage.

With the fog drifting up from town, the air had taken on a damp chilliness and a glass of warm negus was clearly much appreciated by the glum-faced gathering. Cheeks began to glow, though still the silence prevailed. I had no idea who these people were. Across the room I saw Sir Thomas and his son Henry. Beside them, Lady Mortmain stood, neatly encased in tight black silk, a tall, feathered bonnet and heavy veil. The only sound was a bovine moaning that came from the far side of the room. It was Miss Caroline, also starched up crisply in deepest mourning, the flounces and ruffles and bows of her skirt adding to her bulk so that it looked as if she were emerging from a huge mound of coal. She buried her face in her black silk handkerchief and wept noisily. As a maid floated past she shot out a gloved hand, seized a glass of steaming brandy, downed it in one and resumed her sobbing. Beside her, Charlotte Mortmain regarded her with interest, her face pale and mask-like behind her veil.

On a long leather-topped table in the centre of the room sat a large coffin of polished wood. It was draped in a shroud of black velvet and topped by a wreath of flowers. Lilies, their smell filling the room with a heady dizzying aroma. Entwined about them were other leaves and flowers, among them dragonwort, yew, dogsbane. I shivered.

'What is it?' whispered Will.

'That wreath,' I whispered. 'What do you see?'

Will peered at it. 'Yew,' he said. 'Lilies. The yew seems unusual, I admit. And some other stuff. Pink and blue.' He shrugged.

'I wonder who made it. Who decided what it ought to contain.'

'Who knows about flowers? That's a woman's subject, is it not?'

'Perhaps Lady Mortmain, or Miss Caroline? And yet Henry is the one who loves the garden, who has a knowledge that surpasses that of most women on this subject. Why should he not also know their significance? He was familiar with the meaning of the red gardenia.'

'And what is the significance of these particular flowers?' said Will.

'The vipers bugloss – you see those vivid blue flowers on those tall stems? That signifies falsehood. Those small pink spikes you can see beside them is dragonwort. The roots might be used as an astringent, but their meaning here is not medicinal, nor I suspect is it mere coincidence.'

'What—?'

'Horror, Will. *That* is what they signify. Horror of the most violent and appalling kind. Equally, the shrubby leaves of the dogsbane imply deceit, and the lobelia you can see there signifies malevolence, an evil intent from one to another. And you see those leaves and the tall spindly stems that resemble the cow parsley? That's hemlock, Will. Hemlock! I hardly need tell you—'

'Indeed, Jem. But is the message intended for others to read, for those present to interpret, or is it a message to the dead man?'

'A final act of desecration to adorn his coffin with poisonous weeds and flowers?'

'Is it not a possibility?'

'I don't know,' I whispered. 'As you say, one might

assume a woman to be more familiar with the meanings associated with various flowers and leaves, and yet have we not learned to assume nothing? To never fall back on what we *think* we know about how men and women might behave?'

A man carrying a long black pole and dressed from head to toe in black appeared in the library doorway and banged the brass foot of his ebony stick on the ground three times. There was a general murmuring as everyone began to file out. Mr Byrd appeared and shook our hands. He seemed entirely unconcerned by the conversation we had had earlier that day.

'Ah, Flockhart, Quartermain, good to see you, sirs,' he said. 'A terrible, mournful occasion, what?'

'Indeed, sir,' I said. 'It surprises me that Sir Thomas was prepared to spend so much.' I gestured to the shining hearse, the plumes of feathers, the prancing black horses.

'Oh, this is very pared down, I can assure you,' he said. 'Miss Caroline had far more planned, but her father refused.' He swallowed as if suddenly feeling he was on the brink of indiscretion. 'Anyway, all seems to be in order. The undertaker in the village has arranged everything.'

'I assume Edward is to be interred in the family vault here at Blackwater?' I said.

'Yes, sir. I hope everything runs smoothly,' he added. 'Sir Thomas tasked me with taking Caroline in hand. The undertakers were most put out by the conflicting messages. First of all, there was to be black velvet on the catafalque. Then there wasn't. Then an open casket of oak. Then a closed one made of ash. Sir Thomas almost stopped the lead-lined casket due to the expense, until he was reminded that his son was not to be buried underground but was to lie on a shelf with his forebears in the vault. One cannot omit a lead-lined casket for an above-ground interment. And so the expense was increased once more, and corners had to be cut. The number of mutes went from sixteen to six. The hearse was initially glass but has since been changed to the Mortmain private wooden hearse, and so on.' He pulled out a black silk handkerchief and swabbed his face with it. 'It has been both emotional and—'

'Byrd!' a querulous voice cut through the air. 'Byrd, what did I say!' At the doorway, Sir Thomas appeared in his bath chair. He was clad in a thick crust of black wool and silk, his hat tall as a chimney pot. His beady eyes peered out from beneath the brim, his face as white as chalk. He grinned when he saw us. 'Flockhart!' he cried. 'And that other fellow. What's his name?'

'Quartermain, sir,' said Will.

'Yes, you. You two. Come along, come along—' He flapped his arms and fidgeted in his seat. 'Lift me, you fools! Ruskin? Ruskin? Damn the fellow – where is he?' Ruskin appeared from among a group of servants standing against the side of the house. 'Take my chair around to the chapel. I'll need it later. You—' He waved his stick at Will and me. 'Carry me down the steps. Byrd, get the door. That's it. Carefully now! Where's Henry? *Henry?*' He spied his son standing to one side. '*There* you are!' he said. He sounded like a petulant child. 'Get in, boy. Come along! Get *in!*'

Given the number of burly servants and gardeners that I could see standing respectfully nearby, Sir Thomas's choice to be manhandled into his carriage by two comparative strangers seemed an odd one. He held up his arms and stuck his legs out, like some sort of bizarre, man-sized doll. Will strode around to the old man's left side, and between us we lifted the fellow up, carried him down the steps and bundled him into the waiting carriage after his son.

Sir Thomas leaned towards me. 'Do you know who it is, yet?' he whispered. His lips were against my ear, his breath as rank as the grave.

'Perhaps I do,' I replied. 'But I would like to be certain.'

He grinned at me, his teeth yellow against his white papery cheek, his eyes two black holes beneath the brim of his tall hat. The silk weeper that was wrapped about it hung down behind him like the shadow of his own death. His gaze slipped from my face to look over my shoulder.

'Here she comes,' he whispered. 'She's a devil. I met my match with that one! Watch out for her!'

He pulled the door to his carriage closed as Lady Mortmain approached. 'No women at my son's funeral!' He pounded on the floor with his stick. 'And certainly not you! Drive!' he screamed, as if his wife might yet wrench the door to his carriage open and force her way inside. *Drive!*

'Father, wait!' Caroline Mortmain appeared behind us as Sir Thomas drew the blind down over the window. 'Why did he not wait for me? He has Henry in there with him, why could he not take us too?'

'I fear he does not want ladies present, ma'am,' said Mr Byrd gently. 'Women do not attend funerals. You know that. It's . . . unseemly.'

'Oh! You are quite the most impossible—' She turned on her heel and stalked back towards the house.

The hearse lurched forward, the four plumed horses snorting and tossing their heads. Sir Thomas's carriage jolted after it. And behind that, the mourners fell into step. Two 'mutes' – men paid specifically to march behind the cortege looking lugubrious – stood at the back, clothed from head to foot in black bombazine. Each carried a tall ebony pole topped with a festoon of black ostrich feathers. Servants, strangers – more mutes, perhaps as they seem to serve no other purpose – followed on behind. The fog had grown thicker, and even before the hearse had passed beyond the gates it was lost from view. Will and I fell in behind Sir Thomas's carriage with the others. Before us, the tallest and thinnest mute, with a long weeper hanging from his tall hat, kept the time of our footfall with his long black cane. Behind us, Lady Mortmain appeared, riding upon her enormous black stallion. Mr Byrd walked at her side. The two sisters were nowhere to be seen.

We traipsed slowly around the village, the fog obliterating everything, as if we were passing into the afterlife. On either side of the road the villagers had emerged from their houses. They stood in silence like ghosts, half hidden in the fog, their faces pale and blurred. The muted *clop* . . . *clop* . . . *clop* . . . of the horses' feet, the jingle of their bridles, the creak of the carriages and the hearse, were the only sounds. I shivered and pulled my coat tighter about my shoulders, digging my hands into my pockets. I found myself thinking about all we had seen and done over the past few days. I could make no sense of it. Who would want to murder Edward Mortmain? What enemies did he have? Who might hate him so much that they were prepared to poison him, and then set about his corpse, clawing his throat out? The mixture of poison and violence perplexed me, for it was at once complex and outrageous, flamboyant, and yet also enraged.

Will drew my arm through his and squeezed it. The warmth of him against me was reassuring, but my thoughts drifted to a question that had been on my mind a lot of late: whether I would always have his love, his friendship, to rely on. What if he left me and sought love – real love – elsewhere? I had seen the way he'd looked at Thomasina Golightly. Did he think I had not noticed? There was nothing I might do to stop him if that was where his heart lay, and as his true friend it was my duty to help him find happiness. And yet, if it *was* to be her, would I be able to accept it? Did I not want him to be happy? Of course I did. But to share him with another? To be placed second, for a wife would always be first? I would have to make my peace with it, though I did not know how I would do so. I returned the gentle pressure of his hand. I found I was glad about the fog, for once. Glad that I might hide my face, and my feelings, beneath my scarf and no one would wonder at me.

At last we were heading back up to Blackwater. I heard water chattering from the stream on my right. Up ahead, still, silent, invisible, was the pond Henry Mortmain had created, its edges fringed with calendula, watercress, bulrushes, hemlock. We passed Blackwater Hall, now a dark hulking shadow in the fog, and headed to the eastern edge of the estate, where the family chapel stood amid a thicket of oak and yew. Someone had lit the lamps on either side of the door, and they glowed like wreckers' lanterns in the gloom. In the city, the fog has a sulphurous, heavy tang, at once the taste of Thames mud, effluent and coal smoke. The essence of London. Here, the flavour was less tainted, less foul. But it had a rotten, decayed smell to it, as if it had risen from bogs and dung heaps, oozed from overflowing night soil and stagnant ponds. As Will and I stood beside the hearse, waiting to receive the coffin, I saw the white glistening caps of fungi against the damp bricks of the chapel wall – stinkhorn and ink cap I could recognise, but there were others too, soft flabby blobs of seeping black, and a cluster of misshaped stalks and hoods in brown and yellow. The place reeked of damp and beneath that, from deep underground, came the sweetish smell of decaying flesh. It was no later than three o'clock in the afternoon, but the light was dim as mid-winter. A steady drip . . . drip . . . drip . . . was the only sound, as the fog licked wetly against drooping leaves.

The horses stood silent now, formless shadows in the gritty pall of grey. A groom emerged and took hold of the bridle of Lady Mortmain's horse as she leaped down. She dusted off her velvet skirt and adjusted her veil. The fog beaded it in tiny droplets. Her face beneath was invisible. She strode over to the carriage into which her husband and stepson had climbed and threw open the door.

'*You!*' screamed a voice from inside. 'I *told* you—'

'And I told *you!*' she snapped back. 'Ruskin!' she cried. 'Ruskin! Can someone bring the chair?'

Henry Mortmain emerged from the carriage, his face white as chalk. I wondered what his father had been saying to him in their journey about the village. It was unlikely that they had travelled in silence, for he looked as if he would like to bolt, to run away from the funeral, from his family and all the obligations that were now resting upon his shoulders. He put up a hand and touched the flower in his buttonhole – a blue gentian. Had he chosen it himself? Picked it from the garden himself? He fingered it for a moment, as if to steel himself for the ordeal ahead – before moving to stand aside until he was needed. I saw him reach out a gloved hand and pluck a yew berry from one of the bushes that stood sentinel at the porch of the church. He examined it absently, and then squeezed it between his gloved fingers and dropped it on the ground.

Will was watching him too. 'What is he doing?' he whispered. 'The yew is poisonous, is it not?'

'Yes,' I said. 'But I fear Henry Mortmain is experiencing some sort of inner turmoil. Grief. Fear. Loneliness. I suspect he hardly knows what he is doing. At such times he reaches out to nature, I think, plucking a bright berry, like a child would, only to destroy it. Whether there is any more to it than that I can't say. Not yet anyway.'

All at once Caroline Mortmain appeared. 'Miss Mortmain.' It was Mr Byrd. His voice was low and gentle. 'My dear Miss Mortmain, your father expressly said—'

'No women, yes, I heard him too,' she said.

'It is most unorthodox for a woman to attend a funeral. Only gentlemen—'

'I see no reason why "only gentlemen" is the way of it,' she said. Her voice was, as usual, loud and grating. 'And there is nothing you can do to stop me, Byrd. Besides,' she added, 'I see you did not try to prevent my stepmother.'

'Of . . . of course,' stammered Mr Byrd. 'I . . . I . . . '

'Well then.' Caroline tossed her head and stalked into the chapel. Her younger sister, thin and sallow faced, followed in her wake.

'Byrd!' The voice was furious. '*Byrd!* Damn you, can you not *stop* these harridans?'

'I fear not, sir,' Mr Byrd replied. 'At least, not without causing an uproar. And under the circumstances—'

'Yes, yes, man,' snapped Sir Thomas. 'There is nothing to be done about it *now*, I dare say.' His white, wrinkled face appeared in the door of his carriage. Will and I positioned ourselves on either side of him as the chair was brought forward. He weighed almost nothing, and I could feel his bones beneath the wool of his coat. We stuffed him into the wheeled chair. His tall hat had been knocked awry in the kerfuffle and his white hair sprouted from his head like thistledown. He scowled up at us.

'No one should have to put their child into the ground,' he said. 'And yet it was his fate to die. They all die, the first-born. There is nothing to be done about that.' He banged on the flagstones with his stick. 'Wheel me, Byrd!' he snapped. 'And none of that jiggling about you usually do. I need you to make it smooth, d'you hear me? Smooth!'

Behind us, the coffin containing Edward Mortmain was lifted from the hearse. Will and I were spared the role of coffin bearers, as on this occasion that office was undertaken by Henry Mortmain, a sweating Mr Byrd, who rushed back out of the chapel as soon as he had deposited Sir Thomas inside, and a pair of footmen, neither of whom I recognised. They inched their way into the chapel and up the aisle, at length depositing the box on the catafalque, and covering it with a long cloth of black watered silk.

290

At the front, the vicar stood at his pulpit. I had not met him before, but I had seen his face, I was sure of it. The fellow had the living up here at Blackwater, was a relative of some sort of Sir Thomas's. Where had I seen him? Then I remembered – it was outside the Black Bear on St Saviour's Street. I had also seen him coming out of the Burning Post on Peter's Lane in Prior's Rents. And entering the Bull and Bush near Well Court. I knew he had the living at St Bartolph's in Prior's Rents, as well as that of another place further to the north. As far as I was aware, he rarely attended either, preferring to let his curate do all the work. Even now I could smell alcohol on the air, spirits, if I was not mistaken. The fellow had a bloated, bleary look to his face, his crimson cheeks and red-rimmed eyes betraying his state of mild inebriation.

The vicar ran through the service as quickly as might be possible. The words of the last rites I had often found comforting and beautiful, despite my own lack of religious faith. But on the lips of this man they were lacklustre and banal, the words themselves half formed and slurred. His surplice was grubby and stained with what looked like blotches of food and wine. He passed a hand over his hair, flattening the wispy grey remnants to his flaking skull. I looked about at the congregation. From what I could see there were few present beyond Edward Mortmain's immediate family and some aged servants. It was as if the family were determined to shove him into the family vault as quickly as possible. No one appeared to be a friend, from his club or from his other interests and pursuits, and those assembled looked a motley collection of old men in dusty suits.

They seemed perturbed to see women in attendance and had grouped themselves as far away from Caroline Mortmain, her sister and stepmother as possible. My eye caught movement at the back. A tall, veiled woman was standing in the shadows. Mrs Arnold. She inclined her head to me, and then bowed it in prayer. When I looked again, she was gone.

Before us the vicar droned on. The dripping sound that I had noticed outside seemed to have followed us inside and I could hear it now, a constant plopping that served to remind us of the passing of time, as well as the wetness of the day.

All at once Caroline Mortmain gasped. She put a gloved hand over her mouth to stifle a cry. At the same time, a general murmuring began among the assembled congregation. A ripple of anxiety passed though the mourners, looks were exchanged and fingers were pressed to lips. And then Caroline could no longer help herself. She let out a cry. 'Vicar!' she screamed. 'Stop! Uncle! Stop at once!'

A fidgeting and murmuring broke out from among those assembled closest to the casket.

'What's going on?' snapped Sir Thomas, squirming in his chair and looking around for the solicitor. 'Byrd! This is *your* doing. I told you no *women*! They simply cannot stomach it!'

'But I have no idea what's happening, sir,' said Mr Byrd as the commotion increased. Caroline was shoving her way out of the pew. Her vast skirts made hasty passage impossible, and she moved as if wading through a heavy sea. She had dashed her veil to the floor and her face was red, her expression aghast.

'He's alive!' she screamed suddenly. 'Can't you hear him? Edward! Edward!' She lurched forward and flung herself onto her brother's coffin.

'Good Lord, woman, get *back*!' cried her father.

'Listen,' hissed Lady Mortmain. She too had put her veil aside, and her face was white and pale with fear. '*Listen!*'

The chapel fell silent. The candles danced and guttered, the shadows leaping against the walls like imps. And then we heard it. A scratching sound, as if from the frantic fingernails of an imprisoned man. And then a thump. There was no doubt that it had come from inside the coffin. The mourners began to chatter. One of them screamed, another fell back onto the pew in what looked like a dead faint. The vicar's face was set in a grimace of horror.

'Get him out!' cried Caroline. 'He will suffocate! Get him out!' She tore the silken pall aside and worried at the coffin lid with her black-gloved fingers. Outside the sky had darkened. The candles guttered as Will seized one of them and stepped forward. No one else seemed able to move.

'Take her away, Mortmain,' he said as Henry dithered and fretted, trying, and failing, to get Caroline to let go of her brother's coffin. Will held his candle aloft and looked over at me. 'How is this possible?'

'It isn't possible,' I said. 'It *can't* be.'

Between us we managed to prise open the lid. A heavy, polished oak, it had been sealed shut with only two slender nails, and with a sharp blow from the palm of my hand against the lid it sprang loose.

'Open it,' screamed Sir Thomas. He rose from his

wheeled chair and tottered forward, his hands to his face in terror and disbelief. His eyes stared in his head as if they were about to burst from his skull. He reached out, and seized the coffin lid with his spindly hands.

'Sir,' I said, trying to hold him back. 'It cannot be what you think—' But it was no use. He pushed me aside and, with Mr Byrd, raised the lid.

Within, Edward Mortmain had been reassembled by Dr Graves. The doctor was not without some skill, but it was clear to anyone that the man in the coffin was dead. Despite the bandage that had been wrapped about his jaw to keep it closed, his face had a grey lopsided appearance, the grin still fixed in place on his dead lips. The throat that had been so ripped and torn was bandaged tightly, a neckerchief tied over the wound. Beneath the cap of white cotton that was pulled over his head, his skull, I knew, was quite empty, while under his white nightshirt his chest and abdomen were filled with nothing but straw. The pennies on his eyes looked like dark eye sockets in the candlelight. A more hideous and terrifying sight I had never seen. For a moment there was silence. Will and I looked at one another over the open coffin. On all sides faces, white, shocked, horrified, peered over our shoulders. He was dead, there was no doubt about it. But beside him in the coffin, and very much alive, was an enormous black rat.

Excerpt from the Journal of William Quartermain, Esq., surveyor and assistant architect, Metropolitan Sewer Commission.

Yesterday I had another conversation with Thimble regarding the death of 'the Lord', as he insists on calling Edward Mortmain, and the disappearance of the Golconda diamonds. He and I were of the same mind. He informed me that it was dangerous to go in search of them with only two of us. I said that there was no one else I could trust, no one else who had experience of being underground, no one else to whom I could explain my errand and – should we prove successful – with whom I might hope to leave the sewer alive. Should I tell Fox and Badger? They would surely push me under and take anything we found for themselves. What chance did we have of finding anything in that vile soup anyway? 'I can only trust you, Thimble,' I said. 'And it's a dangerous journey too. I cannot find my way there alone.'

Thimble agreed at once to my proposition. He has asked me many questions about 'the Lord' and seems anxious to help find his murderer. I made him swear to tell no one what we are about. I am afraid he might tell his Tosher friends, as it is surely to them that he owes his allegiance. Perhaps I should leave the diamonds to their fate. But as soon as I had mentioned them, Thimble was determined.

By the time the boy returned with his hoe and his sieve, his old, begrimed bowler hat, and his canvas neck protector, I had all but talked myself out of so foolish an undertaking. But seeing him filling his lantern with oil and sharpening the end of his hoe with a whetstone he appeared to have brought for the purpose, I fought against my fear and revulsion, and donned my dreadful sewer costume once more. I had decided that we should go at night – underground there is always a Stygian darkness, so it hardly mattered when we went, though at least this way Fox and Badger had gone home. I did not want either of them asking what we were up to.

We entered the Fleet sewer. Our lanterns shone on the black water, illuminating a web-like layer of scum across the surface. The tide had turned and although we had enough time to complete our search the Thames was nonetheless creeping closer, and there was some urgency to the task. I had none of the skill and surefootedness of the boy and I followed in his wake, sploshing through the filth like a clumsy giant.

Rats are nocturnal creatures. Although underground there is no light for them to see by, they nonetheless seemed to be aware of the rising moon, for they appeared before us more numerous and thronging than ever. Thimble, as usual, was unperturbed. He turned to address me, his grubby face waxy in the yellow light of my lantern. His eyes were shaded by the brim of his hat, his voice a hollow echo. 'Don't fear 'em,' he said. 'You're Mr Cat! Them rats is afraid o' you! Besides,' he whispered, 'they'll smell it if you're afraid. And then you'll be for it!' With this dire warning he continued to wade forward, his lamp throwing a dim yellow light into the endless dark tunnel up ahead. Overhead, the bricks dripped and oozed, as if the fog outside was somehow penetrating down through the earth.

What happened in those dark stinking tunnels will haunt me for ever. I can hardly bring myself to write it down, for to do so is to relive it, to have in my mind's eye the horror as it unfolded around me. My years in London have been not without dangers, but with Jem as my guide and mentor, I believe I have come to understand this teeming city. He has taught me all I know about its cruelties, its deceptions, its wickedness. That night, the night I found myself underground, alone beneath the metropolis, was the night I realised how badly I had underestimated what I knew about human nature. About the city. About myself. I have yet to give Jem a detailed account of what occurred. Perhaps I never will. It is only to these pages that I can confide all. They alone can bear witness to my story, and the terrors that occurred underground in the Fleet ditch that night.

Chapter Twenty-Two

❧

We tramped back towards town in silence. The remainder of Edward Mortmain's funeral had proceeded no better. The rat, as might be expected, had sprung from its lair beside the corpse as soon as the lid had been raised. It had scuttled grotesquely across the body and leaped from the coffin onto the silk-covered catafalque. From there it had scrabbled its way down the drapery onto the floor where it had vanished beneath the pews.

Mayhem broke out, Will and I slamming the coffin closed as the mourners set about after the creature, shouting and clattering boots and sticks fit to wake the Devil. Mr Byrd appeared to have fainted. Henry and Lady Mortmain stood side by side, their hands to their breasts in shock. Sir Thomas had sunk back into his wheeled chair, his hands over his ears at the cacophony, his tall black hat with its long shadowy weeper rolling in the dust. Miss Mortmain had fled, burying her face in her black lace handkerchief as she rushed back down the aisle and out into the fog. Only Charlotte Mortmain appeared unmoved, watching with an amused detachment as her fellow mourners rushed hither and thither. I was reminded of her skill with the ether bottle. Had we not seen her with an insensible rat when we had first met her? What other explanation might there be for the creature suddenly beginning to scrabble about inside the coffin when it had previously been silent? But there had been no time to think about such things, and the uproar had continued until, eventually, the rat had been cornered. Will, surprising everyone by stupefying the creature with the toe of his boot, seized it by the tail and flung it out of the chapel door into the fog.

'Did it bite your leg?' I said now, as he reached down and rubbed his ankle.

'They never bite me,' he said. 'Not anymore. I'm too fast for them.'

'Did you kill it?'

'No. But it will have a sore head.'

We were in luck that evening, for we were able to hail a hansom before we even reached Camden Town. In fact, the fellow almost ran us down he was going at such a clip, and I was glad to be heading back to the city at so brisk a pace. The night air blew into my face, and I was glad of it, for I was feeling somewhat queasy after the tomfoolery with the rat and the sight of the corpse.

'What was that address you gave him?' said Will. 'Aren't we going home?'

'No,' I said. 'Not just yet.'

The Mortmain town house was to the west, some distance away from the rookeries of Prior's Rents. It was at the end of a stately Georgian terrace, its ground floor as pale and bright as sugar, its upper storeys brick. Up and down the street the lamps had been lit early, glowing warmly from tall windows, visible through the fog. Only the Mortmain residence was in darkness, its windows shuttered, as if the place were boarded up from the inside. I put my hand in my pocket and felt the cold iron of the keys Mr Byrd had given me.

'What on earth are we doing here, Jem?' said Will, turning up the collar of his coat. 'Can we not just go home? I can't see why—'

'Well, we are here now,' I said. 'We might as well go inside.' And yet, in my heart I agreed with him. Why had I insisted on coming here? At the back of my mind, something nibbled away at my thoughts. Why *had* we come?

As I looked up at those dark, shuttered windows, felt the fog press its cold lips to my cheek, I felt a sense of dread descend upon me. Edward Mortmain's funeral had provoked in me a profound sense of unease. I had been to many funerals, but this was the first time the coffin had been thrown open and the corpse manhandled; the first time a rat had been almost kicked to death by the mourners while the deceased lay exposed, his jaw bound shut, the pennies on his eyes turning his gaze black and fathomless in the candlelight. I shivered. 'Come along,' I said. 'We gain nothing from standing here.'

The key turned smoothly in the lock, the door opening silently on greased hinges. Neither of us spoke as we stepped inside. The place was cold and silent. It had a still, expectant air, the way old, unloved houses often do, as if the place longed for the lights and warmth that had once given it life and purpose, made it a home, a comfort, a refuge from the world. But the wickedness of the world could not always be kept at bay, and all love and comfort had fled when cholera had crossed the threshold, twenty years ago.

Will had a lantern in his satchel. He often carried one with him, as if his time in the sewers had made him afraid of the dark, afraid of being caught without a light of his own. He lit it deftly, scraping a lucifer on the stonework outside, and touching it to the wick. The harsh smell of sulphur from the match, oil and hot metal from the lamp was somehow comforting. He held it up. Its yellow beam showed us a floor of salmon-coloured marble, a console table sheathed in a dust sheet, its lavishly carved and gilded legs just visible. I lifted the sheet. Beneath was an ormolu clock, the hands frozen at six minutes past eight.

We stood for a moment and listened. Could I hear a sound, slow, rhythmic, coming from deep in the heart of the building? I could not be certain.

'Can you hear that?' I whispered.

Will cocked his head. 'No,' he said. 'What was it?' I did not answer. 'Why are we here?' he said again.

'I don't know,' I said. 'I'm not sure. I think . . . I think we were meant to come.'

'I can't imagine why. Only ghosts live here now.'

'How can you be sure?'

'Only one way to find out.'

We went from room to room. Downstairs, a drawing room with adjoining doors led through to another of equal size. The doors could be opened wide to create a space

301

of ballroom proportions. The rugs had been rolled back and wrapped in oilcloth, and the bare polished boards swept clear. The air smelled stale and dusty, with a hint of camphor and lavender. Despite this, I sensed that beneath the pale sheets the sofas and armchairs, day beds and chaise longues, were slowly mouldering, assaulted by moths and decay as they waited for a family that never came.

In the hallway a staircase stretched up into the darkness. The banister was smooth and warm against my hand. There was no trace of dust on my fingertips – either the caretaker Rintoul was assiduous with the duster, or hands other than ours had recently passed that way. I felt the skin prickle on the back of my neck. And yet I was sure, sure as I could be, that the place was empty.

We walked in silence. I was used to the teeming streets of St Saviour's, my apothecary was rarely silent, even in the dead of night, but here – Will seemed to feel it too, for all at once he started talking.

'Probably built about 1760, 1780,' he said. 'Georgian, but earlier in the period. I could tell straight away. The symmetry of the façade, its simplicity, the exposed brickwork on the upper storeys, of course. It's quite distinctive of these earlier Georgian town houses. The stucco goes to the top in the ones built later, but I prefer it this way. I like to see the stone, the textures of the brick. There's no need for all that plasterwork. And you noticed the ceilings are high but not excessively so? An understated modesty. We should find more of the same up here, and after that, at the top, smaller spaces. Less light. I fear my tastes are somewhat old fashioned, as I prefer an elegant old town house like this to any of those monstrous new villas up in Islington.'

'Shh!' I said. 'Can you hear it?'

'What?'

'Listen!' It was faint, but unmistakeable. The ticking of a clock. Will raised his lantern. Up ahead, at the end of the hall, a light glimmered and pulsed in the darkness.

We drew closer, the two of us, our gazes fixed dead ahead. Around us the shadows seemed to deepen. I felt a growing sense of dread wash over me. Beside me, Will slid the dark lantern closed. I glanced at him. Even in the gloom I could see his eyes were staring, his face white as bone. He looked at me and nodded. I put out a hand and slowly pushed open the door.

The second Lady Mortmain had died of cholera in 1832. After that the family had retreated to Blackwater Hall far to the north in the sweeter air of Hampstead. The house in the city was shuttered, the dust sheets smothering time and memory in every room but one. In one room, time and memory were kept alive. Will and I stood on the threshold of that room now. The light we had seen came from a single candle that had been left on the mantelpiece. In the hearth the remains of a fire, a mound of smouldering coals and glowing embers behind a warm fireguard. There were no dust sheets here, no neglect and abandonment. Instead, there were flowers in a vase on a table that stood before the shuttered and curtained window, a mixture of red river lilies and white chrysanthemums. The bed was made up, the sheets crisp and laundered, a counterpane of damson brocade smoothed and folded back, as if in readiness to receive its occupant. Upon the bed, indented in the feather mattress and pillow, the shape of a human form – no more than five feet in height, the head small, the body narrow. The sight of that woman-shaped hollow made my skin grow cold.

The rest of the room was as any bed chamber might look, adorned with pictures, a dressing table, a pitcher and ewer, the former holding fresh water. A door in the far corner of the room stood open, revealing a shadowy dressing room, the open wardrobes within revealing rails of dresses in bright fabrics and wide skirts in styles popular some twenty years earlier. I took up a book that lay beside the bed – a small, leather-bound copy of *Jane Eyre*. The frontispiece was signed in black ink, now faded to brown, *Elizabeth Mortmain*.

'Elizabeth Mortmain,' said Will. 'The second Lady Mortmain. Obviously this was her room. But it is kept this way by whom? Her husband?'

'Unlikely,' I said. 'He never leaves Blackwater. Besides, he has got himself another wife since this one died. I imagine this shrine – for want of a better word – is kept by someone to whom she was more dear, more beloved, than anyone else in all the world.'

'Henry Mortmain.'

'Quite so.'

'But we saw him at his brother's funeral not two hours ago.'

'Indeed.' I pointed to the candle. There were four inches of it left to burn. 'That was once a twelve-inch candle. You see its thickness, and the spilled wax that has accumulated? A candle of that thickness and quality would be consumed at the rate of an inch an hour. He may well have been here this afternoon, or even this morning. I imagine he is in the habit of leaving it illuminated when he quits the place so that she is not alone in the dark. It is the darkness that everyone fears, Will, you know that much yourself. He could have visited this place quite easily and still been able to present himself at his brother's funeral in good time.' I traced the pools of spilled wax on the mantelpiece with the tip of my finger, examined the wall behind. 'He is in the habit of coming here and doing this,' I said. 'I cannot say how often and for how long, but this is not the first time, by any means. There's too much wax here for one candle, and the wall shows the smuts of an untrimmed wick.'

A miniature in a gilt frame on the dressing table showed a woman of some thirty years old, dressed in a green wide-necked evening dress. Henry Mortmain had inherited his mother's dark hair and soulful eyes, her rosebud mouth. Beside the miniature, a silver mirror, polished and untarnished, and a silver-backed brush. The bristles were still entwined with curling dark hairs. I slipped it into my pocket.

Behind me, Will had opened his dark lantern. He raised it above his head and peered into the dressing room. Here too everything was neat and orderly. Boxes on high shelves for hats, boxes on low shelves for ribbons, lace and silks, drawers for stockings, petticoats, garters, knickers. A pair of tall mahogany doors stood ajar, within dresses hung side by side, like a row of silent women standing in line. The coloured silks of their wide, flounced skirts glowed in the lantern light – midnight blue fringed with black lace, grey with a pink trim, a dark arsenic green with ruffles and bows. But there was something else, too. Something that glowed white, but was also stained a dark diabolical black-red.

Will let out a cry. 'My God, Jem!' He leaned forward, the light directed into a corner of that open wardrobe. 'Can you see it?' The face he turned to me was pale and clammy-looking, dark circles beneath his eyes giving him a sickly, exhausted appearance.

I frowned. 'Are you unwell?'

'A little,' he muttered. 'Just a headache. A fever, perhaps. But never mind that, Jem, look here!' He stepped back. Before us, by the door of the wardrobe, bundled up and rolled into a ball, was a shirt, a neckerchief, gloves and a waistcoat, each of them stiff and dark with dried blood. Beside them, a silver fish fork glittered, its tines crusted with black.

All at once I heard a shuffling step, a cough and a sigh. In that dark, still house we were no longer alone. Will and I looked at one another. Will seized the bundle of clothes, stuffed them hastily into his bag and pulled the wardrobe door closed.

'Who's there?' cried a voice. 'Come out! Come out slow, mind, I've got a dog. And a gun!' There followed a low, menacing growl.

Will frowned. 'Doesn't sound much like a dog.'

I strode forward, across the bedroom and out into the corridor, Will hard on my heels.

'Good evening, sir, to you and your faithful hound,' I cried. I held up my hand to shield my face from the bright light of our interlocutor's lantern. 'Have no fear, we're not intruders.'

'Why, that's *exactly* what you are!' came the frosty reply. 'What are you doing in there? That room should be locked. Come out now and stand where I can see you. You're trespassing at the very least! The magistrate'll hear of this.'

'There's no need for that, sir,' I said. 'No need at all, I can assure you.'

In the hall outside, a man was standing. I could not see him properly as he was holding a lantern of his own. It was far brighter than ours and it dazzled my eyes, so that all I could see were the fellow's boots and the bell-mouthed muzzle of the ancient blunderbuss he carried. It was aimed squarely in my face. I held up the key.

'Mr Byrd gave me it,' I said. 'He did not tell you we were coming?'

'What manner of men come to an empty house at night?' the fellow demanded.

'But you knew we were coming.'

'I did not.'

'You must be Rintoul,' said Will.

'What's it to you who I am?' he replied. 'I'm the one holding the gun. I'm the one who asks the questions. And I am asking *you* who *you* are.'

'That's hardly a gun,' muttered Will.

'It's more than enough to dispatch *you*, sir. And I'll thank you to treat her with respect. She's seen more boarding action than you've had hot dinners and she can split your head in two if she's a mind to do it.'

'She?' said Will.

'Give me one reason why I should not shoot you dead on the spot!' cried the man.

I jabbed Will in the ribs. 'Shut up,' I hissed.

'Where's the dog?' said Will. 'He said there was a dog.'

'Mr Rintoul,' I said. 'There are many reasons why you

307

would be unwise to shoot us dead. The first is that you would find yourself on the gallows if you did.'

'Shooting intruders? Housebreakers? I hardly think so.'

'For goodness' sake, man, we are neither of those things,' I said. 'Put down your weapon. Do we look like burglars?'

His lantern was still shining in our faces. It hung from his left hand, the one he was using to steady the muzzle of his blunderbuss, and the strain of holding both was beginning to show, as both gun and lantern were starting to shake. In the trembling light Will was looking worse than ever. I was sure there must be something wrong with him. The fellow Rintoul was staring at me, however. I could sense him scrutinising my face, and I knew it would look more fearful than ever in the lamplight, the hideous birthmark smothering my eyes and nose as if I was indeed wearing a crimson burglar's mask. It would be hard for him to reach a favourable conclusion.

'If you ain't burglars,' he said, 'then you won't mind me searching your bags and pockets, will you?' I felt my scalp prickle with alarm. In my pocket was the small silver-backed hairbrush I had taken from the dressing table. Even worse, stuffed into Will's bag were the clothes we had found, the shirt and neckerchief, the waistcoat and gloves, the large silver fish fork that had been used to claw out Edward's throat, all with the gore upon them scarcely dried.

Beside me, Will noisily shuttered his lantern. 'Look here, Rintoul,' he said. 'We've stolen nothing. We are here at the behest of Sir Thomas himself. Mr Byrd the solicitor gave us a key – how else might we have got in? Did you see a broken window, or a lock that was forced? Of course you didn't! Well, I can tell you with some confidence that neither Mr Byrd nor Sir Thomas would be pleased to hear that you have shot their agents or violated their agents' persons by rooting in their pockets! Good God, man, show some sense!'

Rintoul lowered the blunderbuss. 'It's empty,' he said. 'And I don't have no dog neither.' He shrugged. 'What might you be wanting here at this hour if you ain't looking for trouble?' He peered into the chamber we had just vacated. Behind us, the candle still danced and flickered on the mantelpiece. 'That room's usually locked,' he said again. 'You got the key to that too?'

'No,' I said. 'Don't you?'

He shook his head. 'There ain't no key to that one.' I could smell whisky on his breath. No doubt there was a bottle of the stuff he was anxious to get back to. 'It ain't never open.'

'Does anyone from the family ever come here?' I asked.

'Only Mr Henry,' he said. 'He comes.'

'Today?' said Will. 'Did you see him today?'

'No, sir. But that don't mean he didn't come. I ain't got my eyes fixed on the place the whole time.'

'So what brought you here at this hour?'

'Just doin' my rounds, ain't I?'

'How often does Mr Henry Mortmain come here?' I said.

'Don't know. Quite regular.'

'Alone?'

'Never seen him with no one else.'

'Do you know why he comes?'

'No, sir. Stays about an hour, usually. Can't say I give it much thought. He being a son o' the family he can come and go as he pleases.'

'Anyone else come here?'

309

'Anyone apart from you?' He raised his empty blunderbuss, as if he'd forgotten he'd said it wasn't loaded. 'No. No one.'

'What about Sir Thomas?'

'No one.' A silence fell. There was nothing more to be gained. And yet, I could not help but feel perplexed. Why *had* we come? I blew out the candle and pulled the door to Lady Mortmain's room closed.

Outside in the street, the cabby was still waiting for us. I wondered how much experience of housebreakers Rintoul had if he supposed they arrived in a hackney carriage at the front door of the property they hoped to burgle. Still, who was I to remark on it? I had other things on my mind – notably the feeling of nausea that had been growing within me since we first entered Lady Mortmain's bed chamber. My bowels gurgled ominously.

'I think I need a dose of calomel,' I said. I put my hand to my brow. Perhaps it was nothing. Nothing that a few grains of opium wouldn't sort out. Besides, I had no time to be sick. I had work to do.

At the apothecary I got out all the things I needed. Will sank into his chair before the stove and closed his eyes. He was as white as a ghost.

'I feel sick,' he said. 'And tired. My head is pounding like a drum.' I mixed him a glass of hot water and brandy. To this I added a few drachms of tincture of ginger and a drop of laudanum. I too took a glass of the stuff as I prepared my workbench. I did not feel well myself, but it would surely pass. I took a deep breath and forced myself to concentrate.

'There is something not right about this case,' I said. I sipped my brandy, as a wave of nausea rose and fell inside me. 'It has become complex and confusing when it should be neither of those things. There may be more than one murder, or there may not. They might be related; they might be entirely separate occurrences. Either way, I think we are being toyed with, made to dance a merry jig by someone. But I *will* catch them. And the clever little trick I am about to perform will help us to do just that. I hope.'

Before the stove, Gabriel was sitting in his favourite chair. He sucked on his pipe and put down his penny dreadful, *Tales of Old London*. There was little that could tear him away from it. The word 'murder' and the promise of 'tricks' were about the only things guaranteed to get his attention. But it was not an audience I wanted, it was help. Jenny scrambled onto her stool at the workbench beside me.

'Don't get too close,' I said. 'This might be dangerous.'

Before me I set out the items I required – a flask, with a long pipe extending from its cork stopper, a porcelain bowl, a spirit lamp. From my satchel I took the small hairbrush I had removed from the dressing table at Sir Thomas's town house. I held it up to the light and abstracted from its bristles as many of the long dark curling hairs as I could. I wound them all together until I had a small pad of hair, some half an inch long and two-eighths of an inch wide. I picked it up between the tips of a pair of tweezers and dropped it into the flask.

'Zinc, if you please, Jenny.' The girl stood on her stool and reached for a jar from one of the high shelves. 'And some hydrochloric acid. I have some in the cupboard

311

under the bench here.' I slipped a small amount of zinc into the flask with the hair and dripped in two drachms of acid. I swirled the hair, acid and zinc mixture.

'Watch,' I said, holding it up. 'You see how it reacts?' In the flask, the mixture began to effervesce. 'The stopper, Jenny. Quickly!'

She grinned at me. 'Jenny Quickly. That's what they used to call me at Mrs Lovibond's Home for Theatrical Girls.'

'Well, you're Jenny Flockhart now,' I replied as I rammed the stopper home. 'And if you can pass your examinations at Apothecaries' Hall you will be Dr Jenny Flockhart, and you will never have to give any thought to who you used to be or what you used to do. Now, pass me the spirit lamp and hold up that porcelain bowl.' She did as I instructed, watching with interest as I brought the spirit lamp's flame to the end of the pipe.

'We must be fast,' I said. 'The bubbles you see in this flask may be poisonous. Do you know what the gas is?'

She shook her head as I touched the spirit lamp to the tip of the pipe. An orange flame appeared, burning gently. I took the bowl and held it close, allowing the orange flame to dance and shiver across the porcelain. Straight away an iridescent black deposit formed on the cold surface.

'Do you know what the gas is now?'

'Arsine gas,' said Will. 'I have seen you perform this test before, Jem. And that black shimmering deposit is arsenic.'

'Quite so,' I said. 'Arsenic. One of the most poisonous substances known to man. And what you have just seen me perform, Jenny, Gabriel, is the Marsh Test. A simple but ingenious way of ascertaining whether arsenic is present. Arsenic is a persistent poison. It lingers in the hair, nails and tissues long after the source of the poison is removed, and the poisoner has fled. John Marsh's test has been performed on the living and the dead; on the recently deceased and the long buried. There is nowhere to hide for the arsenic poisoner since John Marsh devised this little test. All he may do to escape justice is to dress up his actions somehow – pretend death was an accident, or claim the symptoms to be those of some other malady. In this case, I suspect that malady was cholera.'

'The second Lady Mortmain was poisoned by arsenic?' said Will.

'I believe so,' I replied. 'But as the symptoms of arsenic poisoning mimic those of cholera it is easy to see why no one would have doubted or questioned the cause of her death. Thousands died of cholera across the globe in 1832. Besides, there was no Marsh Test at that time, so no one would have been able to prove anything, even if foul play had been suspected – which it wasn't.'

'So what made you suspect that it might have been?' said Will. 'Besides,' he went on, before I could even answer, 'this clarifies nothing, Jem. All it means is that we now have two murders, not one. And one of them occurred two decades ago. They cannot possibly be linked.'

'Is it not the case that Sir Thomas married his third wife soon after the death of his second? The third Lady Mortmain was a companion to her predecessor, I believe. A cousin, or some such. Ambitious, determined, ruthless. What was it Sir Thomas said to us about her? "I met my match with that one!"'

'And what connection might this shameful act have

to the death of Edward Mortmain some eighteen years later?'

'I'm not sure,' I said. 'Not entirely. But I have some ideas.'

Chapter Twenty-Three

∽≈∽

The first indication that I was suffering from cholera was the sudden, violent feeling of nausea that swept over me. I had been struggling with it since we left Rintoul at the Mortmains' town house and got into the cab to return to the apothecary. At first I assumed it was because I had not eaten since the coffee and cold chops Will and I had breakfasted on. Other than a glass or two of negus nothing had passed my lips since first thing that morning. And had we not spent time in the home of a cholera victim the previous day? Cholera was in Prior's Rents. It was in Wicke Street and St Saviour's Street. It was in Bermondsey and Soho, Cheapside and Seven Dials. The city was full of it; I should not be surprised to find that it was now in our own home.

For a short while, after taking a brandy and a few grains of opium when we returned to the apothecary, I had felt a little better. But no longer. Whatever respite that physic had given me, its effect was now spent. When

I looked at Will, slumped in his chair, his face as white as whey, I knew he felt just the same.

'You look ill, Jem,' he said now. 'You look as bad as I feel.' All at once he lurched to his feet. 'I think . . . I think we should . . . '

But I never learned what he thought for all at once he bent double, his arms clutched about his waist as if he were wracked by a violent and agonising colic. And then he sank to his knees, seized the spittoon favoured by Mrs Speedicut, and vomited a thin stream of pale liquid into it. He gasped and retched, and spewed out more of the stuff, and more again. He raised his head and looked at me. Already his eyes were ringed with black, his skin a pale, duck-egg blue.

'My God, Jem,' he whispered. 'My God!'

And so it began for both of us. I have never spewed and retched as much as I did that night, hours and hours of it, even when there was nothing more to sick up, so that I felt as if I would at any moment vomit up my own stomach and see it lying there in the bottom of the bowl. But there was worse to come, for after the sickness came the loosening of our bowels. At first Gabriel and Jenny did not know what to do. Nothing had prepared them for the contagion entering their own home, and I had told them time and again that there was no cure for it, that nothing might save us apart from luck, and the judgement of God.

Somehow, they got us upstairs and into our beds. Mrs Speedicut had once been matron at St Saviour's Infirmary, back when my father had been the apothecary and I his apprentice. I had known her all my life, and although she had undoubtedly been the laziest and most

316

drunken slattern in the entire hospital, there was not much she did not know about the rough management of cholera. And so she took control, placing a bucket and chamber pot on hand to receive our outpourings, mixing each of us a flask of salted water and brandy, with a few grains of opium. After that, she left us to it, ushering Jenny and Gabriel back down the stairs. My head pounded fit to burst; my legs and arms were wracked by spasms and cramps, life draining from my body with every wretched second I spent squatting on the chamber pot or crouched over the bucket.

They say it is feared as much for the swiftness with which it takes its victims, as for the sordid and degrading way it manifests, for the victims of the cholera die in a pool of their own faeces and vomit. Their eyes sink into black hollows, their faces become fleshless, their lips turn blue-black. In less than an hour their skin appears nothing more than a thin layer of vellum stretched over bone. In the next room I could hear Will retch and moan, though as time passed he grew quiet. We would die, both of us, two blue-faced corpses like so many others from Prior's Rents.

But something was not right. Something troubled me about this. I closed my eyes and banged the heel of my shoe on the floor.

'Jenny!' my voice was a whisper. Mrs Speedicut was right to keep her away, but what if my suspicion was right? What then? I beat again, and harder. The effort exhausted me. I sank back onto my tangled blankets and closed my eyes. When I opened them again, Jenny's face was inches from mine.

'You dead yet, Mr Jem?' she whispered.

'No, Jenny.' I put out a hand and gripped the girl's wrist. 'I want you to run the test again. The test for arsenic.' I felt my bowels groan and curdle. 'Take some matter from the bucket. Take it carefully, do not touch it with your hands. Wear a covering over your face. Wash your hands before and afterwards. Take every precaution. *Every* precaution!'

'Arsenic?' whispered Jenny. 'But—'

I leaned forward and retched into the bucket. The thin, gruel-like matter dripped from my lip. 'Do it!'

The girl did as I asked. I heard her tread on the stairs, the *chink* as her spatula went from the chamber pot to the flask. My eyes were closed, but my senses seemed to be heightened. There was a ringing sound in my ears, high pitched, like the echo from a bell. I waited.

At length I heard her footsteps once more. Her face appeared in front of mine. It seemed as if I were viewing her through a mist, and her voice, when she spoke, seemed far away. I could not hear what she said due to the ringing in my ears, but I saw her shake her head and her lips form the word 'no'.

'Do it again,' I whispered.

She shook her head. 'I already did,' she said. 'Twice. I ran the test twice. It's not arsenic, Mr Jem.'

'How's Will?' I said. Her face told me the answer, even though I could not hear her words as the noise in my ears had become a roaring sound. A blackness clouded my vision, as if darkness had fallen, or the candles had been extinguished, one by one. I felt hands upon me, Jenny, perhaps, or Mrs Speedicut, I could not say. I felt as if my entire body was on fire, every inch of me wracked with pain as my muscles dried and atrophied.

I heard voices now, but whose voices they were I could not tell, anymore than I could work out what they were saying. I imagined that I saw Will's face, and the face of Thomasina, though I knew she could not possibly be there. I saw Sir Thomas standing beside his wheeled chair, his wife was at his right side. She was holding his hand even as her gaze was directed elsewhere. I saw that she was looking at Henry. He seemed not to know her, for he turned away and walked into the oak woods at Blackwater. I saw him crawl into a hollow oak beside an old well. And then I heard screaming, screaming, and the faces of Caroline Mortmain and her sister began to circle me, their mouths wide, laughing and shrieking like banshees. I heard a buzzing sound in my head but I felt calmed by it, for I knew it was only the sound of bees.

My eyes snapped open and I found I was lying on the floor beside my chamber pot. Jenny was crouched beside me, sobbing and beating on my chest as if my heart was giving out. 'Mr Jem,' she screamed and wailed, her face wet and puffy. 'Please don't die!'

'Jenny,' I whispered. My lips could hardly move, and my tongue felt huge and soft in my mouth. 'We have one last thing to try.'

She brought what I asked, though her hands were shaking as she set it out before me. I could not do the task myself, and there was none I trusted more than her to do what was required. The physic I had asked for was *Silybum marianum*. Extract of milk thistle. The seeds are crushed and ground with a pestle and mortar, mixed with water and glycerine and left in the dark for five weeks or longer. We strained and bottled the results and sold the bottles for two shillings as a liver tonic (ten drops, three times a day mixed with a little water). It has no efficacy whatsoever against cholera. But I was not thinking about cholera now. Jenny had tears in her eyes when I told her what was expected.

'I can't do it, Mr Jem,' she said. 'What if you die?

'I might not die,' I said. 'But if you do not do it, if you do not at least try, then I almost certainly will die. And Mr Will too, if he is not dead already.'

In her hand she held the hollow needle and the syringe, just as I had instructed. I had to admit, the idea terrified me too. The hollow needle was so new to both of us and neither of us had used it properly. I could tell by the way she looked at me that the sight of me was horrifying. My birthmark had faded to a sickly grey-blue, my skin wizened, my eyes black-ringed. But I had life in me yet and I squeezed her tightly, my fingers clamped like a manacle about her wrist.

'The blood circulates freely,' I whispered. 'We know this for sure. Would it not make sense to assume that what is put into the blood at any one point will eventually make its way to all areas of the body? In this case, I am hoping to reach the liver directly. If I take the *Silybum* by mouth it will take too long, its impact reduced by the action of the stomach. But administered via the blood, why, it will be transported directly to the organs of the body at the speed of the circulation itself. There is no instance of poisoning by milk thistle. Why should it become one now? We must hope that what I propose is a success. There is no other way.'

I forced myself to guide her hand, to make her take up the hollow needle. 'Go on, Jenny, we have no time. Pretend I am an orange.' I pulled up my shirt sleeve and showed her the inside of my elbow. The skin was pale, bluish, the vein a great dark worm. The blood was thickening as the sickness drained the fluid from my body. Jenny's hand was shaking. I put my hand over hers, and guided her fingers to the plunger, the tip of the hollow needle to the flesh of my arm. Was I right? If I was not, we were dead. If I was correct, then there was a corruption at Blackwater that only the hangman could eradicate.

Excerpt from the Journal of William Quartermain, Esq., surveyor and assistant architect, Metropolitan Sewer Commission.

From the outset, my senses were alert. I felt my skin prickle and my scalp itch beneath my sewer hat as a feeling of profound apprehension crawled over me. The waters seemed deeper and fouler than ever, the walls slimier, the red eyes of the rats closer and more numerous. The tunnel became narrower. We turned to the left, and to the right. The route divided once, then again. Already I was lost, I was certain, and I had only the boy to guide me. As if reading my mind, he turned to me and said, 'Lost, ain't ya?' His voice echoed off the brickwork. His eyes had a cruel knowing gleam I had never noticed before, and for a moment it seemed to me that in the lamplight they appeared as red and beady as any sewer rat's. He sniggered. And then all at once his lantern was out and he was gone.

I shouted his name into the darkness, jangling my bell desperately. In my own ears my voice sounded hysterical, wild and frantic, but also flat and dead, and I knew no one could hear me, so deeply was I entombed beneath the earth. I spun around in search of him. The water was higher now, and I wondered whether somewhere up ahead a sluice had opened. The torrent had a redness to it, and the rats were running, squeaking and dashing as if in fear of something unseen. I floundered, my feet slipping on invisible slime, and the air began to move about me in a rushing, stinking breath. And then all at once a skinny hand shot out from a round tunnel high up in the wall on my right and seized my arm. A face peered down at me.

'You're janglin' that bell like a lost cat,' he said. 'Lost Mr Cat! Ha ha ha! Come on, Mr Cat. Fast, or the flood'll sweep us away.' I did as he instructed, finding footholds in the crumbling bricks, and just in time too, for a great wave of dark poisonous water surged past below us.

'This way, Mr Cat,' he said. 'The water's too high to go that way now.' I had no choice but to follow him.

Before us there were steps in the tunnel down which water rushed in a black spluttering torrent, and we had to hang on to a slimy rope and pull ourselves up by it if we were to reach the top. The passage turned left then right. Its roof grew lower so that I was obliged to walk stooped over, looking down at the horrible waters. Thimble turned back to make sure I was still behind him. He stared over my shoulder, peering into the darkness beyond. He looked puzzled, for a moment, but then he shrugged and his face cleared.

'Just rats,' he said. 'Big 'uns, by the sounds o' it. There's a lot o' them tonight.' On and on we walked, against the flow of the waters, deeper and deeper into the bowels of the city.

Eventually, up ahead I saw Thimble staring up at a gully hole high in the wall of the sewer. We were close to the surface now, and as I peered out with him I could see the back of a tumble-

down house. I saw the moon, a blurred crescent, brownish and smothered in fog. Despite the dimness of its light, I recognised the back of Mrs Roseplucker's house. There were the windows with the ugly red drapes drawn, illuminated from within as the girls went about their business. My lantern shone on the vile black lip, the edge of the hole into which the maid flung the contents of the chamber pots every morning. This was the very spot.

Before me, Thimble crouched down in the stream of filth. Soon he was up to his elbows, sifting and squeezing, rummaging and searching. He used to search with his bare toes too, though now he was booted he was obliged to use only his hands. I knew I should help him but I could not. I could not bring myself to do it. All at once the questions that I had pushed to the back of my mind the moment we had ducked into the mouth of the Fleet returned tenfold, my misgivings returning stronger than ever. Why had we come? What was I thinking, bringing the boy into the sewer so late at night to look for something that was not even ours? What point would it prove if we found what we were looking for? And then suddenly Thimble stilled. He was staring down at his hands, illuminated in the light of his lantern. I could not see what it was that he had grubbed up and he did not show me. But someone else saw.

'What pretty thing have you got there then, young 'un?'

Thimble reeled back in shock as Badger plunged out of the darkness. The man loomed over him, his face beneath his sewer hat set in a triumphant leer. He could overpower the boy in an instant and we all knew it. As for me, why, all he had to do was abandon me down there and I would never find my way out. Badger was a big man, and as strong as an ox. He was sure-footed, an ex-Tosher himself, and for two pins he could hold me under.

Thimble tried to dart back the way we had come, but the boots I had bought for him made him heavy and clumsy. I surged forward, hoping to jab Badger back down the tunnel using my hoe like a cattle prod, but he out-manoeuvred me easily, side-stepping my wild lunge and shoving me hard against the black slimy wall. I felt my feet start to slide from under me and I floundered and staggered. He sprang at Thimble, who wriggled and thrashed in his grasp like an eel. The dark water extinguished Thimble's lantern, and I heard its glass eye smash onto bricks. My own light flickered and danced as the foul waters lapped over me, higher and higher as my feet slithered and slipped. Badger twisted sideways and pressed his left boot onto my chest, trying to push me under. At the same time, he was squeezing Thimble by the throat with both hands. All was darkness and flashing light and foul water. I saw Thimble's face, his eyes wide in terror, trying to claw Badger's meaty fingers away. Badger raised his fist and brought it down sharply.

The boy was still. I saw him on his back in the water, his face like a mask, the filth lapping about his cheeks and chin. My fingers, scrabbling against the crumbling brickwork, curled about a loose lump of the stuff and as I pushed myself up and out of the water I swung it at Badger's head, the way he had taught me when he had first shown me how to beat a rat to death.

'Don't give 'em a chance,' he'd said. 'Strike hard and fast. If you don't take 'em they'll remember, and they'll be back.' It smashed into the side of his head, above the ear, with a sickening wet crunch and he dropped like a stone into the water.

Beside him, Thimble was not moving. I saw the red and purple bruises on his neck. I held him in my arms. There was no sign of life, Jem has taught me that much and I know how to look for it. No breath. No pulse. No hope.

Chapter Twenty-Four

Will and I took a cab from the apothecary straight to Blackwater. We were bundled up in hats and coats, with a blanket to keep us warm, as both of us felt the cold through to our bones. Jenny came too, squeezed in between us. She had a flask of warm salt and sugar water in her satchel, along with the hollow needle, the syringe, and a bottle of milk thistle extract.

Will looked drawn and tired, the dark circles around his eyes still showed where the sickness had consumed him, but his eyes were bright beneath the brim of his stovepipe hat.

'You look serious, Jem,' he said.

'We have so little time,' I replied. My head was pounding. Both of us should have been in bed, but we had no choice. We had to go.

'I can't believe you almost left without me.'

It was true, I had pulled my clothes back on as soon as I was able to stand and sent Jenny next door to administer the same dose to Will. I had thought him too sick to come with me, but he had proved as determined as me to see everything through to the end.

'You're not going to that place without me,' he said now. 'Would you have let me go alone?'

'No,' I said. I meant it too.

'You are my greatest friend, Jem.' He squeezed my hand. 'I owe you my life.'

'It's not the first time,' I said. 'The debt is accumulating.'

'I thought it was pretty even, all things considered.'

I shook my head. 'You are quite definitely in my debt. But I have only one requirement for that debt to be discharged.'

'Name it!'

'Make sure you spend your remaining time wisely. Preferably in the company of someone as fascinating and memorable as Miss Thomasina Golightly. Assuming she will have you, that is.'

He blushed. I laughed. 'I'm glad to see there is still some colour in those waxy cheeks of yours. Now, let us rest a while. We must have our wits about us this morning.'

As we approached Blackwater it was clear that all was not well. The building had never looked welcoming, its tiny windows and darkly weathered oak door giving it a prison-like appearance. But today it seemed darker and more forbidding than ever. There were no lights at the windows, and no signs of life or activity. In the gloom of the billowing fog the thick coat of ivy that shrouded its eastern wall looked more black than green, its long tendrils resembling the fingers of a monstrous devilish hand clutching at the brickwork. The place had a lop-sided appearance, its ancient roof sagging and buckled, pierced by tall, twisted chimney stacks. The windows were shuttered, and although it was almost eleven when we arrived, there was no evidence that anyone was stirring.

We asked the cabby to wait. It was a long way back to the city and we had been lucky to find a man who was prepared to take us so far north at that time in the morning.

'Go round the back to the kitchen,' I said to him. 'They are sure to have a cup of tea and a bite to eat. Tell them Dr Flockhart sent you, from Sir Thomas.'

I battered on the door. Had no one seen or heard us coming? I pounded again, as hard as I could. Just as I was about to follow the cabby round to the kitchen the door was jerked open by a pale and visibly shaking Ruskin.

'Oh, sir,' he said, recognising me at once. He seized me by the hand. 'Thank God it's you!'

'How many of them?' I said. 'How many are sick?'

'Miss Caroline, sir. Young Mr Henry. Lady Mortmain, Mr Byrd too, he was taken ill just as he was about to leave. And Sir Thomas too, of course. Some of the servants, sir – Ivor and William the footmen and Susan and Kitty from the kitchen, and several of the guests at the funeral, I believe. I heard reports about them though none of them is staying here, thank the Lord. It's all we can do to look after the members of our own household, so it's a mercy the guests had all gone. The footman Ivor is dead, so is Mrs Grimshaw. Cook and housekeeper, both!'

'But not you, Ruskin?'

'No, sir. At least, not yet.'

'And do you feel well?'

'Quite well, sir.' He put his hand out to stop me from entering. 'You cannot come in, sir. Not while the contagion is upon us. It's not safe.'

'Oh, but I must, Mr Ruskin. I may be able to save them. It's not a certainty, but it is possible. But the longer you leave it the worse it gets. I am surprised there are not more dead. Take us to Sir Thomas. He is by far the weakest and most likely to die. Who's been attending him?'

'Myself, sir. And one of the footmen, as I'm not strong enough to help him to the privy.'

'I see. Well, we must visit all the sick in turn. Will, can you manage the task ahead?'

Will nodded. 'I have salts with me, should I feel faint.' I had shown Will how to inject the *Silybum* into a vein, made him watch while I jabbed the hollow needle into my own arm and depressed the plunger. *Do you think you can do it? Here, practise on me, just a little. Push it carefully. There!* Once the *Silybum* had entered the bloodstream its effects were speedy. When we drank the mixture of boiled water, sugar and salt mixed with a little extract of ginger, and a grain of opium, recovery was faster still. Neither of us felt well, but we both felt better. The worst was clearly behind us. I hoped we were in time to help the others.

And so Jenny, Will and I went from room to room, Will and Jenny visiting the servants, those who were afflicted with all the symptoms of cholera, and I attending to the Mortmains. I gave Ruskin instructions for mixing a draught of warm water with sugar, salt, ginger and opium. All were barely conscious – all but Caroline and Lady Mortmain, both of whom were less sorely afflicted.

And Charlotte, who out of all of them was the only one unaffected.

Mr Byrd, who had gone down with symptoms before anyone else, was by far the worst. He had been lodged in a guest bedroom next door to the room Edward Mortmain had occupied when at Blackwater and had been somewhat neglected by both maids and footmen due to being neither servant nor family. When I went in to see him the smell hit me like a physical blow to the face. The room was close, the candle almost burned down, and the shadows were dark and jumping. The man's face was white as bone, his eyes sunken into black hollows. The sickness had drained fluid from his body and his lips were drawn back over his teeth in a grimace. I spoke his name, but he made no movement, and no sound. Was he dead? I threw the curtains wide. The chamber pot was brimming and foul, the carpet splashed with vomit and other bodily liquids. His clothes, stained and sodden, had been flung into a corner. I went over to the bed and pulled his right arm from the bedclothes, searching for a pulse. There was one, surprisingly strong for one so weakened. The vein was flat and hard to penetrate with my needle, even when I slapped at it, and wound a leather tourniquet around his arm, but I succeeded at last. I propped him up with his pillows and made him drink a glass of warm salt mixture. But I could not stay with him, there was no time for that, and off I went to see to my next patient.

I did not have much hope for Sir Thomas. He was old and fleshless already; what condition would he be in now? And yet the urge to survive cannot be underestimated, for out of all of them he alone still had an angry gleam in his eye. Lady Mortmain and Henry were weak, but managing. Caroline too. Charlotte, with no symptoms at all, was fascinated by the hollow needle and syringe and insisted on following me about the place.

'Devised by a Dr Wood in Edinburgh, you say? And the physic is taken about the body by the blood? It is ingenious, Dr Flockhart. And yet so simple once the circulation of the blood is understood – it is the perfect vehicle for physic.' I could not disagree, though now was not the time for a conversation about it.

Six deaths occurred at Blackwater, all those before we arrived. What the tally might have been had we not arrived did not bear thinking about. I sent the kitchen boy into the city with a note for Dr Graves to come and collect the corpses. Mrs Harbottle and Mrs Grimshaw, the footmen Ivor and William, the maids Kitty and Susan. I offered to help with the post-mortems. I knew what to look for, and what I would find. It would be more evidence, if more evidence were needed, that would send at least one person to the gallows, and it would not be Mr Jobber.

I found Will sitting in a gold brocade armchair in Caroline Mortmain's favourite drawing room. The French windows were closed but the fog had lifted, and I could see the garden once more: the bamboo had been cut back and there was an uninterrupted view across the flower beds. The lawn beyond stretched out to the trees, ancient oaks gathered in a dark thicket, their branches wide and heavy, still in leaf, but brown and yellow now, the earth at their feet moist and rotten. Will's eyes were closed. His face was still pale, with dark shadows about his cheeks and eye sockets, though with every hour that passed he looked more like his old self. I saw he had a glass of the salt water mixture steaming gently in a glass beside him on a golden side table.

'Greetings, Jem,' he said without opening his eyes. 'How are the patients?'

'Doing well,' I said. I pinched the skin on the back of my hand. It sprang back, though not with its usual degree of elasticity. 'The skin is regaining its plumpness. We will hopefully see the same results on everyone here. A few hours and they will all be in the clear.'

When I had told Sir Thomas that I had news of his son's killer his eyes had opened, the lids flickering like the wings of a moth. I heard his breath come in a rough, rasping gasp, so that for a moment I thought I was listening to his death rattle. But I was wrong. The old man was merely laughing.

'Well, well, Flockhart,' he hissed. 'That's something, at least.'

***Excerpt from the Journal of William Quartermain, Esq., surveyor
and assistant architect, Metropolitan Sewer Commission.***

*I laid Thimble on a lip of masonry at the side of the sewer, above
the flow, and I turned to Badger. I had no idea if he was dead
or not, and I didn't care. I propped the fellow up, sitting in the
putrid water, and I left him. Perhaps I would send Fox in to
find him the next day. Perhaps I wouldn't.*

    *I took Thimble in my arms again. I would not leave him to
the rats and the rising tide. And yet how would I find my way
back to the mouth of the Fleet without his help? How would I
be able to carry him all that way, down those slippery passages
and tunnels? Already I sensed a movement in the shadows, a
seething mischief of rats, their eyes red and hungry in the lamplight. I cradled Thimble, wiping the filth from his face as best I
could with my handkerchief. His hat was gone, and his hair was
wet and matted. I could not leave him there. I would not. He
died because of me, for no reason other than to satisfy my own*

vanity. What had I wanted? To prove to Jem that I was capable of succeeding on my own? That I could contribute something meaningful to our enquiries into Edward Mortmain's murder? If I had told Jem my plan he would have stopped me. He would have found another way. He would not have done what I did, a foolish errand with the worst of consequences.

Water drip . . . drip . . . dripped onto my head and a rat scuttled across my shoulder – they were bolder now that we had fallen still and silent, and I could hear one scratching and chattering above my head. And then suddenly I heard a shriek, and a voice cried out, 'Take that, you filthy creature!'

I heard the clang of a shovel striking something, and a limp rat was flung over my head and into the water.

I recognised the voice immediately. 'Annie!' I shouted as I scrambled to my feet. 'Annie!'

The girl screamed as my filth-streaked face appeared in the gully hole. In her hand was an empty chamber pot.

Chapter Twenty-Five

❧

It was late in the afternoon before those who had not succumbed were well enough to listen to what I had to say. The parlour maid had, on my instructions, set a fire in the golden drawing room, and I had banked it up so that its coals roared. One by one they came. Charlotte Mortmain, being in entirely good health, was the first to appear. She seemed surprised to be invited for tea, as if it was rarely offered to her. Everyone was still dressed in black, the mirror was still swathed with black crêpe, something for which I was heartily glad, for the sight of my own face was still alarming to me. Mr Byrd wheeled Sir Thomas, who had refused to put his clothes on and was dressed in his nightshirt and dressing gown, with a night cap on his bald head and a pair of bed socks pulled up to his skinny knees.

'Why can't they all come to my room?' he muttered, his voice querulous. 'I am old and sick. I don't want to be wheeled!'

'Dr Flockhart says the change of scenery will do you good,' came Mr Byrd's measured reply. 'And it will give Ruskin time to arrange for your room to be cleaned. Besides, this room is so bright and cheerful. Is it not a tonic to see the garden, now the fog has lifted?

The old man scowled. 'I buried my son yesterday, Byrd. There is no cheer to be had in this house.'

'Of course, sir,' said Mr Byrd.

'Can't think what you're doing here anyway. Why can't you be sick in your own house?'

'I can assure you, sir, I would have preferred such an arrangement myself.' Mr Byrd sounded irritable. I could hardly blame him. He had spent his life working for the cantankerous Sir Thomas. The only surprise was that he did not sound cross more often. He glanced at me and rolled his eyes. His recovery had been swift, but he had a strained, hunted expression I had not seen before.

'Come over to the fire, Mr Byrd,' I said. 'The warmth will do you both good.'

At length, all were seated, Lady Mortmain alone in a golden armchair, Sir Thomas and Mr Byrd as close to the fire as possible. Henry and Charlotte sat side-by-side on a sofa opposite Caroline, who had spread out her skirts and put her feet up, sprawling back on golden cushions, a cold compress to her brow. She sipped at her draught of warm salt and sugar water and grimaced.

'Get on with it, Flockhart,' said Sir Thomas. He extended stick-like legs towards the fire. 'My feet are cold. Rub them for me, Byrd.'

'Perhaps if I were to move you a little closer, sir,' said Mr Byrd with dignity. The soles of Sir Thomas's socks began to smoulder.

'Not that close,' the old man shouted. 'Back, you idiot. *Back!*'

'Is there something you wanted to say to us, Dr Flockhart?' said Lady Mortmain. She was dressed in a loose dressing gown of black watered silk, her hair caught up in pins. She looked younger than her forty-five years, the sickness had touched her only lightly and her eyes looked huge and dark in her pale angular face. I thought I detected evidence of powder and cosmetics, to enhance her pallor and draw attention to her eyes, but she had done it so skilfully that I could not be sure. I saw Henry Mortmain look at her, and then look away again. His expression was unreadable.

I held up my hands for silence. 'I wanted to speak to you about the murder of Edward Mortmain,' I began. 'As you all know, a man has been arrested and is set to hang for it on Monday. We have spoken to the man in question, and this combined with what we already know of his character—'

'The fellow works in a St Saviour's brothel,' cried Lady Mortmain. 'What can you, or anyone, possibly say in defence of his character?'

'Shut up, woman,' snapped Sir Thomas. 'Let the fellow say what he has to say.' He jabbed his finger at me. 'Proceed.'

'We believe the fellow to be innocent. Of course, still more relevant to this conclusion was the fact that Mr Edward Mortmain had his throat ripped and torn, the flesh clearly bearing what appeared to be the claw marks of an animal of some kind.'

'The rat!' whispered Sir Thomas. 'The rat of the Mortmains!'

'That is precisely what the perpetrator would have you believe, sir,' I said. 'But like any reasonable individual I find I cannot countenance the notion of a murderous supernatural rat, regardless of what your family legend might suggest. What this desecration of the body did tell me is that whoever did this is familiar with the legend and understands the terror and loathing with which it is regarded by this family. But before we get to that, there are some truths that I must share with you, some of which you might find . . . unpalatable. The first of these is the fact that Edward was being blackmailed.'

Caroline put her hand to her breast. 'I beg your pardon? Blackmailed?'

'Yes. I'm sure you know why. *All* of you know why, though you are reluctant to speak of it. It was because he did not visit brothels for the pleasures of women's company, but for the pleasures offered by men. What most of you did *not* know is that I am referring to one man in particular, a young fellow called Charlie who told us that Edward was being blackmailed by someone called "Cock Robin". This was the name used by Mr Byrd who, under instruction from Sir Thomas, sought to terrorise his victim into submission.'

There was a murmuring about the room. 'Good heavens, Byrd!' cried Henry.

'Oh, don't all blame *me*,' cried Mr Byrd peevishly. 'Tell them, Flockhart! Tell then I was only doing Sir Thomas's bidding!'

'Indeed,' I said. 'Mr Byrd was merely carrying out Sir Thomas's instructions.'

'It was his idea,' spluttered Mr Byrd. 'I will not stand here and be accused. Just as it was his idea to use the Golconda stars as bait.'

'And yet he took the bait, did he not, Byrd? Flockhart? He was prepared to steal his own sister's diamonds just so that he might keep his proclivities a secret, so that he might continue to engage in his unnatural passions.' Sir Thomas turned to me. 'Sodomy is a capital crime, a hanging offence. The shame of it, if it were known about beyond his family—'

'Quite so,' I replied.

'He stole my diamonds?' cried Caroline. 'But I had no idea! To thieve? From his own sister? Why was I not informed?'

'I saw no reason for you to know anything,' snapped her father. 'You are such a busybody. Always listening at doors and prying into my business. You think you know all about this family, but you know nothing. You are the last to know anything. D'you want to know what Edward called you? The Virago!'

Caroline gasped and put her hand to her face as if she had been physically slapped.

'On the contrary, sir,' I said. 'I believe your wife was "the Virago".'

'Those were my mother's jewels,' said Caroline tearfully.

'Well, they were too good for the likes of you,' muttered Sir Thomas. 'And your dear brother, my son, obviously thought the same for he did not think twice about stealing them when he thought it might get him out of a scrape.'

'And yet it does not end there,' I said.

'You mean that apart from sodomy, thieving and blackmail there is something else we should be made aware of?' said Lady Mortmain.

'Oh yes,' I said. 'There is murder. We have not even arrived at that bit yet. But let us recap. Mr Byrd blackmailed Mr Edward Mortmain on behalf of his employer, Sir Thomas. Blackmailed him partly to pressurise him into giving up his habits, partly as a test, and a game. Sir Thomas, you are, I believe, somewhat bored by your life as an invalid. Seeing how far your son would go, how high he would jump, was an entertainment to you. And when you learned that Edward planned to marry, a marriage of convenience to a woman who understood him better than any of his family, you were incensed. She knew him for what he was and she accepted him, just as he accepted her. The world of men had not been kind to her, but Edward was. But she was not good enough, was she, Sir Thomas? You could not have your son and heir marry a penniless artist, a widow whose husband had been a well-known philanderer who had died insane in Angel Meadow Asylum. You would not want your name tied in any way to that sort of a woman. And yet he was determined.

'But someone in this room had other ideas. You wrote to the woman – to Mrs Arnold – didn't you, Miss Caroline? How did you know of her?'

'I overheard Mr Byrd talking about her to my father. I waited outside her house so that I could see her. And then I wrote to her. To warn her off.'

'"*You will marry him over my dead body,*" were your exact words, were they not? "*Or over his.*"'

'It's just a figure of speech.' Caroline shrugged and sipped at her water.

'By the way,' I said. 'That water you're drinking, I brought it up from Well Court. It's supplied by the Blackfriars Water Company. Your father's water company. I believe it has a distinctive flavour I thought you might appreciate.'

Caroline spat the water back into the glass. 'Not to your taste, madam?' I turned away.

'Let us turn to perhaps the most important question,' I said. 'Who stood to gain the most from Edward's death? The answer of course, is his brother Henry.'

'Me!' Henry fell back in his chair as if he had been punched in the face.

'Yes,' I said. 'It is obviously you. With Edward dead you stand to inherit.'

'But—'

'Edward was poisoned, and then had his throat torn out. You know where the water hemlock grows, don't you? It is you who worked with the gardener to improve the water supply to the house, who planted the pond with purifying plants, water hyacinth, water cress, flag iris. And hemlock.'

'Yes, but—'

'The indications are quite clear. The mousy smell that came from his lips and oesophagus, the expression on his face, that fearful grin he had,' I shuddered at the memory, the way the muscles had frozen, pulling his lips into a terrible leer. 'You all saw it, all saw that face grinning horribly, its jaw bandaged shut, the pennies resting on its eyes in two dark circles. Which of us would ever forget it?'

'*I* didn't kill him!' cried Henry. 'Yes, there is water hemlock in the ponds. Yes, I might be the only person in this room who knows it, but I did not murder my own brother. I did not . . . tear his throat out, put a rat in his coffin.' He put his hands over his eyes. 'God in heaven, what is going on? What has happened to us, to this family? What have we become?'

'You recognise hemlock when you see it, sir, but you are mistaken if you think you are the only person in this room who knows what it is. Your sisters Charlotte and Caroline are also familiar with it.'

'I beg your pardon!' Caroline's hand leaped to her breast once more.

'The medical books in the library,' I said. 'Who do they belong to?'

'They're mine,' said Charlotte. She scowled. 'I saw you looking at them. I wish to be a doctor. It's no crime to want more than a life lived on a sofa.' She threw her sister a disparaging look. '*I* did not kill my brother.'

'Oh, come, come, Dr Flockhart,' scoffed Caroline. 'You can't possibly think little Charlotte murdered her own brother and desecrated his body?'

'I would not be surprised by anything this family did,' I said, looking at Sir Thomas.

'But there is one person here who *was* prepared to murder Edward Mortmain.' Will opened his satchel and produced the bundle of bloody clothes, the five-pronged silver fish fork with the Mortmain crest on the handle.

'We found these at your house in town,' I said. 'Hidden in the bedroom used by the late Lady Mortmain. The bloody clothes were worn by the murderer, the fork was used to tear out Edward's throat.' I turned again to Henry. 'You alone in this room went to that house. To your mother's room. You went there regularly. The place is a shrine to her memory. Your sorrow at being deprived of her, having her taken from you when you were no more than four years old, has never left you.'

'There is not a day when I do not think of her,' he said. 'She seemed to have been forgotten by everyone –

forgotten by my father, my sister too young to remember her.' He shrugged. 'It gave me comfort to visit her chamber.' He looked at the bloodied clothes, the silver tines of the fish fork still dark with blood, and he closed his eyes.

'But you are not the only person to have keys to your family's town house,' I said. 'Mr Byrd, you have a set too, do you not? You gave them to us not two days ago. Certainly, you did not force us to go, but you implied that it might be worth our while to do so. I wondered why we had gone there, and the answer to that question is – because you suggested that we go. Lady Mortmain's room was unlocked, the candle burning, the bloodied clothes stuffed into a corner. Who else might all this point to but Henry Mortmain? He knew about the hemlock, he had access to the silverware, he appeared to have everything to gain from the death of his brother. It would seem conclusive to anyone who might care to look. Except that it is *not* conclusive at all. In fact, all it did was cement in my mind what I already suspected.

'The final sign of your guilt, Mr Byrd, has been in my pocket since before the funeral.' I opened my satchel and pulled out a fold of thick canvas. A terrible smell filled the room. Hands went to noses, everyone recoiled. I pulled out a glove, flipped open the canvas and between my finger and thumb held up Edward Mortmain's missing pocketbook.

Excerpt from the Journal of William Quartermain, Esq., surveyor and assistant architect, Metropolitan Sewer Commission.

The gully hole was small, but so was Thimble, and between us, Annie and I eased him through into Mrs Roseplucker's back yard. The aperture was not big enough for me, however. I would have to find my way back alone. What else could I do? I told Annie to look after Thimble, that the lad had been a good friend to me, and I would not for all the world see his body treated with anything less than respect. I asked her to wrap him in a sheet, I would come for him as soon as I could.

'And do not sell him to the anatomists,' I said, for I knew she had done such things before. 'Or I will personally see to it that Mr Jobber hangs!'

My return though the sewers, alone, to the mouth of the River Fleet was the worst journey of my life. It is the source of my waking fears, the substance of my nightmares. If I commit it to paper, perhaps then I can exorcise its terrible hold over me – my fear of the dark, of the scrabbling claws and greasy fur of the creatures that live within it, my fear of being lost, lost for ever in those hideous tunnels and passages.

But I had no choice. I took Badger's lamp and headed back into the labyrinth. The sound of my own breathing, the stinking miasma, the way my boots slithered on unseen deposits beneath the brown water, the fact that my light illuminated only a single dim bubble around me appalled me so much that I could hardly put one foot in front of the other. When I shone the light forward, or back, there was only darkness ahead, darkness and shadows that seethed and moved, but always retreated from me, as if whatever lurked there was waiting and watching for my lantern to give out. The walls were streaked with green, ochre, purple, crimson, and festooned with rags, hanging in tattered black strips like widow's weeds.

I turned left into another passage, the dancing light from a hundred beady eyes reflected back at me. I told myself that at least I was not alone, at least there were creatures other than myself down there in the reeking darkness. But the thought did not comfort me. A rat dropped onto my shoulder, but I dashed it away. Another two swam between my boots, brave now that they had realised I was alone. My lamp flickered and dimmed, and I thanked God that I had brought Badger's lantern too.

I walked faster. The water was deeper, deeper than I remembered it. And then, before me, all at once was an iron grating, thick with filth and draped with dark hanks of I-knew-not-what. I had no recollection of ever having seen this grating before. Where had I gone wrong? I had no idea. Beneath the ground, all sense of direction is lost. Without sun, moon or stars, without even the direction of the wind to act as a guide is it impossible to know whether one is facing north, south, east or west. Thimble had seen nuance and individuality in the tunnels, but to me, all the bricks, all the drains and passages, looked the same. Where was the tunnel with the wide bottom and the pointed top? Where was the soft brick wall that told me I was beside the pump shaft in Wicke Street back lane? I looked at the water. Should I follow it downhill? Wouldn't it lead me to the Thames if I did? But what if the tide were coming in? Surely then the water would be flowing in the opposite direction. If I followed its flow I might simply be heading deeper and deeper away from the Thames, away from all hope of salvation. How could I know? I staggered forward again, into that endless stinking darkness.

I turned left.

I turned right.

I came to a gully hole. It was high in the tunnel roof, at the end of a long tube-like drain. The air, for a moment, was sweeter – just a little – and I gasped at it the way a drowning man might gulp for air, for life. I looked left and right. Was it heading uphill or down? I waded forward again. Another gully hole. It was high above my head, some six feet away. Should I shout and scream for attention? But no one would hear my cries over the noise and bustle of the city, even at night-time. I blinked up at it – was that the moon I could see? I could make out a spire, a roof, a building. It looked familiar. I had seen it recently, I knew, but I could not place it. I dropped my gaze. It was no use looking upwards, staring at the moon like a lovesick swain when my only hope was to keep moving forward. To keep hoping. My lantern, still tied to the breast of my filthy sewer coat, illuminated the wall before me. There, wedged in the green and black slime, was something darker that the surrounding area, something dull and lustreless. Upon it, streaked and filthy but unmistakeable, were two letters, 'E' and 'M', embossed in gold. I prised it from the mud and slipped it into my pocket. It was at that point that I closed my eyes and prayed. I prayed for forgiveness. I prayed for Thimble. But mostly, I am ashamed to say it, I prayed that I might be saved.

I turned back the way I had come. The passage narrowed. My lamp flickered again. A rat, larger this time and bolder still, reared up before me on the lip of a spouting drain level with my face. I screamed and lashed out at it, slipping against the tunnel wall. Something moved beneath my boot. Something crawled behind my back. I screamed again and staggered against the other wall, so close it was as if I were trapped in an endless brick-lined coffin. My God! The fear that overcame me was like acid in my mouth, my scalp pricking as if beetles were running across my head, my heart racing fit to burst. The air had grown warm and steamy, as if somewhere upstream a giant bath of hot water had been emptied. I turned and turned again, looking for something, anything, that might help me decide which way to go.

And then all at once a face appeared before me. It was a hideous face, ghastly in the failing light from my lamp, streaked with black and crowned with a hat scabbed with bits of coloured rag and fragments of bone. Hands grabbed at me, I screamed and thrashed them away, sinking to my knees, but they were too strong for me, and I was pulled roughly to my feet.

'Don't fall,' the face whispered. It was not two inches from mine. Its one blinking eye was bright, almost amused. The other was no more than a dark hole. 'I should know, lad. They don't call me One-Eyed Nathan for nuffink. They'll swarm you if you fall. Right, lads?' Behind him I saw the faces of Thimble's Tosher friends, their lights shining yellow in the darkness.

Chapter Twenty-Six

~≈~

It was made of black leather, some five inches by four, and embossed with the initials EM in gold. The room was silent.

'I found this in the Fleet ditch,' said Will. 'I was out beneath the city with my friend and companion Master Thimble. A braver boy I have never known. He would cross any torrent of filth to help a friend, brave any number of dangers and threats. If any of you had but half his courage and honour we might not be standing here now.' He had tears in his eyes as he spoke.

'But where did you find it?' Mr Byrd gaped.

'Beneath Water Street,' I said. 'Right outside your chambers, Mr Byrd. Only you would have thrown it there.'

'But anyone could have—'

'But anyone didn't,' I said. '*You* did. As you said to us not too long ago, Mr Byrd, "one does not choose where one might bestow one's heart". You were in love with Edward, weren't you?'

'Never mind *that*. What about the diamonds?' snapped Sir Thomas. 'Did you find the diamonds?'

Will's face was stony. 'No, sir. The Fleet has them.'

'Confound it, Byrd. You were supposed to retrieve them. Supposed to get them back. What on earth are these fellows talking about? You said you had them. You *lied*!'

Mr Byrd made a curious choking sound. He was as white as alabaster, whatever colour his cheeks had regained with the consumption of brandy and water rapidly draining away. He downed his glass and smiled. His eyes were hard, the apologetic demeanour he habitually cultivated had vanished. Instead, he drew himself up and looked around the room at the faces of those he had served for so long.

'My God, I hate this family,' he said. 'I've hated you for years. All of you. How you humiliated my father, my grandfather, myself. You cannot see it, can you? How your arrogant self-righteous ways are enough to make anyone as sick as those poor bastards in Prior's Rents who are obliged to drink your vile water.' He shook his head. 'I thought Edward was different. He certainly seemed different. And yes, Flockhart, you are right. I loved him – and for a while I believed he . . . I believed he might return my feelings. No fool like an old fool, I suppose.'

He looked down at his hands, wringing them together the way he always had. All at once he seemed to realise what he was doing, and he stopped and balled his fingers into fists instead. 'Of course, I did his father's dirty work,' he said. '*Your* dirty work, Sir Thomas.' His voice was low, hesitant. 'And all the while my . . . my feelings grew – but they seemed . . . they seem twisted and bitter, like toadstools in a dark, unwholesome forest, as if my desire, which I could not own, was tainted with rage and covetousness. I knew where Edward went and what he did, I had him followed, and the fellow reported back to me that he had been to Mrs Allcock's, that he had been to Wicke Street.

'Again and again he went. I asked myself how I could love him when he went to such places? When he wantonly went with men he had no love for? And they had no love for him! I was jealous, of course. What a corrupting emotion *that* is – so violent, so corrosive. Like bile it ate away at me, at my soul, at my love and respect for him. Part of me wanted to punish him, as his father punished him, but at the same time I wanted him for myself.

'When he came to me that last night he was desperate. He told me he was being blackmailed. I listened. I sympathised. I *wanted* to tell him that his father had made me do it, to tell him it was all just a game, a test engineered by his own father. I wanted it all to *stop*. But I didn't. I didn't say anything.'

He squeezed his eyes shut, his fists clenched in his lap. 'I had never seen him so . . . vulnerable. So innocent. And he had come to me for help. To *me*! My heart filled with love and my blood burned like fire in my veins. I had watched him from afar for so long. Had wanted him for so long. And now here he was. He needed me. He was putting himself in my hands. Like a child.' Mr Byrd's chin trembled. 'I don't know what force possessed me, but all at once I took him in my arms. I turned his face to mine, and I tried to . . .'

Mr Byrd seemed to have forgotten where he was, that the eyes of the entire room were fixed in horror upon him. I had the sense that it was a relief to him, to be able to confess at last to what he was, what he had done. 'I tried to kiss him,' he said.

Tears squeezed out from the corners of the solicitor's screwed-shut eyes. 'It was as if he was not the kind of man I knew him to be, as if I had got everything wrong about him. Of course, he had not told me himself that he was a homosexual. I knew because I'd had one of my men follow him for weeks. And . . . and because I just *knew*. I *knew* he and I were alike, why could he not see it? But the look on his face. The expression of horror, of disgust when I touched him. The way he sprang from my arms like a scalded cat.' Mr Byrd's face was ashen, his voice a whisper. 'He leaned towards me then. I could not move, could not speak. And I thought for a moment, for a single delicious moment, that he might have simply been shocked by my intimacy, delightfully shocked, and that he was about to return my kiss.'

He shook his head, his eyes still closed tight. '"*I would no more take you to bed than I would take the Mortmain rat*", is what he said to me. "*You've done my father's bidding all your life, collected his rents, enabled his wickedness, his deceit, his cruelty. There is nothing about you that I could ever love.*"' Mr Byrd pressed a folded handkerchief to his lips. 'He hated me. And . . . he . . . he laughed at me too. And then he left.

'I can hardly begin to describe my feelings. Shame – though you may not believe me. Shame because I knew that he was right. But also fury. And . . . and then hatred.'

He sat up straight and blinked away the tears that had gathered in his eyes. His face hardened. 'A hatred so vast, so deep, so visceral and poisonous . . . I was *consumed* by it. How *dare* he reject me. I who had protected him from the worst of his father's rages, who had defended him countless times. *He is sure to grow out of it, sir. He is young and passionate, sir, a true Mortmain! Were you not a man of wide and varied taste in your youth, sir? Allow him his pleasures, sir, he is sure to return to the path once he has tired of his games.* Again and again and again I spoke up for him, unseen, unrecognised, without even a nod of thanks. And I could not *help* the feelings I had. Why, *he* had awoken them in me, with his dark eyes and his pouting lips and his lascivious glances. Did they mean *nothing*?

'But my fury went deeper than that. Its roots seized my soul and I saw you for what you truly are. *All* you Mortmains – with your cunning ways, your ignorance, your privilege and arrogance, your ill-gotten wealth.'

His face was furious, his lips curled into a sneer, his brow drawn down. The spittle had gathered at the corners of his lips like glue. The Mr Byrd I had always known, the gentle, mild-mannered, affable and gracious man I had liked and respected had quite disappeared. And in his place, a murderer had appeared.

'I could not think of *any* of you without contempt,' he snapped. 'Without loathing. Not one of you is worth a farthing – not Caroline with her noisy chattering about God and idleness, and her ill-informed meddling with the poor. Not Charlotte, an abandoned runt spawned for no reason or purpose. Not Henry, so weak and foolish, always sniffing at flowers and jabbing at the soil. He never wanted to be heir – he wanted to be a curate! Such a lack of ambition. Now he must face up to his family shame – the slums, the water, the lies and greed that are the basis for his very existence. And I hated you, Sir Thomas, the most. Forever belittling me, belittling my father. Forever calling me a "lackey" and a "man of no consequence". One of the "middling sort". A servant, just like any other. And yet it was *I* who ran your affairs, *I* who brokered your marriages, invested your fortune, made you rich.

'And the whole family's superstitions about that bloody rat! Well, I'll give you a rat, I thought. I'll give you the rat you deserve, all of you!'

'You took the silver fish fork,' I said. 'After you'd had salmon for dinner. I heard the housekeeper complaining that it had been stolen.'

'That was easy. Inspired, I thought. I'd not planned to take the thing, but when I saw it at dinner I knew it was perfect for the job that was forming in my mind.' He sat back, contemplating with pride the decisions he had made. He was enjoying it, I could see. To be able to tell the tale as it had happened. As he had executed it.

'It was a good plan,' he said. 'One without fault. And, of course, I had various cards up my sleeve to send you, Flockhart – or anyone who cared to look – on a merry dance. And dance you did, sir!' He grinned. 'To *my* tune.'

Here, at last, in committing a crime all of his own, following his own instructions, Mr Byrd seemed to have found a sense of purpose and pride. The thought chilled my heart. We had always trusted him, and until now I'd had no reason to think ill of him. I knew my partiality had blinded me to his faults. I should have reached my conclusions sooner.

'Edward was poisoned by hemlock,' I said. 'Water hemlock dropwort to be precise. It grows all along the banks of the Fleet where it passes through the grounds via the ponds Henry had created, along with the watercress and calendula and bulrushes. You have a bust of Socrates in your office, sir. You are both erudite and well read. You are aware that Socrates was poisoned by hemlock, and you know precisely how hemlock might affect the body, how paralysis creeps over it until the victim cannot move. A tincture of the leaves and flowers, sweetened with honey and dripped oh so carefully onto the lips of a sleeping man. Administered via a length of silken thread, was it not? I found one such on the floor of the room where Edward died. Some ten inches long. Sticky.'

'Just so,' he said. 'He'd been drinking. A heavy sleeper – perhaps not surprising after his exertions with that man.'

'The way his blood sprayed onto your clothes pointed to only one conclusion,' I said. 'That he was alive when you ripped out his throat.'

Mr Byrd nodded. 'He watched,' he said. 'Opened his eyes but could not move. Could not speak. I thought at first I would have to stab him, that he was about to cry out but – of course he couldn't. He couldn't make a sound. He looked up at me and I saw disbelief in his eyes. Then, what I had not expected, a look of hope – for a single moment – as he thought I might be there to help him.' He smiled. 'And then I saw fear. It was the fear that I especially enjoyed. I knew then what drove Sir Thomas, what kept him alive. That feeling of power. There really is nothing like it.' Mr Byrd closed his eyes again, as if in ecstasy. 'I bent my head and I kissed him,' he said. 'I kissed him the way I had always wanted to.' He shrugged. 'And then I ripped his throat out.'

Will had grown pale. 'When did you become so pitiless, Mr Byrd? So wicked?'

'I have worked for Sir Thomas all my life,' Mr Byrd replied. His face was like stone. 'I learned from a master of the art.' All at once he smiled, as if suddenly enjoying the moment. 'And I didn't finish there, did I, Flockhart?'

'No,' I said. 'You did not, sir.'

'Obviously the constable was going to arrest the nearest person they could find, and that man Jobber was set to hang straight away. But why would a random stranger like that tear at Edward Mortmain's throat? It made no sense. The magistrate would be unlikely to make more work for himself by trying to find out, but the family would know there was more afoot.'

'What in God's name was your intention, sir?' cried Will. 'Edward Mortmain was a good man—'

'My intention?' Mr Byrd held out his hands, as if explaining himself to a foolish child. 'Why, to make them suffer, Mr Quartermain. To take their heir from them in the most brutal and terrifying way I could imagine. To fill them with fear – fear of not knowing who or why. Fear of the unknown. Of the future. Of each other. But then *you* came along, Flockhart. You went to Sir Thomas. He knew perfectly well that it was nothing to do with Jobber. But what alternatives were there? Why, he would look to his family, of course. After so many years in his service I know *exactly* how he thinks. He would make it his business to *know*. I knew he'd suspect Henry. Henry had the most to gain – the title, the lands, the wealth, everything. And he is in thrall to his stepmother, even a blind man can see that. Henry is incapable of achieving anything on his own but she,' he smiled, 'she's a vixen. And who knows what he might attempt with her encouragement. And so it seemed that I could murder the heir and send the spare to the hangman.' He held out his hands. 'Ingenious! And when the rat woke up in the coffin!' He laughed. 'Your faces! I had to pretend to faint so that I could hide my face. I'd used some of Miss Charlotte's ether. The rat was insensible when I slipped it in. But not for long. It woke up at just the right moment. It was quite perfect!'

Everyone was staring at him. Mr Byrd's laughter was brittle and forced, and after a moment he fell silent. I did not blame him for feeling so angry, so frustrated. But to murder a man in cold blood? To attempt to frame his brother for the crime? That was unforgivable, and he knew it. Edward Mortmain had been a good man. He had recognised his family's failings and had intended to remedy the wrongs his father so casually endorsed. He, out of all of them, was the least deserving of his fate.

Mr Byrd stared at me. 'I loved him, Flockhart,' he said bleakly. All at once he looked utterly miserable. Spent and exhausted. His expression aghast, as if only now that he had described his actions did he realise the horror of what he had done. 'For the first time in my life I loved someone. If I could not have him, then no one would.' He screwed his eyes shut once more. 'I am so sorry,' he whispered. 'So sorry.' He slipped his hand into the pocket of his dressing gown and drew out a small blue bottle. In one quick movement he ripped out the stopper with his teeth, spat it aside and downed the contents in a single gulp. I plunged across the room and tore the bottle from his lips. But it was too late. He smiled around at everyone, his face streaming with tears.

'Too late, Flockhart,' he said. 'Nothing you can do now. It takes minutes. I should know, I watched him die.' His face was pleading. 'Forgive me.'

Suddenly he pitched forward, bringing Caroline Mortmain's account books and her golden table crashing to the ground with him. I crouched at his side. He had fallen face down, but Will and I managed to turn him.

'Mr Byrd,' I whispered. 'What have you done?'

'I cannot hang,' he said. 'I have seen it too often. I cannot . . . cannot hang.' His eyes were wide, his breath a terrible gasping sound, the corners of his mouth creeping upwards into that dreadful smile. I held his hand in mine, but it was unresponsive. I sensed a coldness and a heaviness in his limbs, though I could see from his eyes that he was still alive. And then all at once he was gone. Foam bubbled at his lips. I drew my hand over his eyes to close his lids. The room was silent, the faces of the family white and pinched with horror.

'Cover him up,' croaked Sir Thomas at last. 'For God's sake cover him up. I can't look at that . . . that grin!'

I took a coverlet of gold brocade that was draped across the sofa where Caroline was sitting, and I flung it over the dead man.

'Dr Graves is on his way,' I said. 'I've already sent a boy to fetch him. Mr Quartermain and I will return to town with him and inform the magistrate.'

'I had no idea,' said Caroline. 'No idea that Mr Byrd was so full of hate.' She sniffed and dabbed at her eyes. 'At least poor Edward can rest in peace now. At least it is all over.'

I turned to her. 'Oh, but it is not over, is it?' I said. 'Not yet. There are other matters to discuss. The murder of the second Lady Mortmain, for example.'

'What? My mother was murdered?' Henry put his hands to his head, his expression confused and horrified.

'What d'you mean, Flockhart? What are you talking about?'

'It was only a suspicion at first,' I said. 'And since the late Mr Byrd kindly suggested that we might benefit from a visit to the Mortmain town house, and as he had left the bedroom door open for us so that we might find the evidence that would convict *you*, Henry, I thought I might as well see whether my suspicions were correct. The symptoms of cholera are identical to those exhibited in cases of arsenic poisoning,' I said. 'But arsenic is not the friend to murderers that it used to be, thanks to developments in science and medicine. I refer, of course, to the Marsh Test. A simple undertaking that proves beyond doubt the presence of arsenic in any given substance. I can perform it now if you wish.' I held up my hand. 'Please, it is no inconvenience, we have all we need. Will, if you please.'

From his satchel, Will produced the glass flask, the spirit lamp, the pipe and cork, all wrapped tightly in cotton and canvas. The sample of arsenic, the zinc, the oil of vitriol, all went into the flask. I lit the flame and burnished the side of the porcelain bowl with a black shimmering deposit. 'You see?' I held it aloft. 'This iridescence is arsenic. The gas that produced the orange flame is arsine. Yesterday I did the same with a sample of hair from the second Lady Mortmain's dressing table. There can be no doubt about it, the second Lady Mortmain, your mother, was poisoned with arsenic. But today—' I turned to Caroline Mortmain. 'Today, the compound I was testing came from your chamber pot.'

'Mine?' she gasped. 'You mean *I* have been poisoned?' She fell back onto her golden cushions. 'Oh my. Oh, dear Lord. No wonder I have been so sick, so wretched.

I thought I would die—' Suddenly she sat up. 'And have we *all* been poisoned with arsenic?'

'Only you, Miss Mortmain.'

'Only me? But who—?'

'Madam, you poisoned yourself.'

'*I?*'

'If I might explain.'

'I wish you would.' She shook her head angrily, staring round the room as if she hoped to elicit the support of her family.

'It's my belief that you used arsenic to poison the woman who replaced your mother. Who would question it when the cholera was taking so many? The country was terrified. No one knew how the contagion was spread, or who it might afflict.'

'The miasma,' interrupted Sir Thomas. 'It was the miasma.'

'Oh, the miasma,' said Will. 'I am entirely unconvinced by *that* idea, sir. Anyone who has spent time underground, who has seen how the wells and pumps and sewers of the city are all linked would tell you that the stink is not the problem. The water is a much more likely source. Have you seen what people drink? What you supply to their homes?'

'I knew it could not have been the cholera,' said Sir Thomas, ignoring Will completely. 'We are civilised. We are the masters. Cholera is the stuff of slum dwellers who choose to live in wretched conditions of their own making. It is a sickness of savages, from the slums of Calcutta and Bengal. *We* do not have cholera! We did not have it then and we do not have it now.' He turned to his daughter. 'You *viper!*'

Henry was openly weeping now, Lady Mortmain was staring at Caroline, her face inscrutable. Only Charlotte looked intrigued. She clapped her hands. 'Do go on, Dr Flockhart.'

'You hated your first stepmother,' I said to Caroline. 'Hated her for replacing your mother, for replacing you with still more children, another son to push you further and further away from the money.'

'Ingrate!' cried Sir Thomas. He seemed to be no longer listening. '*Wretch!*'

'*No!*' Caroline looked aghast. She had recoiled into herself, her face frozen in terror. She reached out a trembling finger and pointed to Lady Veronica Mortmain. 'It was her. I saw her do it with my own eyes. She was supposed to be my stepmother's companion, but she murdered her. I watched her do it, watched her mix the powders and stir it into the marmalade.'

'I did no such thing!' cried Lady Veronica.

'Oh, but you did,' said Caroline. 'I watched you. But I said nothing.'

'Why not? Why not speak up if you saw me?'

Henry Mortmain was looking at his stepmother with a dawning horror. 'It *was* you,' he said. 'I know it. You care for nothing but your own skin. And you always took my mother her breakfast. I remember it. Always marmalade.'

'I said nothing because who would have believed me?' said Caroline. 'There was no Marsh Test in 1832.'

'Of course there wasn't,' I said. 'But there is now. And you said nothing about seeing your current stepmother poison her predecessor because you did not care. You were glad to have her out of the way. You have a good deal of knowledge about poisons and medicine, don't you, Miss Mortmain? Those medical books in the library – yes, they belong to your sister now, but they used to belong to you, did they not? They are some twenty years old and well thumbed. They are signed *C. Mortmain*. When we first met Lady Charlotte she was carrying a rat in a cage and a book about *Materia medica*. '"*Caroline gave it to me*", she said. You had owned it, and read it, and passed it on. You are no fool, Miss Caroline. The Marsh Test became common currency in murder investigations from 1833. Arsenic would be no use to you now. To be certain, I tested myself and Mr Quartermain. Neither of us was suffering from arsenic poisoning. But *you* were. Just enough to give you some symptoms, but not enough to kill you. I imagine you tested the dose somehow. On a maid, perhaps. Or a footman?

'At first I could not understand it. I was sure we *had* been poisoned by arsenic. When I was proved wrong it seemed that we had all gone down with cholera after all. The city is full of it, it was an entirely reasonable possibility. But I could *not* believe it. Then I remembered the tale you told us about when your mother died. How you ran into the woods and hid. How the toadstools that grew from the stones of the old well surrounded you, like little friends. You described them so prettily, with such affection. But you were a little too familiar with them, with their names and habitats. More knowledgeable and interested than any woman of your class and breeding would normally be. After that it was obvious. You had poisoned us all – except for yourself – with the death cap mushroom. *Amanita phalloides*. The symptoms are almost identical to those of cholera. Who would ever guess? And the Marsh Test, should it be undertaken, would prove an absence of arsenic in the corpses of the dead, thereby confirming, by default, that cholera was to blame.

'I imagine you made a tincture from the mushrooms – macerated them and steeped them in brandy – and put the mixture into the negus at your brother's funeral,' I said. 'I thought the drink was rather strongly flavoured with lemon and cinnamon. To hide the taste, obviously. And of course, you took only brandy and water yourself.'

'There is no cure for poisoning by death cap mushroom,' said Charlotte quietly. 'You must be mistaken, Dr Flockhart.'

'Ah, there I was lucky,' I said. 'The remedy I chose was logical but completely untried. *Silybum marianum*, more colloquially known as milk thistle, is one of the most powerful agents in the pharmacopoeia for cleansing the liver. And I had just taken possession of one of the newfangled syringes, the hollow needle that can pierce flesh and insert physic directly into the bloodstream. Had we all taken a draught of milk thistle in water, the way it is usually administered, we would simply have vomited it out again. Even if we had not, its action via the stomach would be too slow, too attenuated. The only way was to try to neutralise the poison where it was already acting – on the liver itself. If I could get *Silybum* into the system directly, into the bloodstream which passes directly through the liver, then we might just stand a chance.' I shrugged. 'There is no guarantee that it would work if I did it again, if any of us were poisoned again. The method and the dose are completely untried. We are all incredibly lucky.'

I turned to Caroline, who had deflated onto her cushions as if someone had pricked her with a pin. 'And so here we all are,' I said. 'Apart from the six servants who have died. Did you hope to get rid of everyone, your father, brother, stepmother, with a few servants and acquaintances thrown in for good measure?'

She looked up at me. 'Yes.'

'And Charlotte was just lucky?'

'She does not like negus. I knew she would not take any.'

'But then she is no threat to you, is she? You will inherit Blackwater and all its fortunes, not her. Especially seeing that someone else murdered your brother Edward.'

Caroline was on her feet now. Her face was pale, her breath coming in gasps. 'I think I need a little air,' she said. She put a hand to her side and lurched towards the French windows. Outside, the fog still lingered. It had grown thinner, though heavy wreaths of it still drifted about the woodland at the end of the lawn, as if the old oaks had breathed out a vapour all of their own. I knew what she was about, and I stood up to catch her arm. But she was too fast for me and before I could do anything she had flung the door wide and rushed out into the garden.

She would not get far. And yet out of all of us – apart from Charlotte, who made no move to apprehend her half-sister – Caroline had been the least afflicted by the poison she had taken. She was over the flower beds and onto the lawn before I, or anyone, could stop her. She lumbered across the grass, her slippers and gown leaving trails in the dew. She was heading towards the woods. Where did she hope to go from there, I wondered as I toiled after her. There was nowhere she might run to, no one who would take her in or hide her. Ahead of me,

I saw her reach the trees. But the undergrowth was thick with nettles and brambles, and she could not find a way in. She ran left and then right, searching for a path that might lead her into the thicket. She climbed up onto what looked like a low wall of rocks and stones. I saw her bend her head against the clawing branches and shuffle forward, as if she hoped to clamber through to a pathway in the trees beyond.

'Miss Mortmain,' I shouted. 'Caroline. Please, there is nowhere to run.'

She did not reply. She was on top of the stones now, her dress heavy with dew, her hair undone and trailing over her shoulders.

'I had to do it,' she shouted at the sky. 'I had to show them. They had no right to overlook me, to ignore me, to insult me. *Ugly Caroline, no one will marry her! Dull Caroline, no need to ask her opinion. Silly Caroline, always bothering people.*' She turned to face me. 'And when Edward was murdered, well, why should I not take matters into my own hands? Why should I not give them all what they deserved, and get for myself what *I* deserved?'

I was gasping for breath, my head spinning as my legs buckled beneath me. The woman was sobbing now, the branches of an old hollow oak that grew beside the stones became caught in her hair, and she flailed her arms, trying to disentangle herself. All at once she cried out, her eyes fixed on the ground beside her. She stumbled, I heard a sudden sharp 'crack' and a splintering sound, and before my eyes Caroline Mortmain disappeared. One moment she was there, the next she was gone. Had she jumped down into the woods and fled? But I knew in my heart that her fate was far worse than that.

'Jem!' Will was coming across the grass towards me. 'Jem, what happened? Where did she go?' He hauled me to my feet. With our arms around each other we staggered forward.

'Did you see it?' he gasped. 'Beside the tree?' His eyes were wide, his expression shocked. 'There was a creature of some sort. Big and black. A rat, I think.'

'No,' I lied. 'I did not see it.'

The circular wooden lid that had covered the old well was covered in moss and lichen; years of leaf litter had obscured it still further. In the gloaming, with the fog still drifting through the trees, anyone might have mistaken it for a patch of solid earth surrounded by tumbledown stones. But the rotten planks were soft to the touch, the wood consumed by time and decay until it had no more substance than dust. We peered into the hole – into the well. We called her name. No answer came to us from that terrible darkness.

Chapter Twenty-Seven

Will and I sat on either side of the apothecary stove, each of us wrapped in a blanket. We were both exhausted. I had given us another injection of milk thistle and, so far, we both remained well. I was not so naive as to assume that we were both recovered, for the death cap mushroom, like so many others of that kind, can kill days after the original sickness. The poison gets to work deep inside, slowly, quietly, unstoppably, until all at once one drops down dead, and I fully understood that our recovery, and that of everyone at Blackwater, was in no way certain. But I had faith in what I had done, in the strength and appropriateness of the physic I had chosen and in the way we had administered it, though only time would tell if I was correct. In the meantime, we would drink our brandy and opium mixture and hope for the best.

I had instructed Jenny and Gabriel to close the shop early, and they were preparing the workbench for our visitors. Annie, Mrs Roseplucker and Mr Jobber had invited themselves over to say thank you for the release of Mr Jobber, who had managed to remain out of trouble at Newgate by threatening his fellow inmates with my personal retaliations on no less than six occasions.

'I had no idea you were so feared, Jem,' Will had said.

'Of course I am,' I'd replied. 'Let us hope you never fall foul of me.'

Gabriel was an excellent fiddle player, and although I did not have the strength for dancing, I had given Mrs Speedicut instructions for clearing a space between the hop baskets and the tall shelving where I kept the condenser and the leeches in case anyone else was so inclined. We had gin, and ale from Sorley's chop house. We had a warm game pie, a cold pork pie, some hot potatoes roasting in the stove, and two custard tarts for dessert.

Wrapped in a spool of blankets, resting on a makeshift mattress made of hop-filled sacks, lay Thimble. Every now and again Will went over to him to adjust his bedding, stroke his head or make him sip some cordial. Thimble, it seemed, had been knocked unconscious by Badger, and brought back to life by Annie, who'd had some smelling salts in her pocket and had wasted no time in using them. She and Mrs Roseplucker's other girls had carried the lad inside, stripped him, and plunged him into a tin bath filled with hot soapy water. At first Thimble objected, having known only water that was cold and brown. But if there is one thing more frightening than warm water and soap, it is the threat of Mrs Roseplucker rolling up her sleeves and coming forward with a scrubbing brush and a flannel. Thimble had been delivered to us wrapped in a sheet and a blanket, his bundle of clothes tied up with newspaper and string, cleaner than he had ever been in his life.

Now, Will had some of Gabriel's old clothes on his lap and was sorting through them anxiously. He held up a shirt and inspected it for holes, examined a pair of woollen britches and a waistcoat to make sure they were free of snags and stains. He folded them up and put them on the stove top to warm.

'You old nursemaid!' I said. I grinned.

'He saved my life,' said Will, smoothing a cotton neckerchief and putting it to warm with the others. 'I will do what I can for him.' He glanced at the apothecary clock and at the door. He took a sip at his warm physic mixture and looked at the door again.

'You seem a little agitated.' I sat back and put my feet up on the hearth. 'A little nervous.' I sucked on my pipe and regarded him through the blue haze of smoke. Behind us, Mrs Speedicut and Jenny were squabbling about who should look after Thimble when he was feeling better. Gabriel was picking out a jig on his fiddle and staring at the pies lovingly. Thimble's eyes were wide, his gaze fixed upon Will, the way a dog might gaze at its master waiting for instruction. Beside his head stood Will's brass level in its wooden box. Will brushed some imaginary lint from his waistcoat and passed his hand across his hair for the twentieth time.

'You think she's not coming, don't you?' I said.

'Who?' said Will. 'What? No! No, of course not.' His gaze slid to the apothecary clock once more.

'She will come,' I said gently. 'She has our daguerreotype anyway. I assume she would like to be paid for it.'

He gave a nervous smile. 'Yes, of course. That's very true, Jem.'

'I'm joking,' I said. 'If she comes, she comes to see you.' I took his hand. 'You will always have my love, no matter what. And hers, if you are lucky.'

'Thank you, Jem,' he said. He squeezed my fingers. 'And you have mine.'

'In which case, that is all that needs to be said.'

And then all at once the door burst open and Mrs Roseplucker and Annie gusted into the apothecary on a wave of cold smoky autumn. Mr Jobber squeezed in behind them and slammed the door closed making the bell jangle furiously. He was dressed in green velvet, with his cheeks clean shaven and his hair soft and fluffy. He was beaming with delight, and he clapped his giant hands together and danced a light-footed jig to Gabriel's fiddle.

'She's half an hour late,' said Will sadly. 'She's not coming.'

'Found this one outside,' blared Mrs Roseplucker. 'Where's she gone?' She turned about. Thomasina Golightly was standing behind her, eclipsed by the woman's vast flounced skirts and enormous cup-shaped bonnet. Will's face shone as he sprang up, his blanket falling about his ankles so that he almost fell to her feet as he plunged forward to shake Thomasina's hand. She was wearing a blue woollen skirt, hitched up to ankle height so that it did not become entangled in her boots, and a long red military coat. Her hair was short, like Thimble's, who, I saw, was waving to her from his nest of blankets. I nodded a greeting, raising my pipe to her and inclining my head. But I did not get up. I would leave them to their awkwardness. Besides, I was quite happy where I was.

369

The smell of pie and hot potato mixed with lavender and sandalwood in a warm friendly fug. I slipped my hand into the pocket of my jacket, my fingers curling around what felt like a hard cold plum stone. The other of Edward Mortmain's Golconda stars was lost to the Fleet, but even one was more than Will had expected to find, and Thimble's sleight of hand had kept it not only from Badger, but also from the prying fingers of Annie and Mrs Roseplucker. I was sure William Mowbray would know someone who could get us a good price for it. I wondered whether we would be better placed to spend the money on a dispensary for Prior's Rents, or on a cottage hospital? I liked to think there would be enough for both.

Acknowledgements

With deepest thanks to John Burnett and Olga Wojtas, always my first and most valued readers. Thanks also to Lee Randall (a supporter of these books since the beginning) for some important brainstorming conversations about sewers; to my sons Guy and Carlo, who have listened to bits of this being read out for the past two years and reassured me that it wasn't awful; to my mother, for coming to visit so that I could get away from domestic chores and do some writing; and to Mr Mercer-Jones, for always championing my crazy ideas, and for introducing so many of his patients to the world of Jem Flockhart.

Finally, this book would not have happened without my marvellous agent, Jenny Brown, and all the lovely people at Constable, especially Krystyna Green, Una McGovern, Amanda Keats, John Fairweather, Kate Truman, Brionee Fenlon, Jess Gulliver and Ellen Rockell.

Bibliography

Edinburgh, 2023

During the writing of this book, I spent a lot of time reading about sewers and sanitary reform. I drew on the work of many writers and historians and they have been invaluable in helping me get a sense of what the city might have been like above and below ground during the cholera years. Of course, I have taken creative licence with some of the information I gathered and any errors of fact contained in the pages of this book are entirely my own. My characters are not based on anyone, living or dead (apart from the mysterious 'Mr Basilisk' who, as anyone familiar with sanitary reform and the London sewer system will know, is a substitute for Mr Bazalgette).

For anyone who might be interested in such things, below are a few of the 'best books on sewers'. They paint a startling picture and, I must admit, writing about sewers without utterly repelling the reader has not been the easiest thing to do.

Stephen Halliday's work has been particularly useful, and his *The Great Stink of London, Sir Joseph Bazalgette and the Cleansing of the Victorian Metropolis* (Sutton Publishing, 1999) was invaluable. Also of use were his more recent publications, *Water: A Turbulent History* (Sutton Publishing, 2004) and the visually stunning *An Underground Guide to Sewers, Or: Down, Through and Out in Paris, London, and New York* (Thames and Hudson, 2019). The essay 'The Bowels of the City' written by Richard Barnett can be found in his collection of excellent essays *Sick City: Two Thousand Years of Life and Death in London* (Welcome Trust, 2008). This is a book I have drawn on many times for its combination of readability and historical detail. I would recommend it to anyone.

I defy anyone to say that they are not interested in lost rivers and it was a pleasure to immerse myself in Nicholas Barton's detailed study of *The Lost Rivers of London* (Historical Publications, 1992). Also useful on the matter of hidden rivers was Stephen Myers' *Walking on Water: London's Hidden Rivers Revealed* (Amberley publishing, 2011). On the subject of London generally, and the Thames in particular, Peter Ackroyd's *London: The Biography* (Penguin, 2000) and *Thames: Sacred River* (Vintage, 2008) were of great use.

As an account of the link between cholera and water, Sandra Hempel's *The Medical Detective: John Snow, Cholera and the Mystery of the Broad Street Pump* (Granta, 2007) is both fascinating and readable. Other useful books on cholera were Amanda J. Thomas' *Cholera: The Victorian Plague* (Pen and Sword, 2015) and Christopher Hamlin's *Cholera: The Biography* (OUP, 2009).

Last but by no means least, contemporary accounts of the Victorian city and its people have been a sobering source of material – for example, John Hollingshead's marvellous *Underground London* (1862). In particular, I have plundered Henry Mayhew's seminal work *London Labour and the London Poor* (1851), one of the best contemporary accounts of the city above and below ground (the toshers can be found here). Many of the characters we meet in his pages have found their way into my books over the years.